The SERPENT *of* DIVISION

Alyce Chaucer 1

CHRISTINA HARDYMENT

HAUGETUN

First published in Great Britain in 2022
by Haugetun Press, Oxford

ISBN 978-1-7391980-0-8 hb
ISBN 978-1-7391980-1-5 pb
ISBN 978-1-7391980-2-2 eb

COVER IMAGE © Bodleian Library, University of Oxford,
L 1.5 Med., p. 1079; ENDPAPER MAP © Bodleian Library,
University of Oxford, (E)c17:49 (169)

Designed and typeset in 11 on 14 Dante by illuminati, Grosmont
Printed in Great Britain by Henry Ling Ltd, Dorchester

The SERPENT of DIVISION

ALSO BY CHRISTINA HARDYMENT

Dream Babies: Child Care Advice from John Locke to Gina Ford
Arthur Ransome and Captain Flint's Trunk
Heidi's Alp
From Mangle to Microwave:
The Mechanization of Household Work
Behind the Scenes: A History of Domestic Arrangements
Slice of Life: the British Way of Eating since 1945
The Future of the Family
Literary Trails: British Writers in Their Landscapes
Malory: The Life and Times of King Arthur's Chronicler
Writing Britain: Wastelands to Wonderlands
The World of Arthur Ransome
Pleasures of the Garden
Pleasures of the Table
Pleasure of Nature
Writing the Thames
Novel Houses: Twenty Famous Fictional Dwellings

Contents

FOREWORD

The underlying theme of this series of novels is the power of women in a world torn by war and faction. 'To thrive, you must wive,' ran a contemporary proverb. 'The man is the head of the family, but the woman is the neck; she turns the head,' was another. The dynastic webs of wealthy women were woven as intricately and indissolubly as the great tapestries that lined their dwellings. Wives administered great and small estates while their husbands went abroad or to court for months and years. They petitioned the courts against avaricious neighbours and even resisted siege. They jockeyed their spouses into the political lists, manipulating minds, throwing tantrums or using the bedchamber to get their way. Men were often female tools, albeit diplomatically described as their lovers and champions. Early in the fifteenth century Christine de Pisan wrote a detailed guide on how to manage your man, *The Treasure of the City of Ladies*.

The central figure is Alyce Chaucer (1404–1475), only known grandchild of the poet Geoffrey Chaucer (*c.* 1343–1400). She was one of the wealthiest individuals in Britain: herself an heiress and married three times, she had estates in every county of England south of the Trent. After the death of her third husband in 1450 she chose to remain a widow. As such, her power did not have to be veiled in apparent obedience to a spouse. She was notoriously proud and strong-minded. She also loved books, especially her grandfather's works, and had a well-chosen library, which included at least one book by Christine de Pisan.

Alyce lived in great state in the Palace of Ewelme, fourteen miles from the city of Oxford. Little of this now remains, but the church, the almshouse known as the God's House, and the school that she and her last husband built there remain uncannily unaltered. They and the magnificent tomb which describes her as 'Serene Princess' are the inspiration for this story.

Although what follows is entirely imagined, it accords with the scanty facts known about Alyce. When the book opens in 1466 her position is under threat. Loyalty to the house of Lancaster lay deep in her bones: her grandfather and her father had been its servants, and so was she – even though the deposed Lancastrian king Henry VI was more fit to be a Carthusian monk, and was married to a headstrong young French queen whose loyalties were primarily to France. Alyce's vast wealth, retained despite the disgrace and murder of her last husband, William Duke of Suffolk, is being eyed greedily by her enemies, even though her heir is married to Bess of York, King Edward IV's favourite sister. Having held on to her inheritance, Alyce is anxious not to lose it, so she is keen to deny any sympathy with the Lancastrian cause.

Cast *of* Characters

IN AND AROUND EWELME

Alyce de la Pole, Dowager Duchess of Suffolk, a lover of literature and gardens. She is the granddaughter of the poet Geoffrey Chaucer and widow of Sir John Phelip (d. 1415), Thomas Montagu, Earl of Salisbury (d. 1428) and William de la Pole, Duke of Suffolk (d. 1450).

Tamsin Ormesby, an orphaned Ewelme village girl with a stubborn streak.

Simon Brailles, Alyce's secretary, 'twitchy as a hare'.

Ben Bilton, Steward of Ewelme, boyish and boisterous.

Denzil Caerleon, Alyce's man of business, who has a knack of getting into trouble.

Wat, a wild boy.

Marlene Stonor (a flirt) and Eloise Stonor (gullible but well-meaning), Alyce's ladies.

Farhang Amiri, Alyce's Persian physician, much given to quoting Rumi.

Martha Purbeck, Chamberlain of Ewelme Palace, fierce but fair.

Nan Ormesby, Tamsin's grandmother, matron of the God's House, warm and wise.

William Marton, Master of the God's House, pompous and ponderous.

Peter Greene, Teacher of Grammar, fond of malmsey and music.

Gerard Vespilan, Senior Bedesman, formerly Geoffrey
Chaucer's secretary, a skilled limner.

Joseph Pek, Bedesman, a sturdy one-armed veteran of the wars
in France.

Sybilla of Swyncombe, an anchorite, once tiring maid to Alyce,
and before that to her mother.

Sir Brian and Lady Anne Fulbert, of Swyncombe Manor, salt of
the earth.

Thomas and Jeanne Stonor, of Stonor Park, parents of Marlene,
Eloise and William. Loyal friends, for good reason.

IN AND AROUND OXFORD

George Neville, uncle to Kind Edward VI, Chancellor of Oxford
University and Archbishop-elect of York.

John Doll, bookseller.

William Stonor, brother of Marlene and Eloise, studying in
Oxford.

Thomas Chaundler, Warden of New College.

William Waynflete, Bishop of Winchester.

Sir Robert Harcourt of Stanton Harcourt, a bullying braggart
who covets Ewelme Palace.

Lady Margaret Harcourt, his wife but a loyal friend to Alyce.

Sir Richard Harcourt, Sir Robert's brother, 'a snake in the grass'.

Lady Catherine Stapleton, Richard Harcourt's fiancée, envious
and calculating.

Milo of Windsor, a spy.

LONDON AND ELSEWHERE

Mistress Joan Moulton, eminent London bookseller, four times
widowed, as irrepressible as Chaucer's Wife of Bath.

Monique de Chinon, her companion, taciturn and tactful.

John Wenlock, Lord Someries of Luton, diplomat to Edward IV.

Francis Thynne, his secretary, 'close as an oyster'.

John Tiptoft, Earl of Worcester and Lord Constable. A notable
classical scholar but merciless in his pursuit of treason.
King Edward IV of York, crowned aged nineteen in 1461: shrewd
but lazy.
Cicily Neville, Dowager Duchess of York, Edward IV's mother,
cunning and conniving, devoted to advancing her Neville
relations.
Queen Elizabeth, widow of the Lancastrian Sir John Grey,
cunning and conniving, devoted to advancing her Wydeville
relations.
Sir Anthony Wydeville, brother to the queen, as noted for his
jousting as for his love of romantic literature.
John (Jack), Duke of Suffolk, Alyce's heir (Wingfield, Suffolk).
Duchess Elizabeth (Bess), his wife and King Edward's sister;
cleverer than both.
King Henry VI of Lancaster, deposed and imprisoned in the
Tower of London.
Margaret of Anjou, wife of Henry VI (Kœur, Lorraine).
John Massingham, sculptor.

'I first saw the dark imaginings of felony,
and all the scheming; the cruel ire, red as any
glowing coal, the pick-purse, and yes pale dread;
the smiler with the knife under the cloak,
the stable burning with the black smoke;
the treason and the murder in the bed.'

GEOFFREY CHAUCER, *The Knight's Tale*

Ewelme

Few people noticed Tamsin Ormesby as long as she kept her eyes cast demurely downwards and her unruly red hair braided neatly. But she noticed people. Ever since she'd been a small girl, exploring Ewelme's winding lanes, she'd seen how some men would swagger and others slink, how pretty dairymaids made eyes at handsome grooms from the stables, and how the plainer ones wound wool faster onto their spindles when a widowed merchant or an arthritic farmer passed by. 'There's a person and a place for everybody,' her grandmother Nan promised her. 'Though some find theirs easier than others.'

Tamsin didn't want either yet, even though she was now sixteen, old enough to have a husband and babies too. She'd seen her sister Loveday transformed from carefree flirt to querulous drudge after catching the eye of the dashing but penniless Richard à Wood. Settling down before you'd seen something of the world seemed a poor thing. Whenever she crossed Wallingford bridge on market day, she watched the great barges longingly as they sailed and sculled down the Thames towards London. But how could a village girl travel? Easily, she reflected, if she ever found favour with the Dowager Duchess of Suffolk. For everyone knew that Princess Alyce was a journeying woman. Her lands were scattered across the country, from Wingfield in Suffolk to Tintagel in Cornwall. She had even crossed the sea to Calais and Bruges and Paris. She used to spend many months of the year in London and in the ducal stronghold of Wingfield Castle, but now she was returning to make Ewelme Palace her only home. Rumour had it that she had fallen out with her son and heir and had stripped the castle almost bare.

Tamsin was picking blackberries in the hedgerows of Cat Hill when the long procession wound its way past her and down into the village. Princess Alyce looked careworn, a little stooped on her sidesaddle, but her hands, slim and strong, gripped her horse's reins with determination. An alert honey-coloured hound loped beside her, and two fashionably dressed young ladies in riding turbans and fur-trimmed mantles rode close behind on docile palfreys. Tamsin had barely recog-nised them for Marlene and Eloise, the daughters of Alyce's neighbours, the Stonors of Stonor Park. Two years spent at Wingfield Castle had transformed them. Behind them on a mule was the duchess's tiring maid Sarah Osborne. They passed her without a glance, although Sarah, who'd been one of her school friends, usually hailed her when they met. Perhaps she was ailing – she looked pale as a ghost. Tamsin sighed. Theirs was a world in which she had no part. She wandered slowly down the hill until she had filled her basket with blackberries, dreaming of escape from her humdrum life.

Then she saw it. Just where the lane from the school met the road from Britwell, half-hidden in fallen leaves and the slurry of mud thrown up by the hooves of the horses, a glint of coral and gold. She stooped, picked it up, and took it to the great pond beside the road. As soon as it was clean, she recognised it. A rosary of gold-mounted black pearls and large coral beads intricately carved into cages holding tiny figures. She knew it well, had seen it a hundred times in Lady Alyce's long thin fingers as she prayed in church, gave judgment in the courthouse or presided over village feasts. She ran it through her own fingers and realised that one link of its chain was broken. It must have fallen from her grace's girdle as she was riding into Ewelme. Tamsin's heart leapt as she imagined presenting herself at the palace gate, handing it over to Lady Alyce, hearing her grateful thanks, an offer of service, a chance to travel. Lost in a vision of herself on the bow of a ship bound for Calais, she didn't hear the stealthy footsteps behind her. A filthy hand suddenly snatched it away from her, shoving her hard into the sodden reeds at the edge of the village pond.

She turned her head and saw Wat the wild boy racing away from her, crowing and waving the rosary. He ran along the road, turning uphill just before the school onto a steep, narrow footpath that snaked through bramble bushes and led to the overgrown box coverts that rambled over the hillside above Ewelme. It was rough country she knew, home to much worse men than moon-faced, moon-struck Wat. She weighed up her options. Forget she ever saw the rosary and continue down the street to the school where old Mistress Trot was expecting her to oversee the seven-year-olds make their first scratches on wax tablets? Or chase after Wat?

The motto her father had lived by came to mind like a message from his grave: *Grab a chance and you won't be sorry for a might-have-been.* She hooked her skirts up into her girdle and looked up at the slopes of the hill above the village. Wat wasn't yet in sight, which was just as she wanted. He'd hurry less if he didn't know she was after him. She followed cautiously, placing her feet as silently as a deer's. At the end of the footpath the country opened out, and she could see a shambling shape zig-zagging up the hill. He was already two or three hundred yards ahead of her. She ducked down as she saw him stop and turn his head to see if he was being followed. When he saw nothing, he changed pace, began to amble along the ridge leading up to Swyncombe. She knew where he was going. He had a den in the hollow trunk of the biggest of the ancient oak trees that dotted the slopes high above the village. She'd often watched from a distance as the village boys sang rude songs around it and aimed stinking gobbets of entrails through the holes high in its massive trunk. He'd take his trophy there, she was sure. She decided to circle the hillside, using the cover of the clumps of box that encircled the great tree, and then wait until he left the den again before going inside it. She pulled her hood up to hide her face. Now she could pass like a shadow in her dark green cloak and brown dress. Concentrating on stealth, she didn't see the two men following at a cautious distance behind her, moving as soundlessly as she did.

Alyce Chaucer, Dowager Duchess of Suffolk, widow of three of England's wealthiest men and mother of the greatest dandiprat ever to disgrace a dukedom, raised her intricately embroidered skirts and silken undershift, and settled herself on the padded seat of her close-stool. She sighed with relief. Even though they had left Leighton Buzzard soon after dawn, the journey to Ewelme Palace had taken them most of the daylight hours. She had hoped for an opportunity to ease herself at Britwell Salome, but Ralph Boteler, still nursing a long-standing grievance against the Chaucer family, had offered no hospitality. She was exhausted. The long cavalcade of horse-drawn chariots and baggage wagons, riders and footmen, hounds and falcons had spent three days and nights on the cross-country journey from the Suffolks' castle at Wingfield, stopping for the first night at St Edmund's Abbey in Bury and for the second at Someries Castle, near Luton, home of Sir John Wenlock, once an enemy but now she hoped a friend. He and she were almost of an age, and both bore their years well. Though in his sixties, he still had the agility and strength of a much younger man, and she had maintained all her youthful grace. They'd sat up late, talking of old times and of books, and he'd asked her to be a trustee for some properties that he was reassigning.

She'd left Luton at dawn, so that she could spend a night at her Leighton Buzzard hospital and chantry, before taking the Roman road to Oxfordshire. Her right-hand man in Suffolk, Denzil Caerleon, was a skilled stargazer. He had predicted that the good weather would last both for her journey by land and for his own by water to London. He'd been right, too: clear skies and a waxing moon had made it possible to extend her daily rides. The fine new bells of her church pealed a welcome as the long procession wound its way down Firebrass Hill from Britwell Salome, and Alyce's dulled spirit brightened as she took in the gentle sweep of the valley in which she had been born. Her heartland.

Once they reached Ewelme an agreeable chaos reigned. Young and old alike cheered at the sight of 'Our Lady', as she was called by the villagers with possessive pride. The younger Ewelme children made no distinction between Alyce, who often wore the de la Pole colours of blue and gold, and the tall blue and gold cloaked statue of the Virgin Mary in the church. It was a pleasant change from the sidelong glances and embittered whispers that had been her lot at Wingfield. Her decision to remove every stick of her own belongings from the Suffolk ducal seat and leave her son Jack and his royal wife in undisputed possession now rather than after her death would cause widespread rumours at court of a rift between them, but wasn't it true? All that had happened was that she had given up trying to heal it. Jack loathed her, and there seemed nothing she could do to win favour with him. Nor could she take any pleasure in the two little boys on whom he and Bess lavished all their love. She never saw them without a qualm of conscience.

Far more tenants than she'd anticipated had lined the approach to the great north gate of the palace, arms laden with gifts: crocks of cream, nets of eggs, even bundles of kindling. She noticed the trouble they had taken to decorate the baskets and pots that held their offerings; much more than they could spare, she knew. Even the toddlers had carried bunches of dried lavender and cooking herbs, and one little lad had led a squeaking piglet with a wreath of crab apples around his neck.

As she smiled at them and bent down to take the prettiest of the posies, her doubts about abandoning Wingfield dissolved. Wenlock had warned her that it would leave her isolated and vulnerable. But what of that? She was surrounded by well-wishers here at Ewelme. Her steward Ben Bilton would approve her return, she was sure. He had no time for the posturing pomp adopted by the young duke. But where was Ben she wondered as she passed the jesses of her hawk over to the waiting falconer. As essential to the smooth running of the household as salt is to meat, he should have been at the forefront of the welcome, but only her secretary Simon Brailles stood at the gatehouse, his fluttering black gown making him crow-like and ominous.

Just inside the palace forecourt was a shabby-looking pedlar in a wide-brimmed hat, his basket on the ground beside him, lid raised to show a tempting array of trinkets. The slim hound walking beside Alyce's horse gave a low growl as they passed him, and Alyce stung the dog with the tip of her riding crop, smiling apologetically to the pedlar, who touched his fist to his forehead respectfully. Beside the porch to the great hall was the usual line of petitioners eager for her to settle their disputes and solve problems. She dismounted, handing a waiting groom the reins of Larkspur, a dappled jennet with a fine arch to her neck and an Arab flair to her nostrils.

A chair of state had been placed ready for Alyce. Her mother Maud had taught her never to hurry homecomings, to ask questions, to learn as much as she could about what was happening in the lives of the men, women and children to whom she was rather more important than the king himself, so that she would make merciful but just decisions.

'When hard times come, you need them as much as they need you, mark my words. Their respect and loyalty can make the difference between survival and ruin.' Hard times were here with a vengeance now, with Henry VI, the rightful king of England, immured in the Tower of London, his French queen Margaret of Anjou fled home to her father, and avaricious Yorkist eyes upon the lands of supporters of Lancaster.

She put out her hand to Simon Brailles, who bent over it humbly.

'Is all well, Simon?' she asked. Was it just his usual nervousness or was there a shadow of panic in his eyes as he nodded his head?

'Neither Ben nor Farhang is here to greet me. Where are they?'

'Farhang was summoned by Sir Brian Fulbert. Lady Anne is in labour, a hard one. He rode up to Swyncombe with his medicine wallet yesterday. And Bilton galloped away as soon as your harbinger rode in to say you were at Britwell. I've no idea why.'

Alyce sighed. 'No doubt he will return and explain himself soon. He's always been a law unto himself. And it's you I need now. I have quantities of books for you to sort out. They're in the first of the wagons. The most important are my grandfather's, of course – his *Canterbury Tales*, *The House of Fame*, *The Legend of Good Women* and one I am especially fond of, his *Treatise on the Astrolabe*. Put them with my other copies of his writings. Those in white bindings are holy books, some for my palace chapel and some for William Marton's library in the God's House; you can decide between you how they should be divided. The red bindings are for my library. But unpack them all in my cabinet and record them on my catalogue scroll.'

As Simon bowed assent, Alyce noticed a trio of tatter-demalion old men close behind him. They must each be hoping to fill the empty place in the Ewelme God's House left when Nicolas Webb died a month or so ago. A home in her almshouse was much coveted; it guaranteed an old age spent in security and unusual comfort.

She waved a hand towards the old men.

'Are these the candidates for Nicolas Webb's cell?'

'So far, my lady.' Simon's eyes scuttered to them, the sky, the ground, everywhere but to her face. Something was wrong. But what?

'They don't look very promising. What does Marton think? As Master of the God's House, he is going to have most to do with whomever is chosen.'

'He thought it better to await your grace's return before catechising them.'

'I can see why. Well, there is no hurry. Better candidates may yet present themselves. Take them to the kitchen court and ask Martha Purbeck to find them bowls of pottage and a place to sleep. Take Leo too and get him food and water. Now I must see my people.' Simon bowed again, clicked his fingers to the dog, and shepherded the old men and Leo away.

It was an hour before all the plaintiffs had been dealt with, and Alyce gained the sanctuary of her own chamber – and the relief of the privy in its outer turret. She found herself thinking about Nicolas Webb. Sudden death wasn't unusual, particularly among the elderly bedesmen, chosen because of the hardships fate had dealt them. But Webb had only been fifty, and though short of a leg he had been in good enough health to help William Marton with almshouse business. Mushroom poisoning, Simon's letter had said. That was strange. Webb was as learned in plant lore as Farhang Amiri, the aged Persian in charge of the almshouse infirmary, and Nan Ormesby, its matron. He had been a discriminating collector of fungi for years. Perhaps he had been supping with someone more ignorant.

Her dress readjusted, Alyce went back into her chamber, to find that Marlene and Eloise had tidied her bags away into the wardrobe and piled a welcome heap of cushions on the miniver coverlet spread on its canopied bed of state. The daughters of her dearest friends, they had learnt the ways of a formal ducal court at Wingfield, waiting on her daughter-in-law, the new young duchess. Plump little Eloise was a sensible enough chit, though shy, but Marlene, who had the promise of her mother's beauty, had minced about like one of the exotic cranes in the Wingfield aviary. Recently there had been a suppressed excitement about her that suggested an unsuitable liaison. Well, leaving Wingfield would have put paid to that. She settled herself on the bed, then smiled at them both.

'Thank you, my dears. Now leave me. The chamberlain will no doubt have duties for you.'

Alyce watched Eloise bob a curtsey and guessed that Marlene would be rolling her eyes and hissing annoyance as soon as they were out of earshot. Leo, fed now and ready for a caress, slipped through the open door as they left, and stared up hopefully. At her nod, he bounded up and settled at her side. She fondled his silky ears, then reached into the hanging pocket on her belt for her rosary to say some prayers of thanks for her homecoming. And found nothing.

She frowned, sat up and looked around the room. When had she last had it? She thought back to the journey from their last stop, Britwell, where her neighbour Ralph Boteler had refused to receive them. She had been so incensed that she'd calmed herself after they continued on their way by using the rosary to recite a dozen Hail Marys as they filed through the great beech woods that clothed the northern slopes of the long scarp above Ewelme. Perhaps she had absentmindedly tucked it into her girdle instead of safely away in her pocket. It must have been lost somewhere along the track – or after their arrival in the palace itself. She cursed herself for not being more careful with her precious keepsake. Made of corals from the Indies and gold from Samarkand, and fashioned in Damascus for a Coptic abbot, it had been brought to Italy, where her grandfather Geoffrey, then Richard II's ambassador in Milan, had been presented with it by Duke Bernabò Visconti. The coral beads held scenes from Christ's life. It had been in the family for nearly ninety years, and now she had lost it.

The palace seethed like a disturbed ants' nest. Grooms checked Larkspur's harness, the stable and the courtyard. Footmen lifted rush mats off the floor of the hall and peered into dark corners, and Martha Purbeck the chamberlain (Alyce had long ago decided that she preferred a woman to head her household servants) set footmen to search the privy and shake out the rugs and cushions on the great bed. Every other able body was sent off to walk up the hill towards Britwell. Two hours later most had returned, though a few hopefuls stayed out, weaving to and fro on the track, eyes glued to the ground.

Alyce stood by the great north gate looking up the hill, hoping against hope to see an eager running figure. But there was nothing, just the darkening sky and the lowing of the cattle trooping back to the home farm.

Simon Brailles came hurrying up, face pinched and frowning. She turned to him.

'We will walk to the church and pray that it be found.'

They were almost there, followed by a crowd of villagers, when a girl's high screams, panic-stricken but determined and unstoppable, sounded from high on the hill above. Then they were abruptly cut off, only to be followed by a different kind of howl, deep and guttural, and with an unearthly quality about it that made the listeners quake. Then the screams began again. One of the villagers, a tired-looking young woman with a crying baby in her arms, suddenly shrieked aloud.

'That's Tamsin. Mad hobbledehoy, she's in trouble again. Tom, Will, Hugh – go and help her.' A pack of men and boys raced up the hill towards the huge hollow tree that was the source of the grunts and gasps and inhuman howls. At its base they discovered a struggling mass of limbs so closely entwined that it was hard to see who they belonged to until they were hauled apart. The rescuers were left holding two shabbily dressed men with matted beards and the V mark of vagrant branded on their foreheads, a furious red-haired girl with her kirtle torn and her bodice ripped, and a squat, shaggy-haired boy who had to be held in an armlock to stop his tooth-and-nail attack on the men.

An hour later Tamsin, now decently clad in a bodice and kirtle lent to her by a tiring woman, made a clumsy curtsey in front of Lady Alyce's chair of state. The duchess looked appraisingly at her.

'So you found my rosary in the mud, then had it snatched from you by Wat, then followed him up to the oak trees to get it back. That was brave, but foolish. You must know the dangers of those woods. They're a nest of outlaws.'

Daunted by being face to face with the sovereign lady of Ewelme, awed by the splendid tapestries and fine furniture of the great chamber, and unsure whether she was to be praised or punished, Tamsin could do nothing but nod. Her whole body felt bruised, and she felt her eye throb. It would be purple before sundown.

Alyce sighed. 'But you're an Ormesby – with all your family's fighting spirit, it seems. They tell me that you landed one of the outlaws a fine kick in his hangers and bit a chunk out of the hand of the other. Your father Roger must have been sorry you weren't a boy. He died of the pox three years ago, didn't he? As did your mother, if I remember right. Who's looking after you now?'

Tamsin managed to stutter a reply. 'I lived with my sister

Loveday till she got married, but our old cottage was her dowry. Now I live with my grandmother in the attics over the God's House wash house. I help Nan to look after the bedesmen and aid Mistress Trot with teaching the little ones in the school.'

'And do you like it?'

Tamsin hesitated, looking up at Lady Alyce. She had an odd face. Long, straight nose, thoughtful, cool grey eyes a little aslant, high cheekbones, a thin mouth with a one-sided quirk to it. There was a fine web of lines around her eyes, a weary set to her lips. Should she risk saying no? Alyce seemed to guess her dilemma and answered for her.

'Not much, but what's the alternative? Well – for the return of my rosary, I certainly owe you a reward, and Ormesbys have served the Chaucers long and well time out of mind. I shall make it known that I will dower you generously when you come to marry. That will have suitors flocking, for all your freckles and wildcat ways.'

It was, for a girl like Tamsin, the offer of a lifetime. Her mouth gaped, but then closed into a determined line. She shook her head.

'I don't want to marry,' she blurted out. 'At least, not for a long time. I want – I want to journey, to see the world.'

Alyce raised her eyebrows. 'And how do you propose to do that?'

'By your leave, my lady, if you will take me into your service, I would work for no wage but my board and lodging. And I can read and write. I learnt in your own school – under Master Brailles when he was schoolmaster there.'

Alyce looked hard at her, noting the snub nose, the odd eyes, one hazel brown, one green, the determined chin, and the

13

ginger frizz of hair that was already escaping from its braids. Not pretty but brimming with character.

'So he told me when I asked about you. He also told me that you were a harum-scarum miss, forever playing truant, who caused more rumpus in the playground than any of the boys.'

Tamsin coloured. 'But I'm older now. I know what it is to work for my keep. I could... I could keep watch over your rosary. And your precious books. My mother taught me to read, and I love books, though of course I have none of my own.' She looked up at Lady Alyce, took in again the lined brow and sad eyes, and daringly added, 'I could read to you when you are wakeful and worried at night.'

'You presume, child,' said Alyce tartly. There was a long silence. Tamsin's heart sank. Now she'd be sent away, the chance of a lifetime lost.

'My grandmother says I have the sixth sense, knowing what's in men's hearts,' she added desperately. 'But she told me to mate my sharp eyes and ears to a shut mouth.' Their eyes met.

Alyce sighed. 'I can't promise to keep you by me for long, child, nor will I be journeying for a while. But it happens that I am short of a tiring maid. Sarah Osborne was sick as a dog on the journey home, and I've sent her back to her mother in Bensington.'

Tamsin was stricken. 'We grew up together. Is she very ill? Will she get better?'

'Let us hope so, for her and her soul's sake,' said Alyce, a touch of acid in her voice. 'So would you like to take her place? On a month's trial?'

Tamsin's eyes were alight with joy. She saw Alyce smile wryly.

'I think that is answer enough. But you'll need that shut mouth if you're going to last the course in my service, little chit. Go and get your grandmother. I must make sure that she's content with such an arrangement.'

Tamsin whirled towards the door, then stopped and turned. 'Your grace, what will happen to Wat? Please don't punish him. He – he's not quite right in the head, you see. He's like a jackdaw: anything bright and he's drawn to it. And he saved me. I was in his den searching for the rosary when those scurvy pisspots tried to swive me, and he came hurtling out of the woods and threw himself on them.'

'What do you think should happen to him?'

Tamsin thought for a moment. 'Well, he's strong and willing if you know the right way to handle him. My grandmother does – she always calls him off the hill to help her with the fruit harvest in the orchard. And she'll need more help if I'm to work for you. And if he worked in the kitchen of the almshouses and had my bed in the loft over the laundry, the village boys would stop persecuting him. They're that frightened of my Nan. Wat's only mazed, not dangerous.'

Alyce was silent for a beat, then nodded approvingly. 'A Christian thought, Tamsin, and a practical one. Fetch your grandmother, and she and Simon Brailles can put their heads together over the terms of your future – and Wat's.'

Heart full, Tamsin curtseyed jerkily, and dashed down the stairs to find Nan.

Alyce walked to the window and watched her racing off up the hill towards the almshouses, fleet as a hare. If she'd had a daughter of her own, she'd have loved one like Tamsin. 'Wakeful and worried.' The girl had touched a nerve. Great lady though she was, indeed because she was, she had endless anxieties. The Suffolks had once been high on Dame Fortune's wheel but all that had changed after her husband Duke William's murder and a decade of civil war. She had an unwelcome pang of conscience. The root of Jack's distrust and dislike of her lay in her refusal to investigate who was responsible for ordering his father's death sixteen years ago. William de la Pole had been captured on his way into exile, taken aboard a ship called *The Nicholas of the Tower*, and clumsily executed with a blunt axe. His body had been left on Dover beach, his head on a pole in a jeering pun on his name. No trace of the ship could be found. Jack had called her failure cowardly, and it had been. But she had known that William's powerful enemies could break her if she pursued them.

She crossed the room and opened the small wainscot door that led into her private cabinet. Simon looked up from the books that he was unwrapping.

'Did you hear all that, Simon? Have I done the right thing?'

She knew perfectly well that she couldn't have done a worse thing in Simon's eyes. But then he was biased. Though both families were trusted servants of two generations of Chaucers, Brailles and the Ormesbys were as different as night and day. She wondered what he would say.

He hesitated before speaking. 'Time will tell, your grace. She is very inexperienced and, as I warned you, headstrong to a fault.' He paused, then added unwillingly, 'But there's no malice in her, and I think her plan for Wat could be the making of him.'

'I'm sure I can count on you to guide her and check her exuberance,' said Alyce dryly. Then she smiled. 'What I like most about you, Simon, even more than your elegant writing hand and your discretion, is your honesty. That's why I chose you as my secretary.'

She expected a grateful bow, but instead he lowered his eyes in misery. What was wrong, she wondered. At last he managed a tight little smile.

'I'll do my best, my lady. Shall I go down to the God's House and arrange things with Nan Ormesby?'

'Tamsin has already gone to fetch her. Meanwhile, I have a present for you.' Alyce walked over to a leather bag and unstrapped the belt around it. She opened it and took out several carefully folded parcels wrapped in linen crash. Unfolding the first, she revealed two doublets, one russet, one green. A second contained a russet cloak, with a furred trim. A third held three white linen shirts.

Simon stared. Reading his thoughts, Alyce smiled.

'And don't tell me that they are too fine. Your old schoolmastering gown is almost green with age, and black is so gloomy.' She took up the other packages. 'And these are for William Marton. A blue velvet chasuble and two white albs. I intend the church of Ewelme to do as much honour to the name of Chaucer as that of Wingfield does to that of de la Pole. These are fine examples of what old John Lydgate calls ghostly armour in his splendid poem on the Mass. Take them over to Marton now.'

After Simon had left, Alyce crossed the room to a high-backed daybed at one side of the fireplace and sank thankfully back onto its cushions. There was a whimper from the door. Leo. He'd slipped away to visit his old haunts during the hunt for the rosary. Alyce rose again and let him in. Settling back on her bed, she clicked her fingers. As the dog leapt up and settled close beside her, she reached into her sleeve pocket for the little Latin book about chess that Wenlock had given her as a parting gift. It was by a Dominican monk called Jacobus de Cessolis, he had told her, but this copy was written by the renowned Florentine Bartolomeo Sanvito in an elegant cursive script that was far easier to read than the dense northern fashion of lettering.

She thought about Sir John for a moment. They'd played chess, as they always did, and she'd beaten him, as she always did. She was never quite sure whether he lost deliberately or not. You were never quite sure about anything with Wenlock – except for his exquisite taste in books. She opened the Cessolis and began to read. But she had read no more than a paragraph before she had fallen fast asleep.

Someries Castle

Sunlight crept through gaps in the bed curtains, and John Wenlock stirred lazily. Tumbled sheets and the sound of deep snores testified to the energetic lovemaking that had rapidly followed Joan Moulton's evening arrival at Someries. She and Wenlock were old friends and dispensed with niceties when they both had only one thing in mind. After a simple but satisfying meal of cold capon in a quince sauce, they had dismissed the servants, taken a tray of almond tarts and a jug of malmsey, and exchanged the draughty great hall for Sir John's handsome curtained bed. It was a convenient relationship for them both. Sir John's wife had died two years ago. Joan was a buxom widow who had turned her third husband's London bookselling business into a thriving concern, but still kept an eye on the estates in Bedfordshire she'd inherited from her second marriage.

'What I love about you, Joan, is your eagerness,' said Wenlock lazily. 'I don't know another woman who is quite as shameless as you in pursuing her desires.'

'I take that as a compliment. First in a largish field though, I fear.' She stretched out her arms and yawned, pulling her shift together over her breasts, and smacking his hand as he tried to pull it aside again.

'Enough. I have business to attend to this morning.'

'Nothing that can't wait half an hour, surely?'

'And I'm hungry.' She slipped out of bed with impressive

agility and began to get dressed. He watched appreciatively as she rolled on her stockings and pulled garters up her generous thighs. Her fleshiness made his mind wander contrariwise to the angular slenderness of his visitor two days earlier.

'I'm worried about Alyce,' Joan heard him murmur, half to himself, as she pulled her dress over her shift. Her head turned.

'You mean the Dowager Duchess of Suffolk? You told me that she stayed here a few days ago. Her son is married to the king's sister. She has the right to be called Princess Alyce now. I wouldn't have thought she had many problems.'

'More than she realises, I fear. She's burnt her boats with her son and his wife and taken all her worldly goods to Ewelme. It doesn't do to offend the king's family, let alone your own.'

'So what is a notoriously arrogant Lancastrian widow to you, John? You don't often show concern for your fellow mortals. Too busy feathering your own nest.'

Wenlock pursed his lips. 'It's complicated. She's not a lusty woman, of course. And we were once at odds over an Oxfordshire manor. But I admire her.'

'Because she's indecently rich?'

'No. Because of the way she's using her money. She is forever distributing charity to the tenants of her estates. She has been exceptionally generous in endowing almshouses and schools. That's her real passion – education. Especially for women. There are as many girls in her schools as boys. And she loves books, not as valuable objects the way you do, but as companions, the way I do. And she writes poems, I believe, although she won't show me anything she's written.'

Joan raised her eyebrows in amusement. 'This is a new side of you, John. Forgive me if I say I don't believe a word of it. Admit it, you want a slice of her wealth.'

'If anyone gets a slice of her wealth, it'll be the sharks who began circling when they heard she was leaving Wingfield. I warned her when she visited Someries on her way home. But she refused to listen.'

'Her departure was the talk of Cheapside last week,' said Joan. 'She took most of Wingfield's furnishings with her.'

'What the world sees as arrogance is her way of protecting herself. She learnt that during her marriage to Duke William. If she hadn't, he'd have broken her spirit. He knew just how to twist the knife without drawing blood. The truth is that she's done remarkably well to survive the last decade. But she refuses to admit that now she urgently needs friends who are well thought of at court.'

'Something which you certainly are,' said Joan. 'You've feathered your nest nicely by becoming responsible for so many confiscated Lancastrian estates. And how are you planning to help her?'

'I've asked her to be a trustee for some of my properties. That will give the lie to those who say she has no Yorkist allies.'

Joan hoicked a wide woven belt up under her breasts and pulled on her mantle.

'You're making me curious about her. Perhaps I could meet her and make up my own mind. She also sounds a likely customer. If she's brought her library from Suffolk, she might be interested in selling surplus volumes and buying new books.'

She saw Wenlock ponder her words and guessed that he was calculating the advisability of introducing her, a tradeswoman of some notoriety, to the wealthiest and touchiest noblewoman in the land.

'You might just accord fruitfully if I present you in the right light,' he said at last. 'And a friendship between you could be most useful.'

'Useful to you, I suppose you mean,' snapped Joan.

Wenlock shook his head. 'You malign me, my dear. As I said, I'm very fond of Lady Alyce. And she's going to need resourceful friends in the near future. But she and you are as different as chalk and cheese.'

'Opposites can attract,' said Joan cheerily. 'And we have an interest in books in common.'

'True,' said Wenlock. But I doubt if she'll be coming to London for a while. Could you go to Oxford to meet her if I wrote to introduce you?'

'That would be no hardship,' said Joan, as she began to swathe her riding turban over her hat. 'I'd like to see John Doll again. He's got the best book business outside London.'

Wenlock pulled on a loose gown. 'I'm due in Oxford on Monday to consult with William Waynflete, the Bishop of Winchester, and George Neville, the Chancellor of the University, as to who should be the next Sheriff of Oxfordshire. Later that week, Neville is holding a feast in Balliol College. He's bound to invite Lady Alyce; she's a notable patron of the University. Suppose I ask him to invite you as well? Then I can introduce you to her, and perhaps we could visit Ewelme the next day.'

'Why not? Georgie-Porgie and I are old friends. He's been in my shop times without number, buying books the Church would frown upon. I've enjoyed entertaining him as well. Nice young man. A lot to learn in the bedchamber, of course. To be expected, I suppose, given his chosen career.

Wenlock's long, saturnine face creased in a crooked grin.

'You never cease to surprise me, Joan. You'll be telling me you've bedded King Edward next.'

'Not my type,' said Joan. 'Too full of himself. And he prefers spring chickens, anyway. Well, usually. Elizabeth Wydeville certainly succeeded where a good many younger and better women had failed. She showed him what he'd been missing, I suppose.'

'You must call her Queen Elizabeth now,' warned Wenlock.

Joan frowned. 'Only to her face, dear heart. Margaret of Anjou may be in exile, but by my lights she's the rightful queen of England. And her husband Henry of Lancaster is the rightful king, for all he's in the Tower. But I'd like to meet Princess Alyce. I wonder how much she likes a title earned by her compliance with the new regime. Her forefathers were heart and soul for Lancaster.'

'She'd be foolish to follow that dim star,' said Wenlock.

'I wonder,' mused Joan. *What's bred in the bone...* Let me know if you can arrange an invitation for me to Balliol, and I'll meet you in Oxford. I'll bring some books that will interest both Georgie and the duchess. Now, where has Monique got to? It's time we started for London.'

'I wouldn't be surprised if she was keeping my secretary company,' said Wenlock. 'He tells me that he finds her most intriguing.'

Joan chuckled. 'There's more to Monique than meets the eye. She is no ordinary companion.'

'Nor is Francis Thynne an ordinary secretary.'

'He is dauntingly austere, I must say. Where did you find him?'

'He's worked for me since he was twelve. I came across him after the vicar of Hitchin begged a place for him at the grammar school I founded there. He could already write exquisitely. Now he's fluent in French and Latin, and an excellent teacher for my wards when I'm in London, as well as being a useful secretary when I go abroad for the king. Close as an oyster, too. Even I don't know what he's thinking, though he's been with me for thirty years.'

'Does he ever smile?'

'Not often. But then nor does Monique.'

'So they are well suited. How convenient for us. Now – will you break your fast with me, or must you hurry away?'

'I've got some deliveries to make in St Albans before I return to London. I'd best be on my way. I'll go and rouse Monique. Enjoy Oxford.' And, after bestowing a last lascivious kiss full on his smiling mouth, she was gone.

Ewelme

Tamsin adjusted her pitifully small bundle of belongings and gave a shy knock on the door to Martha Purbeck's quarters. The Ewelme Palace chamberlain had a reputation for pernickety fierceness, and Nan had warned her to mind her manners. A sharp voice called to her to come in. Tamsin did so, latching the door behind her. Martha was sitting on a stool by the window sewing. Short in stature but not in girth, she had several chins, a button of a nose and shrewd blue eyes.

'So here's our madcap heroine,' she said. 'Come this way. You're to have Sarah's garret. It's next to Eloise and Marlene's room, and over Lady Alyce's chamber.' The chamberlain headed purposefully away from the main staircase and towards the kitchens. Tamsin was puzzled.

'Isn't Lady Alyce's room up the stairs in the West Tower?'

'Aye, but the likes of you don't take the main stairs.' She led Tamsin through a succession of rooms, then pulled back an arras to reveal a winding stair. It led up two floors to a landing, along which were several doors. From behind one of them, Tamsin could hear a high excited voice.

'And do you know what he said to me, Eloise? He said that...' She broke off as the door opened and the chamberlain and Tamsin entered.

'What did who say?' said Martha.

Marlene looked sly. 'He said that... that... I don't remember.'

'You'd better be careful who you flirt with, my girl. You'll get into serious trouble one of these days, with your come-hither ways.' She turned and put an arm around Tamsin.

'This is Lady Alyce's new maid, Tamsin Ormesby. She is going to replace Sarah for the nonce. Make her welcome. Tamsin, this is Marlene, and this is Eloise.'

Eloise, the younger of the sisters, gave her a shy smile. Marlene scowled.

'So what's wrong with Sarah?'

'She's taken something she shouldn't have. For a problem she shouldn't have had either. She's in the infirmary.'

Eloise looked horrified. 'But Marlene, you said...'

But her sister jumped forward and smacked her cheek. 'Shut up you fool.'

Martha frowned. 'Enough of that, Marlene. I'll show Tamsin where she's to sleep, then I'm going back down to the kitchens.' She looked at the leather trunks and sacking bundles strewn around the disordered room and sniffed.

'You should have unpacked by now. When Tamsin's settled in, she can help you finish. This afternoon the bell will sound for vespers, and Lady Alyce will expect you Stonor girls to accompany her. Don't be late.'

She shepherded Tamsin out, and slammed the door shut.

'Little hussy,' she muttered crossly. 'She'll get more than she bargained for, just as Sarah has, if she isn't careful.' She opened the door of a small dark room. The bed had been stripped to a straw mattress, and the hooks on the walls were bare. All that remained of Sarah's occupation was a musky perfume. Martha wrinkled her nose with distaste.

'What a stench. More fitted to a woman of the street than a decent girl. Open the window, and let some fresh air in. You'll need a pillow and a sheet and a feather bed. I'll go down and look them out and have them brought up. Put your things in that chest, and then help the Stonor girls with theirs.'

She swept out of the room, and Tamsin could hear her firm tread along the landing and down the stairs. She took a stool over to the shuttered window and stood on it, struggling with the rusted latch. It seemed that Sarah had not been one for fresh air. At last she managed to swing it open and leant out. There was the main courtyard, the people in it oddly foreshortened, looking like ninepin men and women. It's a bird's-eye view, she thought, delighted. There was the roof of the great hall, trimmed with stone pinnacles. Over the roofs on the other side she could see the kitchen garden, where cloths lay spread out over rosemary and lavender hedges. Beyond were the brewery and the bakehouse, the great chimney they shared belching white smoke up into the autumn afternoon. On the south side were the high walls of Lady Alyce's private garden; from here she could see its curving hedges and raised flower beds, four tunnels of cordoned fruit trees and the silver sheen of a long canal of water. Then a hand clutched her ankle.

'Come down from there, lazy bumpkin.' Marlene gave a tug that almost made Tamsin tumble on top of her. 'You're supposed to be unpacking for us.'

Tamsin began an angry rejoinder, then remembered Nan's warning 'Watch your tongue. You can't cheek the quality the way you cheek us who know you.' She followed Marlene back into the next-door room. Eloise looked apologetic.

'I said Marlene should give you time to unpack.'

'Unpack what?' Marlene jeered. 'You're a soft-hearted cissy, Eloise. Go and get my last bundle, the red leather one. I think it must have been left in the hall.' After Eloise had gone, Marlene turned to Tamsin with an ingratiating smile.

'So you are going to do Sarah's work now, are you? I hope you'll be as good as she was at braiding my hair. She and I were good friends. She knew when to hold her tongue. See you do too and I'll make it worth your while. Here, take this lace kerchief – it would look good at the neck of that blue dress.'

Tamsin took it hesitantly and bobbed her head shyly. Just then Eloise came into the room with Marlene's bundle. Seeing the kerchief in Tamsin's hand, she snatched it away.

'What are you doing with that? It's mine. I bought it yesterday from the pedlar in the courtyard. Where did you find it? Keep your thieving hands off my things, or I'll have you whipped.'

Tamsin flushed scarlet, and Marlene snorted with mirth.

'Ease up, Eloise. I just gave it to her. It doesn't suit you one bit. Too fancy for a plain Jane like you.' Glaring at her sister, Eloise tossed the bundle angrily into a corner.

'Don't mind her,' said Marlene. 'She's jealous because I was so much more popular than her at Wingfield. When Queen Elizabeth visited, she and her favourite lady-in-waiting

Countess Anne Vere always asked if I could ride with them. And the countess gave me this dress – look, these long sleeves are the latest fashion at court. That's what I'd like more than anything – a chance to go to court. But the old trout always frowns whenever I suggest it.'

Shocked by such lack of respect, Tamsin set about the unpacking. Marlene sat on the window seat winding a long tress of fair hair around her fingers and looking down into the courtyard. Then she gave a whoop of joy.

'I can see him, Eloise! Oh, he's looking up. The rascal.'

Curious, Tamsin edged towards the window to see who she was talking about, but just then there was a light rap on the door and Martha Purbeck's maid Ella entered.

'Marlene, Eloise, it's almost time for vespers. Lady Alyce says you're to bring her cloak and her prayer book. You'd better hurry.'

Marlene turned from the window and pulled a face. 'I'm not going. I've got better plans. Make an excuse for me, Eloise. Or I'll tell mother that you lost her missal.'

She grabbed her cloak and hurried out of the room.

Eloise raised her eyes to heaven, pulled her own cloak around her shoulders, and went out of the door. Ella turned to Tamsin.

'Isn't that Marlene a shrew? But she'll make it worth your while if you keep her secrets. She gave Sarah some lovely things. I've put bedding into your room. I can finish here if you want to get your bed made before we go to vespers. We've got a few more minutes. Lady Alyce always sets off early.'

Tamsin couldn't wait to go back next door to gloat at the luxury of the tiny space that was now home. She marvelled at the downy depth of the feather bed and the sweet-scented sheets. She hung her spare gown and cloak on the wall hooks and put the rest of her things in the chest. Then she looked out of the window again, wondering who Marlene was planning to meet. But she saw only the pedlar, his basketwork trays of trinkets laid out beside him.

Roused from her book by the calling bell, Alyce took only a few minutes to descend the stairs from her chamber to the hall, stride to the inner gatehouse of the palace and click her fingers at a tow-headed young porter to fall in behind her. She crossed the drawbridge, went through the outer gatehouse and walked along the main street to the school, then up past the almshouses to the church, relishing the familiarity of the village in which she had grown up. To the west, the great orange ball of the sun was fretted into a complex web by the branches of the gnarled oak trees that edged the horizon. It was good to be back in this orderly world where the hours were measured out by study and godly observance, rather than being frittered away in gaming and flirting as they were at Wingfield. And there was always peace to be found in the church she had glorified in memory of her parents.

Before she had reached the church porch, Eloise Stonor, panting and clutching Alyce's cloak and psalter, caught her up, and walked demurely behind her as they went up the aisle. The church was already full of villagers, standing in chattering, jostling groups: men to the right, women on the left. One of the musicians up in the gallery hastily blew an erratic fanfare on his trumpet when he saw the duchess appear below him. It was so fartlike that it produced a ripple of laughter among the congregation, but when they too saw their liege lady they fell silent, and made way for her to walk up to and through the rood screen to her chair of state on the left-hand side of the nave. From here she could see across the chancel into the memorial chapel that almost thirty years ago she had commissioned in her parents' honour. Beeswax candles has been lit, clay oil lamps glowed in the alcoves and the setting sun was sending brilliant shards of light through the richly coloured glass of the clerestory windows. Rainbow shadows flickered over the wings of the angels carved on the roof braces and the serene faces of the statues in the chancel arches.

As she sat down, Eloise draped her cloak around her shoulders.

'Marlene has the headache,' she hissed as she tucked it around her mistress.

'How very convenient for her,' Alyce said coldly. 'She looked perfectly well earlier. She has altogether too many of these petty ailments when it's time to go to church.' She saw Eloise colour. How different the two sisters were.

Just then the bedesmen trooped into the Chaucer chapel. All wore long black gowns blazoned with red crosses. Those who could knelt in prayer on the thick rushes laid on the floor; the frailest sat on stools. With relief, Alyce saw the bowed white head of Gerard Vespilan, the senior bedesman. What a survivor he was. Eighty-five years old, he had been at Ewelme since before she was born. He was the bastard of an Italian banker based in London, and his artistic talent had led to his being apprenticed as a scribe and limner with one of London's most successful booksellers. Her grandfather Geoffrey had come across him there in the 1390s and had taken him on as secretary. After Geoffrey's death in 1400, her father Thomas had brought him back to the household at Ewelme.

When she'd been a small child at Ewelme, he had drawn for her endlessly: quick caricatures of everyone in the household; pictures of animals dressed in human clothes to illustrate her Aesop's *Fables*.

As if he could feel Alyce looking at him, Gerard raised his head and met her gaze with rheumy blue eyes. She lifted her white leather prayer book so that he could see that it was still the one that she valued above any other. He had illustrated that for her as well, with exquisite marginal decorations punctuated here and there with absurd grotesques, one a lifelike self-portrait, and had given it to her on the occasion of her second marriage, to Thomas Montagu, Earl of Salisbury, in 1422. One of his eyelids dropped in a brief wink, and she had difficulty in preventing her lips twitching into a smile. It was important not to show favour among the bedesmen, but Gerard was a special case. She noticed how his hands shook and how thin he had become since she had seen him last. Would this be his last winter?

Gerard was not the only bedesman to figure in her distant past. Kneeling on the floor towards the front of the chapel was grizzled, one-armed Joseph Pek, who had served with Thomas in Normandy forty years before. He'd been an archer, captured at Orléans in 1428, soon after Thomas himself had been killed by a ricocheting cannonball. The French normally lopped off the two forefingers of English archers, but, having seen him wield a mace in the melee as dexterously as he had drawn his bow, they had axed his arm at the elbow before they offered him as part of an exchange of prisoners. He'd been lucky to survive at all – only saved, he'd told her, by a comrade-in-arms who knew enough to tie his spare bowstring as a ligature round his upper arm to stop him bleeding to death. He'd returned to be marshal of the stables of her London home, Montagu Inn, but after William's death she'd asked him to return to Ewelme. Now, though nearly sixty, he was one of the most active of the God's House bedesmen, and still helped out in the stables. Four-square and sturdy, with a useful-looking short sword stuck in his belt and a glint in his black eyes, he had discouraged many a casual footpad when he rode out beside William Marton to collect rents due to the God's House.

Scanning the other nine bedesmen, she saw two new faces. Trusting her God's House clergy to choose suitable men, she had sent her assent to their appointments while she was in Suffolk. She must meet them later. There was the high tinkle of a handbell, and silence fell. A surpliced small boy walked up the aisle swinging a perfumed censer. Behind him, striding self-importantly in the sumptuous new blue damask chasuble that he wore over a snowy linen alb, came William Marton, followed by plump, jolly Peter Greene, Teacher of Grammar at the school. Last of all came the choir, boys from the school carrying candles and chanting the introit in haunting trebles: *Jubilate Deo Alleluia laudamus*. Greene, once a chaplain in Dorchester Abbey, loved music, and had taught them well. Alyce settled herself into her seat, absentmindedly fondling the lions' heads carved on the ends of its arms as she had seen her mother do times without number. She was home, among old friends who loved her. With nothing to fear.

Windsor

They were playing chess. Queen Elizabeth was white. She was always white. The thin dark man opposite her was, therefore, always red. They never drew lots, because the queen, heady with her newly acquired prerogative, liked to make the first move. Which suited her opponent well. His nature was all in measured reaction.

The game was at an interesting stage. The white king stood in a thicket of protective pieces, his queen foremost among them. The red king was less well placed. He had lost his most powerful pieces, including his queen, and he was protected only by his knights. Elizabeth moved her queen onto a new diagonal.

'Check,' she said, gleefully.

John Tiptoft, Earl of Worcester and Constable of England, counted twenty to himself to make it seem that the move was a dangerous one. Then, deliberately slowly, he put a hesitant hand towards his queen's knight. In an instant Elizabeth saw her danger. Quick as a viper's tongue her hand came forward and drew the queen back a square. Her opponent leant back with the shadow of a smile.

'You hadn't moved,' Elizabeth said defiantly. 'I'm allowed second thoughts until you move.'

'Of course, your majesty.' He moved his knight to threaten a white pawn, which Elizabeth protected with her bishop. He took the pawn; she took the knight. Now only a single red knight was left. He made it vault into a gap in the line of her pawns. She quickly moved her queen forward again and smiled with satisfaction. He coughed.

'I'm sorry, your majesty. I was about to say check to your king.'

She stared, suddenly seeing that his last knight was holding her king and her queen in a fork. She stood up, and with a petulant gesture swept the chess pieces onto the floor.

Just as one of the queen's ladies hurried to pick up the fallen chessmen, there was a rap at the door. A page went to open it, and a liveried steward entered.

'Sir Robert Harcourt, your highness.'

Elizabeth's face brightened. 'Send him in. Now, Constable, we shall see what treasons flourish in Oxfordshire.'

Burly and florid-faced, Sir Robert bustled in, made a low bow to the queen, and nodded to Tiptoft.

'I bring promising news, your highness. I have said before now that in my opinion Ewelme Palace is a nest of traitors. I had good reason for my suspicions, as a friend of mine has an informant in the Duchess of Suffolk's much-vaunted charity, the God's House. He has already told me of several suspect members of her household. But I decided not to act – after all, to kill the Hydra of disloyalty, we have to crop off all its heads. Now I hear that Lady Alyce has abandoned her son and your sister-in-law and is making Ewelme her permanent home. This is the time to seek proof positive of her perfidy, as well as that of her servants.'

Tiptoft, who knew how much Harcourt coveted the fertile acres and well-stocked forests of Ewelme, raised a sardonic eyebrow.

'Her perfidy? That seems hardly likely given her age and

her position as aunt by marriage to King Edward himself. You should now style her Princess Alyce, remember?'

'Age is no bar to treason, as we discovered when Sir John Fortescue absconded to join the French whore in Lorraine. And the nobility of this realm are so closely intermarried that only ties of blood have real credence.'

The queen gave a malicious smile. 'Well said, Sir Robert. Alyce's Lancastrian sympathies can be assumed. Chaucers served all three Henries. And my lady-in-waiting Anne Vere tells me that Alyce herself was a great confidante of the last Henry's wife, Margaret of Anjou. It wouldn't surprise me if she was party to the great deception, that conveniently timed one-off pregnancy that gave Henry of Lancaster an heir.'

'And shocked him out of his mind,' said Harcourt with a sneer. 'He claimed the boy must have been fathered by the Holy Ghost. My money was on Edmund Beaufort. Margaret and he were inseparable. He had an eye for French wenches.'

'No evidence has ever been found for that particular accusation,' said Tiptoft. 'And the loss of the Talbots and Aquitaine was cause enough for the king's mental collapse.'

'There might be evidence if Alyce, Margaret's friend and mentor, was put to the question with sufficient vigour,' said Elizabeth icily, her green eyes glinting. A vision of her legendary ancestor the serpent Melusine coiled in Tiptoft's mind.

Harcourt spoke again. 'My informant in the God's House is too lily-livered to offer conclusive proof of the duchess's treachery. I am planning to introduce a more ruthless man. He has personal reasons to hate the de la Poles. I have made sure that the almshouse is one bedesman short. All we need do is to get my spy accepted as the new bedesman, and we will have an agent at the heart of things.'

'But the licensing of God's House bedesmen is the duchess's personal prerogative,' objected Tiptoft. 'How can you be sure that Princess Alyce will accept your nominee?'

'Hear me out, my lord. The man I'll bring with me when I visit Ewelme in person will be a pallid scrivener enfeebled by a congestion of the lungs. Such a harmless-seeming man is bound to be attractive to the duchess, given her obsession with books and her much-vaunted charitability. And if he is sponsored by the queen, how could he be refused?' He gave a triumphant smile.

A slow smile wiped the sulkiness from Elizabeth's perfect face. 'And can you get an invitation to Ewelme?'

'I will write to the dowager duchess today, asking if my brother and I can visit her on our way back from Windsor next Thursday, and spend a day hunting there on Friday. She will be hard put to say no. She has to keep on the right side of loyal Yorkist lords like ourselves. Then I'll foist my man on her without warning. If he has your backing, she'll have to accept him.'

The queen hesitated. 'I should at least meet him, so that if needful I could justify presenting him. What is his background. And where is he now?'

'His name is Milo of Windsor, and he has worked for my brother and me for many years, proving himself adept at ingratiating himself with all and sundry. Disguised as a pedlar, he's been getting to know the country in and around Ewelme. With most useful results. He tells me that there are widespread rumours that the Swyncombe anchorite keeps the possessions of passing Lancastrian fugitives hidden in her cell. And, in the hope that you would agree, I brought him with me today. He is in the buttery.'

The queen turned to Lady Anne Vere.

'Anne, seek him out, and bring him here.' Lady Vere curtseyed and left the room.

Ten minutes later a nondescript figure followed Lady Anne into the presence chamber. His features were regular and not unhandsome, though masked by shaggy hair and a straggly black beard. Otherwise there was nothing memorable about his appearance. Milo of Windsor was indeed a perfect spy, Tiptoft reflected, unremarkable in any way, a chameleon who could take on numerous guises. He wondered if, once the present distasteful episode was over, he could persuade him to join his company of intelligencers in the Tower of London.

'Welcome, Milo,' said Elizabeth. 'We have a mission for you.'

The grey-clad figure bowed unctuously, 'I am profoundly honoured, your royal majesty.'

Harcourt stepped forward. 'You are to return to Oxfordshire and continue as a pedlar for the next few days. If all goes as we plan, my brother and I will meet you in Henley on Wednesday and get you shorn and shaven and blench your face so you look suitably sickly. Then we'll take you to Ewelme. We'll say that you are Milo of Windsor, who worked for the queen as a scrivener when young, but is now suffering from a congestion of the lungs, and that her majesty desires the duchess to make you a bedesman. Once you are settled, you will search out any treasons.'

'It will be my pleasure,' said Milo, his peat-black eyes bright with anticipation. 'But what if I find nothing untoward?'

Harcourt smiled unpleasantly. 'One way or another, you need to make quite sure you do.'

The queen clapped her hands in delight. Then she looked at Tiptoft, who was frowning.

'Do you disapprove, Constable?', she asked coldly. 'What is one rich and arrogant old lady between friends? We can all benefit from Alyce's fall.'

Tiptoft composed his features adroitly. 'Indeed, highness. It is long overdue.' He thought for a minute, then turned to Harcourt.

'Sir Robert, how did you make sure that the God's House was one bedesman short?'

'That is my business, my lord. But trust me, it is so.'

Ewelme

After a busy morning overseeing the disposition of the contents of the wagons that had accompanied her from Wingfield, Alyce retired to the solar, where Simon and William Marton waited to give her news of their interviews with the three would-be bedesmen.

'None of them is remotely suitable, my lady,' said Marton in his clipped Scottish accent. 'Two are notorious beggars from Abingdon, and the third rarely seen uninebriated. We need to look further afield. I am leaving this afternoon to spend a week in college now you are safely back. The warden is keen to consult me on various financial matters before the Michaelmas term begins. I could make inquiries while I am there.'

Having seen the three supplicants herself, Alyce could only agree. And Marton had a wide acquaintance in Oxford. Born in Carlisle and educated in Osney Abbey, he had become first chaplain, then a fellow, then treasurer of Queen's College. She'd been introduced to him four years earlier and had managed to persuade him to take up the mastership of the God's House. Under his shrewd management, the foundation's profits had quadrupled. She was delighted to have captured the services of such an energetic and financially competent man, but at times she felt that he was in Oxford rather too often. Just now, newly arrived from Suffolk, she could have done with him at her side instead of advising his old college. As he must surely have known. She couldn't prevent an edge entering her voice as she replied.

'Do so. But bear in mind that we need someone who will get along well with our present bedesmen. Which reminds me – I noticed that there are two new ones since I was last here. Tell me about them.'

Marton looked at Simon, and Alyce again saw anxiety in her secretary's eyes as he cleared his throat with a nervous cough.

'Yes, Richard Malpasse and Thomas Taylor. They are both former tenants of the God's House manor of Ramridge. They were wounded fighting for Talbot in Aquitaine and now too old to survive without support. I know that your grace has sympathy for such men, cast aside when England lost the last of her French possessions.'

Alyce hesitated. She had the uneasy feeling that the God's House was becoming too much a resort of former Lancastrian soldiers. She remembered Wenlock's warning that she should not be seen as harbouring traitors to the Yorkist cause, especially now that she had flounced away from Wingfield. But the appointments had been made. And they were after all merely broken old men. She could only hope that they would be grateful for Ewelme's comforts and speak no treason.

She turned to Marton. 'It would be as well if the new bedesman is not an ex-soldier. And if he had connections with York rather than Lancaster. I must not be seen to favour that lost cause.'

'As you wish, your grace,' Marton said. 'But your father and mother were ever loyal...'

She raised a hand to silence him. 'Loyalty must now be to King Edward and his queen, Marton. And please return from Oxford as soon as you can. There is much to settle.'

Marton bowed and headed for the door of the solar, but not before Alyce had noticed an oddly forlorn look on his pale lardy face. What was that about? she wondered. Or am I imagining things?

Simon stayed behind, fiddling with the quill he had been sharpening. Suddenly wanting to be alone, Alyce grabbed it from him impatiently, and waved him away.

'I need some peace,' she said curtly. 'And something to eat. Ask Martha Purbeck to send some cakes and something to drink up to my turret.' He hesitated, then followed Marton out of the room.

Alyce climbed the stairs to her sanctuary, an octagonal turret on the west side of the palace where her most valued books were kept. It had narrow windows to the north, south, east and west. Below them was oak wainscot, above a vaulted ceiling painted in deep blue and powdered with gilt stars. In two of the windowsills, brick-lined holes provided safe places for charcoal heaters. Sconces for candles stood in the other two. The only furniture was a high-backed, well-padded chair and a prie-dieu. The floor was covered with a plaited rush mat, made to fit it exactly, and between each of the windows were curtains she and her ladies had stitched in gentle waves of contrasted colours. Behind them were sloping shelves, on each of which were books.

She was already regretting her sharp dismissal of Simon. He'd clearly got something on his mind, and she should have cozened it out of him instead of dismissing him so summarily. She knew how sensitive he was. She remembered him as a clever but nervous village child, cruelly teased by other children – Dickon Ormesby among them. He'd been one of the first pupils in the school attached to the God's House, and she'd told Peter Greene to keep an eye on him. Greene discovered his love of music, and soon he was part of the church choir and gaining in confidence. When he was old enough he assisted Peter in the school. Making him her secretary had been a gamble, but it had succeeded. Her beloved books had never been better cared for. But his indecisive nervousness infuriated her. She sighed, reminding herself how privileged her own upbringing had been, the only child of adoring and wealthy parents, while Simon's tailor father had had no time for him.

She sat down on the window seat, from which she had a fine view of the gentle curves of the wooded Wittenham hills south-west of Dorchester. She was happily planning rides there with a hawk on her wrist and Leo at her heels when there was a knock on the door. She smiled wryly at the sight of Tamsin.

'Ah. The black eye is turning a fetching shade of purple.'

Tamsin blushed, then placed a goblet of claret and a platter of sweetmeats on the table beside Lady Alyce's bed. She plumped up its cushions and waited for her to arrange herself on it. Then she spread a fur-lined coverlet over her legs. Alyce watched her quick, competent movements approvingly.

'How are you settling in?' she asked.

'Very well, my lady. And I have a message for you. Gerard

Vespilan gave it to me early this morning when I went back to the God's House for a cloak I'd forgotten. She handed Alyce a small roll of paper, with a knotted cord around it. Alyce untied the cord and unrolled it.

Most admired mistress, it was a gift from God to see you back in your customary place in church yesterday. I had hoped to speak to you privately after the service, but there were too many folk around you. I need to talk to you about Nicolas Webb's untimely death. I cannot believe that he would mistake a mushroom, and the night before he died I saw an intruder in the cloister. I suspect that he was poisoned, though why and how and who by I have no idea. Can we meet?

Gerard V

Alyce stared at his familiar script, a little shaky now but still exquisitely clear. Why on earth would anyone murder Nicolas Webb? But Vespilan, old as he was, could be trusted. Watching her anxiously, Tamsin spoke.

'What is it your grace? Bad news?'

'Perhaps. Did Nan Ormesby say anything about Nicolas Webb's death to you?'

'Only that she thought it very strange. That he knew good mushrooms from bad.'

'But the coroner let it pass?'

'He did. Just gave a warning against eating them.'

'Was Gerard Vespilan at the inquest?'

'No. He had a bad rheum, and Nan kept him in the infirmary.'

'And what did Farhang think?'

'He wasn't there. He'd been called away a few days earlier to treat a patient in Witney.'

There was a sharp rap on the door and a short stocky young man in his late twenties strode in. He had quizzical eyebrows over bright blue eyes, a dented nose above a mobile mouth. He gave Tamsin a broad grin, and she blushed scarlet.

'Well, Tammy, look at you in your finery! Martha Purbeck told me you had been promoted. Well deserved too. Your brother always said you were the cleverest in the family.'

Alyce put down Vespilan's letter and shook her head reproachfully. 'Master Bilton, you're expected to wait after you knock, my fighting cock, as you well know. And why weren't you at the head of the welcome yesterday? You usually are.'

Ben turned to Alyce and made a belated bow with only just enough respectful humility in it. 'Just as your outrider arrived to say that you were at Britwell, I got a message that there were urgent letters for you at Henley, so I clapped spurs to Bayard and rode for them helter-skelter. It was dark when I got there, so I overnighted, and set off in the morning. I thought you'd like them as soon as possible.'

'Not bad news of the barges from London, I hope?'

'No, and there was word from Caerleon. All but one of them passed through Henley on Friday. Which means next Thursday should see them arriving in Wallingford. But Caerleon is on a faster barge, which he's had pulled by four horses all the way. He should reach Wallingford tomorrow.'

Alyce sighed with relief. She had brought her most precious books and jewels with her in locked coffers, but the bulk of her possessions had been loaded on Waveney wherries at Wingfield to be quanted down to Yarmouth, where they had been put into fast sea-going ships to await favourable winds for London. It had been a risky venture, even though she knew that they could not be in more trustworthy hands than those of Denzil Caerleon, who loved tossing about in a storm as much as she loathed it.

'That's a relief. None lost to pirates, then?'

'No. But it seems to have been a close-run thing. Caerleon's messenger said that they had fallen in with two Cornish ships, armed to the teeth and looking for booty. But when their captain heard that the cargo belonged to the Duchess of Suffolk he told Caerleon to pass on John Trevelyan's respects, and to say that he still recalls a certain feast at Tintagel. Oh,' and here Ben looked quizzically at her, 'and to say *Time Trieth Troth.*'

Alyce's eyes widened. So John Trevelyan was on the high seas, and still, doubtless, loyal to Lancaster. She'd wondered where that charming rascal had got to. He'd been a favourite of Queen Margaret in the 1440s, and any cargoes he captured were likely to be going over the narrow seas to Lorraine. But not hers. She had, after all, provided him with an accommodating and wealthy wife in the shapely form of her cousin Elizabeth of Whalesborough, to say nothing of extracting pardons that he ill deserved, first from King Henry and later from King Edward. Seeing Ben appraising what she realised must be a slightly fatuous smile, she composed her features into neutrality.

'Well, he owes me a favour or two. Where are the letters?'

Ben reached into the pouch at his belt and handed them to her. She frowned as she looked at their seals. The first was only too familiar.

My hearty respects to your noble grace, and I beg that you will hear me. We in Norfolk have never known so much robbery and manslaughter as is now within a little time...

44

She ran her eyes down through the clumsily scrawled, ink-spattered letter, and sighed. The latest of Dame Margaret Paston's many impassioned petitions from Caistor accused the Suffolk agents Yelverton and Heydon of committing all manner of mayhem the instant that her grace had quit the county. Likely they had, and likely Jack, damn his eyes, had told them to do so. Well, he'd have to deal with the aftermath too. He couldn't put the blame on her any longer.

Alyce turned to the second missive, which bore the garter-ringed seal of the senior branch of the Harcourts. As she broke it, Sir Robert's face, once handsome, now bloated with high living, rose in her mind's eye. She'd known him since she was a child, and she had hero-worshipped him as a fine soldier until he showed himself in his true colours twenty years ago during the Whitsun festival of mystery plays at Coventry, slashing down the unarmed young heir of the Staffords as if butchering a calf. High in Queen Margaret's favour, he had soon wriggled out of the much-torn net of the law. Now, she knew, he was just as prized by that jumped-up turncoat Elizabeth Wydeville, widow of the loyally Lancastrian Lord Grey and now married to the Yorkist usurper, King Edward. The Staffords were penniless exiles with Margaret in Lorraine, and Dick Stafford's murder had gone unavenged.

Since his main seat was west of Oxford at Stanton Harcourt, Sir Robert did occasionally call at Ewelme on his way to London or Windsor. Alyce didn't trust him an inch. She knew that he coveted Ewelme itself, especially now that it boasted a palace far more splendid than Stanton Harcourt. But the Harcourt star was in the ascendant in the Yorkist court, so she was careful to keep a smiling face towards him whenever they met. Doing so was the easier because she was genuinely fond of his kindly and canny wife, Margaret Byron, and because Jack made no secret of his admiration for the Harcourt brothers' redoubtable reputation as jousters. And Sir Robert had always made much of Jack, especially once he became brother-in-law to the usurper king.

She scanned the neat chancery script of Harcourt's secretary down to Sir Robert's own flamboyant signature. It announced that he and his beloved wife (here Alyce gave a sardonic sniff; it was well known that Robert had married Margaret Byron for her huge fortune and had never been faithful) intended to call at Ewelme late in the day on Wednesday. They would be on their way back from Windsor after a sojourn at court with King Edward and Queen Elizabeth. Sir Robert hoped that they might spend two nights at Ewelme and have a day's hunting on Friday; he had heard that her forest was particularly rich in game this autumn. His younger brother Richard would be with them, as they had a plan about which they wanted to consult her.

Alyce's heart sank. Double trouble. Wednesday was less than five days away. She'd been looking forward to a peaceful week of unpacking and making room for the arrival of the barges. The Harcourts would have a retinue of twenty and more. She considered. It would be politic to agree gracefully. There was plenty of space for the servants in the newly built guest quarters and stable block in the base court of the palace. The Harcourts themselves could occupy the great chamber in the east wing, which had once been her husband William's. There was a spacious anteroom which had been richly furnished for William's boon companion Adam Moleyns. It would be suitable for Richard.

Alyce handed both letters over to Ben, who read them in silence, then looked up. She smiled wryly at him.

'I don't seem to have escaped the world yet, do I? What ill chance that the Harcourts are coming this way so soon after my arrival. We had best delay the unloading of the barges until they leave.' Why was Ben staring down at his still muddy boots so intently. She remembered her father's adage that news travelled faster between the servants of households than between their masters.

'Or is it mere chance? Ben, have you heard anything in Oxford about this?' He hesitated before replying.

'Well, the word last week was that Sir Robert has just been made steward of Oxford University. Oh, and when I was drinking in the Turf Tavern I heard that Sir Richard Harcourt was preparing to remarry – though they didn't know who the lucky lady was.'

'Lucky? Richard appears to be less of a ruffian than his brother, but he's a snake in the grass. He ordered the killing of his first wife, Edith St Clair, two years ago, claiming he'd caught her in adultery. Now he's applied to the Pope for a dispensation to be absolved of murder and allowed to remarry. Whoever he's got his eye on must be rich, though, or with great expectations. He lost everything Edith brought him in dowers from her two previous marriages when she died. Who said he was remarrying?'

'Sir Robert's own squire Hamel Turvey. He was something drunk on Bogo's heaviest ale. Then somebody asked me if Nicolas Webb's death meant there was a vacancy in the Ewelme almshouse. And Turvey laughed and said that there wouldn't be for long as the Harcourts were bringing a candidate for his place.'

Alyce stared at him, eyes narrowed in anger.

'What business is it of theirs? Only I decide who'll be

licensed to pray for the immortal souls of my parents and my husbands.'

Ben looked embarrassed. 'That certainly used to be so. But you've been away a long time, your grace. Nor do you frequent the court, and without favour there how can you have influence in the county? There are even rumours that you may take the veil. These days the Harcourts have a lot of say in what goes on in Oxfordshire. When I said to Turvey that it wasn't likely you'd accept Sir Robert's candidate in the God's House, Turvey laughed and said that you'd have to. Harcourt had gone to Windsor expressly to bring the man back. He's a favourite of the queen's, apparently.'

'But what conceivable interest could Harcourt, or the queen, have in the God's House?'

Ben looked even more uncomfortable.

'Begging your pardon, your grace, I think they are more interested in you – and those they suspect to be your friends. The Harcourts work for Sir John Tiptoft, the Earl of Worcester, now. He's Constable of England, charged by Edward with rooting out traitors.'

Alyce was taken aback. This was not at all what she had thought would happen when she'd announced that she was leaving Suffolk to retire from the world and to become a vowess. It had seemed a most ingenious idea when she had seen the new queen looking at her with a calculating stare and quite transparently planning to cajole Edward into decreeing that Alyce should marry one of her numerous Wydeville relations. Her age would not have protected her – hadn't the dowager duchess of Norfolk, three years off seventy, been led to the altar by the queen's brother John the minute he'd come of age? But a vowess could not marry. She was betrothed to

Christ, although importantly not married to him as was a nun. She could keep control of all her worldly possessions and retain all the other rights and privileges of being a widow.

But anyone convicted of treason would have their possessions forfeited at a stroke of Edward's pen. And the Earl of Worcester was a redoubtable man. Ten years ago it had taken all her influence with King Henry to prevent Tiptoft replacing her as Constable of Wallingford Castle. Influence that was now useless, as Henry was deposed, a prisoner in the Tower of London. She remembered Wenlock's warning. Isolated and vulnerable.

'You mean they want to plant a spy in my household? Why would they think that a good idea? There is nothing to discover. I have been careful to avoid any political actions.'

Ben shrugged his shoulders, a stubborn set to his mouth. Alyce noticed that he was avoiding meeting her eye. What in Jesu's name had been going on while she'd been away? She sighed. God's bones, how she'd needed some peace – but it didn't look as if she was going to get it yet. How unlucky it was that Marton had already set off for Oxford.

'Go and speak to Peter Greene and Simon Brailles, Ben. We need to find a new bedesman before the Harcourts arrive. On Thursday we'll tire them out in the chase and souse them as deep in Bordeaux as herrings in brine. At least the larders are full at this time of year. There will be plenty of venison and pork even if we're unlucky hunting. Send up Mistress Purbeck to talk to me about the sleeping arrangements.'

Ben turned to go, then stopped.

'I almost forgot. The reason that Caerleon is travelling so fast is because he had the Billingsgate fishmongers bring on board a tank of live sea fish for you. Including, he said, the biggest one he'd ever seen – a huge sturgeon. He's transporting it in an elm coffin full of seawater.'

Alyce gasped, then smiled. 'What will he think of next? He's incorrigible. And yet – if it survives, it will amaze the Harcourts.'

After Ben had clumped down the stairs, she turned to Tamsin with a wry smile.

'Well child, you are being thrown into the thick of things. First Vespilan raising doubts about Nicolas's death and now an invasion of my enemies with a spy they intend to foist on me. The wolves are running indeed. If only my father was alive. He had a shrewd way of finding solutions.' She thought for a moment, remembering the happy London years of her marriage to Thomas Montagu, when her father was Coroner of London, and brought problems to her. 'And I used to help him. He said that I had a mind like a gimlet for getting to the point.'

'Then surely you will this time,' said Tamsin loyally. 'And I might help. You could talk to me. And I could spy on their spy. No one notices me.'

Alyce gazed at her thoughtfully, a twinkle in her eye. 'You might well be useful. Who would suspect a chit like you, after all? But take care. Such a man is likely to be cunning and not easily taken in. Fortunately, there is nothing for him to discover. Now, leave me – I need to think.'

Tamsin caught up with Ben as he was walking slowly down the stairs, lost in thought. She tapped his shoulder, and he turned to her with a woebegone look on his face.

'What's wrong, Ben?' she asked. He hastily rearranged his expression and gave her his usual cheerful grin.

'Nothing for you to worry about, Tammy. So how are you finding life in the palace?'

'Bewildering,' she said, relieved to be able to speak frankly after guarding her tongue for so long. 'I thought it would be exciting, but there is so much to learn and I have to watch what I say all the time, and Lady Alyce's ladies, Marlene and Eloise Stonor, seem to think I'm at their beck and call. I don't see that much of her grace.'

He looked at her, and chuckled. 'You need to learn patience, Tammy, not something I ever remember you having. You've been given a once-in-a-lifetime chance to better yourself. You're used to having your own way with Nan, but you've got to earn the respect of the palace folk, not just Lady Alyce. That'll take time.' He touched her furrowed brow lightly. 'Stop frowning. The wind will change and you'll be stuck that way.'

She was hard put not to burst into tears as Ben strode away towards the stables. It had been days since she'd been spoken to so affectionately. She walked up the stairs to her garret with a heavy heart, hoping that the Stonor girls wouldn't hear her. She wanted time to reflect on Ben's words. But she had barely closed her door when it was wrenched open. It was Marlene. She walked over to the open window.

'Who's that handsome fellow down there in the courtyard?' she demanded. 'I saw you talking to him.'

Tamsin joined her at the window. 'Oh, that's Ben Bilton. He's the Ewelme steward. I've known him since I was little. He was a friend of my brother's.'

Marlene turned to look at her, eyes narrowed. 'So do you fancy him, then?'

Tamsin coloured. 'No. Not in the least.'

Marlene smiled slyly, 'Then you won't mind me getting to know him. Tell me about him.'

For all her insistence to Lady Alyce that she wasn't interested in getting married, Tamsin felt a chill of foreboding as she answered as casually as she could.

'He's Suffolk-bred. Son of one of the old duke's squires. He was really popular at Wingfield, apparently. Used to look after Duke John when he was a child. But one day he saw the boy pricking a lame puppy with his dagger, and whipped him. He's always had a hair-trigger temper, my brother said.'

'Surely he didn't get away with that,' said Marlene. 'My father said that Duke William would never hear a word against his son, let alone a whipping.'

'He didn't. He was put in the stocks and banished from Wingfield. But Lady Alyce got to hear about it. She thought he'd been hard done by, and secretly sent him to Ewelme with the next courier. He thrived here; he was in the same class as my brother at school. Under John Saintsbury.'

'What did the old duke do when he found him still around?'

'Lady Alyce made sure he stayed well out of his way. Saintsbury reported well of him, and when she was widowed he joined her household. Now he's steward.'

Marlene looked out of the window again. Tamsin could see her assessing Bilton thoughtfully as he expertly unharnessed the beautiful bay stallion he had ridden into the base court. 'So he's of good family, then?'

'Well, the Biltons are armigered. Their crest is a falcon. But they don't have much land, and there are two older brothers.' She hoped Ben's lack of prospects would put Marlene off.

'He could be fun for a while, though,' Marlene said musingly. Tamsin's heart sank.

Wallingford

In the cramped little cabin of a barge hidden behind an eyot on the Thames near Winterbrook, a wounded man stirred. Denzil Caerleon bent over him.

'Time to dress your thigh again, sir.'

'Where am I?'

'Among friends. And though you're on a boat, you're a long way from the sea.'

'It doesn't smell like it. There's a stench of fish and salt water that reminds me of the hold of a Padstow cog.'

'That's the fish tank. Gift for our hostess. Can you turn on your side? Then I can reach your leg better.'

John Trevelyan winced as Caerleon deftly removed the dressing, and a foul-smelling green poultice, and considered the lacerated flesh beneath it. No gangrene as yet. He swabbed it with warm water and applied another of the thick green poultices supplied by John Crophill, the surgeon who had brought the wounded man aboard the barge in Southwark. Then he wrapped clean linen bandages around it and covered his patient up again.

'Here's a draught for the pain. It should bring down your fever too. And make you sleep well.'

Trevelyan hauled himself upright enough to grasp the cup Caerleon handed to him. He grimaced at its bitterness. 'Are you trying to poison me? And where are you taking me, anyway?'

'To stay with friends. Trustworthy friends of mine. And one of yours too, I've been told. Best not to know more now, just in case we don't reach them.'

'And who are you? You seem no mean leech.'

Caerleon smiled. 'I have some skills. But it is not my profession.'

'What is?'

'That's a good question. I would have been an Oxford schoolman if I hadn't lost my head over a wench. Now I'm a jack of all trades, and master of none.'

Trevelyan drained his cup, then lay back and closed his eyes. Soon soft snores came from his bunk.

Caerleon went up onto the deck of the barge, and threw the old dressing away. It sank slowly, accompanied by flickers of movement of what Caerleon realised with distaste were predatory crayfish. It was a beautiful evening. The river was an inky black mirror, reflecting the half-grown moon. The silvered branches of the great willows that lined the banks of the backwater hung almost to the water, concealing the barge like a curtain. A single swan glided past, its regal head nodding slightly as if in greeting. Caerleon nodded his own head, recalling Bartholomew Anglicanus's belief that the sight of a swan was auspicious and hoping that this meant that Fortune approved his actions. Then he stiffened. Hooves sounded along the towpath and the silhouette of a horseman appeared out of the mist. Then a low double whistle broke the stillness of the night. He breathed a sigh of relief and copied the call. The horseman dismounted, tied his horse to a tree and boarded the barge.

'Bilton, by Our Lady. I hope you have good news of Ewelme.'

'On the contrary. Only bad news. The palace has unexpected

guests. The Harcourts and their train arrive on Wednesday. They are going hunting on Thursday and leaving on Friday. How is Trevelyan?'

'Sore wounded, but he'll survive, I think, given a week or two of careful nursing by Farhang. Can he be hidden in the empty bedesman's cell you sent word of?'

'No. It won't be empty. The Harcourts are bringing their own candidate for the vacancy. They intend him to spy. Rumours of what we've been doing in the God's House have spread, and Sir Robert is hot to prove that the duchess is a closet Lancastrian. To prevent his spy being installed, we are going to suggest she gives the cell to Sybilla, the anchorite of Swyncombe.'

'A woman in the God's House?'

'Women are not expressly forbidden in the statutes, and there is no doubt that she is suitable. We couldn't consult the master of the God's House, Will Marton, as he'd already left for Oxford, but it was his deputy Peter Greene's idea. He's thought for some time that Sybilla is too frail to continue as an anchorite. She's eighty years old now.'

'But Crophill told me that Sybilla worked for the cause in Swyncombe, storing in her cell valuables that the fugitives could not take with them.'

'Sir Brian is loyal to the hilt. He can take over her work. On Monday Peter is going up to Swyncombe to ask her if she is happy to come, and if she agrees Simon will speak to Lady Alyce. She will be brought down as soon as possible, so the Harcourts can be presented with a fait accompli. Which leaves us with nowhere to conceal Trevelyan. Your barge must lie up awhile until they have gone.'

Caerleon shook his head. 'He needs better nursing than I

can give him. The gash the crossbow bolt made in his thigh is festering. Crophill said that Farhang must see him as soon as possible. And what about the sturgeon? Another night in that coffin will be the death of it. Could one of the other bedesmen be persuaded to make room for Trevelyan?'

Bilton considered. 'Dick Lawrence might oblige. He'll do anything for money to get sodden on.'

Caerleon gazed across the water. The swan had disappeared. So much for signs. He turned to Bilton.

'Suppose you got Farhang to give it out that Lawrence has an infectious fever and mustn't be visited. Then we could spirit him away into the attic of a Wallingford taphouse, and tuck Trevelyan into his bed, safe from all comers.'

Bilton sighed. 'It's a lousy plan, but when the ship is sinking any bucket must answer.'

'Does Lady Alyce know anything about what you've been doing while she's been away?'

'Not yet,' said Bilton. 'And now isn't the time. She is all but broken by her experiences at Wingfield. She's not herself. She's wary of seeming a traitor and just wants to retreat into her books and her memories. And now, when she's at her weakest and most defenceless, she'll be appalled that we are risking her heartland.'

'Ewelme is at risk any road if the Harcourts covet it. But we can thwart them between us, Bilton. And this escape route to the coast you have set up is vital to the cause. Stonor, Swyncombe, Ewelme and Donnington are essential links in the chain of safe Lancastrian houses.'

Bilton frowned. 'I don't like it, Caerleon. We planned to suspend our activities on Lady Alyce's return until we were sure she'd approve.'

'You didn't foresee Crophill bringing Trevelyan to my barge with Tiptoft's men close on their heels. He's not just a pirate; he's a known Lancastrian sympathiser. I had to take him on board. But more travelling will be the death of him. Lady Alyce would certainly not wish that. He's her cousin by marriage, and she's very fond of him.'

Bilton grinned. 'I realised that when I gave her the message you passed on from him. *Time Trieth Troth*. Her face was a picture. Pray heaven that Farhang can cure him so that he can be smuggled away quickly. So shall I tell Lady Alyce you are bringing him?'

Caerleon considered. 'No. She'll look guilty if she knows he's in the God's House.'

Ben looked dubious, but Caerleon's confidence reassured him. He gave a nod, mounted, and clapped his heels to his horse's side. As the sound of hooves died away along the towpath, Denzil gazed at the river again. He was charting a perilous course which could end his service with Duchess Alyce for ever. Then a spectral white shape moved towards him across the water. The swan had reappeared. He smiled. A sign, after all. Fortune *is* my friend.

Ewelme

The God's House calling bell sounded for early morning Mass, but this morning Alyce had decided to remain in her own quarters. A reputation for piety had its advantages, she reflected, as with Leo at her heels she entered the turret library in which the household thought she spent long hours in prayer. She was more likely to be immersed in a book which had nothing to do with devotions, but today she simply needed to think in peace. Was Nicolas Webb's death a tragic accident or something more sinister? And what were her most trusted servants up to? She had told Tamsin to bring Vespilan to see her at ten o'clock, but for the moment she wanted to let her inner mind reflect on the problem. It was a trick her father had taught her. Don't stare at a puzzle. Edge towards it crabwise.

To show worship to the Harcourts, Alyce had sent messengers with invitations for Friday's hunt and the feast afterwards to various neighbours. Two were old friends of the Harcourts, Richard Quartermain of Rycot, near Thame, and Ralph Boteler of Britwell Salome. There was another good reason for inviting Boteler. She needed to win his favour. Yesterday he had made it clear how much he resented losing his latest lawsuit against her. He had been claiming that forty years ago her men had destroyed a stone wall close to their boundary but indubitably on his land and used it for the new works at Ewelme Palace, but a dozen or more witnesses had confirmed that his own mother had sold the tumbled stones to Alyce's father for making improvements to Ewelme church.

For her own pleasure she'd summoned her father's former ward and her own childhood friend Thomas Stonor and his French wife Jeanne. Stonor Park was only about seven miles east of Ewelme, and they were her nearest good friends; moreover, they would be longing to see their daughters. That meant at least twelve at her table, and sixty or more in the hall, to say nothing of the extra beds which would have to be fitted into every available nook and cranny. But Ben Bilton, John Cook and Martha Purbeck were used to such occasions, and she didn't doubt that the Ewelme household would run with its customary efficiency.

Alyce looked at the handsome clock hanging on the wall, a wedding present to her and William from Duke Philip of Burgundy thirty years ago. William had been flattered by his generosity – such clocks were rare and highly prized. She had been more than a little amused, remembering another wedding feast six years before that, in Paris. Philip had flirted with her so openly that her then husband Thomas Montagu had challenged him to a duel. The clock was a symbol that Philip hoped the discreet friendship that had grown up between them from that time would continue, and it had. Even now, when Philip was seriously ill, he wrote to her with news of his library and of his hopes for his son and successor Charles. The clock's face showed Fortune couched like a queen at the heart of her wheel. Its single hand, cunningly contrived as her sceptre, was only just nearing eight. For an hour or two, she could retreat into her books.

Yesterday Simon had unwrapped the travelling chest containing Alyce's favourite volumes and laid them out on one of the shelves that ran in three stages around the room. She chose a large folio in a sadly begrimed binding, took it over to her sloping desk by the window, and opened it where her marker lay halfway through. With an almost human groan, Leo slumped down into his basket, resigned to his mistress's inactivity once she was seated at her desk. Alyce smiled. She'd ride out with him later.

Reading a tale from her grandfather's most famous book was a ritual that she always observed on her homecomings. He had died almost exactly nine months before she was born, so she had never met him, but his writings had been a touchstone of wisdom and entertainment for her ever since she had been introduced to them. Her father had commissioned this exquisite copy, illustrated of course by Vespilan, in 1414, on the occasion of her first marriage, to Henry V's favourite brother-in-arms Sir John Phelip. She remembered her mother's dubious face and her father's laughing one. She had after all been only ten years old, too young to understand either the high moral tales or the low scurrilous ones. The book had been meant more for her husband than for her, but he had died at Harfleur just eighteen months later, and the book, along with Grovebury Priory and several valuable West Country manors, had become hers.

The Tales of Canterbury had then been newly bound in the snowy-white skin of a stillborn calf, the finest vellum that her father's money could buy. Vespilan had drawn the portrait of the Knight in Phelip's likeness, stern-faced but kindly and the soul of honour, sitting astride his gilt-harnessed destrier and looking just as he had on the day he came to marry her. He'd bowed before her and kissed her hand as if she was the heroine of a romance, not a ten-year-old girl. The fact that he was then thirty, only three years younger than her father, hadn't worried her at all. He'd been a family friend for many years, and when her mother had explained to her that his wife had died and that he'd asked if Alyce could be his new bride she'd been thrilled, especially when she heard that she would be Lady Phelip, rather than plain Alyce, and would have her own ladies instead of a nanny to look after her. Best of all, Ewelme Manor, which belonged to her mother, was to be part of her marriage portion. 'You won't leave us yet awhile, though,' Maud had explained. 'You're too young to be a real wife to him. And he's off to fight in the great army King Harry is gathering to conquer France.' When she'd heard of Sir John's death a few weeks before the glorious triumph of Agincourt, she'd rubbed soot into the gay reds of the little miniature and smudged it grey with her tears.

But the splendid book had remained to comfort her. As well as celebrating Phelip, Vespilan had drawn her mother as a serene-faced nun in attendance on the worldly prioress, and put in her father Thomas, white-bearded and upright in his much-loved red striped cloak, as the Franklin. Alyce always touched them tenderly when she came to them. The other miniatures in its margins were a pageant of relatives, friends and household servants. Not all had pleased her. She'd rubbed ink into the lascivious red cheeks of the Monk, all too close a likeness of Father Fulke, the family chaplain who'd found every opportunity he could to finger her budding breasts and grope between her thighs. She'd been too naive to complain, believing him when he said that he'd been appointed judge of her nubility by her mother. She'd also smirched the Shipman, a lifelike portrait of the boatswain of the Chaucers' barge, a shifty-eyed man who cuffed the oarsmen brutally when no one was looking, and whom she'd seen toss the barge mouser's litter of kittens into the Thames in a heaving, mewling sack. She'd been right about both of them, she reflected. Fulke had been dismissed after he got a thirteen-year-old laundry maid with child, and the bargee had disappeared with a coffer of plate a few years later.

Finest of all was Vespilan's miniature in the margin of the Tale of Melibeus: an affectionate likeness of her grandfather as he'd been in old age, his once-red hair grey, his finger directing the reader's eye to the start of the story he was telling the pilgrims. His portly girth dwarfed the little bay palfrey he had taken to riding in later life. Alyce wished for the thousandth time that she'd been born in time to talk to him, then reflected, also for the thousandth time, that through his books she knew him as well as if their lives had overlapped. Alive, he'd been as busy and absent as her father, always away on the king's business, his head full of secrets of state.

As it was, his writings had guided her to other authors, stimulated her own pen to spin tales and verses. 'Those libertines you had to mix with in France taught you rather more than I would have you know about,' her strait-laced mother had said, crimsoning and shaking her head after reading her daughter's first authorial effort, *The Life and Acts of the Mighty Queen Hippolyta and her Sisters-in-Arms*. It was a tale which Alyce had written in Rouen while her second husband Thomas Montagu was campaigning in Anjou and Maine. Always fair-minded, Maud had added words of praise that Alyce had treasured: 'But it is light to read and exciting. It's as if at your grandfather's ending, his spirit went into your beginning.'

Hippolyta was tucked away now, as were the literary legacies of her marriage to William: forlorn stanzas on the death of love, and spiky tales of double-dealing and disappointment. How had John Wenlock put it? 'William didn't quite cheat, he just took discreet advantage of whatever circumstances permitted.' Memories of her mother grew more not less vivid now that she was reaching the age at which Maud had died. She was working on a tribute to her. Inspired by Christine de Pisan, it was an allegory about the power of women, set in a garden very like her own here at Ewelme. But she constantly returned to her grandfather's writings, fascinated at the way that as she grew older she discovered new wisdoms in them. She found her marker and settled down contentedly to read of the Wife of Bath, rumbustious and irrepressible, but also pointedly critical of domineering men.

> And I pray Jesus also to shorten their days that will
> not be ruled by their wives. And old, angry misers –
> may God send them a true pestilence soon!

She finished the tale with an appreciative chuckle and closed the book. Now that she was home she could think about having it rebound. She laid the folio reverently back on the shelf and reached into the deep shelf below her sloping desk for *The Game of Chess* and the travel-worn commonplace book in which she jotted favourite lines from the books she read, and ideas for her own stories. While dipping into Cessolis on her journey she'd come across an unusual description of chess pieces in a formal dance that had appealed to her. She sharpened a quill, dipped it into her inkpot, and began to copy.

As Ewelme Palace's gatehouse clock struck ten o'clock, Tamsin helped Gerard Vespilan up the steep stairs to Alyce's turret library. She rapped, gently at first, and then more sharply, at the door. She heard Leo's paws clattering on the floorboards as he jumped up to investigate the cause of the disturbance. But there was no peremptory call to enter from Lady Alyce. Shyly, she lifted the door's latch and opened it. Lady Alyce's head was slumped on top of a stack of cut parchment. Her wimple was askew, and blots of ink trailed across the piece she had been writing on. Leo gave a sudden bark on seeing Vespilan behind Tamsin, and the duchess raised her head. She smiled, abashed.

'Dear me, I must have fallen asleep,' she said, rubbing her eyes. 'It's good to see you, Gerard. I hope the stairs were not too wearisome.' Then she saw the ruined piece of parchment and grimaced. 'That was the finest vellum. Made by the nuns of Syon.'

'Let me have it, my lady,' said Tamsin, eagerly. 'I'll scrape it clean while you are talking to Brother Vespilan.' The duchess nodded absently and led Vespilan to a chair near the reading desk. Tamsin removed herself to a stool in a distant corner and busied herself working at the ink stain with a sharp strigil designed for just such accidents.

She heard Lady Alyce go straight to the point.

'Gerard, your letter said that you saw an intruder in the cloister shortly before poor Nicolas died. Did you see what he looked like?'

Vespilan pondered a while before answering. 'Not really. Just a dark figure in a long black cloak. First in, then out a bit later. I'm not sure how long he was here for. I... I think I nodded off. I'm getting old, you know.'

'I'm twenty years younger than you, and I've just nodded off in broad daylight,' said Alyce, stroking his arm reassuringly.

'It doesn't mean that either of us has lost our wits. Just a sign of weariness. Can you remember anything else about him?'

'There was something familiar about him... but I can't recall what.' His rheumy blue eyes settled on Alyce. Tamsin, watching and listening, saw the deep affection in them, and saw the duchess's face soften in response. She hadn't realised that her carping and demanding mistress had such a capacity for love.

'They said it was the mushrooms Nicolas collected,' said Gerard. 'That there was a death cap among them. But he was a rare chooser. Always careful, he was. Horrible his screams were while he lay a-dying. And the smell...' Sweat had risen on the old man's forehead, and he wiped it away with the sleeve of his grey gown.

Tamsin caught sight of a skeletally thin wrist and forearm, and realised how old he was. She saw the duchess rise from her own chair and kneel at Gerard's feet, holding both his hands in her own as she spoke.

'Gerard, what you've told me is very important. One day we may need to get it written down officially. But for the moment, just knowing that it could have been murder is a help. My father used to say *praemonitus, praemunitus*: forewarned is forearmed.'

She turned to Tamsin. 'Help Vespilan down the stairs, child. And take him to the kitchen for a posset before you escort him back to the God's House. He's my oldest friend, saving only Sybilla of Swyncombe. When they die, so will much of my past.'

She paused, then turned back to her desk, saying in a murmur that Tamsin thought she was not meant to hear, 'Which may be as well.'

Oxford

Comfortably settled in a high-backed chair, Lord Wenlock watched George Neville sipping wine from an ornate Venetian goblet as he lounged back on a bed piled with velvet cushions. They were in a tapestry-hung chamber in the great tower of Balliol College, and George, like Alyce, was planning hospitality. But on a far grander scale: nothing was too good for his Oxford celebration of his new appointment as Archbishop of York.

'The masters of the largest colleges are coming, of course. And the abbots of Osney and Rewley and the prioresses of Frideswide and Sandford. Bishop Waynflete. And the Duchess of Suffolk, if we can persuade her out of Ewelme. I sent her an invitation on Thursday but have had no word back. John Doll, Luke Tabarder and Walter Godfrey will come, of course. It's important to acknowledge such eminent townsfolk. Sir Robert and Sir Richard Harcourt will be there. And Master Chaundler of New College. Set him at a little distance from me. He is a great scholar but I dislike his watchfulness. How many is that, Frith?'

His secretary ran his eye down the columns of names on a scroll of parchment.

'Twenty-five on the dais, your grace, and about two hundred in the hall. There will be musicians in the gallery, of course.'

'Excellent. We should have replies to the invitations in the next few days. But we must make sure there are places for latecomers, both on the dais and at the lower tables. Wenlock, you'll be welcome of course. Have you any friends you'd like to invite?'

'There is someone,' said Wenlock. 'You already know her I believe. Joan Moulton, the London bookseller. She's keen to find new customers in Oxford.'

'John Doll will have to look to his laurels,' said Neville. 'Joan has some splendid books for sale. And a splendid body. I'd be delighted to see her again. But now let's think about food.' He turned to the beefy man who had been waiting patiently by the door.

'Crawford, what can you get hold of? Game aplenty, of course, but what about beef and pork and fish and fowls?' Just as Crawford began to suggest suitable courses, the heavy tapestry arras behind Neville trembled. Through a gap in it, a tall man dressed in black velvet slipped into the room. Wenlock's eyes widened in surprise, but he quickly composed himself, making a courteous bow and receiving one back. Neville looked up, disconcerted.

'My Lord of Worcester. I had not known you were in the city. I am planning a feast to celebrate my elevation to York. You are of course invited if you are in Oxford next week.'

'As it happens, I will be,' said Tiptoft. 'Thank you, my lord.' Then he glanced towards Frith, Crawford and the other servants and his high forehead wrinkled as if he was in pain.

Taking the hint, Neville dismissed them with a wave. After the door had closed behind them, he turned again to Tiptoft.

'Well, Constable, no doubt you are honouring us with your presence because you have your eye on some turncoat or other. Who is it?'

Tiptoft's ice-blue eyes, hooded like a raptor, blinked twice before he spoke.

'Are you inviting the Dowager Duchess of Suffolk to your feast?'

The chancellor's face fell. 'But surely you don't suspect Lady Alyce of treason? Of course I'm inviting her. But I don't know if she'll come. She is a sad recluse these days. But loyal surely. After all, her son is married to...' His voice tailed away, as Tiptoft gave a sardonic smile.

'Her son and she are not close, Neville, as her quitting of Wingfield has confirmed. But I hope that you are right. No, I asked after her mainly because I respect her great learning. If she accepts, then let me sit beside her. We can talk of books.'

George Neville looked relieved. 'How foolish of me to think that you are always in pursuit of traitors, my lord. Your learning is legendary, and your gifts to Oxford's libraries splendid.'

Many of them confiscated from those that the constable had accused of treason, Wenlock thought to himself, but he too relaxed. Then he tensed as Tiptoft spoke again.

'Yet there may be cause for concern. I come from Windsor, where Sir Robert Harcourt has been telling me and the queen that the duchess is disloyal, pointing to the number of supposedly needy folk in the God's House who have ties to Lancaster, and reminding us of her father's closeness to that house. Now, he says, she has cast off her son and left Suffolk because he is married to Bess of York. And that Ewelme is "a nest of traitors". Her majesty would I fear be only too pleased to be able to declare Princess Alyce unworthy of her title, but I told Harcourt that he would need very positive proof of her disloyalty.'

Wenlock decided to intervene. 'Young Suffolk and Bess of York have been married for eight years, and for the dowager duchess to retire to her childhood home is natural at her age. Nor is housing a handful of war veterans who served with her husbands in France necessarily disloyalty. Countless ex-soldiers could be tarred with that brush. Myself among them.'

Tiptoft looked impassive. 'We'll see. But enough of politics. I would welcome a tour of your library, Chancellor. I hear you have acquired some Greek texts.'

'Yes,' said Neville eagerly. 'From the Sign of the Mole in Paternoster Row. Moreover, its owner Mistress Moulton herself may be at the feast. Lord Wenlock says that she is planning to bring some very fine texts to Oxford next week. She has lately been to Bruges and she has as fine an eye as her late husband had for an interesting book. I want my college to become renowned for scholarship, with the best library in the University. Incidentally, if you ever need a place to lodge your own splendid collection, you will I hope consider Balliol.'

Giving Neville the vaguest of smiles, Tiptoft turned to Wenlock.

'It is good to see you, Wenlock. What brings you to Oxford?'

'It's always a pleasure to visit England's greatest centre of learning and catch up with old friends. And this morning the Archbishop-elect and the Bishop of Winchester and I decided on a candidate to recommend to the king as the next sheriff of Oxfordshire. Thomas Stonor retires in November.'

'Indeed?' said Tiptoft. 'Who did you decide on?'

Wenlock glanced at Neville. 'Sir Richard Harcourt. I was dubious as there are rumours of his mistreatment of his late wife. But his grace felt that his many local connections were in his favour. Waynflete agreed.'

'The Harcourts are hot for York,' said Tiptoft. 'There is no doubt of their standing in the eyes of the queen, at least.

I suspect King Edward has his reservations, however. But in this, as in so many things, he will be swayed by his wife.'

Admiring Tiptoft's ability to sit on the fence, Wenlock picked up his cap and cloak, and bowed to both men.

'God be with you, my lieges. I must depart. Bishop Waynflete asked me to dine with him.' As he left, he saw Neville turning to the constable with an ingratiating smile.

'Shall we go to the library, now, Tiptoft? It is I believe the finest of any college in Oxford.'

Wenlock hummed to himself as he walked along Turl Street to the High Street, where he turned left. There was clearly no way of preventing Sir Richard becoming sheriff. George Neville had recently pocketed a generous contribution to college funds from him, and he suspected that a similar donation had been made to Waynflete's Magdalen Hall. But it had been reassuring to discover that Tiptoft had his doubts about the Harcourts – and that he admired Lady Alyce. Surely what he had just said amounted to a warning, one that he knew Wenlock and Neville would pass on to the duchess. Not that the constable would let admiration get in the way of his commitment to rooting out treason. Or of any chance of adding to his splendid library. He shook his head sadly. Alyce was trebly vulnerable. The Harcourts wanted her lands, the queen her head, and Tiptoft would happily commandeer her books. And she seemed obstinately oblivious to her peril.

When he reached the scaffolded frontage of the much-enlarged Magdalen Hall, Wenlock looked up at the cunning sculptures that decorated the stone course above its windows. Faces he recognised alternated with grimacing monsters.

A saintly looking Henry VI embraced a despondent lion, and there, in a prominent position, was Waynflete himself, with broad brow and eyes raised to heaven. He ducked through the wicket door in its massive oak entrance gates. Inside was a chaos of building, with labourers busy everywhere. A porter greeted him, bowing respectfully when he said that he had an appointment with Bishop Waynflete, and led the way past the scaffolded chapel and into a cloister.

'His excellency is occupying the rooms usually used by William Tybard, who has presided over the governance of the college since its foundation,' he explained, as he rapped on a door on the far side of the cloister. 'They look over the River Cherwell. Both the president and his excellency are very fond of fishing. You may well find him dangling a rod in the river.'

The door was opened by a black-clad cleric, who showed Wenlock into a luxuriously furnished room, with high windows along its eastern wall. Waynflete sat on the wide cushioned seat that ran the length of the windows, a rod propped on the sill of an open casement, and a book in his hand. His face was the twin of the handsome stone head outside the gatehouse, but his eyes were tired and watchful. He smiled as Wenlock entered.

'Lord Wenlock, it is very good to see you again. I didn't have time this morning to ask you what you were up to in Calais.'

Wenlock shrugged modestly. 'Making diplomatic advances to France and Burgundy turn and turn about, and failing to achieve very much, I fear. How sensible you have been in retreating from the tangled ways of politics and concentrating on education at Eton and in Winchester. And now at Magdalen. I hear you have the best choir in Oxford and you plan a school across the river.'

'Yet even here in Paradise we have snakes in the grass. Before we go to dine, I want to ask your advice on an embarrassing situation. Books are going missing from the University Library. And just when I was hoping that the return of Duchess Alyce to Ewelme with all her Wingfield library would result in more of her generous gifts. If she gets to hear of it, then *vale et omnia quae*. What makes matters worse is that one of the missing books was a gift from her: an illustrated copy of the treatise on the astrolabe that her grandfather made for her uncle Lewis Chaucer.'

'Maybe you should confess its loss to her,' Wenlock replied after a momentary hesitation. 'She'll be shocked, but she respects frank speaking above all things. You could even ask her to look into it. Though it is some time since she's been in Oxford, she has the goodwill of Oxford scriveners and booksellers and is well able to wheedle information from them. She also needs support from her friends just at the moment, among whom I know you to be one of the most eminent. The Harcourts are apparently intent on blackening her name. It would help her if she was seen to have such a powerful ally as your grace.'

Waynflete's face cleared. 'You're right,' he said. 'And it will be a pleasure to see her. I'll write to her straightaway and invite her to see how my new buildings are getting on. Especially the school. She's as interested as I am in the education of the young.'

London

Joan Moulton felt a surge of pride as she rode under the freshly painted coat of arms (three sable moles *courant* on a green field) that hung in front of Moulton Inn and into its busy courtyard. She enjoyed coming home. Thomas Moulton had been sixty when they married, and she had accepted that she was to be more a nurse than a wife. He had known her parents well and had been amused rather than shocked by her previous headstrong excursions into matrimony. Joan had loved books ever since her father had trusted her with the many treasures in his library, and Tom's trade and his huge top-heavy house in Paternoster Row had attracted her at a time when she was desperately in need of a place to mend her broken heart after her second husband Martin of Hungerford had been killed in France.

By the time Tom died seven years later, an honoured citizen of London with his own coat of arms, she'd learnt all he could teach her about bookselling. She'd continued running the business with her stepson William, a steady hard-working man only twelve years younger than she was. Last year they had set up a second workshop in Westminster, conveniently close to both the abbey and the royal palace. Handsomely illuminated genealogies and prophecies became a speciality, as did presentation bindings. They also had a network of chapmen who roamed all over England south of the Trent hawking their books and broadsheets, each stamped with their emblem of a scampering mole. The chapmen had another purpose. They carried messages between the fugitive Lancastrians who had scattered over the country since the final defeat of the Northern rebels two years ago at Hedgeley Moor. Joan owed all she had to Thomas Moulton, and in gratitude she had remained as loyal as he had been to Henry VI, despite the king's capture a year ago.

A tall thin man with a cadaverous face took the bridle of her horse and held it steady as she dismounted.

'Is all well, Guy?' she asked.

'The better for your return, mistress,' he answered. 'Which is well timed. Master Matthew is in the shop with Lord Scales, the queen's brother. He's already refused a dozen or more of our finest books.'

Joan's face lit up. 'Sir Anthony Wydeville? He's a noted collector. Now, let me think. What would appeal? He's a mixture of a man. Loves tournaments and all the stuff of chivalry but wears a hair shirt and talks of making a pilgrimage. And he's just come into property through his stick of a wife, Lady Scales. King Edward made over the Isle of Wight and Carisbrooke Castle to him on the queen's urging.'

'Wydeville said that he came on the advice of Lord Wenlock.'

Joan beamed. 'Lord Wenlock is a friend indeed. And I know just what will appeal to Sir Anthony.'

She bustled through the great hall, ducked behind the arras that hung behind its dais, and along a narrow passage into a large room with a high raftered roof and gable windows on the north side that allowed light to flood in. It was warmed by charcoal braziers, each with a bucket of water beside it in case of fire. Curtained shelves lined the walls, and there were four double-seated chairs with reading slopes in front of them. Her head bookman Matthew Cobham was standing anxiously beside one of the slopes watching a strikingly handsome young man dressed in murrey velvet slashed with yellow silk leaf through the pages of a splendid book of hours with a dissatisfied air.

'I have prayer books aplenty already,' he was saying. 'Have you anything lighter? Sir John Paston said that he bought an amusingly illustrated Ovid from you a fortnight since.'

As Joan entered, they both looked up, Matthew with evident relief. Wydeville rose to his feet and gave a slight bow. Joan sank into a curtsey.

'I am honoured to see you in my shop, Sir Anthony. My journeyman tells me that you are in search of interesting reading matter.'

'Yes. Lord Wenlock has long recommended Moulton's as the best bookseller in London. And he said that you would be able to advise on what would suit me.'

'I can indeed. And I have just the thing – I acquired it from the Countess of Stafford last month. It is a collection of tales and proverbs and wisdom from the East, translated into French and little known in England. Bound with it is a thrilling account of the campaigns of Alexander of Macedon. Matthew – could you bring in the *Dîtes Moraux des Philosophes*?'

Wydeville's face brightened. 'That sounds just the thing. Short readings are much more amusing than long tracts.'

'It needs rebinding,' Joan warned. 'But that's an advantage if you like the book. You can specify how you would like it to look.'

She drew him over to the large table in the centre of the room. 'Come and look at these specimen bindings and choose a style that pleases you. I suggest something in line with other such volumes in your collection. Would you like your own arms combined with those of Lady Scales on the front cover?'

Sir Anthony sighed. 'My wife has little interest in philosophy. But I might get her a blank book she could fill with household recipes. To take her mind off expensive fashions.'

Matthew returned, a shabbily bound quarto book under his arm. He placed it on a reading slope near the window and opened it up, turning one page after another. Sir Anthony's eyes gleamed as he took in the lavish ornamentation around the small blocks of text. As well as gilded arabesques and gay wreaths of flowers and fruits, there were tiny landscapes, in which knights and their ladies trooped towards turreted castles. He smiled with delight.

'This is wonderful, Mistress Moulton. Exactly the sort of thing I love. I favour red bindings tooled in gold. Could you also give it lateen clasps? How long will it take? And how much will it cost me?'

'It's a rare treasure. And I wonder if you might also be interested in a copy of this?' Joan took a scroll from a nearby shelf. 'It is Sir John Tiptoft's newly indited *Ordinances for Jousts and Triumphs*. I don't want to sell my exemplar, as I foresee considerable demand.'

Sir Anthony's face lit up. As Joan knew, he had challenged the Bastard of Burgundy to a tournament to be held in London next summer. Nothing could suit him better than a copy of Tiptoft's book. As constable, Sir John was president of the Court of Chivalry, and he had drawn up a special series of rules of combat for the event.

'I am indeed. How soon could you have a copy made for me? Bound as a small book.'

'What do you think, Matthew?'

'Would you like it decorated or simple, Sir Anthony? And what sort of binding?'

'Red and gold again. With my coat of arms on the front, and illustrations as handsome as your limners can manage,' said Wydeville. 'In fact, perhaps you could make two copies, and I will send one to Anthony of Burgundy. Blue and gold for his copy, with his crest on the front. The tournament has been postponed because of the ill health of his father, so we'll both have time to con it.'

'Excellent,' said Joan, wreathed in smiles. 'I am planning to go to Oxford next week, but our binders and text writers can get started on both the *Dîtes* and the *Ordinances* straight away.'

'To Oxford?' said Wydeville. 'I would have thought it had booksellers aplenty already.'

'Indeed it has. But Lord Wenlock has promised me an introduction to a notable collector, the Dowager Duchess of Suffolk. She has retired to her childhood home at Ewelme, which I believe is some fifteen miles south of the city.'

'I have heard it is now a palatial residence,' said Wydeville. 'Well suited to Princess Alyce.'

'Do you know her well?' asked Joan.

'Only by repute. She had some superb hawks in her mews at the Suffolks' London home, the Manor of the Rose, and my parents often went hunting and coursing in Epping Forest with her. But she does not now frequent the court as she used to when she mothered Margaret of Anjou and was a bosom friend of Cis Neville, the Duchess of York. In truth, my sister the queen has a deep dislike of her – and of any former confidante of Margaret of Anjou, except of course our own mother, Jacquetta of Luxemburg. She tells me that there are

77

rumours of treasonous goings on at Ewelme and steps are being taken to discover them. The dowager duchess may not be styled Princess for much longer.'

Joan kept her face blank. 'Indeed. Then should I be wary of befriending her?'

'I think you should. Folk are judged by the company they keep, especially in these uncertain times.'

After Wydeville had left, Joan turned to Matthew. 'That was a useful piece of gossip. I shall pass it on to Lord Wenlock so that he can warn Lady Alyce. She begins to interest me greatly. It seems she might also be the ideal customer for the beautiful treatise on falconry *Ars Venandi cum Avibus* that I brought back from Bruges. And I must gather together some tempting treasures for the wealthy folk I'll meet at Bishop Neville's feast. Selling books cannot be counted a crime – depending of course on what they have between their covers.'

Matthew shook his head disapprovingly. He was a profoundly cautious man. She laughed, knowing he disliked both the political risks she was taking with her network of chapmen and the salacious sideline in books banned by the Church that she was just beginning to explore.

Ewelme

Simon Brailles tapped apprehensively on the door of his mistress's closet. He heard the scrape of a chair and then her voice.

'Come in.'

He went in, almost wishing he was still assistant schoolmaster in the God's House, well removed from responsibility in situations like this. He had been dragged willy-nilly into helping with the Lancastrian fugitives by Ben Bilton, damn his eyes. And now he was having to deceive Lady Alyce, who had shown such faith in him by making him her secretary.

Alyce smiled warmly, which made him feel even worse.

'It is good to see you again, Simon. I've spoken to Martha Purbeck and Bilton, and the four of you seem to have kept everything in good order since I was last here. Thank you.'

She wouldn't thank him when she found out what had really been going on, he reflected gloomily, but managed to bow gratefully.

'But,' she continued, 'I know that you will need help now that I am going to manage my estates from Ewelme instead of Suffolk. Caerleon will be my man of business, coming and going between my estates. You will at the very least need a new text writer. Do you know of anyone who would suit you?'

He felt a stab of anxiety. She must think that he wasn't competent. And he had tried so hard to justify her trust in him. Moreover, at present any newcomer would present a security risk.

'Thank you, my lady,' he said. 'I am managing at present. But next month when the quarterly rent rolls arrive, some temporary aid would be welcome. I could ask John Doll of Oxford if he knows of a clerk who could take on such work.'

'An excellent idea. Let me know his answer.' She made a nod of dismissal.

Simon knew it was now or never. 'One more thing my lady...' He hesitated.

'What is it?' asked Alyce, frowning impatiently.

He cleared his throat, then gabbled out words so fast that she could hardly catch them.

'We have considered the three candidates for the God's House, your grace, as you directed. Two are derelict sots from Wallingford, and the third is a notorious thief. Given that your grace has insisted that we fill the empty place before the Harcourts arrive with their candidate, we have come up with another possibility – if she meets with your approval.'

He got no further.

'*She*?' repeated Alyce, aghast. 'A woman in the God's House? Surely you know that there is no provision for that in the statutes.'

Brailles blenched, mentally cursing Ben Bilton for leaving him to deliver this bolt from the blue. But he had worked for Alyce long enough to know that he would get a fair hearing if he persevered.

'The statutes do not forbid women in so many words. In many legal situations, as in theological literature, the Latin word *homo, hominis*, includes both sexes. And this is a most deserving case.'

'But surely Will Marton will reject a woman out of hand? As will Peter Greene.'

Simon plunged bravely on.

'Please hear me out, my lady. The woman in question is Sybilla of Swyncombe, and this was in fact Peter's own idea. He has been worried for some time about her health now that winter approaches. As you know, she turned eighty in the spring. And although she is, as she always has been, patient in adversity and uncomplaining, the Swyncombe servants who look after her bodily needs say that they can hear her cough-ing in the night. She is uncommonly thin, too, abstaining as she does from all meat and fasting on Fridays and holy days besides. Greene says that there are mixed communities in your other almshouses. And were Marton only here, we think he would agree. He has great respect for Sybilla.'

He saw a faraway look come to Alyce's eyes and could guess what she was thinking. She had often told him how important Sybilla was to her. He knew she had been her mother's tiring maid, and after Lady Maud had died thirty years ago she had looked after Alyce herself. But soon after the death of Duke William she had expressed her wish to become a recluse. When the incumbent of the Swyncombe hermitage had died a few years later, she had replaced him. Since Simon became assistant schoolmaster twelve years ago, he had often accompanied Alyce up to the ancient church, then visited the Fulberts in the manor house while Alyce spent several hours with Sybilla, her most trusted guide and mentor.

At last the duchess spoke. 'Well – it is certainly a solution. But will she agree? She values her peace and independence highly.'

Simon could answer confidently. 'Peter Greene walked up to ask her yesterday. She was staying in Swyncombe Manor as Lady Fulbert was in labour. She said that if your grace approved, she would find it a relief this winter, as long as she could find someone to keep an eye on her bees. But that she would wish to return to Swyncombe in the summer months to tend her garden. You know how she has toiled to make the plot around the church an offering to God's glory. The flowers are thick as a carpet now, scarce a blade of grass between them.'

Alyce nodded slowly. 'Simon, I should have trusted you, and not been so quick to anger. I do approve. In truth, it is a happy chance. It will be a comfort to have Sybilla closer and it solves our problem with the Harcourts very neatly. Send someone to help her to move down this afternoon. No, wait. I think I will go myself. I'll take the Stonor girls and Tamsin with me. And a cart for her belongings.'

Relieved, Simon bowed and left the room. He went down the stairs, across the hall, and into the steward's office next to the kitchen.

Ben Bilton looked up anxiously. 'How did she take it?'

'Badly at first, but when I told her how frail Sybilla now was, and that she was willing to come, she came round. She's even counting it a blessing. She's going up there this afternoon herself, with Tamsin and the Stonor girls.'

'Better and better. That'll give us time to get Dick Lawrence away to Wallingford and install Trevelyan in his cell. I'll ride down to Wallingford and find Caerleon.'

The door opened and the conspirators jerked round guiltily. But it was only Peter Greene, his cheerful face full of glee.

'Mistress Purbeck has been baking. Here, I've brought you some saffron cakes.'

'Don't you think of anything but your stomach?' teased Ben. But he reached eagerly for a bun. So did Simon.

In the private pleasaunce at the heart of her garden, Alyce was pruning unneeded branches of the interlaced fruit trees that had been trained to form four short tunnels leading to the central fountain. The garden was reached by a steep outside staircase from her own apartment. From there a narrow bridge crossed the moat, then a path led to a door in the south wall of the orchard. The only other entrance was a gate in the east wall which opened into the base court for the convenience of the gardeners, but it was always locked. The key was held by Ben Bilton, who opened it for them, and locked up again when they left.

She remembered how often she had found Sybilla bent over plants in her garden at Swyncombe, staking the weak, thinning the rampant. A lesson for life, the gaunt old woman had called them. Balance was what men and women needed, to be rooted in place, given strength by neighbours, and supporting them in turn. Although she had always loved the contemplative pilgrimage up to Swyncombe, it would be good to have her old mentor close by while she settled into the new, more retired life that she had chosen. And no one could question Sybilla's chastity and sanctity. Saving her sex, the perfect candidate. And what barrier was that, in truth? Holiness is what men and women alike associated with Sybilla, not sex. The statutes could be amended. Alyce began to look forward to justifying her decision to admit a woman to the community. She could quote her favourite author Christine de Pisan's belief that women should be given the same opportunities as men, as well as citing any number of almshouses with mixed communities – among them her own Charterhouse in Hull and her almshouses at Leighton Buzzard. Indeed, she wondered that she had not thought of appointing bedeswomen to the God's House before.

Alyce snipped deadheads off fading germanders, picked a few spears of rosemary, and sat down on the turf seat beside the fountain. She was pleased to see that the gardeners had kept its grass beaten down hard. Then she paused. Something about their interview had suggested that Simon was not being altogether frank. What was it? She cast her mind back over the conversation but couldn't put her finger on it. She shrugged. Best not to belabour her wits. Like the mystery of Nicolas

Webb's death, it would out anon. And sometimes the most unpromising of situations could turn out for the best.

She took her tools and put them away in the hut just beside the entrance to the garden from the courtyard. Then she heard a clatter of wheels. Opening the ironbound oak door, she saw a cart had rumbled into the courtyard. A tall sunburnt man with high cheekbones, bright blue eyes and wiry black hair springing up from his skull in a halo of surprise leapt down from his seat beside the driver and began to pull the cover off the cart's load. Her spirits lifted. It was Denzil Caerleon, in clothes still encrusted with sea salt by the look of the stains on them. She took off her gardening apron and put that too into the hut. She took out an old silvered mirror she kept there, and adjusted the folds of the scarf she had wound around her head. Then, feeling a little foolish, she bit her lips to make them redden, and emerged into the courtyard, head held high.

Caerleon and John Cook were both peering into the cart, their voices raised in argument. She tapped Denzil lightly on the shoulder with her silver cane. He whirled round defensively, then saw her, raised his clown's eyebrows in a delighted smile, and made a low bow.

'Your grace, I must apologise for my appearance – I am in dire need of a bath and a change of clothes. But there was no time to lose if I was to get the fine sturgeon I've brought you from Billingsgate here in time. It's a female, caught near Deptford and hopefully full of the most toothsome roe. And though I brought her in a coffin, she's very much alive. Now I am trying to explain to John Cook that she must be kept in salted water or else she will perish. But he wants to put her straight into the great stew filled from the spring.'

Alyce looked into the coffin at the huge fish and shuddered. The fish was almost 5 foot long, but slender in proportion to its length, with a long pointed snout and rows of bony plates overlapping each other along her back. A small malevolent eye rolled, and stiff whiskers dangled from below a long gash of a mouth.

'I thought she had a look of you, your grace,' said Denzil with a wicked grin. He was spared Alyce's wrath by John Cook, who was shaking his head.

'Water's water, your grace. And we'll be eating this 'un soon enough, won't we? With the Harcourts arriving on the morrow.'

She found herself smiling at the honest countryman's ignorance. 'Do as Denzil says, John. He's right. The feast is not until Friday, and the longer we keep her alive the better eating she will make.'

'She won't fit into a fish kettle, that's for sure,' said Cook. 'I could chop 'un into chunks and stew 'un in a cauldron. Or cut through 'un into steaks and fry them.'

'Steaks would look dramatic,' said Denzil. 'Roast the head whole on a spit, put a pomegranate between its jaws and arrange the steaks around it on a great platter. With watercress from the brook and damascene plums. That'll be a centrepiece indeed.'

He turned to Alyce. 'My lady, after I've bathed I must return to the other barges and keep them downstream of Wallingford out of the Harcourts' way.'

'Can't that be left to the watermen? I want to hear all about your voyage, especially your encounter with John Trevelyan.'

'I'd rather stay with them myself,' said Denzil. 'Truth to tell, I dislike the Harcourts. I came across them many years ago when I worked for John Doll. And one of my men is unwell. I need to go across to the infirmary and ask Nan Ormesby if there is a place for him.'

Alyce watched him as he strode away, so sure of himself and so careless of what the world thought of him. He was the most adventurous man she had ever come across. Too adventurous for his own good, she sometimes thought, but the world was always more interesting when he was around. She'd first seen him a year ago in John Doll's stationers in Oxford High Street. He'd been reading a Tale of Tristram aloud for a group of scriveners to copy, declaiming it with a relish and vitality that delighted her. Doll had told her his story.

'Best journeyman I've had, but I'm beginning to think he's more trouble than he's worth. He'd have been high in the University now if it weren't for his wayward temper. The word is that he eloped with an heiress and lost his place at New College. She died in childbirth, sobbing for her mother, and I think that something in Denzil died too. He has a restless mind, that's the trouble. Obsessed with the night sky and dabbles in alchemy too. Gets dead drunk more than he ought to and disappears altogether from time to time.'

'Let me know if you tire of him,' she'd said. 'I could find a place for a text writer with an interest in star-gazing.' A month later, Denzil had appeared at Ewelme, all his worldly goods in a small bundle, carrying a terse note from Doll: 'I've tired of him.' He was now just as essential as Ben Bilton and Simon Brailles to the smooth running of her life, apt with the horses, hounds and hawks, sharp on points of law and a connoisseur of fine books.

Was she getting too dependent on him, she wondered? No. She had made him, and she could unmake him. Not that she would. His certainty gave her strength. And though she had no intention at all of remarrying, she found the company of such an attractive and clever young man lit up life considerably. One day, she supposed, he would get over the loss of that first love of his and find himself a wife. Meanwhile, it was good to have him back at her side.

Tamsin woke with a start. The sun was already high in the sky. She wasn't used to such quiet, comfortable sleeping quarters. There had been no summons from the duchess that morning; she must have sent for the Stonor girls to help her dress. When she went down to break her fast in the buttery, she saw Alyce in the distance, heading towards her garden. She scurried across the courtyard and caught her mistress up just as she unlocked the oak door to the orchard of her pleasure garden. Alyce turned at the sound of her running feet and stared at her blankly, mind evidently far away.

'I'm sorry I'm late, my lady,' Tamsin blurted out breathlessly. 'Can I be of service in any way?'

Alyce blinked slowly as if waking from a trance, then shook her head.

'No, child. There's nothing I need. I'm going to my garden. Go and see your friends in the God's House. But I'd like you to be ready to go with me to Swyncombe after dinner. We're going to collect its new resident.' She gave Tamsin an unexpectedly mischievous grin and disappeared into the orchard.

Bemused, Tamsin stared after her. The duchess's sudden changes of mood mystified her. Still, she was to go with her to Swyncombe. And it would be lovely to see something of Nan and Wat.

She found them both in the infirmary garden. Nan was hanging out sheets, and Wat was digging up carrots and skirrets. He dropped his spade when he saw Tamsin and ran to greet her, flapping his arms as if trying to fly and crowing with delight.

'Wat!' Nan shouted. 'What did I teach you about greeting? Stand straight and bow your head. Then wait to be spoken to.' Abashed, Wat slowed down, peering hopefully at Tamsin from under his heavy brow.

Nan chuckled. 'He's been missing you something awful.'

'I miss him,' said Tamsin with feeling. 'And you.'

Soon they were all sitting in the infirmary kitchen, eating saffron buns that Martha Purbeck had brought over from the palace kitchen's baking.

'How are you managing?' asked Nan. 'Is Lady Alyce impressed by you?'

Tamsin sighed. 'I don't know. There's so much to learn. And I overslept today. I've never had a room to myself before. This morning Lady Alyce looked at me as if I wasn't there.'

'Don't worry, child. When Martha Purbeck came over, she told me that you were getting on fine. Lady Alyce has a lot on her mind just now. She can be unpredictable, and sharp-spoken at times, but she's fair-minded. Trust her, and you won't go far wrong.'

'Then there's Marlene. She keeps excusing herself from her duties, and I think she's up to something. And she's very unkind to her sister.'

'Marlene is a little minx,' said Nan flatly. 'My advice to you is to keep out of her way.'

The bell sounded for the bedesmen's midday dinner. 'Stay and eat with us,' said Nan. 'It's my own venison stew. And the roots that Wat's been digging up. Or do you have to be back in the palace?'

'Not until later,' said Tamsin. 'I'd love to.'

After the meal, she hurried back to the base court of the palace. A cart was being unloaded and a tall thin man with an angular face and a shock of thick dark hair seemed to be arguing with Lady Alyce.

'Who's that?' Tamsin asked a stable hand, a friendly snub-nosed lad called Jem who had just come in from the courtyard.

'Master Caerleon,' he said in awe. 'He's a legend. Been acting as my lady's steward in Suffolk. Now he's come to Ewelme to be her travelling man of business. They say he has the sight. Knows your fortune just by looking at you. He was in charge of the duchess's ballingers that went by sea to London. Everything in them was put on barges at Southwark, and they've been sailed and quanted and towed up the Thames. Caerleon has brought a great sea-fish on the fastest barge. It arrived at Wallingford this morning and now it's here. The other barges will get there today or tomorrow, but they won't be unloaded until after the Harcourts leave. I heard that Caerleon'll be off again on the instant to take charge of them.'

The duchess was evidently worried. She kept shaking her head, but the dark-haired man just shrugged his shoulders, clearly pressing his point. At last Alyce gave him a curt nod and headed back into the hall.

Tamsin hurried after her, nipped past, then turned, curtseying awkwardly.

'My lady, you said I was to go to Swyncombe with you.'

Alyce looked at her with a frown, then her face softened. She had forgotten she'd told her new tiring maid to ready herself for the ride to Swyncombe.

'That's right, child. We're going to escort Sybilla the anchorite down to the God's House. She is to be our first bedeswoman. You know of her reputation for godliness, I am sure. Martha is going to tell Nan to prepare for her the cell left vacant by Nicolas. Go up to Marlene and Eloise and tell them that I would like them to come too. We'll ride, of course, but we'll bring a cart for Sybilla and her possessions.' She disappeared towards her chamber.

Tamsin went up to give the Stonors Alyce's message, then went into her room to collect her cloak. She could hear the girls arguing through the thin partition between her own room and theirs.

'I covered up for you yesterday, Marlene, but you'll have to come with me to Swyncombe.'

'Oh, Eloise, please. This is our only chance for a little privacy before the house is swarming with guests. You can tell her my fever is worse. She doesn't need both of us now that she's got Tamsin. I'll let you wear my new blue dress for the feast after the hunt.'

Tamsin wondered who Marlene wanted to have a little privacy with. There was no one suited to her rank or age in the household. She prayed that it wasn't Ben Bilton. Not that she wanted him for herself. Nor had he ever been more than kind to her in an older brotherly way. She'd seen him chaffing the Stonor girls in like fashion about the amount of baggage they'd brought back from Wingfield. But he'd looked hungrily after Marlene when they'd disappeared into the palace, staring as if he'd seen a vision. She strained to hear more, but the voices had sunk to whispers. Perhaps they had remembered she was next door. She gathered up the russet cloak that Mistress Purbeck had given her the day before, and walked through the wardrobe, down the staircase and out into the courtyard. Lady Alyce was already mounted on her beloved jennet Larkspur, and Leo was prancing at the prospect of an outing. Adam, an elderly groom, was sitting on the driving seat of a capacious cart pulled by two horses. The Stonor girls' palfreys were being held by stable boys, and Jem was holding the harness of a mule that she guessed was for her to ride. He grinned, and motioned her to mount, cupping his right hand low as a foothold.

'She's a sweet-tempered little thing,' he whispered as he helped her into the saddle. 'You'll hardly need the reins; she'll amble after the other horses as if she's on a leading rein.'

She gave him a small, tight smile. She'd told Lady Alyce that she could ride, but, as Jem well knew, she'd only ever been astride Nan's placid old donkey.

Just then Eloise came out into the courtyard, walked over to them and looked nervously up at Alyce.

'Marlene has a fever. I think she'd best stay in bed.'

Alyce sniffed in annoyance.

'Malingering again. Oh well. No time to see her now. Take her horse back to the stable, Jem, then join Adam on the cart. We must be off if we're to be back before dusk falls.'

She gave a sign to the groom who held Larkspur, and he let go of the reins. Then she clapped her heels to the jennet's flanks and clattered out of the courtyard, followed by Eloise and Tamsin. The cart rumbled along behind them. To Tamsin's relief, the mule Jem had chosen for her proved to be a good deal easier to ride than Nan's donkey, which had a tendency to stop whenever a tasty thistle presented itself. She settled herself in the saddle, enjoying being able to see so much more than she could when on foot. Most of the fields were stubble after the harvest, and the village women and children were gleaning for heads of wheat that had fallen from the stooks. If she hadn't found the rosary, she would have been among them. In Marlene's absence, Eloise was good company, telling stories about childhood escapades in the forest with her brother William.

'He's studying at Oxford now,' she told Tamsin. 'I miss him. He always stood up for me when Marlene was unkind.'

Over to the north-east, thick woods marked the beginning of the great hunting forest that spread from Ewelme almost to Stonor, and Leo, glimpsing a deer, began to race away, front paws aping the deer's terrified leaps. Alyce pulled out a bone whistle and gave it two sharp blasts. He veered back, regretful but as always obedient. The lane sloped upwards, then veered to the south between two high ridges.

Swyncombe

Half an hour after leaving the palace, they reached Swyncombe church. St Botolph's was the oldest church for miles around, built by the Saxons for travellers on their way from the ports of Norfolk to King Alfred's capital at Salisbury. Attached limpet-like to its north-western corner was the anchorite's cell where Sybilla lived. Her worldly needs were provided for by Sir Brian Fulbert, the tenant of Swyncombe Manor, as part of the terms by which he held his lease from Alyce. His kitchen staff were entrusted with the duty of taking food, water and fresh rushes to the cell, and receiving in return a bucket of slops to empty out on the nearby dung heap. And if anyone in the Fulberts' household ailed, Sybilla left her seclusion and tended them.

Fulbert came out to greet them, grinning from ear to ear.

'Welcome, my lady. You are our new daughter's first visitor. She was born in the small hours. As she decided to approach it contrariwise, she was fortunate to have both Sybilla and Farhang helping her into the world.'

'Farhang is a master of his craft,' said Alyce, 'and I'm eager to see Lady Anne. But it's Sybilla I've come to see. Simon tells me that she has agreed to retreat into the God's House.'

'That's a relief,' said Sir Brian. 'She has earned such comforts in the evening of her life. She'll be asleep, I suspect. She was up all night.'

'Could I go and see the baby?' asked Eloise. 'I promise not to wake Lady Fulbert.'

Alyce nodded, and told Adam and Jem to take the horses to the little pasture across the road. Then she went inside the church with Tamsin. It was a cave of colour. Thomas and Maud Chaucer had renovated it, adding armorial windows in glowing reds, blues and golds, retiling the floor, putting in two more lancet windows and hiring an itinerant Flemish painter to give it a fine Doom on the east wall. For good measure the artist had painted a riot of flowers and birds and beasts over the walls of the aisle, and the sunlight striking through the stained glass made rainbows dance in the air. Alyce knelt in prayer for a few minutes, then went over to the squint in the south wall of the chancel through which Sybilla could watch the celebration of the Mass.

'Sybilla, I'm home,' she said. There was no reply.

Alyce frowned. 'Sybilla,' she repeated, a little louder. Her voice echoed from the round vault of the roof. She peered through the squint, but the angled wall showed her only a small section of the opposite side of the cell.

'Sybilla!' she called a third time. But there was no reply. Was that a groan from inside? She strode out of the church, followed by Tamsin and Eloise, and walked round to Sybilla's single window and peered in. Ominously still, a dark heap lay on the floor. She tried the narrow door, but it was bolted from the inside. A furious buzzing came from the shelf of bee skeps set in alcoves in the outside wall of the anchorhold. Something was seriously wrong. She called for Adam and Jem, and they came hurrying over.

'Adam, Sybilla seems to have collapsed. Go up to the manor house and get Sir Brian. Tell him to bring crowbars and heavy mallets. And the smith. We need to break this door down. Tamsin, go with him and get some women from the house to tend her when we get her out. And Farhang, if he can be spared from Lady Anne's side.'

Fifteen minutes later, men were levering crowbars against the hinges of the door of the anchorhold while the smith, a giant of man, swung a mallet against their ends. The door splintered and broke away from its frame. The smith stepped into the cell, then uttered a curse and stepped hastily out again.

'Adders, he said. 'I heard them hissing. They must have bitten Dame Sybilla, God rest her soul.'

'She may not be dead,' said Alyce. 'I thought I heard a groan when I was in the church. Jem – you have thick boots and leggings. Pull on your riding gauntlets and bring her out.' Jem stepped inside, looking warily about him as he picked Sybilla's body off the floor and carried her out of the cell. Tamsin shuddered in sympathy. Everyone feared snakes, the descendants of man's oldest enemy, the serpent in the garden. Just in case, she attached Leo's leash to a fence post.

They all watched with horror as Jem gently lowered Sybilla

onto a cloak that Hugh had spread out on the ground. Suddenly there was a blood-curdling howl and a black shape scuttled out of the door of the cell and disappeared into the woods. Eloise gave a screech and Leo jerked at his leash.

'Her cat. Scared out of its wits, no doubt,' said Alyce quickly, hoping to forestall rumours of attendant familiars, but knowing that whispers of a pact with the Devil and his creatures would soon be spreading round the parish like dry rot in damp wood. She bent over Sybilla's stick-thin body in its coarse anchorite's robe and felt under her wimple for a pulse in the swollen neck. She felt a flicker of movement.

'Carry her into the church. Brian, could Farhang attend her? I think she still breathes.'

'I'll go for him myself,' said Fulbert, staring at Sybilla's unhealthy grey pallor. 'But I fear I should bring Father Jerome as well.' He strode away.

Tamsin followed Alyce into the church, where Hugh and Jem made Sybilla as comfortable as possible on a bed of cloaks spread out on the wide bench just inside the south door.

'I think her lips are moving, my lady,' said Hugh. Alyce bent over the old woman. Like a whisper of wind, there came a croak. 'Scrrak. Bur…'

Alyce froze in alarm. Was her old friend going to betray her greatest secret?

'What did she say?' asked Jem.

'I – I'm not sure. Perhaps she's calling on St Botolph.' To her relief, Sybilla stopped trying to speak.

There was a rapid step behind them and Tamsin turned to see Farhang Amiri hurry in, clutching a little wooden medicine chest. He was in his seventies, olive-skinned, with a neatly trimmed beard following the lines of his sharply sculpted jaw.

His green physician's gown was stained with weather and age. He bowed briefly to Alyce, and Tamsin saw in his deep-set brown eyes the same affection for her that Gerard Vespilan had shown. Admiration akin to adoration.

Behind him followed Jerome, the Fulberts' chaplain, carrying a silver box containing a communion wafer and the tiny bottle of oil required to save Sybilla's soul from hell in the final sacrament of extreme unction. Bustling after them were two competent-looking maids and Eloise.

Farhang bent over Sybilla, running long sensitive fingers over her face and neck. He had a thin-bladed knife between thumb and forefinger. Suddenly he stopped, made a small incision into her neck, stooped and began sucking hard at it. Tamsin shivered. The black-robed figure hunched over Sybilla was altogether too like the tales of blood-sucking devils that Nan used to scare her with on winter evenings. He spat out a mixture of saliva and blood and stooped again to suck and spit. Then he felt along Sybilla's arms. As he did so, he called to one of the Swyncombe maids.

'Esther, bring water from the cauldron on the kitchen fire. As hot as possible.' He made another small incision, this time to Sybilla's left arm, stooped and again sucked vigorously.

He was feeling slowly and carefully along Sybilla's feet and shins when Esther bustled up with a steaming wooden bucket. Farhang dipped a cloth in it and squeezed the hot water over both wounds, then sucked at them again, and finally sluiced the remaining hot water over them. Then he pulled Sybilla towards himself and cradled her upright in his arms. He turned to his medicine chest and took out a small blue glass bottle. After shaking it, he removed the stopper, forced its narrow neck through Sybilla's clenched lips, and poured its contents down her throat, muttering prayers as he did so. Her eyes flickered, and she gave a choking cough, but he put his hand firmly over her mouth so that none of the medicine could be expelled. She gave a croak and went horribly limp. Tamsin's heart stood still. She was surely lost. But no. Her eyes flickered again, then opened. They rested on Alyce, and a great look of peace came over her face. Tamsin felt tears streaming down her cheeks. Farhang gazed critically at the calm face, then nodded with satisfaction.

Sir Brian stepped forward. 'Master Amiri, the whole parish is indebted to you. Sybilla is much loved for her kindness and patience, and her gift of healing. Do you think we should take her back to the manor house for the night? She looks terribly weak.'

'No,' said Alyce. 'Farhang has brought her back from death, and from now on I want her close to me at Ewelme. Brian, do you have a palliasse and a coverlet that we could put into the cart for her?'

'Of course, my lady.' Sir Brian turned to the housemaids. 'Jenny, Merryn, fetch bedding from the house.'

When the cart had been padded well, Hugh and Jem carried Sybilla over to it. As Alyce herself tucked a coverlet around her, Tamsin saw that she was blinking back tears. Then she turned to Sir Brian.

'Brian, could you set a guard you can trust outside her door until I send men up from Ewelme to collect whatever's inside. Whether or not the rumours of the hoard of treasures Sybilla kept safe is true, I suspect that her cell might be ransacked, snakes or not, otherwise.'

'Best put some poisoned fish inside,' said Merryn, the older and more assured of the Swyncombe maids.

'In a day's time it'll kill off any of them evil serpents.'

Alyce nodded approvingly and mounted Larkspur.

'I'll see that it's done straightaway,' said Fulbert. 'And I think that Farhang should go with you. Sybilla needs him close by. My wife is doing well and has her women to tend her and the baby.'

'My thanks, Sir Brian,' said Alyce. 'Truth to tell, Ewelme needs him sorely.'

She was remembering how ill Vespilan had looked. Her favourite people in the world were both under threat. Her most trusted servants were concealing something from her. And, if Bilton's information was right, her heartland was in jeopardy, threatened by the machinations of the Harcourts. But she had risen to many challenges in her life. She'd rise to this one.

'To me, Leo,' she called as she clapped spurs to her horse and set off homewards, the hound loping at Larkspur's side. Tamsin and Eloise mounted hurriedly and did their best to keep up with her, Tamsin almost falling off more than once. She saw the determined set of Alyce's mouth and her preoccupied gaze.

'Is anything wrong, your grace?' she called shyly.

Alyce glanced across at her worried little face and gave a wry smile.

'I fear so. But quite what I don't know. If this was a chess game I would fear that my opponent had devised a sustained mating attack against me.' She sighed. 'A double bind.'

'Is there anything I can do?'

Alyce looked around before answering. Eloise and the cart had fallen behind.

'I don't know. Keep your eyes and ears open, and your mouth shut, as your grandmother recommended. And trust no one.'

Ewelme

The sun was low in the sky by the time the little cavalcade reached Ewelme. Alyce had sent Jem ahead to make sure that Nan was prepared, and she was relieved to see her in the porch of the infirmary when they drew up by the school.

Nan hurried out as soon as the litter stopped, nodded to Alyce and Farhang, and frowned as she stooped over Sybilla's unconscious form. She turned to Hugh and Jem.

'Carry her into the infirmary. Wat will show you the bed we've prepared for her. But how on earth did adders get into her cell? Its door is rarely left open, and the scent of her cat would have scared them away.'

Alyce was taken aback. In the excitement and horror of finding Sybilla and getting her down to Ewelme, she hadn't thought about how the snakes had got into her cell. She looked down at the ashen face of the old recluse, relieved to see a vein pulsing gently under the skin of her bony forehead.

'God knows. We must pray heaven she recovers. Look after her well, Nan. Farhang will instruct you. And let me know as soon as she is well enough to be moved. If possible, I want her settled in to the God's House by Thursday, so the Harcourts see we have no place for their spy. Vespilan can keep a close eye on her, and let you know if she has need of you or Farhang. I'll go and tell him what's happened. Eloise, to me.'

Eloise gave an anxious glance towards the palace and Alyce guessed that she was wondering what had become of Marlene.

'But I am being thoughtless. Eloise, go and see how your sister does. Tamsin can come with me.'

She headed for the arched south gate of the almshouse cloister, and Tamsin followed. They walked across the central courtyard to Vespilan's room on the north side. Alyce tapped at the door, and there was a shuffle of footsteps. When Gerard opened it, his face lit up.

'Welcome, your grace. Peter Greene said you were bringing Sybilla to the God's House. She could have no better refuge in her old age. And I'm looking forward to her company. Make a change to have somebody worth talking to. When will she be moving in?'

'We have brought her down from Swyncombe, but she is very ill. Adders had somehow got into the anchorhold, and she was bitten. Farhang is tending her in the infirmary, but as soon as she is well enough she will be moved into Nicolas's room next door to you, and I hope you will keep an eye on her.'

Alyce saw the old man tremble. She took his arm and helped him back into his room, and onto a chair. He was pale with shock. She pulled a joint stool close to Vespilan's chair, and perched on it, stroking his arm to calm him.

'Snakes? Bitten? But how?' he asked.

'We don't know,' Alyce said. 'But I fear evil doing.'

'These are evil times,' Gerard said, staring at Tamsin. 'I warned Bilton and Marton. First Nicolas eats a death cap, then vipers worm their way into the anchorhold.' He shook his head. 'Two mysteries. Which betokeneth a third. There is devilry afoot.'

Tamsin stared at the old man in horror. Noticing, Alyce bent down and whispered to her.

'Go to the infirmary, child, and ask Farhang for a restorative cordial for Brother Vespilan.'

After Tamsin had hurried away, Alyce took her place on the stool, and held the old man's shaking hands between her own.

'Gerard, we need your aid over the next few days. The

Harcourt brothers and their train are visiting us on Thursday and staying for a day's hunting on Friday. They have a mind to foist their own candidate on the God's House, which is why we decided to bring down Sybilla. I can now say that there's no room for him. But I'd rather they didn't find out that I have a woman among my bedesmen. We'll need to prevent them poking around if we can. If they find her, I'll defend my decision, of course. But I'd like to avoid confrontation just now if I can.'

'I'll do my best,' said Gerard, gazing past her. 'Where's the little maid gone?'

Alyce chuckled. 'You scared the child, Gerard, staring at her and talking of evil and mysteries. Shame on you. But I know you didn't mean to. I sent her to fetch Farhang.'

Before Gerard could reply, his door opened, and Farhang Amiri appeared, followed by Tamsin. He looked assessingly at the old man, took his hand and felt his pulse. Then he nodded to Alyce.

'He just needs rest, my lady. I've brought an infusion which will make him sleep. And I could come over to the palace later and tell you how Sybilla is. She is still unconscious and Nan is just settling her in. But you might like to see her cell for yourself before you go.'

'I would, Farhang. And I'll expect you this evening after vespers. Come, Tamsin.'

Reassuring Vespilan with a last gentle stroke on the arm, Alyce went out of his room and into the one next door. The spartan little chamber had been thoroughly scrubbed and scattered with fresh rushes. There was a stack of kindling on one side of the fireplace, and a black iron pot standing on a trivet on the other. Soft young shoots of ladies' bedstraw and rosemary had been mixed in among the rushes on the floor, scenting the air pleasantly. Nan would have put them there to take away the sour smell of old men typical of the cells. A rough sheet lay on a fat straw palliasse on the bed frame, and a thick wool blanket was folded at the bed end. Alyce nodded approvingly.

'That will do for now. For the moment we'll keep her cell the same as all the others. I don't want to draw attention to her. But once the Harcourts have left, we'll bring down some of the fine linen I brought back from Wingfield, and a goose-down quilt. And perhaps that folding shrine to St Botolph that stands in my tower room. It was my mother's. Sybilla will treasure it.'

They walked down to the school, hearing chanting voices through its open windows, then turned right along the main street to the palace. Alyce was musing on Vespilan's words. Was he right in believing that Webb's poisoning and Sybilla being bitten by adders were mysteries, not chance happenings. 'Which betokeneth a third.' Was there worse to come?

Later that evening, Farhang tapped on the door of Alyce's chamber. Trained in Shiraz, he had had to flee Persia after converting to Christianity. He'd settled in Angers, where he established a reputation as a marvellous physician, highly valued by René of Anjou. In 1445, when René's fifteen-year-old daughter Marguerite was married by proxy to King Henry VI, he travelled to England with her, because she was far from well. Alyce had soon realised how gifted he was. When he was summarily dismissed by the cabal of English doctors who regarded care of the royal family as their own prerogative, she persuaded him to come to Ewelme.

'Come in!' she called. He entered soundlessly, as he always did, soft-shod in the sandals that he wore all year round. He put back the hood of his striped wool gown, made for him by the palace tailor in the style of a Moorish djellaba, and held out a small bottle.

'Attar of roses, my lady. Imported from Damascus. Inhale it: it will lift your spirits and calm your mind.'

'How well you know me,' Alyce said with a sigh. 'My mind certainly needs calming at the minute. Sybilla nearly dead and the Harcourts about to arrive to snoop out supposed treasons in the God's House and my palace. Bilton heard in Oxford that they are planning to foist a bedesman on me, a spy in our midst. Not that it will do them any good. There is nothing treasonous going on here. And since Sybilla has survived, there is no vacancy in the God's House.'

Farhang paled. 'I hadn't heard that the Harcourts were coming to Ewelme. That is an unlooked-for trial.'

'And what about Nicolas Webb's death? Did Vespilan tell you that he suspected that he was poisoned deliberately?'

'Yes, he told me that he saw a night-time prowler in the cloister shortly before Nicolas died. I wondered about that. Nothing was disturbed.'

'I fear it was murder. The deliberate removal of one of my bedesmen to make way for the Harcourts' spy. If only there was a way to find out the identity of the prowler. Gerard did say that there was something about him that jogged a memory.'

Farhang thought for a moment. 'I will talk to Vespilan again, my lady. When he is a little stronger. It could be that I could coax something more from him. But don't bother him. Let's wait and see. Remember the words of Rumi: *Patience is the key to joy.*'

Alyce smiled wryly. Farhang had a proverb from the old Persian philosopher Rumi to fit every occasion. But she had suffered too often from waiting on the wishes of others. Now that she had the power to do so, she was determined to steer an independent course.

Ewelme

Soon after eleven on Thursday, there was a commotion of barking dogs and shouting voices on the road that wound up from the king's highway, and the Harcourts came clattering into Ewelme. Liveried guards swung the great doors of the outer gatehouse open and two richly dressed men on high-bred coursers rode into the base court, followed by two ladies in extravagantly embroidered riding habits on pretty white palfreys. All had hawks on their wrists and hounds at their heels. One of the riders who clattered through the gatehouse after them was evidently their huntsman; draped around his shoulders was a feathered yoke of dead birds strung together by their beaks and claws. They were ordered by size, with the plump corpses of pheasants in the middle and the tiny body of a skylark at each end. Grooms ran to the heads of the horses, falconers handed the hawks onto perches, the dog boys whistled the hounds to the kennels and footmen helped the ladies to dismount.

Tamsin had put on a soft woollen green gown that the Ewelme tailor had remodelled from an old one of Martha Purbeck's to fit her slim figure. With a snowy white stomacher under its bodice, and a fillet of leather holding back her well-brushed red curls, she proudly followed Alyce out of the east wing, where the duchess had been checking that Martha had prepared the guest chambers properly. She noticed that there was a stooped figure swathed in a dark grey cloak among the retainers being guided towards the servants' guesthouse at the far end of the base court. He was being helped along by a page. The would-be bedesman, no doubt. She resolved to watch him like a hawk.

The Harcourts strolled across the drawbridge, each with a lady on his arm, both well wrapped up against the chill autumn wind.

'That's strange,' Alyce murmured to Tamsin. 'I wasn't told that Sir Richard would be bringing a lady. She must be his new wife.' She stooped to calm Leo, whose teeth were bared in a snarl at the newcomers.

Sir Robert bellowed a greeting, and hastened up to her, grabbing her in a bear hug. She jerked away from him instinctively, and all but lost her balance. Fortunately Tamsin was close enough to save her from falling.

'You clumsy fool, Robert.' Shaking her head in disapproval, Lady Margaret stepped forward, and kissed the duchess affectionately.

'Forgive my oaf of a husband, Alyce. His only excuse is that he's been longing to see you.'

'Indeed I have,' exclaimed Robert. 'It's been months since you've been to court. And the Garter ceremony was poor stuff without its most eminent lady. Begging your pardon, Margaret, but she is, you know. But you look blenched, Alyce. Have you been unwell?'

'Just weary from the long journey from Wingfield. As you probably know, I'm going to make Ewelme my home for good now. If I return to Suffolk, it will be as a visitor.'

'That is excellent news for your many friends here in Oxfordshire,' said Sir Robert. 'But who is this pretty wench? Don't think I've seen her before, have I? Just out of the nursery, by the look of her. Tender little pullet, I don't doubt.'

His eyes wandered down Tamsin's trim figure. She felt a blush rise to her cheeks. Alyce frowned. She gestured to Tamsin to stand back beside Martha, then turned to Lady Harcourt.

'Margaret – it's good to see you. How long have you been on the road? Let's go inside.' Avoiding Robert's eagerly proffered arm, she took Margaret's and led her guests into the small central hall of the guest wing. Tamsin followed with Martha. Once inside, Alyce turned to Robert's brother Sir Richard Harcourt. A head shorter than his brother and half his girth, he had narrow watchful eyes under a hood rolled into a turban-like hat, its exaggeratedly long tip looped over his shoulder. He always adopted the latest fashions, relying on them to distract from the meanness of his person. Thin-faced, thin-lipped, likely thin-hearted, Tamsin thought to herself as the duchess held out her hand for him to kiss.

'It seems that I must congratulate you on two counts, Richard – your knighthood and, I presume, your wife. Please introduce me.' But as Alyce turned to his companion, who had now unwrapped the long silken hood tied around her head and much of her face, her jaw dropped in shock. So did Mistress Purbeck's.

'Who is she? Tamsin whispered to the chamberlain.

Martha stooped to whisper in Tamsin's ear.

'Lady Catherine Stapleton – de la Pole that was. Her grace's least favourite lady. One of the reasons she left Wingfield. She's second cousin to the late duke. Always whining that her father had been done out of his inheritance by the duke, and that she deserved compensation from her ladyship's Suffolk jointure. She married Sir Miles Stapleton, a Yorkshire knight with lands near hers in Suffolk. Sir Richard Harcourt's son William is married to their daughter.'

'I must apologise, Lady Stapleton,' they heard Alyce saying. 'I had heard that Sir Richard was planning to remarry.'

'So I am,' said Richard. 'And you are not mistaken: Lady Stapleton and I are indeed espoused. My wife – er – died recently, and Sir Miles died in January, and we thought the match an excellent way of keeping together our children's inheritance and providing for our own support and comfort into the bargain. Always understood each other well, Catherine and I. We are waiting on a dispensation from Rome, but we are already keeping company. Given our age and good standing, there is no likelihood of vulgar gossip.'

Clearly lost for words at this unexpected development, Alyce looked round for help. When she saw Martha Purbeck standing in attendance by the sideboard, with Tamsin beside her, she beckoned them forward.

'Martha, please show our guests to their rooms. Lady Stapleton had better have the chamber we intended for Sir Richard, and Sir Richard can be accommodated in the small chamber next to Sir Robert. Tamsin, run over to the kitchens and tell the potboy to take hot water to their rooms, and to stoke the braziers: our guests will want to refresh themselves after their journey.'

Tamsin saw a conspiratorial glance flit between the brothers. Then Sir Robert spoke.

'I'm sure the ladies can settle in on their own with the help of your servants. Meanwhile, perhaps Richard and I could have a tour of your famed almshouse before the meal. I am planning a chantry of my own at Witney, and I would be grateful for your advice on its layout – and on the ideal number of occupants.'

Alyce frowned again, but nodded assent.

'Of course. Let us walk over to the God's House. So you have seen the light at last, Sir Robert?'

He chuckled self-consciously. 'Nothing like age for bringing a man to a consciousness of his immortal soul. Not that age seems to touch you, my dear. As lovely as ever. Do you think on another husband at all? There would be a long line if you did. With me at the head of them if it wasn't for my dear Margaret.'

As Lady Alyce and the Harcourt brothers walked through the gatehouse towards the God's House, Tamsin noticed that the grey-swathed figure was now sitting in the sunshine on a bench outside the servants' guest house. She turned to the housekeeper.

'Can you manage on your own, Mistress Purbeck? Lady Alyce asked me to keep an eye on that man. He's the one the Harcourts want in the almshouse.'

Martha hesitated, then nodded. 'Alright, dear. But be careful. Don't let him guess we suspect him.'

Tamsin set off purposefully as if going into the great kitchen, separate as was usual from the rest of the palace in case of fire. When she was almost there, she hesitated, then turned towards the bench where the still-hooded man sat. She walked boldly towards him.

'Can I help you find your companions, sir? You seem a little lost.'

The man looked up and drew back his hood. Tamsin found herself looking into a pair of compelling dark eyes. He answered her in a warm, slightly husky voice.

'That's kind, little maid. I have been ill a long while, and I am resting myself in this welcome sunshine before going inside. It is a long ride from Windsor, and we set off betimes.'

'Can I get you some refreshment?' she asked. 'I was on my way to the kitchen.'

A gentle smile spread over a pale face lined with weariness. She had judged him to be around forty, but realised he was rather younger. And very handsome.

'That's kind. A cup of ale would be most welcome.'

She nodded, and walked away, discomposed. She had not expected the spy, if that is what he was, to be so... so attractive. But it was a disturbing kind of attraction. Kin to the weaving of a weasel in front of a rabbit. She shivered and went into the kitchen.

As Alyce led the Harcourts out of the gatehouse and along the high street towards the God's House, she pointed to the high-roofed building that fronted on the street.

'That is our school. I recommend you add one to your foundation in Witney. I have heard from Bishop Waynflete that there is far too little provision for the children of its townsfolk. Our statutes include provision for a Teacher of Grammar to educate the children of my tenants and I make sure that any other worthy mites get learning there too. Girls too. This is a new world, you know; reading and writing in our own English tongue is necessary for everybody who seeks to rise in the world. It is the cause closest to my heart. The children do arithmetic too, sing in the choir, and learn practical skills by helping the bedesmen with their chores.'

Neither of the Harcourts showed any interest in the school.

They turned left past its handsome oak door and headed for the arched entrance gate that led up to the door to the almshouse's enclosed courtyard. Inside, a narrow cloister with a low wall ran all around a central garden in which raised brickwork beds were bright with marigolds and bushy clumps of thyme and sage. One or two curious old faces could be seen at windowpanes, and two sturdy lads in the blue and yellow tunics of the school were winding up a bucket of water from the well. A few bedesmen were pottering among the herbs with trowels, carrying trugs for weeds. One of them was Vespilan, who gave Alyce a tiny reassuring nod as he bowed respectfully to the visitors.

'Very neat and seemly,' said Sir Richard, his cod-like eyes darting around as if in search of something or somebody. 'I believe that you have provided for the support of thirteen poor men. Are all these rooms occupied?'

'They are,' said Alyce. 'We did have a death in August, but a very worthy case presented itself on Tuesday, so we now have our full complement.' She turned aside at a tug at her sleeve. It was Vespilan. The old man was holding out a fragrant posy: spikes of rosemary, a few heads of lavender, some peppermint stalks and a sprig or two of lemon-scented thyme.

Alyce took the posy and sniffed appreciatively. As she did so, she heard an explosive bark of sound from Sir Robert being suddenly cut off and guessed that Richard had pressed warningly on his arm. On the whole, she reflected wearily, she preferred Robert's open bragging to Richard's devious wiles.

'Our new member does well,' Vespilan murmured. 'Deep asleep.' Then he raised his voice. 'My lady, Dick Lawrence two cells along has a fever, and we are taking precautions against it spreading by discouraging visitors from now on.'

A little puzzled at this news, Alyce turned back to the Harcourts. 'This is Gerard Vespilan, our oldest resident, and so Minister of the Bedesmen. From what he says, it would be wise to cut short further inspection, and I'm afraid that the master of the God's House Will Marton is away this week. But you can meet his deputy, the Teacher of Grammar Peter Greene.' Yes, Robert's colour was dangerously high. She would have to be careful not to goad him any further.

'As to numbers,' she added, 'that rather depends on the size of your proposed foundation's income. We endowed our almshouse in perpetuity with three manors. That has been adequate for thirteen up until now, but there is no knowing whether their yields will be enough in the future. I am think-ing of adding another manor to the endowment.'

'Another?' snapped Sir Robert, glad to be able to vent his frustration. 'I would have thought that you had already been more than generous with Suffolk's lands. And more than one of those manors were quite unfairly inherited by that grasping husband of yours. You should be planning bequests, not putting more lands out of the reach of your right heirs.'

'Can we be too generous in the matter of providing for the immortal souls of our progenitors?' Alyce asked innocently but provocatively. She knew that more lay behind Sir Robert's outburst than anger that there was no vacancy in the God's House. Catherine Stapleton had never forgiven Duke William for not willing her the Buckinghamshire manor in which she had grown up. Instead, he'd prevented Marsh Gibbon from ever reverting to her branch of the family by making it part of the endowment of the God's House, and so protected in perpetuity. It had been ungenerous of him, but then he had been an ungenerous man. Doubtless Catherine had told the

Harcourts that not only Marsh Gibbon but Ramridge and Conock, the other two manors that William had added to the endowment, ought to be hers.

They mounted the short flight of steps up to the master's first-floor chamber. Alyce knocked at the door. It opened immediately. Peter Greene must have seen them from the window. He beamed a welcome, and Alyce had the uneasy feeling that he had steadied his nerves for the Harcourts' visit with a cup or two of ale. But she managed a chill smile in return.

'Peter, you know Sir Robert and Sir Richard Harcourt of course. They are eager to find out about the running of the God's House. Sir Robert plans to found a similar chantry and almshouse in Witney. Can I leave them with you while I look in on our new resident?'

Greene bowed. 'Certainly. Would you like some refreshment, your honours? I have a demijohn of sack that has just been breached.'

'Excellent idea,' said Sir Robert, cheered by Greene's welcome after the austere reserve of Alyce and Vespilan.

'We will see you at dinner, Alyce,' he said, striding into the pleasant chamber and settling down beside the corner fireplace on the only cushioned chair in the room. Richard sat on a chest under the long window that overlooked the cloister and looked around him.

'What luxury: a hearth and chimney. But this is no doubt an exceptional chamber.'

'It is certainly the most spacious,' said Greene. 'But all the bedesmen have a brick fireplace that they can cook on, though they generally eat in the common hall. And another fireplace warms their bedrooms at night. It's the usual thing, these days.

Her ladyship used the same architect for the almshouses and the palace – and before that he worked on the king's college at Eton.'

'The usurper's college, you mean,' Alyce heard Robert snap as she was going down the stairs. She hoped that Greene would watch his words. Gullible and well-meaning, he was hugely popular with the schoolchildren, but utterly unversed in diplomacy.

Alyce re-entered the cloister. There was no sign of Vespilan, but as soon as she reached the door of Sybilla's cell it opened, and Gerard smiled out at her, a bunch of strangely shaped earth-covered roots in his hands.

'Welcome, my lady. I've just been digging up some white bryony roots for Farhang's potion against pain. Would you like to see how Sybilla does? She said a few words this morning, but Nan has given her another draught of mandragora, and she is fast asleep now.' Alyce entered and sat down on the bed. She took Sybilla's thin wrist and felt her pulse. To her relief it was steady. She tucked the hand under the bedcover and gave her old nurse's cheek a gentle caress.

'What a blessing that she was chosen for the God's House, my lady' said Vespilan. 'Else she would surely have died.' They sat in silence, Vespilan telling his beads in prayer, Alyce's mind chasing back to the past. If Sybilla had died, so too would the secret that she alone knew, the truth about Alyce's marriage to William.

She had first come across him in France. As the wife of Thomas Montagu, Earl of Salisbury and the English commander, she was the first lady of Rouen. William had then been a lieutenant under Montagu's command. Elegant, good-looking and an excellent dancer, he also shared her love of books. Thomas had issued frequent warnings that he was not to be trusted, but she had dismissed them as his usual jealousy whenever a man spoke to her. So it was that in 1430, lonely in her widowhood, she'd enjoyed William's visits to Ewelme. Her mother Maud was charmed by him. He frankly admitted that he was in desperate need of money. In June 1429 he had led his troops into a disastrous defeat at Jargeau. A few weeks later, both he and his brother John were captured by troops led by the legendary Pucelle, Joan of Arc. He was put in the custody of the French commander Count Dunois of Orléans but allowed to return to England to raise a ransom, leaving his brother John as a hostage. Her father also approved of the match. Even with the ransom to pay, William had much to offer: an earldom with estates close to Alyce's own, both in the Thames Valley and in Suffolk.

After their marriage he had not seemed in any particular hurry to return to France and redeem his brother. Given a place on the royal council thanks to the influence of Alyce's father, he spent most of his time in London and Windsor, setting himself to charm the boy king Henry VI, and soon succeeding. It wasn't until 1433 that he found it convenient to return to France, only to find John mortally ill. Dunois was sorry for him, and reduced the ransom demand on the condition that William do his utmost to get Henry VI's council to agree ransom terms for his own brothers Charles of Orléans and John of Angoulême, who had been captured at Agincourt in 1415. William did his best. He even became Charles's guardian, bringing him to Ewelme. But he soon realised that Charles's genuine literary brilliance put his own slight talents in the shade; nor had he liked Charles's unconcealed admiration for Alyce – or the verses he penned for her. After a couple of years, he passed him on to Sir Reginald Cobham.

Their marriage had limped along for the next decade. As the years passed and no children were born, Alyce had seen his calculating eyes become increasingly impatient as he looked at her. His marital attentions, always perfunctory, lapsed entirely. He had never desired her, he told her frankly. He liked earthier, more flirtatious women in bed. She had had the uneasy feeling that he was willing her to die so that he could marry his preferred paramour, the curvaceous and uncritically loving Elsbeth de Burgh, whom he had imposed upon her as a lady-in-waiting.

What had changed everything was Elsbeth's pregnancy and Jack's birth at Newton Montagu, the remote Dorset manor to which Alyce and Sybilla had taken her while William was away in France. And Elsbeth's death days later. On William's return, she had presented the boy as her own child. Since then, William had been a model husband. For very good reason. At last he had it all – an heir for his dukedom without losing access to Alyce's vast inheritance.

With a sigh, she turned to Vespilan. His faded blue eyes were assessing her thoughtfully, wondering what preoccupied her.

'How ill is Dick Lawrence?' she asked, seeking to distract him.

Vespilan hesitated. 'Farhang believes that it is the sweating sickness. He says he is not to be visited.'

He was opening his mouth to say something else when he glanced out of the window. He stopped short.

'But here is Sir Richard Harcourt coming in search of you.

And I promised to take these roots over to Nan Ormesby in the infirmary.' He picked up his crutch and hobbled out of Sybilla's room.

Although she sensed that Vespilan was keeping something from her, Alyce sympathised with his wish to avoid Harcourt's company. Walking to the small casement window, she too looked out at the garden. Sir Richard was approaching along the cloister. He must have seen her go into Sybilla's cell. He gave a perfunctory knock and entered.

'Ah. The new resident,' he said, looking keenly at the humped shape under the blankets. 'When did he arrive? And who is he?'

Alyce was glad that she had not yet introduced the little luxuries she planned. Could she also avoid revealing the new occupant's sex? Though she was ready to defend her right to choose whom she would, she suspected that matters would go more smoothly if things were left vague.

'Yesterday. The former anchorite of Swyncombe, with an inflammation of the lungs that will benefit from the milder airs down here now that winter advances on us. But you must not risk infection.'

She led him firmly out into the cloister and through the door that led out of the almshouse.

'Was Master Greene able to help you with your plans?' she asked. 'He is not so well versed in money matters as Will Marton, I'm afraid. Where exactly in Witney does Robert plan to build his chantry and almshouse?'

'Well, it is not entirely decided. It has been most useful talking to Greene. Although my brother favoured an arrangement like your own, he had not realised quite how much support in the way of lands it required. He might achieve such a foundation in time, especially if Bishop Waynflete contributed – it could be attached to his episcopal manor in Witney. But Robert is still financially embarrassed after raising troops to fight in the north for King Edward four years ago. For the nonce he has decided to limit his endowment to a small chapel for a hermit at Newbridge, where prayers for the family could be combined with taking tolls for crossing the Thames.'

He offered her his arm as they strolled back to the palace. After a few minutes silence, he cleared his throat and began to speak.

'My lady, I will be frank with you. We have with us a former scrivener who was wished on us by the queen. He is presently weak in body, but he has been a faithful servant to her, and she wants to ensure he is well cared for. Robert had thought that he could be the first of our Witney bedesmen, but knowing it would be some time before such a foundation could be set up we brought him with us. His squire Hamel Turvey had heard in Oxford that there was a vacant place in the Ewelme almshouse. The queen would take it most kindly if he were to be installed here.'

Alyce bristled. 'Sir Richard, the right to appoint bedesmen is mine and mine alone.'

She saw the shadow of a sneer cross Sir Richard's face, but he quickly composed his expression.

'If there is no vacancy, we are in a quandary. Milo is in no state to travel further. The journey from Windsor exhausted him. It would please her majesty very much if he could stay in your guest lodgings until we establish a permanent position for him. Or perhaps until another of your bedesmen breathes his last. I know of your great benevolence to the deserving poor, and he might be useful to you. Though enfeebled, he writes a fine hand. I imagine you will have a great deal of bookkeeping and organising to do, what with all that you have brought over from Wingfield. Remember, it is not wise to oppose the royal will.'

Laced though it was with courtesies, the threat was unmistakable. Nor was this the time to gainsay either Queen Elizabeth or men so much in Yorkist favour as the Harcourts. Bend like the willow to avoid snapping like the elm, her mother used to say. And they did in fact need a text writer. She looked Richard straight in the eye.

'As I said, Sir Richard, the right to license bedesmen is mine and mine alone. But Milo may stay here for the present. There is room enough in the guest lodgings. And you are right in thinking that we could do with an additional clerk. Indeed, if the God's House officers and I find him suitable, we might even consider him for the next vacancy. If he doesn't prove suitable, I will undertake to find a safe escort for him to Chalgrove or Stanton Harcourt.'

'Thank you, Lady Alyce,' said Richard, as eager as she was to avoid confrontation. 'I'm sure you will find Milo most obliging.'

Tamsin emptied a fifth jug of hot water into the lead-lined wooden tub beside the hearth of the guest chamber, watched critically by Lady Catherine Stapleton, who had settled herself in a chair padded with embossed leather. She was turning to leave, but Lady Catherine called her back.

'Just a minute, you pretty little thing. I'd like to ask you a few questions. Have you been in attendance on my cousin for long?'

'No, my lady,' said Tamsin. 'I grew up in Ewelme village, so I've known of her all my life. But I'm on trial. Her usual tiring maid has been taken ill.'

'I thought you were new to her service. You weren't with her at Wingfield, and, though you've a taking way about you, you lack the normal polish of her attendants. Her last maid Sarah and I were great friends. Perhaps you and I can also be useful to each other.'

Tamsin felt her colour rise but managed a vacuous smile. The simpler Lady Catherine thought her the better.

'Tell me – I'll make it worth your while – have you noticed any unusual comings and goings in the God's House, especially since Lady Alyce's return from Suffolk? I am going to be frank with you. One reason for our visit here is that my husband-to-be and his brother are uneasy about the duchess's loyalty. There seem to be so many old soldiers among the bedesmen, men who fought for Lancaster in the troubled years before King Edward came to the throne. And there are rumours of a countrywide traffic in traitors who seek to escape to France to join the rebels in Lorraine. A secret route with safe houses along the way – and the Ewelme God's House is thought to be among them.'

Tamsin swallowed nervously, aware she was being asked to betray her mistress.

'I've heard nothing of that,' she said. 'As to unusual comings and goings...' She thought quickly. Best to seem stupid.

'The pedlar from Henley came about a week ago,' she said slowly. 'But he's a regular. Nobody out of the ordinary.'

Then she had an idea. She changed her expression to one of awed amazement.

'Oh but there was something unusual.'

Lady Catherine leant forward eagerly.

'The fish. As long as I am, and ugly as sin. Lady Alyce's steward Master Caerleon brought it up the Thames yesterday on the fastest of the barges carrying the duchess's chattels that came by sea from Suffolk. It's been kept alive in a great coffin of seawater, and it's to be cooked for the feast after the hunt tomorrow.'

The future Lady Harcourt sat back impatiently. 'You foolish girl. That isn't what I meant at all. I want to know of any traitors who have been given shelter here.'

'Traitors?' said Tamsin, genuinely startled. 'What would they want with us in Ewelme?'

'What indeed? Time will tell.' Lady Catherine felt in her pocket and took out a silver farthing.

'Here, sweeting. There'll be more of these if you find anything out. And don't worry about losing your job. I'll take you into my own service if needs be. Now leave me and go and find Marlene Stonor. I haven't seen her since she left Wingfield, and I want a word with her.'

Inwardly boiling with rage, Tamsin meekly took the coin, made a clumsy curtsey and left the guest chamber. How dare the nasty vixen think she would betray her mistress for a farthing? And what, she wondered, did she want with Marlene? As she climbed the winding stair up to the attic, she heard whispering voices from the Stonor girls' room. One was recognisably Marlene's, but the other was a man's, deep and amused. She turned and went down again, meeting Eloise on her way up.

Thinking quickly, she said, 'Eloise, Lady Stapleton says that she would like to speak to Marlene. Could you ask her for me? I thought I had better not interrupt her.'

'From what?' said Eloise, puzzled.

Tamsin blushed. 'I think… I think she has a visitor.'

Eloise cocked her head and listened. Then she nodded her head slowly.

'You were wise not to go in. But nor will I. Lady Stapleton will have to wait on her. Like the rest of us always have to. Let's go down to the kitchen. Then split up in case she follows.'

She turned and clattered down, deliberately loudly. The whispers ceased. Eloise grinned.

'Quick, we need to disappear fast. Then she won't know who heard her – and him.'

'Do you know who it is?' asked Tamsin, heart sinking at the idea that it might be Ben Bilton.

'Wouldn't tell you if I did,' snapped Eloise. 'It's more than my life's worth to sneak on my sister.'

They descended quickly and silently and hurried over to the kitchen. Eloise saw Martha Purbeck's maid Ella stirring a huge black pot hanging over the fire and went over to her. Tamsin went straight through the kitchen and out into the stableyard. The first person she saw there was Ben Bilton. So it wasn't him in Marlene's room. What a relief. He had evidently just returned from a ride and was patting sweat off his horse's back as it drank eagerly from the water trough.

Shyly, Tamsin approached. 'What a beautiful horse, Ben.'

'That he is,' he answered proudly. 'Bayard is named for the horse in the legends who understood human speech. Which he does, I'm sure. I saved every penny I could for three years to buy him.'

Once the magnificent white horse had drunk his fill, Ben led him into a stall in the stable, filled a manger with hay, and closed the door on him. Then he turned to Tamsin.

'How are you doing, Tammy? Getting on with the duchess? She's a hard taskmistress but a fair one.'

'Alright, I hope,' Tamsin said. 'But there's so much I don't understand. Especially why she's cut herself off from her son and his wife and her grandchildren.'

Ben looked at her thoughtfully. 'Happen you'll do better if you know more about it. That way you won't speak out of turn. But don't tell her I told you.' He led her out of the stableyard and over to a bench by the wall of the base court.

'It's her son Jack who's behind the rift. He was brought up at court, the darling of all the ladies and especially of King Henry, who'd have loved a lad like him as his heir. But then the duke was murdered – you'll have heard that story – and Jack came to Ewelme. Not overpleased to find me here, and as prickly as a hedgehog. Actually, the only person he got on with was your father Roger, who taught him to tilt at the quintain and wield his pretty little sword. He was downright insulting to Lady Alyce – told her to her face that she'd caused his father's death.'

'Surely that wasn't true,' said Tamsin.

'Of course it wasn't. I never properly understood why she put up with so much from him. Anyway, when he was fourteen or so, Richard, the then Duke of York and Protector of the Realm, as King Harry was having one of his mad fits, happened by on his way home to Fotheringay Castle. He stayed a night, and was very taken with Jack, who served at table. Next day, he saw him practising swordplay with Roger, and offered to take him away and train him up. Jack was wild to go, begged and begged. So Alyce agreed, though with a heavy heart. She had no option, really. Two years later, she was told he wanted to marry Duke Richard's daughter Bess. Their marriage was supposed to end the wars between York and Lancaster. But then the Duke of York was killed in an ambush. Within months, his son Edward took London and won the bloody battle of Towton. He was crowned King Edward the Fourth, by right of his descent from Edward III's fourth son, Edmund of Langley.'

'But surely Alyce's son would be a loyal Lancastrian? His father was King Henry's most trusted adviser.'

'You'd think so. But he was very happily married to Edward of York's sister. The good thing about that was it meant that when Edward became king, Jack – and Lady Alyce – kept all their lands. He came of age three years ago and was allowed to enter in on the dukedom of Suffolk. Her grace had to make the best of things. She divided her life between Ewelme and Wingfield and seemed content. Once the wars were over, the young duke and duchess set about having babies. Two boys so far, and there'll be more on the way, I don't doubt. They're real lovebirds, those two.'

'So why did Lady Alyce leave Suffolk for good?'

Ben shrugged. 'I don't know what caused the final rift. But I wouldn't put it past the Harcourts to have poisoned the young duke's mind against her. Sir Richard has lands in Suffolk, and he often visits Wingfield. Smarmy outside, devilry inside, that's him.'

'His wife-to-be is no better,' said Tamsin. She told Ben about Lady Catherine's suggestion that she spy on her mistress.

'I won't of course. But I thought I'd play along with her. Telling her petty things that won't harm my lady. Like that ugly fish coming on the barge!'

Ben frowned. 'Be careful, Tamsin,' he said warningly. 'You may be playing with fire. If Lady Alyce thought you were less than loyal, you'd be back to teaching the little ones. Or banished entirely.'

Tamsin reddened, then remembered something else. 'And she wanted to speak to Marlene.'

Ben raised an eyebrow. 'She did, did she? That's interesting. I wonder why.'

Ewelme

The feast was a success, reflected Alyce, as she looked around. The sturgeon steaks had been acclaimed by the Harcourts and her neighbours. Her cellarer had decanted jug after jug of the strongest ale and wine from the palace's best barrels. She had enjoyed riding that morning with Richard Quartermain. He was a clever and experienced chaser after hounds, generous in giving way at fences, admiring of her falcon's training, and watchful of her safety. She had even managed to resign Ralph Boteler to the loss of his lawsuit. During the morning quest for quarry, Boteler had commented on the hordes of rabbits scurrying away from their hawks and hounds, and she had offered to give his coney-catcher an annual month of trapping rabbits in the ancient warren in Ewelme Chase.

She had seated the two men on either side of her on the dais, not least so that she could avoid being too close to the Harcourts, who were both now dozing in their chairs. Her minstrels had made the company rock with laughter through long and scurrilous ballads, then weep over ancient laments. She looked down the long table to see how the Harcourts were faring. Exhausted by his hectic and successful chase after one of the wild white bulls that were such a renowned feature of Ewelme Great Park, Sir Robert was so drunk that he could hardly lift his glass to his mouth. Even the self-controlled Sir Richard had a boss-eyed look as he waved away a proffered jug with a glare. Alyce rose, a signal for Margaret, Catherine,

Edith Quartermain and Jeanne Stonor to follow her to the great chamber to join the two Stonor girls, who had been dispatched from the hall as soon as the minstrels became bawdy. All the men still capable of standing did so, bowing courteously.

'Now the real roistering will begin, I do not doubt,' said Margaret as they settled themselves close to the blazing fire. 'We're well out of it.'

'Indeed,' said Edith Quartermain. 'Now we can talk of more interesting things. 'How is your new kitchen, Margaret? I hear that it is as splendid as that of Osney Abbey.'

'Not quite on that scale, but it suits us very well,' said Margaret. She looked appreciatively around the candlelit room. Two floor-to-ceiling silk tapestries in rich reds, blues and greens, and gleaming with silver and gold thread, lined its long north wall, one on each side of the door from the hall. They showed the seven liberal arts personified as queens being greeted by Boethius, whose *On the Consolation of Philosophy* Alyce knew well from her grandfather Geoffrey's translation of it into English.

'I remember you commissioning those in Rouen twenty years ago,' Margaret said, and sighed. Alyce knew why. They had both been in Rouen. William of Suffolk was then first and foremost among King Henry VI's counsellors, and he'd taken Alyce with him to France to bring back the French king's niece Margaret of Anjou to be England's queen. The Harcourts had also been in the escorting cavalcade. She and Margaret had both become close to the fiery-hearted sixteen-year-old, so eager to be the most glorious queen that England had known. Her head was stuffed with the romances that were common currency at her father René's sophisticated court, and she had brought with her a chest of splendidly illuminated French books from his library. She had given several to Alyce, including Christine de Pisan's *City of Ladies*. But the dream had gone sour. The English had not taken to the scant-dowered French girl, especially after she persuaded her besotted husband to return Anjou and Maine to the French. Now Henry was in the Tower of London and Margaret was a fugitive in France with their son, rightful heir to the throne of England. How the wheel of Fortune whirled.

'But what happened to the Fall of Thebes?' Margaret asked. 'It used to be across the west wall.'

'I'm going to hang it in Montagu Inn. It is more suited to London. Here I want only harmony, to show that my palace is a woman's world. To fit that space between the windows I had an amusing bedcover of men and women playing cards in a garden made into a hanging. Upstairs in my chamber of state I have the great tapestry of Dame Honour which Queen Margaret gave me as a reward for my service to her. And when they've been unpacked, the series showing the Amazonian queens and the defeat of Hercules and Theseus by their warriors are to hang in the great hall.'

Alyce had settled herself in her favourite chair with her current piece of needlework, a purse embroidered with falcons. Leo, exhausted from the hunt, lay couched at her feet.

'You are obsessed with those mannish women,' snapped Lady Catherine acidly. 'They are inventions of diseased imaginations. You should be surrounding yourself with more spiritual themes. The life of Our Lord, and of his many saints. At your advanced age, you should be considering making your peace with your maker.'

She was staring covetously at the great sideboard loaded

with gold and silver plate and translucent Venetian glasses. Alyce could read her thoughts. If William had not had a son, the de la Pole inheritance would have climbed back up the family tree to William's father's youngest brother Thomas – and down again to Catherine. But then Jack had made his belated appearance. And his wife Bess was just as fecund as the other children of Richard of York and Cicely Neville. Which gave Catherine the inspiration for the most annoying question she could possibly ask of her hostess.

'How are your grandsons, Lady Alyce?'

Edith Quartermain tutted reprovingly. Catherine was well aware of the rift between Alyce and her heir. Jeanne frowned, and went over to Marlene and Eloise, who were playing nine men's morris at a table. She made a sign towards the door; they stood up meekly, curtsied and left.

Alyce didn't allow her long fingers, busy with an intricate couching stitch, to stop for a second.

'I miss them,' she said simply, and with finality.

Catherine was undeterred.

'It is very unnatural that your son does not have more respect for his mother. Particularly one as generous as you have been. Many a parent would punish him by willing away what he assumes too lightly to be his rightful inheritance.'

Alyce raised her head and looked her straight in the eye. 'What of your own grandchildren, Catherine? Will we see them in Oxfordshire soon?'

The prospective Lady Harcourt had the grace to blush.

'Perhaps not for some little while.' She gave a brittle laugh. 'In truth, my son William is not entirely resigned to my marrying his father-in-law.'

'It will certainly mean the postponement of his own

inheritance,' said Margaret Harcourt dryly. She was not fond of her sister-in-law to be.

There was silence for a few minutes as the peace-loving Edith cast about for an uncontroversial subject and Catherine pondered on how to make more mischief. Jeanne Stonor came to the rescue.

'Well. Alyce, I thank you for returning from Suffolk. It will be very merry to have my girls closer to me. You must all come over to Stonor, so that they can see their brother William and their old nurse, who has missed them sorely.'

'I'd love to,' said Alyce. 'Give me a week or two to settle in, and we'll ride over.'

There was a tap on the door. 'Come in,' Alyce called. It was Eloise. She peered around the room and then retreated. Jeanne called her back.

'What is it, child?'

'I was looking for Marlene, Mother,' Eloise stammered. 'I thought perhaps she had forgotten something and returned.'

'Perhaps she went to the privy,' said Jeanne. 'When you do find her, please thank her for the jug of germander she left in my room with a most loving little note. So thoughtful of her. I do believe that she is growing out of her wild ways at last.'

Alyce frowned. 'I wonder where she found germander. There is none except in my own garden. Which is always locked.'

Eloise looked confused. 'I... I think she did pick it there. She told me that Ben Bilton showed her round.' She dropped another curtsey and closed the door behind her.

'What time are we leaving in the morning?' asked Margaret.

'Soon after breakfast, I believe,' said Catherine. 'Richard says that he can't wait to quit this drowsy backwater. Windsor was so glorious. There is always so much going on there. Edward and Elizabeth have refurbished it most splendidly. The old pretender and his harlot wife had let it go to rack and ruin.'

Alyce felt her nostrils flare but managed to control herself. Just say nothing, her mother had taught her. Silence is more infuriating than the hottest of answers. Don't show you care.

Respite came in the form of a tap at the door. It was Tamsin, looking dishevelled and scarlet-cheeked. Had she been drinking? Alyce wondered.

'Your pardon, my ladies, but Sir Robert is on the point of retiring, and asked if his lady would be so good as to accompany him.' She bobbed a curtsey and disappeared up the stairs leading to Alyce's chamber.

Margaret pursed her lips and sighed as she rose.

'Count yourself lucky you don't have to obey the commands of a husband any longer, Alyce.'

Catherine stood up as well, yawning ostentatiously, but pleased to have been presented with one last dart to send home.

'That depends on the husband of course. I'm for bed as well. We'll have so much to do in the morning.' She swept out of the room.

Jeanne also rose, gave Alyce an affectionate hug, and followed her. But Edith lagged behind.

'Alyce, I must warn you. There is gossip abroad that you are under suspicion at court. Your precipitate departure from Wingfield has caused tongues to wag. Don't give them further cause to do so. And don't trust the Harcourts and Lady Catherine.'

'I am all too aware of their connivings against me, Edith,'

Alyce replied. 'But I thank you for your concern. Rest assured, I am doing nothing to justify their suspicions.'

After she had gone, Alyce sighed. It seemed that the world and his wife were gathering eagerly to witness her downfall. Wearily, she followed Tamsin upstairs – and was much cheered by what she found. A fire was burning brightly in the hearth, and a small cauldron of water heating over it on a trivet. Her nightshift was warming on a clothes horse in front of the fire, and candles were lit on the table beside her bed. The splendid hangings were half-closed, ready to be drawn completely when Alyce had climbed inside.

Tamsin hooked the cauldron off the fire and poured the warmed water into a silver-gilt basin, and Alyce swished it over her face and hands with a small sponge. Then Tamsin handed her a linen towel. As she dried herself, Alyce noticed that the colour was still high on her new maid's face – and suddenly guessed the cause.

'What is it, my child? Did Sir Robert make a lunge at you?'

Words burst from Tamsin in an angry torrent as she re-moved Alyce's coronet and pulled out the pins that pinned a gauzy veil over the jewelled net around her coiled braids.

'He would've had me in the passage if Master Bilton hadn't come round the corner. He told me afterwards that he'd seen Sir Robert follow me out and guessed why. The old goat had got me against the wall and had one hand up my skirt and the other groping for his laces. I tried to knee him, like my gran taught me, but he was too strong for me. He smacked my cheek and went on unlacing himself. I was nearly sick all over him, his breath was so foul. Wish I had been. When he saw Ben, he pretended he'd just stumbled against me, and shambled off. I do pity Lady Margaret.'

'So do I, Tamsin. But I suspect that one day she'll have him taken off her hands for good and all. He has more enemies than any other turncoat of our time.' She shook her hair loose and tied her lace night bonnet over it.

'I heard something else about him, my lady. I was sitting next to his valet at dinner. Apparently he's hugger-mugger with my Lord of Warwick. He's going to join the earl in his latest campaign to scour the seas of pirates. They're to set sail from Southampton as soon as the ships are ready.'

As she knelt by her bedstead, Alyce added John Trevelyan to her customary prayers. But surely he would be in some French port by now, offloading his booty to be taken to Queen Margaret at Kœur, the castle in Lorraine that her father had given to her as a refuge. God speed him safely back to Cornwall before Warwick's famously well-armed fleet strung itself across the narrow seas. Devotions over, she snuggled down into her feather bed, her toes enjoying the warmth of the hot stone wrapped in thick flannel that Tamsin must have placed in it earlier. Tamsin closed the curtain, pulled her own truckle bed out from under the bedstead, and slipped out of her clothes and under its covers. Her gentle snores lulled Alyce to sleep. It seemed that she had acquired a maid in a million. Imaginatively thoughtful, sensibly reticent and, she suspected, true as steel. But perhaps, she thought, remembering her pursuit of Wat, dangerously impulsive.

Ewelme

Next morning thick mist swathed the valley. Ralph Boteler and the Quartermains were the first of the guests to leave. They had decided to go to the Watlington market together and knew every inch of the road. The Harcourts waited impatiently for the mist to clear. It was an hour before they too left, clattering out of the village to join the king's highway to Dorchester and Oxford. After returning to Stanton Harcourt, they were planning to spend a few days at Minster Lovell, being entertained by William Lovell, an old crony of Richard's. It had rights to fine hunting in Wychwood Chase. Alyce, relaxing against cushions on the wide window seat in the great oriel window of the solar with Thomas and Jeanne Stonor, watched them go with relief.

'*Pourquoi sont-ils venus?* What were they after?' asked Jeanne.

'What do you mean?' said Thomas. 'Something more than hospitality and hunting?'

'I think so,' said Jeanne. 'I heard Lady Catherine asking Sir Richard "if he had been successful". She is a *coveteuse*, that one.'

'What did he say?'

'"Yes and no. And hold your tongue." Not very courteous for a betrothed. But then it is after all a business arrangement between them.' She shivered a little. 'How do they manage without warmth and love in their lives? I know I couldn't.' She leant in towards Thomas, who moved closer to her, and put a brawny arm around her now buxom body.

How differently adversity affected people, thought Alyce. Jeanne too was a de la Pole. Alyce discovered that Jack was not her husband's first bastard when in 1445 she and William had journeyed to bring back Margaret of Anjou. Charles of Orleans, freed five years earlier, was at the final celebratory feast, and had approached to renew their old friendship. After half an hour of literary talk, he had motioned over a lively looking girl of sixteen who had been standing patiently nearby, and announced that Jeanne was William's daughter, conceived on a high-born French woman called Marlène de Cay during the weeks he was held captive after the battle of Jargeau. Marlène had given birth to Jeanne and then entered a nunnery. Alyce took one look at Jeanne's uncanny likeness to William and accepted her charge enthusiastically before her husband could say anything. The girl had returned to England with them and learnt how to run a household from Alyce. Thomas Stonor had met her soon after they brought her to Ewelme, and they had fallen head over heels in love. Alyce had seen to it that William provided Jeanne with a generous dowry, and she and Thomas were now happily settled at Stonor with a bevy of children.

'How is your dear William?' she asked Jeanne. 'He must be sixteen now. Is he enjoying Oxford?'

'He's a muser and a dreamer. He talks of nothing but Cicero's rhetoric and the verses of John Lydgate. He was seventeen last month; it is high time he left the university and started at a London Inn of Court. He'll have to bend his mind to more practical things when he succeeds his father at Stonor.'

'Time enough for that,' said Alyce. She had a soft spot for her godson, a thoughtful, clever lad, and preferred his studiousness to Jack's obsession with tournaments and hunting.

There was a tap on the door, and she saw Simon Brailles put his head round it.

'A messenger from Denzil Caerleon has just arrived from Wallingford Wharf, my lady. He says that the barges are unloading, and the first carts will get to Ewelme by noon. He has some business in the town, but he'll be back before dark. Shall I send down our carts to make things easier? I doubt they'll have more than four at the wharf.'

'That's an excellent idea. Send two men on each to help them with the loading.' After he had left the room, she turned to Thomas Stonor.

'Can you and Jeanne stay another day, Thomas?'

'Thank you, but no,' said Thomas, always the soul of tact. 'I suspect you have more than enough to cope with. We'd love the girls to come and visit us for a few days when you can spare them. And I'll summon William from Oxford, if that would please you. He'll enjoy seeing you, I know.'

'And I him,' said Alyce. 'He'll marvel at all the books I've brought back.'

'He'd do better getting to grips with the wool trade.'

'He will when he needs to, I am sure,' said Alyce abstractedly, looking out at the courtyard below, where she could see Simon deep in conversation with Ben Bilton. She could read baffled indignation in his gestures, mulish defiance in Ben's. Bilton suddenly turned on his heel and disappeared through the gateway. What were they up to? And how was it that Denzil already had business in Wallingford? Then she remembered Milo of Windsor. She'd told Martha to make up a room for him in the guest lodgings. Presumably he would have gone there. At some point she needed to see for herself what manner of man he was.

And she must get Peter Greene to tell her what questions the Harcourts had asked about the God's House. And what he had told them. She sighed. When would the elusive peace she sought settle around her?

Just then the sun broke through the last of the mist, lighting up the brilliant colours of the trees that clothed the slopes of the high hills to the east of Ewelme. Scarlet and gold and sharp acid greens. Irresistible – and she had an excuse. She turned back to the Stonors.

'Can I ride with you up to Swyncombe, Thomas? As I told you yesterday, Sybilla is now living with us. But I want to organise the bringing down of her possessions. Tamsin, you can come too. Tell Hugh and Jem to saddle their horses and ours, then bring me a warm cloak and my riding boots. Oh, and tell Marlene and Eloise that their parents are about to leave. Perhaps they would like to ride with us as well.'

Tamsin dimpled with pleasure and dashed away.

'What an attractive wench,' said Jeanne. 'Brimming with energy.'

'Rather too much at times,' said Alyce drily.

As Tamsin raced up the winding stair to Alyce's wardrobe, she met Marlene on her way down.

'Your parents are leaving, my lady. Have you bidden them farewell?'

'What business is it of yours to tell me what I should be doing?' hissed Marlene, punching Tamsin's upper arm viciously. Tamsin winced and shrank back against the wall of the staircase.

'Lady Alyce told me to ask you if you would like to ride

part of the way with them. I'm just going to collect her cloak and boots.'

'Maybe Eloise would. She's upstairs. I have fish of my own to fry. Tell them I am still suffering from my ague.'

She flounced down the stairs and disappeared. Nursing her arm, Tamsin went on up the stairs and knocked at the door of the girls' chamber.

'Who is it,' Eloise called out in a shaky voice.

'Tamsin, my lady. Lady Alyce asks if you would like to accompany her and your parents some of the way to Swyncombe.'

There was a silence before Eloise answered.

'Yes, I would. Tell them I'll be down in a minute.'

Tamsin opened the great press in which Alyce's fur-lined cloaks were stored and selected a dark green one and a pair of green leather riding boots. Then she went into her own room to get a cloak for herself, and returned to the solar, but found only Thomas and Jeanne there.

'Eloise will join us presently,' she told them. 'Where is my lady?'

'She wanted a word with her chamberlain,' said Thomas. 'We are to meet her beside the gatehouse. What of Marlene?'

'She says her fever has returned,' said Tamsin, blushing.

Jeanne looked sharply at her. 'Is that true or just an excuse?'

Thomas intervened. 'Don't cross-question the girl, Jenny. Marlene seems much improved – remember the germander? She may well be feeling frail after the feast. We'll have Eloise's company while we ride.'

They went down to the gatehouse, where Alyce donned her riding boots and mounted Larkspur. Hugh sat astride the horse hauling the cart, and Jem held a sturdy rouncey. Grooms were holding the Stonors' horses and Tamsin's mule. As they mounted, Eloise came running up, the hood of her cloak pulled well up, and a groom helped her up onto her horse. Jeanne looked at her sharply.

'Eloise, have you been crying? Put down your hood; let me see you properly.'

Shamefacedly, Eloise pushed back her hood, to reveal reddened eyes and a nasty double scratch down her cheek.

'Who did that?' said Thomas, shocked.

'It was my new kitten, father. It was my own fault. I was teasing her.' She clapped her heels to her horse's flanks and led the way through the gatehouse. Thomas and Jeanne exchanged anxious glances and rode after her. They were soon beside her, heads bent in conversation.

Alyce and Tamsin followed at a little distance. There was silence for a while, then Alyce spoke.

'Was it Marlene, Tamsin? Tell me the truth.'

Tamsin hesitated. 'In truth, I don't know, my lady. She was coming down the stairs when I went up to the wardrobe.'

'Not, then, prostrate in bed. She is always making excuses to avoid her duties. I'm fond of Eloise, but Marlene worries me a good deal. I hope you will tell me if you think she is in some mischief.'

Tamsin was silent, which Alyce was beginning to realise was an unusual state of affairs. She looked sharply at her, but then reflected that it might go hard on the child if the Stonor girls took against her. She sighed and thought instead of Sybilla. Now she had had time to reflect, she realised how very unlikely it was that a clutch of adders would have made their way into her cell. But if it wasn't an accident, whose doing was it? A godless wight for sure. A passing vagrant? She remembered the barred door. When did Sybilla start locking herself in? She didn't remember her doing that in the old days. Perhaps as she became frailer. And as the king's peace was less and less upheld. But it was a strange coincidence that the snakes had appeared just after she had agreed to become a bedeswoman in the God's House. No one could have known about that – unless Peter Greene or Sybilla herself had told them. She decided to ask Sir Brian if any strangers had passed through Swyncombe. But what would he know about casual passers-by, preoccupied as he had been with his wife's labour? She slowed Larkspur so that Tamsin was riding beside her.

'Tamsin, when we get to the manor I'll make an excuse for you to go to the kitchens; I'd like you to see what you can find out from the servants about visitors at Swyncombe on Tuesday.'

Tamsin's spirits rose. She knew that her silence on the subject of Marlene had annoyed her mistress, but now she was being trusted.

Swyncombe

When they reached the clearing in the trees near the church, the Stonors, who had already dismounted, were waiting for them.

'Would you like me to stay and help you with Sybilla's things?' asked Thomas.

'No,' said Alyce. 'Sir Brian's men will help load the cart I'm sure.'

He bowed over her gloved hand, then turned to Eloise, who had just risen from kneeling for her mother's blessing.

'Be a good child, my sweet. And don't let that sister of yours drag you into mischief.'

Jeanne came forward and embraced Alyce. As she did so, she whispered in her ear. 'There is something amiss with Marlene. Eloise won't tell us what it is, but I know she is holding something back.'

Alyce hugged her in return. 'I'll find out, worry not. And once we've sorted out the Wingfield chattels, they can both come to you at Stonor for a while.'

She watched them disappear into the copper and gold of the beech woods that capped most of the long ridge between Swyncombe and Stonor Park. As she did, Sir Brian Fulbert came striding along the path from the manor house, followed by a twelve-year-old boy with a head of blonde curls and bright blue eyes. They both bowed to her.

'Welcome, my lady. You'll remember my oldest son.'

'He's grown a good deal since I last saw him,' said Alyce with a smile. 'Do you still raid my orchard, Humfrey?' The boy blushed and looked down at his feet.

'He'll get a good tanning if he does,' said his father sternly. 'I hope he's grown out of such childish pranks.'

'Don't scold him, Brian,' said Alyce. 'Set him to amusing his new sister.' She felt in her hanging pocket and pulled out a small object wrapped in a soft silk cloth.

'Here, this is for the baby to cut her teeth on.'

He unwrapped the gift, a stumpy stick of coral with a silver bell attached to it.

'Thank you, my lady. From what I remember of Humfrey's bawlings, it'll be much needed.' He tousled his son's hair affectionately, then handed him the coral.

'Have you named the baby yet?' said Alyce.

'We would like to call her after you,' said Fulbert. 'Anne and I are hoping that you will be one of her godmothers.'

'I'd be delighted. Let me know when the christening is to take place.'

Fulbert's stern face broke into a smile, and he gave a low bow. 'We are indeed honoured. But to business. I have kept a guard on Sybilla's cell since you left. The maids put poisoned fish through the squint, and this morning we found three dead snakes. We poked about in the cell's corners and dragged Sybilla's bedding out. Even so, your men should be wary – there could be more among the bundles still inside.'

'Thank you, Sir Brian. My men have thick gloves and stout boots.' She nodded to Jem and Hugh, and they followed her round to the door of the cell. A yeoman in Fulbert's livery who had been sitting against its closed door stood up as they approached.

'Open up, Robin,' said his master. 'And then give Lady Alyce's men a hand with Sybilla's chattels. We'll haul them out with rakes, just in case.' He turned to Alyce.

'I have another favour to ask you. As you know, the relics of St Botolph that draw so many wayfarers to Swyncombe inspire many donations to the upkeep of the church and the anchorhold. Though they are kept in a locked and chained reliquary in the church, they are Sybilla's own property. She was given them, she told me, by a particularly grateful patient. Could we keep them here?'

'I don't see why not,' said Alyce. 'When Sybilla recovers, we can ask her what she wills. But until then keep them here. They couldn't be anywhere more appropriate.'

Fulbert smiled with relief. 'Thank you, my lady. And we'll keep an eye on her cat, too. Came mewing back this morning, eager for milk. Now, would you like to come over to the manor while they load the cart?'

'Thank you, but no,' Alyce said. 'I'd rather watch them empty the cell. But Tamsin would I fancy welcome some refreshment. Can she get something in your kitchen?'

'Of course.' Sir Brian turned to his son. 'Take her over to Cook, Humfrey.' Humfrey made a cheeky little bow to Tamsin and led the way to the back of the manor. The kitchen was bustling with kitchen maids, watched over by an enormously fat man who was standing by the great hearth with a mighty ladle in his hand. On a great iron spit a pig was slowly revolving; its skin, criss-crossed with long slits, crackled merrily.

'Milk for Princess Alyce's maid, if it please you, Cook,' Humfrey cried out.

The cook turned to look at Tamsin. He pointed his ladle at a stone seat set deep into one side of the hearth.

'Sit there, maid, where you can warm your feet. They'll be cold as puddocks after your ride, I don't doubt.'

Then he shouted to a girl who was sweeping the floor.

'Jenny, take a cup to the larder and fill it with milk. And bring a crust of bread. Happen the wench'll be hungry. Then you can take over this basting. I'll to the mistress to see what her orders are.'

As she nibbled the hunk of still-warm bread and sipped the creamy milk, Tamsin eyed Jenny, noticing a bright yellow ribbon that tied back her dark hair.

'That's pretty,' she said. 'Looks new.'

'It is,' said Jenny proudly. 'My sweetheart bought it for me from the pedlar who came by early last week.'

'I'd love to buy one like it. Which way was he going?'

'To Henley, he said. It's market day there on a Tuesday.'

'So he was here on Monday?'

'Yes, in the afternoon. He asked me which way would be least muddy, and I said the easiest road was the lane along the ridge to Stonor. Master Greene came soon after, to speak to Sybilla.'

'And have there been any other visitors?'

Jenny looked at her sharply. 'Why are you asking? Sir Brian asked us that on Wednesday. Is it something to do with Sybilla? But surely that was mischance. Cook said that the snakes must have been seeking somewhere warm, and Sybilla must have left her door open when she came over to the manor house to tend Lady Anne.'

Tamsin was interested in the fact that Cook had thought fit to offer such an idea. If there had been no other visitors, might Sybilla's attempted murder have been the work of one of Sir Brian's household?

'So there were no other passers-by?'

Jenny shook her head. 'No one anyone saw. Though the dogs did make quite a commotion on Monday night. But it was probably the fox taking the chicken we found gone on Tuesday morning.'

Or someone who wanted to be taken for a fox, thought Tamsin. She drained her cup, thanked Jenny, and left the kitchen.

Alyce was watching her men load the last of the sacks that had been stacked at the back of Sybilla's cell on to the cart when Tamsin returned to her side. She raised her eyebrows questioningly.

'A pedlar passed by, but that was on Monday, before Peter Greene had asked Sybilla if she'd come down to Ewelme. And there was a commotion among the dogs on Monday night, but it was probably a fox as a chicken was missing next morning. And Cook thought the snakes must have slipped in while Sybilla was over in the manor house tending Lady Anne, who was poorly.'

'Sir Brian said that Sybilla was with her all night,' said Alyce. Tamsin stared, then understood.

'So she didn't go back to her cell until early on Tuesday morning. She would have been in the manor house when the pedlar came by on Monday. Shall I go back and...'

Alyce shook her head. 'Not now. But it's something to bear in mind. I wonder if Peter Greene saw anything of that pedlar on his way from Ewelme.'

Ewelme

As they followed the loaded cart down the steep descent from Swyncombe, Alyce could see the gleaming ribbon of the Thames winding through far-away water meadows. It was now past noon, and sunshine streamed across the valley, glinting off the glass windows of her palace and the gilded weathercock on the church tower. From here it seemed such an orderly little paradise. Was there, though, corruption at its heart? Something established before her return, which was causing her most trusted servants to behave so strangely?

When they reached the base court they found a cluttered mass of carts, horses, drivers and yeomen. Ben Bilton was directing the unloading of the carts. Everything was being taken into the courthouse at the end of the lodgings, to be sorted out by Martha Purbeck. Alyce told Ben to put Sybilla's possessions in a separate place, then beckoned Tamsin to follow her into the courthouse. Furniture was stacked at one side, rolls of carpet and tapestry hangings on the other. Chests and bundles variously labelled 'Books', 'Linen', 'Wardrobe', 'Buttery', 'Kitchen', 'Chapel' occupied the middle of the room. Several barrels of wine were grouped near the cellar door. Alyce began to regret her insistence that every single stick of her furniture, every shred of tapestry and all her chapel furnishings should be taken from Wingfield. She had experienced considerable satisfaction at the time at the bare walls and half-empty chambers that resulted. But she was beginning to realise that in the eyes of its people she must have seemed an eccentric old harridan, a witchy figure who frightened her own grandchildren.

Tamsin looked round in amazement. 'Where has it all come from?'

'The law awards widows the use of a third of their dead husband's lands for their lifetime. Chattels are allotted according to the marriage contract. My father insisted on legal settlements that endowed me with a more than generous share of their worldly goods. All my husbands agreed to them because of the size and value of my dowry.'

'But there's so much.'

'As there should be,' she said, a little defensively. 'I brought each of my husbands a fortune in land, and the lands I was granted as jointure after their death will pass back to their heirs when I die. But any moveable property remains mine absolutely to dispose of as I wish. Moreover, these things are the lining of my life, memories in solid form. Everything holds a story.'

She saw Tamsin's eyes lingering over the piles of possessions that she had accumulated over the last five decades and felt a little ashamed. There was a king's ransom in furnishings, tapestries, plate, books and jewels. And, much as they meant to her, she was approaching an age when worldly goods should be despised. It was high time that she began to give things away or made a will directing dispositions. If she died untimely and intestate, Jack would inherit everything. Which was the last thing she wanted to happen. She sighed and turned back to Tamsin.

'Now, why don't you go and see if you can be useful to Ben and the people unloading the carts? I won't need you until dinner time.'

Tamsin left the hall and walked over to where Bilton and a group of men were unloading the carts that had arrived from Wallingford. Marlene and Eloise were nudging each other and whispering as they watched. Ben nodded to her.

'Come to help, Tammy? Undo the straps round those bundles. They're altar cloths. You girls can take them over to the chapel.'

Alyce looked around the courthouse. Once everything had been put somewhere, an inventory could be taken and decisions made about what to keep and what to give away or sell. Not that she liked selling. It would be better to will chattels inherited from her first two husbands to their descendants. Of whom there were plenty. Her favourite among the Phelips was Viscount Beaumont, grandson of Sir John Phelip's older brother and still ardent in the cause of Lancaster. As for Thomas Montagu's descendants, most of them had lined their own nests more than thoroughly by bowing the knee to the usurping Yorkist king Edward IV. Especially his grandsons

George Neville, soon to be Archbishop of York, and Richard Earl of Warwick, who was, foreign envoys reported, wealthier and more powerful than the king himself. Much more to her liking was their little sister Meg Neville. The men had wealth enough, she decided. Meg should have everything she'd been given or had inherited from Thomas. She smiled at the thought of her much-loved step-granddaughter.

Then an idea struck her. She turned to her chamberlain.

'Martha, when exactly did Nicolas Webb die?'

Martha shook her head wearily. 'August the eighteenth. I remember because it was the feast day of St Hugh the Little, the poor mite murdered in Lincoln, and all the schoolchildren came up to the palace. Nicolas was in the infirmary by then. Guts like water, sick as a dog, sweating and dribbling. Nan made him a posset of milk thistle, a sovereign cure for poisonings, but it didn't save him. He was slow a'dying, too, God rest him. Two days it took.'

'Who said it was mushroom poisoning?'

'Nan Ormesby. She said Nicolas had gathered a basketful earlier and taken them to the God's House kitchen to make a stew. When Farhang returned after Nicolas had died, he thought maybe Nick'd plucked a young death cap by mistake. They look harmless enough without their stalk, but they'd kill a stronger man than him in a trice.'

'Wouldn't Nicolas have known a death cap?'

'He used to, for sure. But his eyes were not what they were. Mayhap he didn't have his spectacles by him. He was always losing them.'

Chance or a ruthless way of making place for an intelligencer? Alyce wondered. It was unlikely that they would ever know. Unless...

'Martha, did any of the Harcourts' men pass through Ewelme around the time that Webb died? Or any strangers at all?'

The chamberlain thought for a few seconds.

'We had quite a few asking for bed and board in August, as we always do. Folk are on the road then. And the pedlar came by, as usual. But no one I knew for a Harcourt man has been here since early in August, when Sir Robert came through with his usual train on his way to Windsor. Wanted to know if we knew when you'd be back. We told him not before September.'

'Did he go into the church, or into the God's House?'

'The church, for certain. He attended a Mass and talked very graciously to some of the bedesmen and to the master. Then off betimes, thank goodness.'

Thanking Martha, Alyce was about to set off for her own quarters when a group at the other side of the courtyard caught her eye. Ben Bilton had loosened the hides strapped around a bundle of tapestries and was showing them to the Stonor girls. They were admiring the weaving – and showing off to the men. Eloise was giggling, and Marlene's usual bored expression had altered to a suggestive simper. Alyce frowned. Ben ought not to be wasting time on giddy chits like the Stonor girls. Or showing Marlene round her garden and letting her pick germander. She called sharply over to them.

'Marlene, Eloise, take those hangings into the courthouse. Then ask Dame Purbeck how you can help her.'

As the girls each took a strap of the bundle of hangings and carried it away, Alyce saw that Denzil Caerleon was standing by another of the carts, deep in conversation with Tamsin. So he had returned. Why hadn't he come straight to her?

she wondered. She watched him, expecting him to turn and see her, but he didn't. A little annoyed, she turned to Ben.

'Bilton, I'm going into the solar. Please tell Master Caerleon to meet me there.' Then she swept away.

It was a good quarter of an hour before Denzil joined Alyce in the solar. She sensed his eyes assessing her thoughtfully as she waved him to a chair. Was he too part of the conspiracy of silence that surrounded her?

'Denzil – I want to hear all about your journey, but first I have to tell you something. A terrible thing has happened. I expect Bilton will have told you of Nicolas Webb's death, and my decision to bring Sybilla of Swyncombe down to replace him.'

Caerleon nodded. 'He did. I thought it a very good idea. No doubt Vespilan is delighted.'

'He was. But when we went up to Swyncombe to bring her down, we found her close to death – bitten by adders in her cell. And I doubt if they got there by chance.'

Caerleon frowned. She watched thoughts chase across his strange seer's face. Relief, then puzzlement.

'Who in God's name would harm Sybilla?' he said at last. 'She is all but a saint. Was anyone seen? Was anything stolen?'

'We couldn't tell. But I've brought all her possessions down here now. She's safe in the God's House under Farhang's care, and he thinks she should recover.'

'When she does, you can ask her if she has any idea why it should have happened.'

'I will,' said Alyce. 'And, by the way, we have one remaining visitor.'

Denzil looked inquiringly at her.

'He's a scrivener called Milo of Windsor, a favourite of Queen Elizabeth, apparently. The Harcourts wished him on me – they said they had heard I was a bedesman short and they wanted him given a cell in the God's House. But by then we had chosen Sybilla to replace Nicolas Webb. Fortunately, she wasn't killed, so Milo is here only temporarily, as an assistant to Simon Brailles.' She stopped short, struck by the implications of what she had said.

'God's bones, Denzil, do you think that the Harcourts had a hand in the snakes in Sybilla's cell?'

He considered. 'The timing's adrift, isn't it? How could they have known that you were planning to bring her down to replace Webb? My money is on it being the work of a Lollard with a spite against such dedicated servants of God as Sybilla.'

'I suppose you might be right. We'll have to wait until she recovers. Perhaps she was in correspondence with such a fanatic. She was ever hopeful of making converts.'

'By the way, your new maid is an interesting child, isn't she? Very hot in your defence when I was joking to Bilton about your stripping Wingfield. I assured her that I needed no convincing of your rights to your inheritances, but she gave me as mulish a look as I've ever seen and marched away. Then Bilton came over and ticked me off for flirting with her.'

Alyce chuckled. 'Ben knew her brother Dickon well, and as both Dickon and her parents are dead, God rest their souls, he regards himself as her guardian. He'd like to wed her in time, but she's an adventurous little soul and determined not to dwindle into a wife before she has to.'

A sonorous bell began to toll from the church. Alyce felt a wave of relief. Vespers. A blessed pause to reflect on the day.

'Are you coming to church?' she asked.

Caerleon shook his head. 'I need to wash the grime of my journeying away. And when I'm presentable I'll take a look at your new scrivener. Or whatever he is. I wonder...' He broke off, then looked at her a little shyly.

'Perhaps we could talk things over at greater length after supper? It's a clear night. We could watch the full moon rise.'

'A lovely idea,' Alyce said. 'I've missed our star-gazing. But not tonight. I have other matters to deal with. After midday dinner tomorrow. In my garden. I'll tell Bilton to unlock the gate in the orchard wall. Then you can tell me about your encounter with John Trevelyan at sea.'

Oxford

'I've taken two rooms for us at the Mitre,' said Joan Moulton, as she and Monique rode through Oxford's East Gate, followed by two grooms and a packhorse loaded with bundles. 'We'll be here for a few days, and it's central and comfortable.'

'Surely there was no need for a second room,' said Monique, who had a parsimonious streak.

'I've also arranged to meet Sir John Wenlock as soon as he arrives in Oxford. He'll be staying at his old college, but...'

Monique raised a hand. 'Say no more. I'll enjoy the luxury of solitude.'

The Mitre's grooms hurried out to stable their horses, and two porters took their luggage up to their rooms, one splendid and looking out on the High Street, the other smaller, but comfortably furnished and in a quieter part of the inn.

'Tomorrow is Sunday, so I want to go to Catte Street today

after we've eaten and see what Paul More's bookshop has to offer,' said Joan. 'Next to Doll's, it's the best in the city. And I'll take some of our books to tempt him with.'

Paul More dealt mainly in copying exemplars for the benefit of students, but he was becoming increasingly interested in illustrated books, for which prices had soared in the last decade because of the ending of the flood of French books brought back by bibliophile commanders during the war. More had been one of them, decamping from Caen with the rest of the Duke of Somerset's army, bringing with him as much literary booty as he could carry, and settling in Oxford because it was the obvious place to find a market. He was a lively, bright-eyed man in his thirties with a ferret-like face, not averse to under-paying his scriveners and using second-rate binding materials to save costs. Twenty years younger than John Doll, he was keen to replace him as official University stationer. To do so meant building up a reputation for honest dealing, and he was abandoning his old practices. But Joan was well aware that he was still accepting valuable books of doubtful provenance in the hope of a quick turnover and a fat profit.

When Joan and Monique entered his shop, he was standing at a table on which several books were lying, all open at striking images. Two were psalters, one a herbal, the third Aristotle's *De Animalibus*.

'Tell your master that I'd be happy to let him have all of these in exchange for the Chaucer treatise he showed me yesterday,' he was saying to a strikingly good-looking young man. 'Nor will I ask inconvenient questions as to where he acquired it.'

The young man flushed. 'He's not my master. He's my friend. And he didn't "acquire" it anywhere. As I said, it was left to him by his mother. That's why he knows it is valuable. She said that it was worth more than all her chattels and the house itself.'

Joan saw More suck his cheeks in to stifle a smile of disbelief. He nodded blandly. 'When can I see the book?'

'Now, if it suits you. He is hard by, in the Turf Tavern, and has it with him. I'll fetch it.' He vanished.

'A treatise by Chaucer?' asked Joan. 'Not the *Conclusions on the Astrolabe* that he wrote for his son?'

More nodded.

'I have never seen a copy.'

'Nor I,' said More. 'The only one I know of is in the University's own library. Pray heaven that this is not that one. It would be too hot for a respectable bookseller like me to handle – here in Oxford.'

Their eyes met. 'But if a way of selling it elsewhere arose? In London, for example?' said Joan in sly inquiry.

'Then, for a consideration, I'd be happy for you to buy it. The seller wants payment in coin, but I myself do not have enough ready money in my coffer to do that. Which is why I offered books.'

Joan turned to Monique. 'My purse, Madame de Chinon. What would you say was a fair consideration, Paul?'

A few minutes later the young man returned, a slim packet in his hand. Paul More unwrapped it and handed it to Joan. She opened its red leather cover. Inside were about forty octavo pages written in an elegant script.

'*De Astrolabio*,' it began, then continued in the old-fashioned English of the previous century: 'Little child Lewis, my son, I perceived well by certain evidence thine ability to learn science touching numbers and proportions.'

Turning its pages carefully, she saw that inserted between the pages were diagrams of the workings of an astrolabe, one showing it set for Oxford's latitude. She closed it, unable to conceal her excitement at happening on such a treasure.

'John, I have to thank you. Rest assured it will go with me to London, where I will find a discreet buyer for it after I have had a few copies made.' She turned to the young man. 'Could you ask your master if he would prefer coin to the value of the books he was offered by Master More?'

The young man's handsome face looked nervous. 'As I said, the book is my friend's to sell, inherited from his mother, God salve her soul. As to remuneration, I know that he would prefer coin.'

Joan opened her purse and began to count out gold angels. When she had handed them over to the young man, he gave her a radiant smile and left the shop. Monique stepped outside and watched him walk away down Catte Street. As he reached its junction with New College Lane, a cloaked figure appeared and went to meet him, She saw the lad hand over the purse of money – and be wrapped in a bear-like hug.

She returned thoughtfully to the bookshop, where Joan was gloating over her purchase. 'This is worth a fortune to the Sign of the Mole,' she crowed. 'Copies are as rare as hen's teeth. I suppose Duchess Alyce has one, but she might well covet another. I must thank you, John, for giving me the chance to buy it. Though I can see why you passed it up. I doubt whether your secretive supplier acquired it legitimately.'

'I doubt if he has a very legitimate life,' remarked Monique. 'He emerged from concealment in New College Lane and gave his triumphant emissary an embrace that suggested they are not merely master and man.'

Joan shrugged. 'Then no wonder they are living in the shadows. I have no problem with such liaisons; indeed a great many scriveners and limners indulge in them, as do players. Nevertheless, anyone with a respectable social position to uphold must needs be wary. The Church would condemn them in a trice, as would the civil authorities.'

Bidding More good day, she and Monique continued down Catte Street and then turned west towards the North Gate.

'I'd like to call at Brasenose College to ask whether Lord Wenlock has arrived,' said Joan. 'If he hasn't, I'll browse in the book stalls along North Wall.'

'Then I will return to the Mitre,' said Monique. 'Shall I take your prize with me?'

'Thank you,' said Joan. 'Have you any other plans?'

'If you do happen on Lord Wenlock, you might mention to his secretary Francis Thynne that I will be at vespers in St Mary the Virgin, and that it has a very fine choir at present.'

Joan chuckled, and waved a farewell.

Ewelme

On Sunday, Alyce at last achieved the tranquility she sought –
the sense of a house without care – like Sans Souci, the dream
castle in the old French romance which Charles of Orléans had
read to her long ago. Life with Jack and Bess had been all too
full of care: care in speech, in dress, in financial transactions.
Minding what she said about her grandsons, who racketed
around the castle at all times of day and night and copied their
father's offhand rudeness to her. Oddly, it was Bess, fond wife
and mother though she was, who more often than not took her
side, telling the boys not to invade Alyce's private sanctum and
chiding her husband for neglecting his mother. But nothing
could mend the deep rift with Jack that the loss of his father
in such terrible circumstances had created.

Now that she was back in her own home and could choose
her companions and decide for herself what to do, life would
be altogether pleasanter. The suspicious death of Nicolas and
the attempted murder of Sybilla cast dark shadows, but her
visitors had left and she could concentrate on finding the right
places for her Suffolk chattels. As to Milo, even if he was a royal
spy, there was nothing amiss for him to report. He might even
prove useful, if he was indeed a skilled scrivener.

Alyce had a peaceful breakfast in her chamber, then went
up to her turret to read. She turned to Venetius Fortunatus's
life of the saintly Saxon princess Radegund, who, like Sybilla,
had ended her days as an anchorite. William had given her

the book to mock her. 'More nun than wife,' King Clothair had complained of the woman he had abducted as a child and groomed to be his queen. But Alyce had relished Radegund's subtle revenge on Clothair: an exhibitionist concern for the most pestilential and leprous of the poor, and neglect of her appearance and her personal hygiene. When the king reached for her in bed, Radegund pleaded a call of nature, disappeared into the privy, and stayed there praying audibly until the matins bell sounded. Fortunatus had been Radegund's chaplain, and his sardonic telling of the ancient tale still made her chuckle.

At twelve o'clock she led the Stonor girls and Tamsin into the church for a special service in Radegund's honour. It was led by Peter Greene as William Marton was still in Oxford. She noticed Milo was sitting on a stool, a little removed from the bedesmen. After the service was over, she walked out of the west door of the church and collected Leo from the boy who had been minding him during the service. She told Tamsin to go over to Milo and tell him he was to join her in the master's chamber, where it was her custom to take a glass of wine after special services. Then she dismissed the Stonor girls, opened the door that led from the west porch into the God's House and mounted the stairs to the master's sanctum, where Peter Greene was already pouring her a glass of Rumney wine, her favourite midday refreshment.

'How is Milo getting on?' she asked, stroking Leo's head.

'Wouldn't trust him an inch,' said the normally charitable Teacher of Grammar with unusual rancour. 'Keeps himself to himself, but then turns up in unexpected places. And he's not the broken-down old man he seemed to be when he arrived with the Harcourts. But he is certainly an accomplished scrivener.'

'Well, we have his measure. Let's make what use we can of his talents. Who knows, we might be able to convert him into a friend. A tempting and well-paid position in my scriptorium might wean him away from his present masters. But what of the Harcourts' questions about the God's House?'

Greene beamed. 'They praised it to the skies. Said they'd like to copy it exactly. I told them that it took three valuable manors to provide for it, and Sir Robert frowned somewhat. But when I explained that we had two chaplains and an infirmary as well as the school to finance, Sir Richard nodded approval.'

Alyce was about to ask Peter if he had met anyone on his way up to Swyncombe to invite Sybilla to be a bedeswoman when Milo came in, leaning, Alyce thought, rather too heavily on Tamsin's shoulder. A low, rumbling growl came from Leo's throat, and she gave him a warning tap on his muzzle. Seen close to, Milo was younger than he had looked when he arrived, and his pallor had lessened. His strikingly dark eyes darted from side to side, taking in every detail of the chamber. She signed him to a chair. As he sat down, he looked hopefully at the flask of wine on the table and coughed ostentatiously. Peter Green rose with a smile and poured him a measure.

'Are you comfortably settled, Milo?' Alyce asked.

'I could not be better lodged,' he answered with an unexpectedly charming smile. 'I cannot thank you enough, your grace. And I will do anything you wish in the way of copying or recording in return; I would count it a favour. My hands are stiffer than they used to be but have not lost all their cunning.' Nor have you, thought Alyce to herself. What better way to ingratiate yourself with me and poke around at the same time.

'I am obliged to you,' she answered. 'Peter Greene says you

have great talents. And we do have a good deal of copying to do. The accounts from the manors that pay for the God's House must be copied in triplicate – one for Ewelme, one for the manor in question, and one for the trustees. I'll pay you, of course. Simon Brailles will find you a place to work in my scriptorium. It will be in the palace, rather than the God's House.'

'I will do so willingly. In fact, your grace, I would also like to eat meals in the palace at the common table rather than with the bedesmen in their hall. Since I am not to be of their number.'

'That can be arranged,' she said. His eyes met hers blandly, then he bowed and rose, looking around.

'Perhaps your maid could assist me back to my lodgings. I am still very weak.'

Tamsin glanced at Alyce, who nodded her assent, and she lent him her shoulder once again.

Once they had left, Alyce sighed. 'I suspect he thinks he will find my servants easy to suborn,' she said to Peter Greene. 'And I fear he's right. He has a wheedling charm about him. I saw one of the gardeners laughing with him earlier this morning.'

Peter nodded. 'And he's got a way with the women. Ella told me he gave her some pretty ribbons that he said he'd bought from a pedlar.'

'Hmmm,' said Alyce. 'I trust she will be wary. But how does poor Dick Lawrence? Is he well enough for me to visit him?'

'No, my lady,' Greene said quickly. 'Master Farhang says that it is probably the sweating sickness and that we should keep away. He wears a mask when he goes in.'

'Poor Dick. We must add him to our prayers. Pray heaven he survives. And how is Sybilla?'

'Still not conscious,' said Greene. 'But Nan says that she is improving. Her pulse is more regular.'

'Let me know the instant she wakes.'

'I will, my lady.'

After inspecting the orderly little cloister garden and exchanging a few words with the bedesmen tending them, Alyce returned to the palace, Leo at her heels. Feeling that she had done her duty towards her dependants, she sent Tamsin to ask the kitchen to send her dinner to her private apartments. As she headed towards the courthouse to find her chamberlain, another low growl came from Leo's throat, and she saw that Milo was now sitting on the stone bench in the porch of the hall. A fine vantage point, she reflected. From there he could see exactly who was coming and going. At the sight of her, he stood and bowed. Leo's growl deepened, and he suddenly dashed over to Milo, snarling, hackles raised. Milo aimed a panicky kick at him, but the hound went on barking fiercely.

Alyce pulled out her whistle and blew it sharply. Leo returned to her side.

'My apologies, Milo,' she called across the yard. 'I can't think what came over Leo. I'll whip him if it happens again.'

Milo's face was a mask of fear. But he recovered himself and bowed humbly again. 'I'd be grateful, your grace. I have always been afeared of dogs.'

Alyce entered the courthouse, where she found Martha inspecting the recently arrived linens. When she saw Alyce, a guilty smile spread over her apple-cheeked face.

'Shouldn't be at it today, I know my lady, but I couldn't help myself. Just admiring things, really. Wondrous fine, these sheets of Rennes flax. And so many! I hardly know where to put them all.'

'I want Sybilla to have two sets of them,' Alyce said. 'You take two sets as well, Martha. You deserve them. And I'd also like two sets sent over to Gerard Vespilan. And goose-feather beds for him and Sybilla.'

Martha was taken aback. 'My lady, we must be careful not to give preferential treatment to some in the God's House and not others.'

Alyce thought for a moment. 'Then let them be an entitlement to those of a certain age. She and Vespilan are our only octogenarians.'

She led the chamberlain outside and nodded in the direction of Milo. 'What do you make of him?'

Martha pursed her lips. 'Pleasant enough to me, my lady. Eats well. Says his chest ails him and his eyes are dim without his spectacles. But I've seen him spry enough when he doesn't know I'm watching, and he shows a deal of interest in what he supposedly can't see. He's been chatting to folk a good deal. Do you want to speak to him, my lady? Shall I call him over?'

'No. I spoke to him lately in the God's House. He asked to eat his meals here rather than there. More chances to spy, I fear. But I'm hoping we can persuade him to our side. Keep an eye on him, but be friendly.'

'I will, your grace. You can count on me for that. Oh, and a letter came for you this morning. Master Caerleon was given it in Wallingford. Looks to be Lord Wenlock's seal. Three Moors' heads.'

She handed Alyce a thin packet and turned back into the courthouse.

Alyce stuffed it into her pocket and walked back to her own

apartments. After Tamsin had served her midday meal and taken away the leavings, she mused on what had happened since her return. A death and a near death. Two accidents – or a murder and an attempted murder? Looking down from the window of her solar, she saw the alleys and neatly trimmed hedges of her garden. Soon it would be time to meet Denzil there. She decided to go down early. She needed to think, and in it she could be sure of being alone, without interruption. It was a *hortus conclusus*, an enclosed walled space with only two entrances. Then she remembered the bunch of germander that Marlene had given Jeanne and frowned. She must reprimand Ben Bilton for letting her in.

Marlene Stonor murmured with pleasure. Putting down the cup of sweet malmsey wine she'd been sharing with her companion, she leant back on the velvet-smooth surface of the turf seat at the heart of Alyce's garden, enjoying the warmth of the afternoon sun – and the strong hands fondling her breasts. Then the man beside her stopped his caresses and stood up. He placed the cup of wine carefully on a low wall and knelt in front of her. Putting both his hands underneath her skirts, he ran them slowly up her thighs. She shivered with pleasure.

'You rascal,' she giggled. 'Not here. Not on the Sabbath. You wouldn't have the nerve...' Then she mewed with pleasure as he moved his fingers higher. She allowed him to explore for a few minutes, then slapped his hands away and sat up abruptly.

'What do you think I am?' she scolded. 'A common slut to be taken at your will? I'll have you know I aim much higher than you.'

But the man pushed her sideways on the seat until she was

flat on her back. Holding her arms high above her head, he straddled her. Gasping, she wrestled to escape, but there was no stopping him. Soon she no longer wanted to. Until she heard the sharp bark of a dog.

'Leo!' Alyce called peremptorily. She was examining the medlar trees in her orchard. They were resplendent with scarlet leaves, their fruits hard and fat. They wouldn't be ready to eat until they had been touched by the frost and rotted into mush inside their skins. She remembered her mother's delight when her father had brought the saplings back from France. They were old now, almost too tall for the orchard. But this was a heavy crop, which would ensure fresh fruit for the whole household, as well as quantities of the tart medlar sauce that gave such a fillip to fish dishes. To say nothing of her own invention: a dense medlar cheese spiced with cloves and lemon. It was time she wrote down such recipes, although she wasn't sure who for. She sighed. If only she had a daughter of her own. 'A son's your son till he gets him a wife. A daughter's your daughter for the rest of her life.' And a daughter-in-law whom you know you have wronged is no company at all.

'Leo!' she called again, and the dog emerged from the neatly trimmed hedges that surrounded the garden's central plaisance. He whined as she strolled towards the fountain where the four tunnels of espaliered fruit trees met. Apples and pears hung in profusion. She sat down on the wide stone edge of the fountain and took a deep breath of the sweet-smelling air, enjoying the garden's quietness, its inviolable peace. Leo, still for some reason alert and uneasy, laid himself down at her feet. She bent down and soothed him by ruffling the spot behind his ears that she knew he found especially pleasurable.

As she did, she saw a scrap of fine muslin, edges bound with black and gold thread. A woman's kerchief, muddied and wet. Not her own, though. The Stonor colours. She remembered the posy of germander that Jeanne had boasted of being given by Marlene. A vision of Ben proudly showing Marlene around the garden came into her head, and a cold anger seized her. Tomorrow she would summon the pair of them to account for themselves.

Deciding to cut herself a bunch of flowers for her book room, she unhooked her little Aleppo steel scissors from the huswife on her girdle. Carrying the posy, she headed for the water garden. Huge, sullen carp nosed their way along the canals that ran along its length. They would be fine eating for the Christmas season.

The thought reminded her of Denzil arguing with Tom Cook about the sturgeon, and it struck her that she hadn't asked him what his business at Wallingford had been. Presumably some scheme of his own, as he hadn't mentioned it. How much didn't he mention to her? she wondered. Still, she could ask him in a few minutes. She watched the great carp absent-mindedly for a few minutes, then, feeling chilled from inactivity, walked back into the little orchard and nuttery, Leo at her heels. Seeing some ripe apples on the ground, she put down the posy and stuffed them into the stout leather wallet that she always slung round one shoulder while gardening. Then she saw that there was still one perfect white rose lingering on the bush that Farhang had bought from a Levantine merchant. She cut it off carefully and placed it in the heart of her bunch, only to wince as the dense thorns on its stem made a jagged wound on her thumb. Scarlet blood oozed from it. She swore roundly.

'What ails you, my lady?' Denzil Caerleon had appeared

from nowhere. Leo ran up to him eager to be petted, and he stroked his head. Alyce put down the flowers and showed him the ugly scratch. He took out a large linen handkerchief and dabbed it gently. 'Farhang would quote that old Persian poet he thinks so much of: that a rose's rarest essence lives in its thorns. Quite what he means by that I've no idea. But I rather like another of his proverbs: that he who dares not grasp the thorn should never crave the rose.'

What did he mean by that? thought Alyce. She looked up half eagerly, half with dread. Could he be...? But then she saw that he was busying himself wrapping his kerchief around the flowers with no thought of her at all. Feeling like a fool, she composed her features in a casual smile and gave a light laugh.

'You have a ready answer for everything, Master Caerleon. But what can you tell me about your meeting with that rogue John Trevelyan? He'll dare too much one of these days.'

She noticed Denzil hesitate a beat before answering and wondered why.

'He seemed in high spirits, my lady, and his ships were well-found. Hopefully, he is on his way down channel by now. His ships are faster than anything Warwick could chase him with.'

'That's a relief. And did you have any misadventures on the Thames?'

Caerleon launched on an account of a near-run thing with a savage current at Kingston Bridge, a broken rudder at Reading, and an argument he'd had with the miller at Goring who charged them 5 marks to winch the barges over his weir.

'Even though he knew the barges were mine?' Alyce said indignantly. 'I'll send Joseph Pek to berate him tomorrow.'

'Was the letter I brought up from Wallingford bad news?' said Denzil.

Alyce realised that she had forgotten all about Wenlock's letter. She felt in her pocket and pulled it out.

Dated 19 September in the sixth year of the reign of Edward the Fourth of that name.

Right trusty and esteemed Princess Alyce, I greet you heartily. I write to renew my warning to you on your last visit. I have had news from a friend who wishes you well that the word at court is that you be a traitor to York, and proof is being sought to arraign you. It is said that royal coursers have been dispatched to nip at your heels. I pray you to be cautious, if you value your home, perhaps your life. And trust no one. I can say no more here, but I would that I could see you privily in Oxford or come to Ewelme itself. Watch your step. I would not see you tried before your peers, few of whom would dare oppose the will of those who now guide the king.

Alyce stared at Wenlock's elegant handwriting in disbelief. The pit of her stomach clenched. She handed the letter to Caerleon.

'What do you think of this, Denzil. Who does Wenlock mean by "those who now guide the king"?'

'The queen, of course. Her father Lord Rivers and her brother Anthony.'

'So are the royal coursers the Harcourts? That would explain their recent visit, and their clumsy attempt to foist Milo of Windsor on me as a bedesman. But what have I to fear? I've done nothing.'

'Innocence never saved anyone,' said Caerleon bitterly. 'Moreover, the Harcourts have a formidable master. Lord Tiptoft, the Constable of England and the head of the royal intelligencers.'

'John Tiptoft? I had thought he and I were on good terms. He took my refusal to concede the constableship of Wallingford Castle with remarkably good grace five years ago, and we have corresponded about books amicably since then.'

'Tiptoft would not let personal liking interfere with obedience to the Crown. Having chosen York over Lancaster, he is loyal to the bone.'

'But what of my step-grandson the Earl of Warwick? He has always been a good friend to me. I thought that he was King Edward's most trusted adviser.'

'Not any longer,' said Caerleon. 'He retreated to Middleton in high dudgeon after receiving scant thanks from Edward for his efforts against Lancastrian rebels in the north. And now he's being moved sideways, sent to scour the Channel of pirates.'

Alyce was startled. If the Earl of Warwick, the man who'd won Edward his throne, could fall from favour, then so could she. Wenlock was right. Separating so publicly from Jack and Bess had probably offended Edward deeply. She felt profoundly foolish.

'But all is not lost, my lady,' Caerleon said. 'You just need to rally new allies. You've done well to win Lord Wenlock's support. And you have many influential friends in Oxford. Churchmen, who have great weight at court. And renowned bookmen. King Edward is a great lover of literature. Perhaps a generous gift?'

'You're right,' said Alyce. 'It's time to act. I shall go to Oxford tomorrow. When I passed through Someries, Wenlock told me that George Neville is staying at Balliol, winding up his affairs before he goes to York to be installed as archbishop. I know he's fond of me. So is wise old William Waynflete,

Bishop of Winchester. He's spending September in the city, overseeing work on new buildings for the college he's founded on the banks of the Cherwell. He sent a letter a few days ago suggesting I visit, in fact. Then there's Thomas Chaundler of New College. There's something fell about him, but he has his finger in all manner of pies. All three of them are eager for donations for their new buildings and largesse from my library.'

'Neville and Waynflete sound excellent prospects. But I'd avoid Chaundler. He's a nasty two-faced piece of work. He had a hand in my losing my fellowship. Wanted to get rid of me because I knew too much about him visiting the Cowley stews.'

'Does he indeed? I'd never have taken him for a lecher.' She thought for a moment, then drew herself up, every inch a princess.

'Denzil, if I write a letter to the Bishop of Winchester, could you ride to the city with it now and deliver it to Magdalen Hall?'

'Of course, my lady. And would you like me to attend you tomorrow?'

She shook her head. 'It's time you had a rest. I'll take Ben Bilton. It'll give me a chance to ask him how things have been on my Oxfordshire estates.' And, she thought to herself, to tell him not to take visitors into my garden. She clicked her fingers at Leo and turned to go. Then she stopped and looked back. It was a trick she often used to startle erring servants into betraying themselves.

'Denzil, what was your business in Wallingford just after you arrived with the great fish?'

Caught off his guard, he coloured. 'Who said I had business

in Wallingford?' Alyce could sense that he was prevaricating. This was all of a piece with Simon Brailles' skitterings and Ben Bilton's evasions.

'Simon Brailles. He is usually reliable,' she said coldly.

'Ah, Simon... yes, I told him I was going to Wallingford, but I only meant I was going down to pay off the barge haulers. And to warn them that there would be one more barge in a couple of days' time – as I told you, it lost its rudder at Reading.'

Their eyes met. He held her gaze for a few seconds, then looked away. She decided not to probe more deeply, but the conviction that he was lying lay coldly in her heart. Unbidden, a phrase in Wenlock's letter came into her head. 'Trust no one.' Clicking her fingers at Leo, she walked out of the garden, her mind in a whirl.

Much later that evening, Denzil strode into the great hall. It was empty except for Simon Brailles, who sat gazing morosely into the dying embers of the fire. He looked up wearily.

'Where have you been, Caerleon? We need to talk.'

'The duchess asked me to take a letter to the Bishop of Winchester in Oxford. She's planning to rise early and go to the city to talk to him and others of her friends there. But why so gloomy? Has anything gone wrong?'

'Not yet,' said Simon. 'But I'm tired of all this deceit. I can't look her grace in the eye.'

'I know what you mean,' said Denzil. 'She asked me about Trevelyan this afternoon, and I had to lie through my teeth. I'm sure she could sense that I was holding something back. And why did you tell her I had business in Wallingford? I had to cobble a story up about that too.'

'I couldn't very well say that you were taking Dick Lawrence to his new quarters, could I? What did you tell her you were doing, by the way? We need to sing off the same song sheet.'

'I said I had to pay off the bargemen. And warn the bridge bailiff that there was another barge on its way. Which was true as far as it went. Except I'd already done both. By the way, what of Milo of Windsor? Is he behaving himself?'

'He's going out of his way to charm everyone he talks to. Specially Lady Alyce's girls. Who don't know what he's up to, of course.'

'Nor do we want to tell them. Tamsin is a staunch young wench who knows how to keep a still tongue in her head, but Eloise is a feather-brained innocent, and Marlene…' Denzil paused ruefully. 'Marlene is far too worldly for her years.'

Oxford

Early next morning Alyce set out for Oxford, with Ben Bilton and Jem jog-trotting behind her. Taking the initiative instead of being knocked about by events had restored her sense of self. She nodded amiably to other travellers on the Oxford road as she recalled Waynflete's letter.

> I would like you to see the new chapel and cloister taking shape, and the start we have made on integrating Magdalen Hall and the former St John's Hospital into a great whole. William Orchard, the Headington mason and quarryman you recommended to me, has drawn up splendid plans. When built, my cloister will put Chaundler's at New College quite in the shade. As for advising you, I will do what I can, but I would also value your advice on a worrying matter.
> Yours with admiration and respect,
> Waynflete

'A worrying matter.' What could that be? she wondered. The Oxfordshire manors attached to his Winchester bishopric meant that Waynflete was besieged with local problems as well as having to negotiate the tricky waters of court politics. She hoped she could help, though she feared she was sadly out of touch with both.

An hour later, they were looking down at the city from Rose Hill. Its spires and towers, many scaffolded, could be seen in all their splendour from here. Never had there been a busier time of building. The noble families who had profited from the war with France were racing to establish colleges and chapels to pray for their immortal souls. Descending to St Clement's, they rode over the bridge across the River Cherwell and through the East Gate as the bells of St Mary's were sounding for nones.

At the Magdalen Hall gatehouse Alyce dismissed Ben; he had a list of commissions from Mistress Purbeck and Farhang Amiri and needed to go to the apothecaries' quarter. Jem hailed the porter and the college's great oak doors opened wide. A sharp-featured clerk in a lawyer's bonnet and a cloak fastened with Bishop Waynflete's badge rose from a stone seat inside the gatehouse, brushing its dust from the back of his gown fastidiously.

'Welcome to Oxford, Princess Alyce,' he said. 'I trust your journey was without incident. I am Lionel, the Bishop of Winchester's secretary. His lordship is in the chapel. Please follow me.'

Leaving Jem to take their horses to the stable, Alyce followed the fussy little man into the new vaulted antechapel, from which the chapel itself would lead away through an intricate loggia. Bishop Waynflete was watching a stonemason carve a flowing beard on the chin of an effigy of a saint. He looked up with pleasure when she entered, holding out his episcopal ring for her to salute.

'Princess Alyce. It has been much too long. I'm so glad to see you. Indeed, I was about to follow up my first letter with a visit to Ewelme, but then I heard that Bishop Neville had invited you to his feast on Thursday.'

Alyce frowned. 'I have had no word from Bishop Neville.'

'That's strange,' said Waynflete. 'He told me he sent the letter by episcopal courier early last week.'

'I haven't received any such letter,' she said, wondering uneasily if it had been deliberately intercepted. But by whom? And why?

'Well, that matter can easily be settled. We will see George over dinner, which we are to eat at New College at noon. Thomas Chaundler has invited him as well as you and me. We must be on our way now; there will be time later to show you the plans Orchard has drawn up.'

With two clerks ahead to shoulder the townsfolk out of the way, and two liveried retainers behind them to watch for cutpurses and other such chancers, Alyce and Waynflete walked along the High Street and into a twisting lane that curled around the back of Queen's College, then turned sharply right to New College. Once through its towering stone gateway, they crossed the cloister to the warden's lodgings. An elderly man answered their knock, and led them upstairs to a handsome vaulted chamber, hung with Flemish tapestries illustrating the Acts of the Apostles. Chaundler and George Neville were playing chess at a table by the window, Chaundler soberly dressed in a high-collared black gown and a tight-fitting clerical cap, Neville more flamboyant in a fur-trimmed robe of deep blue velvet figured with gold embroideries, its sleeves slashed to show a gold satin lining. She smiled at the sight of him. George had always been a genial friend to the Suffolks, sharing their interests in fine furnishings and books.

'My dear Princess Alyce! Just in time to save me from disaster,' said Neville, rising with relief and holding out a beringed hand. 'We're playing by Cessolis's rules, and I can't get the hang of them. I've lost two pawns already, and Thomas has my bishop and my knight in a pin.' Alyce curtseyed, kissed the Bishop of Exeter's episcopal ring and bowed her head for his blessing. Then she walked over to the board and looked at it with interest.

'It's his queen you to need to watch out for, your grace. The pin is easily broken. Can I suggest...' She whispered in his ear. Neville looked again at the board.

'I see what you mean. She's the one to watch in play as in life, it seems.' He slid a pawn forward to where it threatened Chaundler's queen but was protected by his own bishop.

'You shouldn't have told him,' protested Chaundler, put out. Then he remembered his manners. Standing up, he knocked his king over to concede the game, and came forward to make her a deep bow.

'It is an honour to see you here within the walls of New College, your grace. You have done so much for the University – your contribution to the building costs of the new Divinity School, your gifts of books for its library. I had lunch with the master of your God's House, William Marton, yesterday; he said that you had brought many treasures from Wingfield. If you have any surplus to your needs, New College would be only too grateful. Your generosity is legendary.' He walked over to the sideboard and poured three glasses of wine.

'I'll see,' said Alyce, curtly. She disliked flatterers, especially devious ones. She couldn't fathom the true loyalties of Thomas Chaundler. Simply by being the only person who properly understood the intricacies of college politics, he had managed to hang on to power in the University even though George Neville was officially chancellor. Was he the scholarly peacemaker he pretended to be, or a royal ferret? She didn't know. Waynflete lauded his intellect to the skies, but what, she wondered, were his principles?

Contented at having won for once, Neville tidied the ivory and jet chess pieces away in their box.

'Perhaps you and I could have a game before long, my lady?' he said. 'I'm sure I would learn from it. And I hope that you can accept my invitation for next Thursday. I would value your presence most highly.'

How lucky that she had made this spur-of-the-moment decision to come to Oxford, Alyce thought. To have ignored Neville's invitation would have been interpreted as a deliberate slight. Now she could be gracious.

'My apologies for not having answered, your grace, but I never received your letter. But the Bishop of Winchester told me this morning that you had bidden me attend, and I shall be honoured to do so.'

Neville looked puzzled. 'But I sent my own courier last Monday. He said he handed it to one of your bedesmen.'

'Then it is passing strange. I can only suppose it was forgotten or mislaid. Some of the bedesmen are sadly wanting in wits. I'll make enquiry on my return. Thursday, you say? I don't see why not. I'll bring a small household, and we will overnight in the city. Where do you suggest?'

'I'd be honoured if you stayed in the Balliol guest house, Princess. I was waiting on your answer before I offered it to anyone else.'

'My thanks. That will do very well. I have some flibberti-gibbet young ladies who will relish visiting the city's shops.'

Glass in hand, she wandered over to a long oak table in the centre of the room, and began to look at the books laid out on it. A slim quarto volume, its leather cover intricately tooled in gilt, was propped up on a stand.

As she stretched her hand out to pick it up, Chaundler hurried over.

'Your grace, I'm not sure that is suited for your eyes.' He made to take it away, but Waynflete forestalled him.

'Let the duchess see it, Chaundler. She is a woman of experience after all, with great literary nous. Her reaction will help us to decide what to do with it.' He handed it to Alyce.

'It is Thomas's renowned morality play, *A Defence of Human Nature*. It tells of the never-ending struggle between man's head and man's heart, between Reason and Sensuality. It is a presentation copy which he had planned to give to Bishop Beckington on behalf of the college, but the bishop died in January of last year, just a month before it was completed. Thomas has kindly offered it to the University's ever-growing library, as he has another copy for New College. The text is of course impeccable. But the limner has perhaps overstepped the mark of discretion.'

Alyce took the book over to a sloping desk and opened it at the title page. Facing it was the usual drawing of the book being presented by the author to his patron. She pulled her spectacles out of the leather case in which they hung from her belt, perched them on her long narrow nose, and studied it in silence. Then she looked up.

'This illustration is very fine indeed. I love the restrained effect of grisaille drawing – indeed, it is very similar to the frontispiece of my own copy of Deguileville's *Pilgrimage of the Life of Man*. Did you have the book made by John Doll's limner, Denis Pailton? I believe he learnt his craft in Bruges.'

'You are most discerning, your grace. Yes, Doll is by far the best of the Oxford stationers, and his limner Pailton has a rare eye for portraiture.' He gave a snigger.

Alyce looked more closely at the frontispiece. Although the kneeling image of Chaundler was made rather more slender than Thomas actually was, the face, with its shaggy eyebrows and bulging eyes, was a speaking likeness; as was that of Beckington, the late Bishop of Bath and Wells. She turned the pages respectfully, then froze. The third drawing in the text showed a haggard woman with a crown and the hawk-like profile of the king's mother Cicely Neville pleading with an enthroned king, even as he is being handed an apple by a revealingly dressed woman. There was no mistaking Edward of York's long fair hair and florid face framed in a short beard, or the high forehead and pouting lips of Elizabeth Wydeville. Alyce leafed to the next illustration. It showed the king naked on a bench, his miniver robe fallen from his shoulders and barely covering his loins, a broken sceptre and the bitten apple at his feet. The woman, now next to him on the bench, leaned lasciviously towards him. The elderly queen, banished to a corner, is weeping. The drawings unmistakably represented the uneasy moment when Edward revealed his secret marriage to a Lancastrian widow and Cicely Neville famously berated her son for his choice of wife. Edward was coroneted. Cicely wore the elaborate crown she had once adopted as her due as Queen Mother. Elizabeth wore no crown – her coronation had been later in 1465, a year after the book's completion.

Fascinated, Alyce turned to the fourth picture. It showed the erstwhile king naked and alone in a wilderness. A prediction of, or a prayer for, Edward's fall from the throne? She glanced up to see all three men watching her intently. She thought for a beat. There was no doubt that Beckington, hot for Lancaster all his life, would have loved tucking such a book away in his episcopal library in the West Country, but it was now a perilous possession in the extreme. She closed it firmly.

'It is very fine work, but it makes a laughing stock of the king. And the queen. I can see why the warden wants it to disappear into the University's book chests, but that would surely be risky. It would be a shame to destroy it. Better perhaps to find a brave buyer who could export it. Perhaps Master Doll could act for you; find a middleman who would pay the college well for it with a view to taking it to Bruges, where it would find a ready market.'

'An excellent verdict, your grace,' said Chaundler. 'I will send it to Doll to do so.'

'Please congratulate him from me on a fine if dangerous piece of bookmaking. I intend to visit him later today. I want to thank him for recommending his former journeyman to me. Did you ever meet Denzil Caerleon? He is now acting as my man of business. He has that rare combination: practical competence and literary learning.'

She was startled to see Chaundler's lip curl in an almost feral snarl.

'Have I met him? I certainly have. He has a long history of wrongdoing. As a favour to his parents, I took him in as a scholar at this college, but he was thrown out for disgraceful behaviour with a woman. Did you know of this, your grace?'

'I did,' said Alyce with icy calm, disliking the degree of venom with which Chaundler laced the word 'woman'. 'John Doll told me all about his past. But that is now behind him.'

'Can you be sure of that, my lady?' said Chaundler. 'What's bred in the bone will not out, they say.'

'Give a dog an ill name and hang him,' Alyce quipped in

return. 'He has been working for me for two years now, and I find him loyal, resourceful and clever. What more could one want in a servant?'

'Honour,' said Chaundler, flint-eyed.

Just then a servant entered to announce the meal.

'I thought that we would eat up here in peace rather than with the raggle-taggle mob of scholars in the hall,' said Chaundler. 'Excuse me for a few moments; I must make sure that they haven't forgotten anything.'

After he had gone out, George Neville fanned himself in an ostentatious dumbshow of relief, and Waynflete gave Alyce a most unepiscopal wink.

'Did I detect hackles rising between you and Thomas, my dear? I should warn you that he's a dangerous man to cross. But enough of politicking. You have been away from Oxfordshire for too long. Are you planning to stay awhile?'

'For good, I hope,' said Alyce. 'I have given overall responsibility for my eastward lands to John and Elizabeth, and I will have charge of those here and in the West Country. To be honest, I hope that I never have to visit Wingfield again.'

George Neville heard the suppressed anger behind her words and raised his eyebrows.

'But John and Elizabeth are all the family you have, Lady Alyce. And what about your grandsons? Most widows find them a solace in their old age.'

'Not when hovering over them is their other grandmother. Your aunt Cicely is the biggest busybody in creation,' said Alyce tartly. 'Anyway, I am not most widows. Thank the Lord I have a more than adequate livelihood and plenty to busy myself with. Which reminds me, I want to ask your advice. I am thinking of becoming a vowess. Not to retreat from the world, but to protect myself from being required to marry.'

Neville gave a slow nod of understanding, having immediately guessed who might do the requiring. But before he could reply, the door opened and Chaundler returned, followed by four servants carrying loaded trays. There was a dish of chicken and almonds cooked with rice, a pot of steaming soup, and a salad of celery, watercress and slivers of lemon. The servants spread white cloths over the chamber's central table and laid four places. Richly scented muscatel wine was poured into tall, gilded glasses.

Chaundler smiled benignly.

'Let us give thanks for what we are about to enjoy. William, will you say grace?'

Waynflete rose and said a blessing over the food, and as they sat down to enjoy it pages brought round bowls of warm water, then soft white towels scented with lavender. How well these churchmen lived, thought Alyce, as she dried her hands and pulled her steel eating knife from its sheath. Few but princes of the blood could equal them. Chaundler courteously offered her choice titbits from the chicken dish, and a valet handed her a golden goblet, a ceremonial cup gifted to the college by Henry VI. She raised it to pledge her companions, took a sip herself and passed it to Waynflete's waiting hands.

After the pledges were done, the meal enjoyed, and the bowls and towels once again circulated, the servants withdrew, leaving the four of them alone. Alyce again raised the subject of her becoming a vowess. Frustratingly, they all had different views on the matter. Neville objected on the grounds that it was irreversible, and she might change her mind about remarrying. Chaundler was all for going further, becoming a nun.

'You would speedily be raised to great state in the Church,' he pointed out. 'Look at the Prioress of Amesbury and the Abbess of Syon.'

Waynflete shook his head. 'It depends on what kind of a life you want to lead. Being the head of a religious house will entail far more nuisance than pleasure or profit. You will find yourself nannying a flock of addle-pated old hens. Simply becoming a vowess seems to me the best solution. But the sooner the better. If you want to prevent unwelcome interference in your future.' By which, they all knew, he meant Elizabeth Wydeville's greedy eye for wealthy wives for her indigent kinsfolk.

As they walked back to Magdalen, Waynflete pointed to the high spire of St Mary's, the University Church. 'The other matter I wanted to consult you about concerns the library that we have established above the Chapter House in St Mary's. At first the books were chained along reading slopes, but there are so many now – gifted by such benefactors as the Duke of Gloucester, God rest his soul, the Earl of Worcester Lord Tiptoft and indeed you yourself – that they have to be kept in locked chests. We keep a careful catalogue, and there is always a librarian on duty when the room is open. But some seem to be going missing. Especially rare ones. Prices for fine manuscripts are soaring these days, as collectors invest in them, and books are now among the University's most valuable assets.'

Alyce pondered. 'Who has the keys of the book chests?'

'Only the librarians. As usual, the chests are exceptionally secure, with at least two locks on each. But I think the thefts are during the day, while the chests are open and the books being consulted. We didn't notice at first, because the number of books stayed the same. What was changing was the books themselves. Two-penny primers instead of serious works. Even one or two blank-paged books. There is clearly an exceptionally cunning thief at work. And he must be one of our own scholars. Someone with every right to use the library.' He paused and swallowed nervously. 'What decided me to tell you about it is that one of your own gifts has been purloined: the copy you gave us of the treatise on the astrolabe which your grandfather wrote for your Uncle Lewis when he was a boy. It was one of our most treasured possessions. We only discovered its loss this week. I mentioned it to Lord Wenlock and he said that I should tell you. That you had a talent for unravelling mysteries.'

Alyce stared at him with disbelief. She had been exceptionally fond of the little book that her grandfather Geoffrey Chaucer wrote for his oldest son Lewis when he was a child because he had so loved the night sky. It had been in English to make it easier for a child to understand. Lewis had died before it was finished, and Geoffrey had been so saddened that he put it aside. But what remained had passed into the possession first of her father Thomas and then of herself. John had shown no interest in star-gazing, so she had decided that the University library would be the most appropriate home for the copy she had had made for him. She couldn't control her anger.

'This is shocking news. I wouldn't have dreamt of giving a copy of *De Astrolabio* to Oxford if I'd thought there was a risk of it being stolen. I certainly won't give any more books to the University. When was it last consulted?'

Waynflete cringed from her wrath, wishing he hadn't taken Wenlock's advice.

'Three weeks ago. But a deft thief could have taken it while they were returning another book to the chest.'

'Surely books should be handed back to librarians. Not put back into a chest by a reader.'

'We have instituted that practice now.'

'Locked the stable door after the horse has bolted, you mean.' She sighed. 'Have you alerted the Oxford booksellers?'

'That is an excellent idea. And the college librarians. And we will send word to London. If it is offered up for sale, there's a chance of getting it back. Or if copies appear taken from it. Its illustrations are unique.'

'How did you discover its loss?'

'It was asked for by a student, Thomas Holbroke, last week. But it could not be found.'

Alyce remained frostily silent until they reached Magdalen again, and Waynflete took her up to his room to look at the college plans. They were magnificent, making one architectural whole of the old hospital, the former Magdalen Hall and the new chapel and cloister.

Alyce looked at them critically. 'Are you going to have a tower?'

'Of course,' said Waynflete. 'But not for some time. Funds, even mine, are not bottomless.' Was that a hopeful glance he gave her? Well, a donation was the last thing she intended making after the loss of her treasured gift. Then she relented. Waynflete had contributed so much to the cause of learning in every one of his many estates. After all, his college was a worthier cause than lending money to the king on uncertain terms.

'I'll see what I can do. I don't want it spent on a vanity project like a tower, mind.'

'Any contribution would be welcome,' said Waynflete gratefully, relieved that her anger had subsided. 'Would you like it to go towards the school I am planning? I'm negotiating for a site for it across the river.'

Alyce brightened. Schooling children was much closer to her heart than showy stone pinnacles. 'That is an excellent idea, Bishop. I'll attend to raising funds on my return.'

She hesitated, then spoke again. 'It wasn't just the advisability of becoming a vowess that I wanted to ask you about. I'm worried by what I've come back to in Ewelme. There has been a death and a near-death. Both unexpected. Nicolas Webb, one of my bedesmen, died of eating poisoned mushrooms a month ago, and I decided to replace him with my mother's old gossip Sybilla – you will remember that she became an anchorite up at Swyncombe. But she was bitten by adders in her cell, and nearly died. I suspect that the Harcourts could have contrived Webb's death, perhaps even arranged for snakes to be put in Sybilla's cell, though I can't imagine how. Both Harcourt brothers visited me a few days ago, and tried to foist a new bedesman on me in the name of the queen. It seems likely that he is a royal spy. Wenlock sent me a warning that I was being watched.'

Waynflete pondered for a few minutes before speaking.

'As to the death of your bedesman, that sounds like an accident. At this time of year there are many such, and it was well before your return. The Harcourts are however to be feared; they are certainly not among your well-wishers. Worse, they are highly thought of at court. Sir Robert is especially close to the queen. And I suspect that it is the queen you must needs fear most. Elizabeth wants to fleece former Lancastrians of everything they have to bolster the importance and wealth of her own kindred. Edward is all for forgiveness and mending bridges between York and Lancaster – however, he will not take a slight to his sister lightly. You have made yourself doubly vulnerable by falling out with your son, you know. It would have been wiser to move away with less ostentation and fewer wagons.' He paused, then added, 'To the world it must look like spite.'

Alyce coloured. 'But that would have been the last I would have seen of the furnishings that have lined my life for so long, the memorials of all that I have achieved – and suffered.'

'Worldly state is worth less than peace of mind, Alyce.'

'I intend to have both,' she replied obstinately.

He shook his head. 'Then you must walk a narrow road between the evils pressing on every side. Beginning on Thursday. The Harcourts will also be at George Neville's dinner at Balliol. Yet they are I think less to be feared than the Earl of Worcester. He may seem amiable, but as Constable of England he is dedicated to unearthing treasons. And he too is to be at George's dinner. He has apparently asked to be seated beside you.'

Alyce nodded slowly. 'Thank you, William. Forewarned is forearmed. The memory of saying just that to Gerard flashed into her mind, and she sighed, her newfound confidence somewhat sapped. And what of George Neville's letter? Had it just been mislaid or deliberately intercepted?

There was a sharp rap at the door, and Ben Bilton marched in, a heavy bag slung over his shoulder. 'What cheer, my lady?' he said. 'You said you wanted to visit Master Doll's bookshop. I think we should go now if we're to be home before dark.'

Alyce frowned and nodded towards Waynflete. Ben bowed belatedly. Alyce shook her head.

'I must apologise, your grace. Bilton's father died before he could be taught manners and he was left too much among churls.' She saw Ben's face fall and regretted her choice of words. He was touchy about his childhood.

'Fortunately, his mother's gentle blood survived his stepfather's abuse,' she added quickly, 'It's rare for him to forget his manners. And he is now among my most trusted servants. In truth, I prefer rough-hewn to silver-tongued.' Ben coloured, and she wondered why. But in a trice his cheeky grin returned, and he made an exaggeratedly low bow to them both.

John Doll's bookshop was only a short distance from Magdalen, so they left their horses in the college stable and, attended by two Magdalen porters, walked down the High Street past a jumble of shops and college frontages, some modest, some grand. There was a long table outside the shop laden with student necessaries, guarded by a wary-eyed old woman sitting on a joint stool with a bundle of raw wool on her lap, from which she teased a thread of yarn onto a spindle. When she saw Alyce and Ben stop in front of the shop, she put her work down on the books table and hurried inside. A moment later she emerged, bringing with her a pale young clerk. He bowed low, ushered them into the shop and up a winding stair. Alyce smiled at the sight of John Doll sitting at his usual desk by a large window, more stooped than he had been when she had last visited his shop three years ago, but otherwise little changed. He stood up and bowed, brushing back what little remained of his wispy grey hair and blinking at her through thick glass spectacles.

'Lady Alyce. Or should I say "Princess"? What an honour and a delight to see you again.'

'Lady Alyce will suffice. I feel something of a fraud at being called Princess, and who knows how long such a title will be proper.' Their eyes met in silent understanding.

There was a cough from the far corner of the room. Alyce started. She had assumed they were alone when she had made such an incautious remark. It came from a tall thin gentlewoman dressed in dark grey, her face veiled. She was standing at the side of another woman, seated at a table, and too absorbed in what she was reading to have noticed them.

John Doll gestured towards them. 'Mistress Joan Moulton is the owner of London's famous Sign of the Mole. Undoubtedly the most interesting bookshop in Paternoster Row. She is spending several days in Oxford, buying and selling books to the colleges. She is attended by her companion, a most erudite lady.'

At the sound of her own name, Joan looked up. Alyce almost laughed. The bookseller was the image of the Wife of Bath in her copy of her grandfather's *Tales*, generously built and flamboyantly attired. The jut of her chin suggested obstinacy but there was shrewdness in her brown eyes. Seeing Alyce and Ben, she stood up.

'Introduce your friends, Master Doll. They are I hope book-loving customers of yours whom I might tempt with my own acquisitions.'

'You might indeed, Mistress Joan. This is Alyce, Dowager Duchess of Suffolk, who has a considerable library in her palace at Ewelme, especially since she has now added her

Suffolk books to it. And her steward, Ben Bilton. Not a reader, I fear, but a doughty man of his hands.'

Joan made a half-hearted gesture towards a curtsey, then sat down with a grunt of relief when Alyce signed her to do so.

'This is a happy accident, Duchess. We have a mutual friend in Sir John Wenlock. I was staying at Someries last week, and he said that I might meet you in Oxford as we were all bidden to Bishop Neville's feast on Thursday. He said you are to make Oxfordshire your home in future. I myself have a manor at Charlbury and I hope to entertain you there one day. Most of my books are in London, but I keep certain rarities there under lock and key. Thieves abound in these troubled times.'

Alyce stared. So this startlingly unlikely bookseller had been staying at Someries? She was well aware of Wenlock's fondness for voluptuous women. What intimacies had they exchanged? she wondered. She felt a flush rising to her cheeks and turned away to hide it. She hoped that Wenlock had not said too much about her new circumstances. But Joan was too busy extracting a book from the capacious leather wallet on the floor beside her feet to notice.

'I say fortunate because Lord Wenlock told me that you are the granddaughter of Geoffrey Chaucer, our greatest English verse-maker. I've recently acquired a copy of a little-known book that he wrote for his son, Lewis. Perhaps the boy was your father? It is a treatise on using an astrolabe. Very prettily illustrated too.' She handed the book to Alyce, who took it in silence, instantly knowing it for the copy that she had given to the University's library – which Bishop Waynflete had just told her had been stolen.

'Hmm,' she said neutrally. 'And did you acquire it from Master Doll, by any chance?'

Doll shook his head, looking over her shoulder as she leafed through the slim volume.

'No, though I would have relished the handling of it. It is most exquisite. Mistress Moulton has several sources of supply in Oxford, I believe.'

Alyce turned to Joan. 'So where did you get it? Because I should warn you that I gave this book to the University's library myself, and that it was stolen recently from Great St Mary's. I'm afraid it will have to be restored to it.'

Joan silently cursed her misguided impulse to offer the treatise to Alyce. She hadn't been able to resist such an appropriate customer, but she should have realised that the duchess was likely to be extremely well informed about Oxford copies of her grandfather's books. She struggled to save the situation.

'But I paid good money for it,' she said defensively.

'Which does not mean that you can keep stolen goods,' snapped Alyce. 'Who sold it to you?'

'As to that, I cannot and will not say,' said Joan, bridling at Alyce's haughty manner.

'You will have to when this matter is brought before the University authorities. As it will be, I assure you.'

'What I say to them is my affair,' said Joan, in high dudgeon. Remembering what Anthony Wydeville had told her of the court's suspicions of Alyce's loyalty, she summoned up a counterattack.

'As to wrongdoings, London is rife with rumours that Ewelme Palace is a nest of traitors, fugitive Lancastrians who are being succoured by you and your people.'

She turned to John Doll, nodded a farewell and swept out of the room, followed by her veiled companion. Alyce was left, the book still in her hand, shaken to the core. There was an uncomfortable silence.

'I am so sorry, Lady Alyce,' Doll said at last. 'But I am sure that Mistress Joan would not knowingly have bought a stolen book. And she is bound to protect her supplier. Any bookseller would do.'

Alyce stifled the urge to curse Doll roundly. Instead, she handed him the book.

'John, I wanted to stay longer, but we have a long journey to make, and time presses. Could I ask you to take the book to Bishop Waynflete with my compliments, and tell him how it came to be recovered? But until we discover who sold it to that woman, there could be more losses.'

'Doubtless the Chancellor's Court will raise the matter with Mistress Moulton,' said Doll.

'And by then she will have fabricated some plausible lie,' said Alyce tartly. 'Laced with her honeyed words and come-hither looks.'

Doll looked unhappy. 'I have to say that I have always found her an honest dealer.'

'Perhaps you should reconsider. I had thought to look round your shop, but I have no mind for that now. I'll be back to Oxford in three days' time for the feast, and I'll visit you then. Or on Friday.'

She turned to leave, then paused. 'John, have you heard any such tittle-tattle of traitors at Ewelme in Oxford?'

She saw Doll glance at Bilton, and a flush rise on the young man's cheek. Her heart sank.

Ewelme

Wondering what had made Lady Alyce rush so precipitately to Oxford, Tamsin decided to make the most of her absence by tidying up her inner sanctum. She was ordering the pens and papers on the table in the turret window when, glancing out into the courtyard, she saw Milo of Windsor sitting on a stool on the gallery of the guest lodgings. It was a sheltered sunny position, from which everything going on in the courtyard could be seen. His eyes must have caught her movement, for he raised his head and seemed to be gazing straight at her. She shivered. Eyes like a snake. Nor did she like the familiar way he patted her on the arm, or, worse, her lower back, when she was near enough to him to be touched. She backed away from the window and went on with her task, marvelling at the lovely things that Alyce used every day when writing. Curving swan quill pens, which it was one of her duties to sharpen. Little earthenware jars of ink, each tightly corked. A round silver box holding fine sand to dry up excess ink. A thin-bladed, razor-sharp knife for slicing paper or vellum. Sticks of sealing wax. Heavy lumps of sea-smoothed stone, which Alyce had told her she had picked up from the beach below the great Cornish castle of Tintagel, where the Atlantic breakers smashed into the cliffs with a never-ceasing roar. Alyce held lands close to it, so perhaps one day they would go there and she would see King Arthur's birthplace.

Her drifting thoughts were brought abruptly into the present by a hesitant knock at the door. Simon Brailles, she guessed, come to check up on her. She crossed the room to open it. But it wasn't Simon. It was Milo, his habitual sly smile more marked than usual.

'Tamsin, my dear. My apologies for disturbing you. But I saw you at the window, and I wondered if you would do me a favour. My chest is paining me, and I don't think I can walk as far as the infirmary.'

He sat down heavily on a cushioned stool near Alyce's desk.

'Could you get me some liniment from Nan Ormesby. I have used up what she gave me. See, here is the pot it was in. He handed Tamsin an empty jar made of clouded green glass. She took it from him, shying swiftly away from the move his now free hand made towards her bottom.

'I'll go as soon as I have finished tidying my lady's cabinet,' said Tamsin. 'But you can't stay here. Only Lady Alyce's personal servants are allowed in her upstairs quarters. They are always kept locked.'

'And rightly so, I realise now,' said Milo, looking round at the richly furnished room with an assessing eye. 'I will go down straight away. You will find me in the courtyard when you return with the liniment.'

To Tamsin's relief, he stood up and went out. She finished tidying up, leaning out of the window to shake the little sheepskin rug that kept Lady Alyce's feet from the chill of the floor, and sweeping the floor before replacing it. She scattered dried penny royal lightly into the rug to deter fleas and moths and to scent the room pleasantly, refilled the charcoal burner on the windowsill, and put fresh candles and tapers into holders on the walls and the desk. Satisfied, she smiled. Lady Alyce would feel properly welcomed on her return in the evening. Then she left, closing and locking the door behind her. She went into her own room to fetch a warm cloak to wrap round herself, then set off for the infirmary.

As she crossed the courtyard, Simon Brailles and Denzil

Caerleon came out of the stable. Denzil, who was leading a saddled horse, gave her a welcoming smile, but Simon frowned.

'I saw Milo of Windsor coming down Lady Alyce's stairs,' he said crossly. 'What was he doing alone in her chamber?'

'He was never alone there. I was preparing it for her return, and he knocked at the door. I thought it was you. He wanted some more of Nan's ointment. But I told him he couldn't wait there.'

'I should think not. Next time you're in there, lock the door, and make sure it is me before you open it. It's locked now, I trust?'

'Of course it is,' snapped Tamsin, cheeks hot with anger that he was talking to her as if she was a fool. Especially in front of Master Caerleon. She glanced at him, and was relieved to see that he was still smiling. He was the most exciting person she had ever encountered. Perhaps one day Princess Alyce would take them both with her on one of her journeys. Leaving the fussy, ever-critical Simon behind to nitpick about niceties to his heart's content. Her thoughts brought an answering smile to her lips. But Caerleon didn't see it. He was staring over at the porch of the hall, where Milo was sitting as usual. But he had a companion. Marlene was on the stone seat beside him, showing him a piece of paper. They were deep in conversation. Then Milo looked up, and saw them. He said something to Marlene, and tucked the paper away into a fold in his doublet. Her lips twisted in a malicious smile, and she gave Tamsin a little wave. Tamsin nodded back, feeling uneasy at their evident closeness.

'I'm for Wallingford, Simon,' she heard Caerleon say. 'I'll be back as soon as I can.' He mounted, and clattered off through the gateway without a backward glance.

When Tamsin reached the infirmary Nan was bending over a patient so swathed in bandages that Tamsin couldn't see his face. 'Who's that?' she whispered.

'A clumsy fool who fell against the bee boles and got stung all over his face. I've teased all the stings out, and applied cider vinegar. It's a sovereign remedy for stings. What do you want, child?'

Tamsin pulled Milo's jar out from under her cloak and showed it to Nan. 'Milo asked me to get some more of the liniment you gave him. His chest is bad again he said.'

Nan raised her eyebrows. 'Has he used what I gave him up already?'

'He says so.'

'He must have been rubbing it all over himself twice a day, then. Oh well, it was only pig's lard scented with juniper. Smells nicely medicinal and does no harm. I'll refill it and bring it over when I take the laundry over to Martha Purbeck.'

'Are you managing without me?' asked Tamsin.

'We miss you but we'll survive,' said Nan. 'But how are you getting on? Are the other servants being nice to you? They may be jealous that you've risen so high of a sudden.'

'Everyone is very kind, Nan. Mistress Purbeck has shown me around, and Eloise Stonor has given me some of her old clothes. I don't like her sister Marlene much, though. She glares at me, and she pushed into me as she was going down the turret stairs, and almost made me tumble. And... and she seems very friendly with Milo.'

'Does she indeed? Not too friendly, I hope. I've heard she's an incorrigible flirt. Still, you do your best to make a friend of her and Eloise, dear. Don't let that hot little head of yours get the better of good manners.'

She came over to Tamsin and wrapped her in her arms. Tamsin felt tears pricking her eyes at the warm familiarity of Nan's hug, sweet-scented with balsam and wormwood and honey. She realised suddenly how lonely and scared she had been feeling for the last few days. Though all her daydreams seemed to have come true, she still feared that her new life might of a sudden vanish away. She hugged Nan back, drying her eyes on the rough cloth of her capacious apron.

Nan chuckled, then thought of a sure way of cheering her granddaughter up.

'While you're here, dear, could you go and see Wat? He's chopping wood, but he's been asking for you. Misses you sadly.'

'Of course I will,' said Tamsin. 'I hoped I'd have a chance to see him.' She sprinted away to the woodyard.

Wat's round face lit up when she appeared. He put down the axe he had been using and called out her name joyfully. Then he came towards her slowly, reaching out a hand in wonder to stroke the soft blue cloth of her cloak, then raising it to touch the fine cambric of her kerchief. Then he knelt at her feet, his hands clasped as if in prayer. Tamsin couldn't suppress a chuckle of laughter. She raised him up to his feet and shook her head in mock reproach.

'What's this, Wat? I'm still just Tamsin. No need to kneel to me.' Head still bowed, he looked up at her under his brows. Nan had cropped his shaggy head of hair into a trim pudding-basin shape, exposing pale skin at the back of his neck. He was wearing a tough leather jerkin that looked as if it had been cut down from a much larger one.

'That's a fine jerkin,' said Tamsin. 'Who gave you that?'

Wat smiled with pride and jabbed a grubby forefinger towards the woodshed. Adam Sawyer, one of the bedesmen, was coming out of it with an empty log basket. He came up to them and gave Tamsin a welcoming smile.

'Well, Mistress Tamsin, you're a fine lady now. Happen too fine for us folk.'

'Never, said Tamsin, with a warm smile. 'How could I forget the toys you made for me when I was a little girl. I've still got the hoop and the top and the wooden doll.'

'Maybe one day your own little one will play with them,' said Adam, winking.

Tamsin shook her head firmly. 'Not for a good while, I hope. I want to see the world before I settle down.'

'See the world you will with Lady Alyce,' said Adam. 'She's resting from bruising times just now, but she'll recover and be venturing again soon. It's in her blood to wander.'

Wat had filled the empty basket and taken it into the woodshed while they were talking. When he reappeared he held something in his fist as if it was very precious. He thrust his closed hand towards her and opened his fingers slowly. Inside nestled a baby dormouse. It was lying on its back, tiny paws clenched and eyes tight shut. Tamsin smiled with delight and stroked its plump belly gently.

'Wat, it's a darling. Where did you find it?' He nodded his head towards the log pile, then gestured to her pocket.

'Oh, Wat, I'd love to keep it, but I wouldn't be able to in the palace. You look after it here, and I'll come and see it soon. Has you got more of them?'

He nodded eagerly and held up four fingers.

'Four! Quite a family. And a mother?' He shook his head sadly.

'He's feeding them on drops of milk squeezed from a rag,' put in Adam. 'He's that gentle with them. You were right about his coming here, Tamsin. He's a changed lad. That was a good deed of yours.'

Tamsin returned to the palace, her heart warmed by the knowledge that she would always have loyal friends in the God's House. There was no sign of Marlene, and Milo was back on his stool in the gallery. She called up to him to say that Nan would bring the liniment over on her next visit. He nodded his thanks with a knowing leer that brought back some of her earlier unease. But she managed to give him a polite smile as she went over to the courthouse to find out what chores Dame Purbeck had for her.

Alyce and Bilton rode back to Ewelme in silence. Alyce had asked him about taking Marlene into the garden, and he had flatly denied doing so. It was another mystery to add to the sidelong looks that she'd noticed Ben exchanging with Farhang and Simon Brailles' evident anxiety. She was beginning to wonder if there was any truth in the rumours of treasonous goings-on in her absence. She must speak to Caerleon. He at least was free from suspicion. For the last year he had been as far away from Ewelme as she had.

Ben also wanted to talk to Caerleon. Shopping done in the apothecaries' quarter, he'd visited the Turf Tavern again, and been generous with rounds of ale. He had heard much talk of the duchess's imminent undoing. Clearly someone was leaking information about the goings on at Ewelme. But who? Had Milo already unearthed evidence that would damn them? Could he have sent word to the Harcourts? Damn Denzil for preventing them winding up their operation on Lady Alyce's return.

Tamsin was the first to greet them when they returned. Alyce nodded absently at her, and looked around the courtyard, clearly seeking someone else. At last, she turned back to her.

'Tamsin, could you find Marlene and Eloise and tell them we are going to Oxford early on Thursday. We'll stay the night in the Balliol College guest lodgings and come back on Friday.

Tamsin hesitated. 'Will I be going to Oxford as well?' she asked shyly.

Ben saw Alyce think for a moment. Then she looked at Tamsin's eager young face.

'You as well. And Master Caerleon will come with us. Where is he, do you know?'

'He went to Wallingford this morning, my lady. I haven't seen him since.'

Ewelme

William Marton returned to Ewelme next day. Alyce beckoned to him to follow her into the solar. He followed with his usual ponderous tread. He was a heavy-set, immensely dignified man, with thick hair newly trimmed around his head and his slab-like cheeks smoothly shaved. He never used one word when several could be employed, and he spoke so slowly that Alyce had to bite back the urge to finish his sentences snappily for him. Which she knew annoyed him intensely.

'William, it's good to see you back. So much has been happening. You'll notice a new face in church and around the palace. He's a scrivener called Milo of Windsor. He was wished on me by the queen herself, and brought here by the Harcourts, who asked me to make him a bedesman. They'd heard of Webb's death. To forestall that, I've appointed Sybilla of Swyncombe.'

She paused, expecting Marton, a stickler for tradition, to protest. Rather to her surprise, he merely nodded.

'Yes, your grace. I heard the news. Peter Greene wrote to communicate your decision about Sybilla to me. An excellent idea in my opinion, bringing the God's House in line with practice in several of your other almshouses. He also told me that she had been assailed by vipers in the anchorhold. What an unfortunate mischance. I trust that she has recovered.'

'She is doing so, thanks to Farhang's care,' said Alyce, relieved that he accepted her announcement so calmly. 'And

Milo may be useful to Simon. After all, we have nothing to fear from his spying. But as he has the Harcourts' ear, I don't want him given access to any confidential documents.'

Marton bowed his assent. 'You can of course count on me, your grace. I will ensure that he is limited to such mundane matters as...'

Alyce couldn't stop herself cutting him off before he began on a long list of harmless tasks for Milo.

'Thank you, William,' she said with her sweetest smile, ignoring his pained look. 'One more thing: I'd like you to make enquiry among the bedesmen about a letter which was delivered to one of them a week ago, on the Monday you left for Oxford. It was an invitation to a feast this Thursday from the Bishop of Exeter. Luckily I dined with him yesterday, and he naturally asked me if I was planning to come. It would have been extremely insulting if I had appeared to ignore it.'

Marton was all concern. 'I will do so immediately, your grace. All I can think of is that it was one of the more slow-witted brethren who received it. How very fortunate you came across his grace on your visit to Oxford. Which I trust was as fruitful as you had hoped it would be. Did you acquire any new books?'

Alyce shook her head wearily. 'Unfortunately not. I did visit John Doll's shop, but I had a very unpleasant encounter there with a brash London bookseller who had the effrontery to offer me a stolen book.'

Marton raised his eyebrows. 'What led you to surmise that it had been illegally appropriated?'

'It was one of my own. My grandfather's treatise on the astrolabe, written for my uncle. I decided last year to donate it to the University library.'

Marton paled. 'I recall your generosity well,' he said. 'Did the bookseller say where she acquired it?'

'No. She refused, most rudely. But she had the grace to leave the book. Doll is returning it, and she'll have to answer to the Chancellor's Court for her possession of it.'

Marton shook his head solemnly. 'I did hear that there had been books stolen recently. I hope they catch the malefactor. Else Oxford's well-wishers will hesitate before giving books. Now, I must return to my duties. I fear that there is a great deal to be done.'

Just as Marton took his leave, Martha Purbeck bustled into the solar. 'Excuse me, my lady, I think you should come to the great hall and make sure the hangings depicting the Amazons you brought from Wingfield are being put in the right places. They look wrong to me.'

She was right to be worried, Alyce discovered. The men who had hung the exquisitely woven hangings along the long rods positioned close to the ceiling behind the dais at the north end of the hall had made no attempt to make sense of the sequence.

'Take them all down,' she directed. 'Queen Orythia has to be on the far right. Then her daughters Queen Hippolyte and Queen Menalippe. Then the Amazon warriors preparing for a joust. *Then* the vanquishing of Hercules.'

Just as the final hanging was being set into position, an elderly man in a travel-stained cloak was shown into the hall by one of the gate guards. He looked flustered and dishevelled and had his arms wrapped tightly around a long leather bag.

Alyce turned to greet him. 'Master Massingham! How good to see you. Are you come with the drawings for my tomb? The alabaster has already been ordered from Tetbury.'

Then she noticed his distress. 'What's wrong? You are clutching your drawing roll as if you thought it was going to be snatched from you.'

'So it was, your grace, so it was. Four men-at-arms on horseback came out of the woods as I was coming over the hill from Stonor Park. Wearing black cloaks with the hoods pulled up, and their faces muffled. They shook my saddlebags out, and grabbed my roll, undid its lacings and pulled out the drawings. In the pouring rain!'

Alyce was incensed. 'Did you say that you were under my protection?'

'I did. But they just jeered. And when their leader saw what the drawings were, he laughed and said – begging your pardon, Princess Alyce – "The sooner the old harridan gets this under way the better." Then he threw them back at me saying "It's well for you that there's no sedition here. If you be a loyal subject to King Edward, then let him know if you find any at Ewelme." Then he shouted to his men to mount, and they rode off. Some of the drawings are sadly stained and torn, I fear.'

'Whose livery were they wearing?'

'They had their cloaks pulled over their badges. But as their leader tossed down the drawings I saw his. It was a white rose on a golden sun.'

Alyce was silent. So the ambush had involved the king's own men. Or the queen's. They, not the Harcourts, were the royal coursers Wenlock had warned her about. Her mind raced, but she managed to conceal her anxiety from the old sculptor.

'That road is notorious for drunkards and ruffians, Massingham,' she said reassuringly. 'They were no doubt mercenaries, returned from France and now with no future.

The badge was probably a trophy from another raid. Our sovereign Lord Edward fears traitors, but he will find none here.'

She took the old man's arm. 'Let's go up to my great chamber where there's a fire burning and spiced ale on the trivet. You can show me just how you plan the housing of my mortal remains.'

Thirty years earlier she had ordered a seemly tomb for her parents in Ewelme church; six years ago she had commissioned one for William. The one that united Thomas and Maud in death was simple and dignified. William's was humbler than he had envisaged, but anything elaborate would have been vandalised; to make its survival more certain she had waited ten years before having it erected in Wingfield, far from the Londoners who loathed him. Both experiences had made her reflect deeply on apt memorials, and during the last miserable months in Suffolk she had found much satisfaction in imagining her own. It would of course be at Ewelme, despite the willed requests of both Montagu and Suffolk that she be buried at their sides. At the thought of Thomas Montagu, she had a twinge of conscience. His directions for his tomb had called for him to be flanked by both his first wife Isabel and his *dearest* wife Alyce. Though flattered by the distinction, and much as she had loved him, she had long resolved that in death she intended to be true to her deepest self. Ewelme was where she had begun life, and where she desired to spend the rest of her days. Its gently rolling hills and wooded acres, its palace, its church, its almshouses and its school were her heartland, her legacy to future generations.

It would be no good leaving orders for what she wanted to be made after her death – she knew how rarely the wishes of the dying were met in such matters. Wise men and women set sculptors to work on their tombs while they lived, so that it was impossible to ignore their wishes. The most splendid she had ever seen was the monument created in St Mary's, Warwick, for her childhood hero Sir Richard Beauchamp, dubbed by all Europe the Father of Chivalry. In July, when she had been staying at the Suffolks' Manor of the Rose in London, she had asked John Massingham, a London sculptor who had worked on Beauchamp's tomb with his father, to sketch a few options for her own, and to bring them to Ewelme.

Massingham spread out his designs on the long table in the centre of the room. She liked the elaborate canopy. Angels stood at attention along the sides of the tomb, each in a heraldic surcoat that signalled her numerous connections to families of rank. She also liked the loving gaze of the winged spirits who lay curled on each side of her head. The effigy pleased her less. Massingham's sketch showed her in elaborately embroidered robes of state, vividly coloured and bejewelled, and with a headdress and veil like those currently sported at court. Her face was perfectly proportioned, with a high forehead, a small, fat pursed mouth and meekly downcast eyes. It looked nothing like her.

'The canopy and the sides of the tomb chest please me much, Master Massingham,' she said. 'And the small angels by my head. But not the effigy. I want it to have my long jaw and thin cheeks, and to be dressed much more plainly, with my widow's wimple under my coronet. I plan, before I die, to become a vowess.'

Massingham protested. 'Most of my female patrons opt to be portrayed as they were in their prime, my lady. Before the – er – twilight of widowhood descended upon them.'

'For me widowhood has been a dawn, not a twilight,' said Alyce. 'And I would rather that those who held me dear and their descendants were given an honest picture of both what I was and what I became. Make my gown simple, my mantle blue. Make me as I am now. As for jewels, include just one for each of my husbands: the ring that Sir John Phelip gave me on our espousal (on my right hand, as befits a vowess), the coronet which my Lord of Salisbury gave me on our wedding day, and the jewelled armband that my Lord of Suffolk gave me to display the Order of the Garter which the king awarded me in my own right. Oh, and I want the rosary that I inherited from my grandfather looped on my girdle.'

Massingham took out a wax tablet and a stylus and made rapid notes, then looked up.

'If it is to be an accurate portrait, I will need to make some drawings of you, my lady,' he said.

'So be it,' said Alyce. 'You can make them now. I'll lie still as death on my daybed. And I have a new idea. John Golafre of Fyfield's tomb has a *memento mori* cadaver underneath it. It shows him in his shroud, all but naked, raddled and repentant.'

'Like to Archbishop Chichele's tomb in Canterbury?' said Massingham. *'I was a pauper born, then to primate here raised, now I am cut down and served up for worms. Whoever who may be who will pass by, I ask for your remembrance.'*

'Yes. For that is how we meet our maker. But not with worms wriggling from the belly like Chichele. That's overdoing things. So is his inscription. I'd like hopeful images above my cadaver: I want to look upon the Annunciation and have my patron saints, John the Baptist and Mary Magdalene, close by.'

Massingham made more notes.

'And I want work to start on it as soon as possible. There is no need to stint on materials or skilled workmen. Who knows when we will be called to meet our makers?' She crossed herself pensively, and turned to Tamsin.

'Bring us refreshments from the buttery. The oldest malmsey wine that we have, and spiced gingerbread. Lying down for one's effigy requires the finest comforts.' She walked over to her daybed.

Massingham was still at work when Denzil Caerleon returned from Wallingford and strode into Ben's office.

'Ben, the last London barge, the one that lost its rudder at Reading, is at Wallingford Wharf. We need to unload it.'

Ben jumped up from his chair. 'I'll summon some men. How many carts will we need?'

'Four should do it. And half a dozen men.'

By dusk, the last load had been hauled up the hill. Massingham had retreated to work up his drawings, and Alyce stood in the base court to greet the men with Tamsin at her side.

'Supper is laid out for you all in the great hall,' she announced. 'You can wash it down with the new-brewed ale.' A cheer rose from the exhausted men.

'Tamsin, go and tell Mistress Purbeck that the men are ready to eat. Ben, go with her and help her bring in jugs of ale.' Then she turned to Denzil.

'Caerleon, I'm charging you with keeping order. But first a word.' She retreated towards the entrance to the solar until they were out of earshot of the men.

'Denzil, things get worse. Master Massingham was attacked

by the king's men on his way here. They jeered at him and talked of treason at Ewelme.'

He pursed his lips in a silent whistle. 'They must have been the coursers that Wenlock warned you about in his letter.'

She nodded. 'That's what I thought. I hope they don't return. I am planning to go to Oxford on Thursday. I've been invited to the Chancellor of Oxford's farewell feast. I'm going to take the Stonor girls and Tamsin with me, and they will need a man to squire them while they tour the shops. I want you to come.'

His heart sank. 'Doesn't Ben normally accompany you on such trips, my lady?', he said. 'I have much to attend to here.'

'So has Ben, what with the arrival of the barge,' said Alyce, too loyal to voice her suspicions about Ben's feelings for Marlene. 'But I need a trustworthy attendant for the Stonor girls.'

The shadow of an emphasis on 'trustworthy' led Denzil's quick mind to jump to her motive for omitting Ben from the expedition. 'Could it be that Ben been seeing some things – especially one very shapely thing – more often than he ought to?'

Alyce hesitated, then gave a rueful nod.

'I'm not sure, but I suspect he has. Marlene seems curiously elated. Let us hope that out of sight will be out of mind. But, in truth, I'd value your company myself.'

She looked up at him quickly with a tentative little smile, only to draw back like a sea anemone poked with a stick at the sight of the naked misery in his eyes. She gave a step backwards before continuing in a slightly louder, much cooler tone.

'I hope that the expedition will be something you'll find interesting. You've earned a reward after your arduous journey. We'll be visiting Doll's bookshop to see what new treasures he has on offer. I'm sure Master John would like to see you again.'

Cursing his inability to hide his feelings, Denzil managed a grateful smile.

'I thank you, my lady. As I am sure you know, there is nothing I value more highly than the trust you put in me.'

She stared at him. 'I hope it is not misplaced. Now I must away and see how Master Massingham does. He's understandably eager to return to London and the safety of his own studio.'

Denzil looked after her as she left the hall for the solar. Her shoulders were slumped, and she looked profoundly lonely. 'In truth, I'd value your company myself.' She must have been shaken by the attack on Massingham and the threats of the royal soldiers. And he had brought new danger with him. Could word of the Cornishman's presence have leaked out? He decided to go down to the God's House after the meal and see how Trevelyan was.

As he left the palace gatehouse an hour later, a man came out of the shadows and fell into step beside him. Milo of Windsor. Denzil cursed inwardly, but he managed a polite nod. It was important not to raise suspicion.

'Master Caerleon, may I walk with you?' said Milo. 'I have some copying to return to the master of the God's House, and you seem to be going there too.'

'I am,' said Denzil. 'Perhaps I could save you a journey?'

'No, I need to query one or two details with him. What business do you have there?'

Denzil thought quickly. 'I want to ask Farhang about a rash

I've developed. I'm hoping it isn't the start of the same fever that Dick Lawrence is suffering from.'

Milo recoiled, and Denzil thought for a moment that he was going to be rid of him. But though he made a little more distance between them, he recovered himself and padded along beside him. He's like a burr, thought Denzil. Hard to shake off. When they reached the archway leading to the cloister garth of the God's House, Denzil pointed through it.

'That's your quickest way to the master's room. I'm heading over to the infirmary. I expect I'll see you back at the palace for supper.' He nodded and turned left. But when he reached the door of the infirmary, he looked back, and saw that Milo hadn't moved from where he had left him. He waved, motioning again to the archway. Milo waved an acknowledgement and disappeared into the cloister.

Suddenly uneasy, Denzil decided to check that Milo was indeed going to Marton's quarters rather than snooping into the bedesmen's rooms. But when he looked into the cloister he saw to his relief that the door of Vespilan's room was open, and Gerard was seated protectively between the doors to Sybilla's and Trevelyan's cells. He saw the old man smile vacantly at Milo, who raised a hand in salute and walked towards the stairs. Once he had disappeared up them, Gerard looked round, saw Denzil, and beckoned him over.

'I saw the two of you coming from my bedroom window, and after you parted I thought it would be as well to happen to be in the cloister myself. Just in case our friend had any Christian ideas about visiting the sick.'

'How are they?' Denzil asked.

'Farhang says Sir John's wound is healing well. He's hoping that he can be smuggled away to Donnington soon. And

Sybilla has recovered consciousness. Will you tell Lady Alyce? But she isn't to visit yet, lest she catch Lawrence's fever.' He winked conspiratorially.

Denzil breathed a sigh of relief. *Fortune be my friend*, he whispered to himself as he headed for the infirmary. It seemed that they had got away with their leaky plan after all. Neither he nor Vespilan saw the man concealed in the shadows at the top of the stairs. Outside Marton's rooms. Which, having seen Marton disappearing into the church a few minutes earlier, Milo knew full well were empty.

Most of the men who had brought up the baggage from Wallingford had left the hall for their own homes, but Simon Brailles sat on gloomily, swigging beer. Bilton paused beside him, just as he gave a long belch. Ben laughed.

'Where are your manners, Master Secretary? What would our mistress say if she could see you now?'

Simon took another gulp of the heady brew before he answered with unusual anger.

'What would she say if she knew we were risking her heartland? Who knows what that spy of the Harcourts will discover? Or when? He's making himself pleasant to everyone in the household. He even said to Pek that he's a friend of Lancaster at heart. Not that Pek believed him.'

'Don't worry, Brailles. Caerleon and I know what we're doing. Everyone in the palace is loyal to the duchess.'

'But too many of them know what we've been doing while she's been away. I think it's time we confessed to her. She'll know the best course to take.'

Bilton looked thoughtful. 'You may be right. Let's go over

to the infirmary and ask Farhang how Trevelyan is doing. If we can only get him away, we'll be safe.'

'Safer, not safe,' said Simon miserably. 'That weasely little man is making up to the maidservants. And some of them know what's been going on over the last year. Late-night comings and goings in the God's House and the infirmary.'

In the infirmary they found Farhang in his medicine closet, pounding spices in a mortar. He looked up with a smile, then saw their long faces.

'Come for a potion to restore good humour?' he said teasingly.

Bilton shook his head. 'No. To hold a council. Simon thinks we should tell the duchess about Trevelyan and what we've been doing here.'

Farhang was silent. Then he said, 'What does Caerleon think?'

'Of what?' came Denzil's voice from the door.

'Of telling Lady Alyce what's afoot,' said Bilton. 'Brailles thinks we should. He's losing his nerve. Thinks that Milo could uncover proof of what's been going on at any time.'

'That's true enough,' said Caerleon. 'When will Trevelyan be well enough to travel, Farhang?'

'Not for at least three days.'

He saw Ben's face fall. 'What's the matter?'

'Lady Alyce is getting suspicious.'

'It'll be over soon. Milo is snooping around, but he hasn't discovered anything. One of us can escort him to Donnington on Saturday.'

Oxford

Joan Moulton and Monique de Chinon left their rooms in the Mitre Inn and walked along the High Street to St Mary the Virgin, the University's church and the home of its library. They had been summoned to account for Joan's possession of the stolen treatise on the astrolabe. Monique paused to admire some lengths of exceptionally fine soft woollen cloth hanging in the window of a mercery.

'Perhaps it's time you had a new gown,' said Joan. 'That's the blue you used to favour, isn't it? I expect they would make it up for you while we're in the city.'

Monique shook her head. 'I like to see fine fabrics, but my day for wearing them is past. I prefer not to draw attention to myself.' She smiled wryly. 'And it is endlessly amusing, discreetly observing in your shadow. What are you going to say to the chancellor?'

Joan blew out her plump cheeks and let loose a hiss of air. 'Not the truth, for sure. Have you any ideas?'

'It struck me that you might say a chapman approached you with it when you were browsing outside a bookshop in Catte Street. That you have no idea who he was.'

'Suppose they ask me to describe him?'

'I'm sure you can invent something suitably misleading.'

'I can indeed.'

'And if you mention how much you have lost in the

transaction, but that you don't begrudge it in the great cause of learning at Oxford…'

An hour later they were bowed out of St Mary's by a grateful librarian and made their way to John Doll's bookshop. Doll hurried forward.

'Mistress Joan, what a pleasure. Have you resolved the unpleasant business of the stolen book? It was no doubt sold to you by a complete stranger.'

'It was,' said Joan with a broad wink. 'The chancellor George Neville and Bishop Waynflete are only too delighted to have it returned. Especially as I have generously forgone half what I paid for it.'

'I did assure her grace of Suffolk that you would never knowingly have bought a stolen book. But she was as angry as I have ever known her.'

'A pity,' said Joan. 'Wenlock told me she would prove an excellent customer, but that seems unlikely now. She's someone who stays on her high horse far too long. Still, I'm restored to the chancellor's good graces. And his feast tomorrow should prove an excellent opportunity to tempt other purchasers of books. I went to Bruges last month and have brought some wonderful things with me.'

'Bruges,' sighed Doll. 'I envy you such an opportunity. I haven't crossed the narrow sea for two decades. And then I only went from Calais to Rouen. The Duke of Gloucester wanted me to assess the books he had acquired during the wars. I travelled back with chests full of treasures that he wanted the University to have.'

'What became of them?'

'They, and the ones he bequeathed the University after his death, should be in the library in Great St Mary's. But Sir

Anthony Wydeville has a great lust for literature and has I am told "borrowed" a good few. Whether the University will ever see them again I doubt.'

'That's interesting,' said Joan. 'Sir Anthony visited my shop last week. He brought some books he wanted copied, and I noticed that the Gloucester coat of arms was on the frontispiece of two of them. Of course, he asked for his own arms on the copies. When he collects his order I could tactfully mention that you were looking forward to the originals being returned.'

'You'll be lucky to winkle anything out of a Wydeville, I fear.' The tall figure in black had entered the shop so quietly that neither they nor Monique had heard him. Behind him came a heavily built grey-haired man in a clerk's gown.

'My Lord Tiptoft,' exclaimed Doll, with a bow. 'And Dr Hurleigh. You are both welcome. Have you met Mistress Moulton of the Sign of the Mole in Paternoster Row?'

Tiptoft bowed to her, a smile transforming his austere face.

'I know only of her reputation. The chancellor mentioned that you were in Oxford, Mistress Moulton, and that you were bringing some new acquisitions.'

Joan smiled in return. 'That's right. I'd be happy to show them to you. And I sold Sir Anthony one of your own books a few days ago in London. He fell on *Jousts and Triumphs* greedily. We are rebinding it for him. And making another for him to send to the Bastard of Burgundy.'

'A courteous gesture, indeed,' said Tiptoft. 'But it will take more than courtesy to beat such a formidable adversary as Burgundy.'

He paused for a moment, then added with a slightly arch look, 'I believe you are a friend of Sir John Wenlock?'

Joan dreaded to think what the king's notorious spymaster knew of her romps at Someries, but managed to reply blithely.

'Yes – he is, like you, a great lover of books. I am rebinding an alchemical treatise by Paracelsus for him, decorated on its frontispiece with that curious charge of his of three Moors' heads. He says it's inherited from a crusading ancestor.'

'And what of the Dowager Duchess of Suffolk?'

Joan hesitated. 'I met her briefly on Monday, and I'm hoping to get to know her better tomorrow. She is coming to Oxford again for George Neville's feast. I've brought an exceptionally fine copy of Frederick II's *Ars Venandi cum Avibus* which Lord Wenlock thought would appeal to her.'

'It certainly will. She's a fine huntress herself, with some splendid hawks in her mews,' said Doll. 'Trained by herself, too.'

Tiptoft was silent for a beat, then said 'Mistress Moulton, I'd be grateful if you could sound out Lady Alyce as to her intentions.'

'Intentions? Of what sort?'

'In especial, whether she intends to remarry.'

Joan was flabbergasted. Was Tiptoft planning to make a bid for Alyce's hand? She thought quickly. Though they shared a scholarly passion for literature, he was twenty years younger than the duchess, and in need of an heir. And from what Wenlock had said, marriage was the last thing that Alyce had in mind. Nor was there any prospect at all of Alyce confiding such intimacies to her. Given that unpleasant scene on Monday, she'd be lucky to get a chance of offering her the *Ars Venandi*. She opened her mouth to prevaricate politely, but Tiptoft raised his hand.

'I can see from your mazed look that you have misunderstood

me. My interest is not personal. It stems from something the queen was saying to the king when I was last at Windsor. If I was in a position to do so, I would strongly advise her to protect herself from a pre-emptive command to marry by becoming a vowess.'

Joan was relieved. 'My apologies, Sir John. I see that you spoke as a disinterested friend. If I get a chance to suggest it, I will certainly do so.'

She watched as Tiptoft left the shop, then turned to Monique.

'There goes the most unreadable lord of my acquaintance. But Wenlock will be reassured that he does not seem to ill-wish the duchess.'

'When I knew him at court I judged him to be a fair-minded man,' Monique said thoughtfully. 'But he is a watcher and waiter. Hence his shrewdly judged absence on pilgrimage when it came to taking sides in the late wars. He's one to make his own decisions rather than to be governed. But once he has, he is like granite.'

Oxford

Thursday dawned fine and clear, and the dozen riders in the duchess's cavalcade set out for Oxford as the sun rose. They rode through Bensington, and crossed the Thames at Abingdon, where Tamsin's mule cast a shoe. After half an hour's wait at the forge, they made good speed. The road was kept in good repair between there and Oxford, and they were too big a company to be troubled by the notorious brigands who haunted Bagley Wood. Tamsin's heart thrilled as the city's towers and turrets came into sight behind its ancient wall. She hadn't been to Oxford since her parents died.

Soon they were crossing the first of the dozen or more arches that carried the causeway across the marshes to the south gate of the city. The road was crowded with handcarts and wagons. Jem and Hugh went ahead to clear a passage, but, even so, their progress was slow.

'Of course – it's market day,' said Denzil. 'All the country will be in town.'

'I'd forgotten that,' said Alyce, flicking her whip at the flies buzzing around her horse's head. 'We must watch for cutpurses and hookmen. Still, there will be much to amuse the girls.'

The last and longest arch crossed the Thames itself, after which the guards at the south gate bowed them through. St Aldate's, the High Street and the Corn Market were thronged with stalls of all sizes. Shouting their wares, costermongers wheeled barrows piled high with fruit and vegetables. Just as they reached Carfax, the great crossing of the east–west and north–south highways at the centre of the city, bells of all sizes began to peal the hour for nones. Foremost amongst them was the single deep note of St Mary the Virgin, in the High Street.

The Balliol College guest house was just inside the north wall of the city, a hundred yards beyond Carfax. Once a tavern, it had a courtyard and stables behind it. An outside staircase and a covered gallery gave access to the first-floor rooms that looked over the courtyard.

'Your grace – you are most welcome,' said a burly man, who stepped forward to take the bridle of Larkspur as she dismounted. 'I'm Alan Jerrid, the custodian. How was your journey?'

'Easy going, happily,' said Alyce, shaking her cloak into place and loosening the long scarf that she had wrapped around her hat while riding.

'We'd have been here earlier if Tamsin's miserable nag hadn't cast a shoe,' said Marlene. 'We left at dawn, but we had to wait in Abingdon until the smith got his fire hot enough to shape another one.'

'Well, you're safely arrived, that's what matters,' said Jerrid. 'What's your pleasure now? Warm water to wash in? Something to eat? A rest in your chambers?'

'I need to recruit myself, then I will go to vespers in Balliol,' said Alyce.

'Can we go to the shops?' begged Marlene. 'I saw some beautiful woollens being sold in North Street. Eloise and I both need warmer dresses with winter on the way.'

'Did you see the ribbons and laces on the stall just past the Carfax crossroad?' said Eloise. 'And the shoemaker's shop?'

'Don't you want to eat?' asked Alyce.

'We can buy food from the stalls,' said Marlene. 'There was a stall selling pancakes by the Carfax conduit, and I could smell spiced fritters cooking somewhere.

'Well, if Master Caerleon is happy to squire you, you can wander about for an hour or two.' She looked questioningly at Denzil, who rolled his eyeballs, but gave a nod of assent.

'But get your things unpacked first, and mind that you are back here by four o'clock. I will go to Balliol for vespers at three, and I want to see you all safely back in the guest house before I leave for the feast.'

Giggling excitedly, the girls disappeared up to their chamber. Alyce noticed that Tamsin looked longingly after them.

'What about you, Tamsin? I can manage without you. Denzil, can you manage all three of them?'

His mouth twisted sardonically. 'In for a penny, in for a pound,' he said, with a mock sigh. Tamsin's face lit up, and she followed the Stonor girls upstairs, lugging as many bags as she could manage.

Half an hour later, Tamsin was trailing behind Marlene and Eloise, who had linked their arms into Denzil's as he led them along Oxford High Street. When they came to a bakery he bought them each a crisply cased meat pasty, fragrant with saffron and mace. He elbowed a vagrant off a bench beside the great conduit that dominated the crossing of the High Street and Corn Market, and they sat and munched in companionable silence, dazed by the busy whirl around them. As soon as they had finished, the Stonor girls set off down the High Street towards a promising-looking table outside a mercery. Tamsin followed them. It was piled high with bales of gaily dyed cloths.

Marlene stalked inside and headed for the silks stacked under the watchful eye of the shop's owner. She pulled out a length of azure blue sarcenet and held it up to her face.

'What do you think, Eloise?' she asked her sister.

''It matches your eyes marvellously. With a cream bodice, edged with that wide riband you're embroidering, you'd be the equal of any court lady.'

'I think I'll buy it. She turned to Denzil, who was leaning in the entrance to the shop reading a small battered book.

'Denzil, can you deal for me? Lady Alyce will pay you back. I'll need ten yards.'

Tamsin saw him give a sigh and push the book into a pocket in his doublet. He turned to the shop's owner, a middle-aged woman who was examining the cut of their clothes and shrewdly assessing the profit she could extract from them. Soon he and she were in hot dispute as to the value of the cloth, but it was not long before she shrugged her shoulders in defeat, got out her long steel shears and cut off the dress length. Next it was Eloise's turn to choose. She found a fine dark red wool that contrasted well with her dark hair. Tamsin looked longingly at the materials, but as she had no money of her own wandered to a small stall opposite the shop's entrance. It was hung with prettily carved animals, intended for children no doubt. She examined a hunched little mouse nibbling at a nut and thought how much Wat would love it.

Denzil came over to her. 'What about you, Tamsin? No dress fabric? Is that mousekin more to your taste?'

'I love the way its maker has carved its tiny paws,' she said, turning it up to show him. 'He must have watched mice close up to know just how their little claws look when they are clutching a nut. But I can't afford to buy anything. I have 'no money.' Denzil looked down at her, an amused look on his lean, hard face.

'You'll be earning money soon enough now that you are in her grace's service. Let me stand you treat.'

Tempted, Tamsin stroked the mouse again. How Wat would love it. But then she shook her head.

Earn what you spend and never lend was what my father taught me. Thank you, Master Caerleon, but I'll wait until I've got money of my own.'

He looked at her, eyes narrowed, assessing. 'You'll go far if you keep such resolves, child, and don't let anyone persuade you from your own truth.' Then he offered his arms to Eloise and Marlene again, and they dragged him off to the next stall.

Tamsin wandered after them for a while, but when she found herself in front of a bookseller's window she came to a stop. There was a table in front of it piled high with shabbily bound books and scraps of parchment and paper. She began turning them over and opening them up. They must be students' exemplars, copies made for scholars to con for their examinations, and then brought here to be resold. After a few minutes, a balding, bespectacled man in a dusty fustian doublet came out of the shop and spoke to a groom who was lounging against a wall, while the three horses he had charge of drank thirstily from a nearby trough.

'Piers, your mistress said to say that she wouldn't be much longer, but that you'd have time to purchase a pie to eat while you're waiting.' The groom touched his forehead, and walked over to a nearby pie stall.

The bookseller turned to Tamsin. 'Good day, little mistress. Are you looking for something to line your shoes with or are you a scholar in disguise?'

She coloured, then stammered a reply. 'I love reading. But I was just looking… I'm not able to buy anything.'

The old man smiled reassuringly at her. He was going to say something when he looked over her shoulder and started in surprise.

'Denzil Caerleon, by all that's wonderful. What brings you back to Oxford? I thought you had gone to Suffolk with her grace long since.'

Denzil, who had left the Stonor girls by a glover's stall, bowed.

'Master Doll, good day to you. I want to thank you for recommending me to Lady Alyce. She's brought me back to Ewelme with her now that she has decided to quit Suffolk. She is in Oxford for the Balliol feast George Neville is giving later today.'

'As am I – we talked of it when I saw her on Monday.' He turned to Tamsin.

'Pardon me, my child, Master Caerleon worked for me once.'

'No need to ask pardon,' said Tamsin. 'I came to Oxford with him.'

The old bookseller raised his eyebrows. 'So do you too serve the duchess?' Tamsin nodded shyly.

'And, it seems, you share her love of books. Would you like to come inside? I'm busy with a customer, but you could look around the shop.' Nothing would have pleased Tamsin more, but just then Marlene advanced on them, and pulled at her arm.

'Oh no you don't, Tamsin. We've only an hour before we're due back at the lodgings. We're not going to waste time in a dreary old bookshop. Denzil, you said that we could go to that haberdasher's we saw as we rode in. Eloise needs trimmings for her veil. And the glover. I want new gloves.'

Denzil grimaced. Tamsin could see that he was running out of patience with nannying wenches round town. One less might seem a good idea to him. She plucked up her courage.

'Could I stay here, Master Caerleon? It isn't far to the Balliol guest house. I remember the way and I could easily find it on my own.'

Denzil was shaking his head to refuse, when John Doll interrupted.

'She'll be safe with me, Denzil. In fact, I even have a duenna for her. Joan Moulton, a London bookseller, is inside, and she said she is going to vespers at Balliol when she leaves. She could take the lass to your lodgings.'

'Joan Moulton of Paternoster Row? I'm not sure what kind of duenna she will make for little Tamsin. Is she as exuberant as ever?'

'More so, if it were possible.' He gave Denzil a wink. 'She is much seen in the company of Lord Wenlock. They too are going to the Balliol feast. She has brought down some samples of the books that her London workshop has been making. The most unusual marginalia and decorations you can imagine, inspired by exemplars from Italy brought back by the Earl of Worcester.'

'Then keep Tamsin by all means. Meeting Mistress Moulton is an experience a book-loving girl shouldn't miss. In fact, that would work well. Simon Brailles asked me to get a pint of oak-gall ink from you. Tamsin could bring it with her.' Denzil turned away to catch up Marlene and Eloise, who were already heading for St Aldate's.

Tamsin followed John Doll into the low-ceilinged bookshop.

Wide sloping shelves lined its walls. A young man in a crumpled scholar's gown was leaning against the window frame, deeply absorbed in a small volume. He looked up as they came in, blushed and closed the book hastily. John Doll chuckled.

'Are you still salivating over that Ovid, Master William? Well may you redden – and not just because of this young lady. You'll have read the whole of it without paying me a penny by next week.'

The young man looked abashed.

'I'm sorry, sir. It's true that I haven't any money at the minute. But I'm hoping to get some from home before long. My mother has sent me a letter to say that their friend and patron the Duchess of Suffolk is coming to Oxford, and they are sending my next month's allowance with her.'

'Then you must be William Stonor,' said Tamsin. 'Your sisters were lately outside the shop – they have gone to the haberdasher's with Master Caerleon. I am due to meet them and Lady Alyce at the Balliol lodgings.'

William looked at her with new interest. 'So who are you? I don't remember seeing you at Ewelme Palace.'

'I'm Tamsin Ormesby. I used to work in the God's House. I'm only lately of the duchess's household. In truth, I may not be part of it for long. It's just that her usual maid was taken ill, so I am taking her place for a while.'

'Ormesby? Not the little sister of Dickon Ormesby? Who rode north with Warwick four years back and never returned? Dickon and I were good friends. But what does that dry old stick Simon Brailles think of you being in the household? Not pleased, I'll be bound. His father and yours were ever at loggerheads, and Dickon used to lead him a merry dance when he was a schoolboy.'

'No, not pleased. To him Ormesbys are t–troublemaking r–roisterers unfitted for a g–gentle household.' She imitated Simon's slight stutter and they smiled at each other.

'What's this? Lovebirds?' A trumpet of a voice burst in on their ears, and like a ship in full sail Joan Moulton swept into the showroom from the bindery, followed by a tall thin woman dressed in grey with a stiff, high wimple.

'Don't mind us; don't let us interrupt true love, even if its course rarely runs smooth.' With a knowing wink, she slapped Will on his buttocks, tweaked Tamsin's ear and disappeared into the bookseller's inner sanctum. Suffused with embarrassment, Tamsin could hardly bear to meet Will's eyes, but when she did she saw only laughter in them. Joan's strident voice could still be heard, even though she had closed the door behind her.

'John, I have asked your binder to package up all the books that I agreed to buy, and have a porter take them to the Mitre. I am particularly pleased with that splendidly illustrated *Pilgrimage of the Life of Man*. I've already thought of a discreet customer. I have left you the ones of mine that you chose in exchange. I think we are about even, but we can tally up precisely later. Monique, make a note. I must go to Balliol now to greet Georgie-Porgie.'

The door swung open again, and she and her attendant swept past them and out of the shop, sudden as a whirlwind. A few minutes later, John Doll came out of his office, smiling.

'There's a fine example of a woman who knows her own mind. I wish all my customers were as decided and discriminating.' Then he noticed Tamsin and frowned.

'I quite forgot. I told Denzil that she would escort you back to Balliol. Run and call her back, William.'

'There's no need for that,' said William quickly. 'I'll escort Tamsin. I want to greet my sisters and pay my respects to my godmother. But not yet; she's hardly had time to read anything.' He turned to Tamsin.

'Now, Tamsin, what are your likings? Not Latin or Greek, I suspect. How about a book of legends. Or a romance of Arthur?'

Tamsin looked gratefully at him. 'A romance of Arthur, if there is such a thing. But in English, please. I can't read French.'

'Most of them are in French,' said William. 'But there's a rhyming one in English, isn't there, Master Doll?'

'I have something better,' said the bookseller. 'An English telling by a Warwickshire knight called Malory. It's very little known as yet, because it's unfinished. Sir Thomas is still working on it, but he brought me the first part to be copied a few months ago. He was on his way to Newbold Revel to celebrate the birth of his grandson. The boy's to be named Nicholas, which Sir Thomas only half likes. He'd have preferred Lancelot, no doubt. He lives in London now, but his wife still rules him with a rod of iron. I've got to have it finished before he returns next week, so you can't take it away. But you can curl up on a chair here and read it until William is ready to go.'

Tamsin's eyes shone. 'I'd love that.'

Doll smiled indulgently, and disappeared into his cabinet, emerging with a sheaf of handwritten pages tied into a roll with a lace of leather.

'Don't muddle the pages,' he warned her. 'Sir Thomas hasn't numbered them yet. He's forever adding new tales, so he leaves that until last. Now, I must get that ink ready for Master Brailles.'

Tamsin settled down into the padded chair Doll waved her towards. It was tucked at the end of a narrow space between two high bookcases and lit by a small square window above it. She carefully untied the lace around the roll and began to read. The writing was spidery and uneven, and there were many crossings out and insertions. But she could make it out easily enough.

> It befell in the days of Uther Pendragon, when he was king of all England, and so reigned, that there was a mighty duke in Cornwall that held war against him long time. And the duke was called the Duke of Tintagel. And so by means King Uther sent for this duke, charging him to bring his wife with him, for she was called a fair lady, and a passing wise, and her name was called Igraine.

Soon she was lost to the world.

Escorted by two grooms, Alyce walked the short distance from the guest lodgings to Balliol College itself, enjoying the bustle of the market. As she waited outside its massive oak doors while one of the porters knocked for admission, a company of horsemen and women came briskly up the street, kicking up foul water from the many puddles. Alyce groaned as muddy splashes fouled her deep-red velvet cloak. She looked indignantly up at the riders, but the great doors had swung open, and they had passed her, led by a flamboyantly dressed woman with a wide riding hat tied down with a green scarf. Her companion was very thin, dressed all in grey, with a gauzy veil. Alyce frowned, recognising them from her visit to Doll's bookshop on Monday. It seemed that Joan Moulton and her companion were also visiting the college. Perhaps even going to the feast. No, surely a London tradeswoman would not be set among Oxford's most eminent citizens.

Then, to her horror, she saw Bishop Neville himself descending the short flight of steps from the porch of his lodging, his arms extended in welcome. He wrapped them around the substantial form of the bookseller, and planted a smacking kiss on her cheek. She planted one in turn on his great jowl, and they mounted the steps together, talking eagerly. Neither had seen her, and she was tempted to turn on her heels and slip away. But before she could, there was a gentle touch on her arm. She turned to see the reticent woman who had been in Doll's shop with Joan on Monday. She had lifted her veil, revealing an anxious, pockmarked face.

'My apologies, Princess Alyce,' she said with a deep curtsey. 'My mistress was too intent on her purpose to see you. She and the chancellor are old friends.'

'That much was obvious,' said Alyce tartly. Then she stared at the woman and blinked.

'You look familiar. What did you say your name was?'

'I am Monique de Chinon. We last met twenty years ago at the court of Queen Margaret in Greenwich Palace.'

Alyce peered at her. She remembered the breathtakingly lovely Monique de Chinon, in whose honour the court poet Sir Richard Roos has composed countless elegant couplets. How changed she was.

'I remember now. You were the most beautiful of Margaret's ladies.'

'Until I caught the pox. I would have died of it had Mistress Moulton not taken me to the hospital at Syon Abbey. She had come to court to fetch the body of her husband, who had died of it.'

'That was good of her,' said Alyce.

'The more so since her husband and I were lovers. I owe her everything. She is vulgar and brusque and a ruthless businesswoman. But she has a heart of gold. I fear that on Monday she was – *comment dire bouleversée* – much upset by your accusation. She is quick to anger.'

'Yet she is happy to buy stolen goods? Has she appeared before the Chancellor's Court yet?'

'Yes, yesterday morning. She explained that she had bought the treatise from a travelling chapman, and was shocked to hear that it had been stolen from the University's collection.'

'Which the chancellor of course accepted without question. Being such an old friend,' said Alyce sarcastically.

'Their friendship may well have encouraged him into a benign interpretation of the incident,' Monique answered neutrally, but with a wry twist to her lips. 'But the book is restored. Your servant, Princess.'

She gave Alyce an elegant curtsey, and turned back into the college. Alyce stood still for a moment. She certainly didn't want to go to vespers in Balliol if Joan was going to be there too. Although what Monique had said made her realise that there might be more to the buxom bookseller than she had thought, she still bristled with anger at her insolence. She turned to her grooms.

'I've changed my mind about attending vespers. I feel too weary after our journey. Be so kind as to escort me back to our lodgings.'

Tamsin felt a hand shake her shoulder, interrupting her reading. She looked up, frowning fiercely, then saw that it was William, and gasped an apology. He laughed.

'What have I done to deserve such a glare? Come on, Tamsin, we must be going.'

'Already? Can't I finish it?'

'You were so deep in it that I left you as long as I could. You've been reading for almost an hour. But I've got a class in half an hour, and I must greet Lady Alyce and my sisters and then get to it. We'll have to hurry as it is. Tie it up and give it back to Master Doll. Maybe you'll find time to go on with it later. How long are you staying in Oxford?'

'Not long – we'll be going back to Ewelme tomorrow. But I know Lady Alyce is planning to visit Master Doll. She has some books that she wants rebound. Perhaps I could read some more then.'

As she followed William through a maze of back alleys and snickets, Tamsin's head was spinning with the story she'd been reading. Merlin struck her as a little like Denzil Caerleon, all mysterious hints and disappearances. The Harcourt brothers were like the bullying northern kings whom Arthur successfully defeated, and the devious Marlene reminded her of the ruthlessly persistent Morgause, determined to seduce Arthur. Who to her mind bore a close resemblance to William Stonor.

When they reached the Balliol lodgings, Eloise ran up to her. 'Where have you been, Tamsin? Lady Alyce has been asking for you.'

Suddenly she noticed William, and her face lit up. She flung her arms around him. 'Will, by all that's wonderful. I was hoping we'd see you. Mother sent all manner of treats for you. Come and greet Marlene and Lady Alyce.'

Taking his hand, she dragged him away towards the double doors that led into the great chamber. Tamsin trailed after them, hoping that she was not in disgrace. She needn't have worried. Any annoyance at her tardiness was forgotten in the general delight at William's appearance.

'How you've grown,' said Alyce, shaking her head in amazement, as he rose from a deep bow. 'Why, I have to raise my eyes to you now. Are you enjoying your studies?'

'Greatly, godmother. I can't thank you enough for persuading my father to let me stay in Oxford for an extra year before I go to an Inn of Court in London.'

Alyce turned to Tamsin. 'Where have you been, chit? Not out on the streets on your own, I trust?'

Tamsin began to stammer an answer, but William interrupted.

'No, she's been in John Doll's shop, lost in legends of Arthur. I walked back with her so that I could greet you.'

Alyce frowned. 'Denzil said he had left her in the care of a respectable tradeswoman, who John Doll had said would bring her back here. What happened to her?'

'That was Mistress Moulton, a London bookseller. She whisked past us and out of the shop before Master Doll could ask her to take Tamsin with her.'

Alyce shook her head wearily. 'Mistress Moulton. Typically high-handed and thoughtless behaviour from what I experienced of her on Monday. It was fortunate that you were in the shop too, William. Tamsin, have a care. Don't forget that you are on trial only. Now go and lay out my clothes for tonight.'

After Tamsin had hurried away, Alyce turned again to William.

'What legend of Arthur was she immersed in?'

'A new telling that Master Doll was copying for one Thomas Malory. He's a Warwickshire knight, apparently.'

Alyce blinked in surprise. 'Malory? Abroad in England? I thought him in France.'

'Not now, it appears. Master Doll said he lives in London. A few months ago he passed through Oxford on his way to Newbold Revel to celebrate the birth of his grandson. He left his telling with Doll to be copied. Do you know him then?'

Alyce's memory flashed back twenty years to a war-hardened soldier knight in his forties who had arrived at Ewelme Palace as escort to a scared little girl.

'We met briefly twice. He brought Jack's first wife-to-be to Ewelme in 1446. Anne Beauchamp was only two, but was the sole heiress of the vast estates of Henry, Duke of Warwick. He died untimely, aged only twenty-one. Malory had been high in the young duke's favour and was devastated by his death. He admired my books greatly and asked if I had any that concerned King Arthur. Said he had a vision of penning an English version that would inspire a new age of chivalry.'

'When did you meet again?'

'Little Anne died three years ago.' William saw tears well up in her eyes. 'I'd become very fond of her. Malory came for her funeral in Reading Abbey and spent a few days here, copying a rhyming Death of Arthur I'd inherited from my grandfather. So he's still writing tales about him?'

'So Master Doll said. Apparently he acquired a notable library of the legends while he served with the Duke of Bedford in France.'

'And his telling is good enough to keep little Tamsin transfixed. How interesting. I'd like to look at it myself.'

A sonorous bell began to toll, and William started. 'Time for my class. I must go back to my college. Will I see you tomorrow, godmother?'

'Yes. Can you come to Doll's shop at noon?'

'Willingly.' He bowed over the hand she extended to him, then pulled on his scholar's cap and hurried away.'

Ewelme

Ben Bilton gently shook the arm of the sleeping man lying in Dick Lawrence's bed.

'Are you feeling strong enough to get up, sir?'

Trevelyan opened his eyes. For the first time since he had crashed to the deck of his ship and lost consciousness, he could think clearly. He remembered being slung into a pinnace, which must have taken him away from the unequal battle off Dogger Bank between his two Cornish ships and the king's Channel squadron. And he remembered waking up on a barge and suffering agony as a wound in his leg was examined and dressed by a dark-haired man with strong but gentle hands. Then nothing until now. He looked up at the anxious young man.

'Who are you? How did I get here? I remember a barge...' his voice tailed away, and he closed his eyes again.

'I'm Ben Bilton. Steward to the Dowager Duchess of Suffolk. The man on the barge was Denzil Caerleon, her man of business. You hailed him when you went alongside her ship off Yarmouth three weeks ago. Caerleon brought you up the Thames.'

Memories stirred in Trevelyan's fogged brain. 'The barge. It stank of fish. He gave me something to ease the pain in my leg... But how did I get there?'

'You were hit by a crossbow dart. Your sailors got you out of the sea battle and to a Southwark surgeon called John Crophill, who's as loyal as we are to the red rose. Tiptoft's spies were skulking around, so Crophill took you to Three Cranes Wharf, where he found Caerleon transferring the duchess's goods from the Ipswich ships on to barges to take them up the Thames to Ewelme. He gave Caerleon some dressings for your wound and told him to put you in the care of Farhang Amiri, the infirmarian here.'

A slow smile spread across Trevelyan's face. 'Ewelme. Paradise on earth. What does Princess Alyce think of my coming?'

'She doesn't know of it,' said Bilton. 'Caerleon was told there was a price on your head, and we thought it best not to tell her.'

'But surely she is a loyal Lancastrian?'

'That may be so, but she has powerful enemies eager to accuse her of treason. Rumours have leaked out about the escape route we've been providing for fugitive Lancastrians. Lady Alyce knows nothing about it; she's been at Wingfield for the last two years. But her enemies heard the rumours, and forced a royal spy on her. It's best that she knows nothing about your being here. As soon as you're well enough, we'll smuggle you away.'

'Where am I now?' asked Trevelyan, looking around at the bare little room.

'You're in a bedesman's cell in the God's House, the foundation for the needy that Princess Alyce and the late duke established here. It belongs to one Dick Lawrence, who's now tucked away in the attic of a Wallingford tavern. Farhang has announced that the old man has an infectious fever, and fear of it is keeping everybody away except Farhang and the God's House matron, Nan Ormesby.'

'You should have left me to my fate.'

'We know how highly she thinks of you. You should have seen her brighten when I passed on the message you gave to Caerleon. *Time Trieth Troth.* So we thought it worth the risk. Once you've recovered a little more, we'll get you away to Donnington. From there we can arrange horses to take you to Southampton, and so to France.'

'I'd prefer Cornwall,' said Trevelyan. 'High time I was back in the warm arms of my wife.'

'Crophill advised against that,' said Bilton. 'Your Cornish manors will be watched.'

Trevelyan frowned. 'I don't like this, Bilton. If I'm discovered, then the duchess will be implicated. The sooner I'm away from here the better. Give me your arm, and we'll see if I'm recovered enough.'

Using Bilton's arm as a prop, Trevelyan hauled himself up to a sitting position, and slowly swung his legs off the bed. Once both his feet were on the ground, he tentatively placed his weight on them, and rose to his feet. The world swam before his eyes, and he sank down again.

'It might be a day or two before I can travel.'

Suddenly the door of the cell was wrenched open. Milo stared in, a leer of satisfaction on his face.

'So this is the sick bedesman, is it? You don't look like a bedesman to me. From what I overheard Caerleon saying to Farhang in the infirmary, you're John Trevelyan. A notorious pirate. But worry not. I'm as sympathetic as you are to the cause of Lancaster, especially if I'm well paid for supporting it. What's it worth for me to keep silent?'

Trevelyan struggled groggily to his feet, still holding on to Ben, who was trying to reach the exultant scrivener. But Milo moved well out of his way.

'Come on, Bilton. I was listening just now. I gather that Princess Alyce knows nothing about your treasonous activities. If you don't want me to tell her when she gets back from Oxford, and have her dismiss the lot of you from her service, you'll need to pay me well.'

Ben thought quickly. All was not lost. Milo clearly had no idea that they all knew he had been planted at Ewelme to spy out treasons by the Harcourts. The man was bluffing, pretending he was just a man on the make, probably planning to profit both from them and from the Harcourts. He raised his hands in a gesture of surrender.

'Alright. How much do you want?'

'How much are you offering?'

Ben looked at Trevelyan, who shrugged, and pointed to the doublet that hung from the back of the door.

'There's a purse in my inner pocket. My share of our prize moneys. Probably forty nobles. It's about what Judas settled for; maybe it will satisfy this churl.'

Milo swiftly reached around the door, grabbed the doublet and went out, slamming the cell shut behind him. They heard the key turn in the lock. Then running footsteps. They stared at each other in consternation. With a curse, Ben began battering on the door of the cell. Then he tried the window, only to find it was rusted shut. He went upstairs and managed to open the one in the bedroom. Leaning out, he started shouting.

It seemed an eternity before the door of the next cell opened, and Sybilla called out in a quavering voice.

'What's going on?'

'We're locked in,' shouted Ben. 'Can you open the door?'

He saw her emerge, a shawl wrapped around her thin shoulders, and totter towards Trevelyan's cell with painful slowness, using the wall as support. But when she reached the door she shook her head.

'There's no key in the keyhole.'

Milo must have taken it with him, Ben realised. He called down to her.

'Can you get Farhang or Nan Ormesby from the infirmary, Sybilla? They'll have spare keys.'

'I'll try,' she said. 'But I'm still very weak. It may take me some time.'

It was another half an hour before they heard running footsteps on the flagstones of the cloister. The lock clicked, and Farhang swung the door open.

'What happened? Who locked you in?'

'Milo. He must have followed me when I came to see how Trevelyan did. He knows who he is and will be taking word to the duchess's enemies for certain, though he pretended that he was acting on his own account.'

Farhang stepped across to Trevelyan's bed, and gave him a swift examination.

'He is not strong enough to ride as far as Donnington. Nor can we risk pursuers catching up a wagon. It'll have to be Swyncombe. The escape route in reverse. You and Pek must take him up in the wood cart. Pile bundles of straw over him. We can rely on Sir Brian to hide him away in the manor's attics. Sybilla collapsed at the infirmary door, I'm afraid. It was much too soon for her to be getting up. Nan has put her to bed and is looking after her. Pray heaven she recovers.'

Oxford

George Neville finished saying grace and beamed complacently. Every significant dignitary in the University and a dozen distinguished visitors to Oxford were seated at the long dais table high above the body of the hall. Their servants and the students were crowded together on long trestle tables. On the dais, snowy damask cloths set off a splendid array of gold plate, some laden with artfully arranged heaps of fruit and nuts, others awaiting the arrival of the fantastical subtleties dreamt up by the college cook, a culinary genius whom Neville had bribed away from the London Company of Mercers to Balliol. Candles in many-armed gold sconces lit up the glittering gold and silver threads that embellished the gorgeous velvets and silks of the diners at high table. They were now subsiding into their seats in a chattering mass.

He looked around, noting that Princess Alyce, whom he had seated on his right, was deep in conversation with the Earl of Worcester. They were talking about his latest translation, Cicero's essay on friendship. Lady Margaret Harcourt was on his left, listening to William Waynflete boasting about his new college buildings. All was just as it should be. Except... He frowned. In front of him were two empty seats, announcing to all and sundry that two guests were absent. The scholars closest to the dais were already nudging each other, and one or two were whispering, despite the injunction that students of the college must remain silent while eating in order to benefit from the wisdom of their betters on the dais. He cursed inwardly. He had taken a chance in seating them there, as he particularly enjoyed their company. He signed to the college steward, who hastened to his side.

'Gregory, has Lord Wenlock arrived in college yet?'

'He arrived this afternoon, your grace. But he went out into the town almost immediately. Shall I ask the porter if he has returned? Perhaps he was fatigued after his journey.' Neville was about to nod when there was a commotion as the double doors at the far end of the hall swung open. Joan Moulton swanned in, splendid in a scarlet velvet gown with a tightly laced bodice that thrust up her thinly-veiled bosom into a sumptuous frame of downy feathers. A gauzy veil floated over the twin peaks of her hennin, under which her hair had been intricately plaited, except for a few artfully arranged curls. Lord Wenlock followed in her wake as she processed the length of the hall, beaming down on the admiring ranks of young scholars. She stepped up to the dais and took the empty place opposite Neville, nodding familiarly to Waynflete and Lord Tiptoft as she sat down. Bowing to George and Alyce, Wenlock took the chair beside her.

'Apologies, Chancellor, Your Grace. Mistress Moulton and I became immersed in examining the unusual books that I had commissioned her to bring from London, and lost track of time.' He winked at George Neville, who gave a deep chuckle.

'Quite understandable, John. I know how engrossing Mistress Moulton's arcane volumes can be. She is a lady of infinite resource and charm.'

Beaming, Joan put her shoulders back to hoist up her breasts even higher.

On her right, Sir Robert Harcourt hopefully extended an

arm. Joan intercepted it skilfully with a raised goblet, and shifted herself out of his reach with a teasing smile. Wenlock greeted his neighbour, Lady Catherine Stapleton, but his attention soon turned back to Joan.

They were, thought Alyce, like bees greedily swarming around a queen. Only Tiptoft remained aloof, watchful, faintly amused. When she saw that Wenlock's right hand was out of sight under the table, and that Joan's left side had shuffled closer to him, her anger mounted. Crisp as frost, her voice cut through the jests and laughter.

'Mistress Moulton, I hope you have settled the matter of the stolen book?'

Waynflete looked put out. He had not wanted the theft to be talked of. Putting a finger to his lips, he leant across Lady Margaret, and whispered.

'Indeed she has, Lady Alyce. She explained to the Chancellor's Court that she acquired it from an itinerant chapman in Catte Street. It was most fortunate for the University that she offered it to you. We have it safe under lock and key now, and I assure you and...' – he looked past her to Lord Tiptoft – 'any other prospective donors that we will set up a better policed system for lending books out.'

Alyce opened her mouth to object, but Waynflete was determined to justify the Court's action.

'Perhaps you do not know how eminent and trustworthy Joan Moulton is. She's the widow of Thomas Moulton, the founder of the famous Paternoster Row bookshop, at the Sign of the Mole. Her knowledge of the book trade is legendary. She is lately returned from Bruges and has brought back some fine examples of Flemish printing. You might be interested in adding some to your collection.'

'It is high time that we began printing here in England,' said Joan, after nodding to Alyce with a smile that was an infuriating mix of innocence and triumph. 'We are lagging behind in what is a most lucrative trade. The absurd restrictions which the Company of Scriveners and the Stationers' Guild have put on importing print books, and the laws against presses in England, mean that foreign competitors are far ahead of us. I met an interesting merchant venturer called Caxton in Bruges who is eager to diversify into printing and to open a press in London.'

Tiptoft interrupted her. 'Printing brings with it all manner of abuses. Particularly at times of disaffection and rebellion.'

Joan flashed him a brilliant smile. 'My Lord of Worcester, I would have thought a scholar like you would be an advocate of the new learning, not a philistine. And surely these days the whole country is loyal to the new king. After all, his marriage to a notable Lancastrian's widow has done much to unite the two causes.'

'Would that it had,' said Tiptoft. 'In fact, the servants of Margaret of Anjou are scattering around subversive tracts printed in Lorraine, both in London and in the north country. My agents apprehended a chapman in Lincoln only last week. Before he died during – er – questioning, he told them that he was only one of a small army of Lancastrian sympathisers. They nail their accursed lies up on church doors faster than we can tear them down. I wish we could discover how the tracts are getting into the country.'

Servants began to bring in dishes heaped high with delicacies. Scarlet lobsters were wreathed in samphire; scallops peeped enticingly orange and white out of the shells in which they had been steamed. They must have been brought up the

Thames like her sturgeon, thought Alyce. As one elaborate course after another was carried in with ever increasing pomp, the early polite conversings swelled to jovial uproar. She replied gratefully to Lord Wenlock's intelligent questions about the running of her school, all the while enviously noting the way in which Joan's prattle seemed to fascinate everyone in earshot, her easy manner with men far above her in rank. Envy shifted to anger when she saw her expertly extract the plump flesh from inside her lobster claw, tap Wenlock's shoulder, and pop it whole into his mouth, distracting him from what he had been about to say to her. Aware that it was absurd to feel so wrong-footed by this pushy nobody, she turned back to Tiptoft, but found him deep in conversation with Lady Catherine Stapleton. She was about to turn to Waynflete when she felt a hesitant tug on her sleeve. It was one of the serving boys.

'My Lady of Suffolk,' he stuttered nervously. 'There is a messenger come for you.'

She looked past him to the door of the great hall. Tamsin stood there, her eyes huge with anxiety. Behind her stood Jem. What could they be about? Some disaster must have arisen to bring them to intrude on the feast. She turned to George Neville.

'A thousand pardons, your grace. I fear that something is seriously amiss with my company. I must needs excuse myself.'

Neville beamed and jovially waved her away, only half-hearing what she said. He was befogged by the heady wine that had accompanied the latest subtlety, a huge schooner of spun sugar crewed by live mice tied to its spars with tiny harnesses. She doubted if he would remember anything about her abrupt exit on the morrow. Distracted by Joan's sallies of wit, few noticed her leave. But Tiptoft's ice-blue eyes followed her thoughtfully as she disappeared behind the arras that lined the entire hall, and made her way, sheltered from sight, to the open door.

'What on earth is the matter, child?' she said crossly to Tamsin.

'It's Marlene, my lady. She has disappeared. Eloise has been drugged.'

'Why didn't Denzil come to get me?'

'We don't know where Denzil is. Jem and Hugh escorted me.'

If she had been enjoying herself more, Alyce might have sent Tamsin away with a flea in her ear. Marlene was a giddy young fool, who deserved whatever comeuppance she might be getting. But the feast was all but over, and she owed a duty of care to the daughter of her old friends. Cursing Denzil for not keeping a better guard on the girl, she followed Tamsin out into the night.

Twilight filled Oxford's streets with shadows, and pitch-soaked torches blazed on each side of the great oak double doors that closed the colleges for the night. A few tardy students scuttled towards their lodgings, and a handful of wayfarers slumped on the benches around Carfax.

When they reached the Balliol guest house Alan Jerrid hurried forward.

'Thank you for coming, my lady. We've hunted everywhere for the girl. Her sister is still dead to the world. We found a cup beside her bed with a posset laced with henbane.'

'Could anyone have entered the lodgings? Or do you think Marlene slipped out on her own?'

'The postern gate was unbarred from the inside,' said Jerrid.

'So she went of her own accord. And until Eloise recovers, we have no idea why.'

'And Caerleon?' asked Alyce.

Tamsin looked embarrassed. 'We can't find him. He seems to have disappeared as well.'

Alyce suddenly recalled Marlene's air of suppressed excitement when she had waved the three girls goodbye. Was it Denzil, not Ben, she had been flirting with? But surely he was not fool enough to meddle with the Stonors' daughter?

Just then, a sleepy-eyed Eloise staggered out into the courtyard. 'Where's Marlene?' she asked. 'She can't have gone without me. She promised...'

'Promised what?' demanded Alyce.

'That I could be her maid of honour.'

'Maid of honour? Who did she plan to marry?'

'Denzil Caerleon. She's expecting his baby.'

Alyce felt as if the bottom had dropped out of her world. Her most trusted man of business had betrayed her. And she had failed in her duty of care towards her oldest friends' daughter.

'Do you know where they have gone?'

'To Stanton Harcourt. Marlene said that Sir Robert knew all about it. He's going to give them shelter and make things right with our parents. She said that Denzil would be seen as a fine match if he had a good position in Sir Robert's household.'

Shock on shock. Caerleon retained by her greatest enemy. Alyce had never felt more alone.

Ewelme

The journey back to Ewelme next morning was a sober one. All thoughts of an enjoyable day among John Doll's books were forgotten. Jem had been sent ahead to alert the palace to their return, and Tamsin and Eloise rode in silence behind Alyce.

Her thoughts were a tangle of dead ends. She felt profoundly lonely. Waynflete had offered scant comfort, and she hadn't had time to consult Sir John Wenlock – who had anyway seemed entirely engrossed with that vulgar London bookseller. She recalled with distaste how confident and full of herself Joan Moulton had been. And how blooming with sexuality. How brief her own fulfilment as a woman had been – the few years, much interrupted by war, of her marriage to Thomas Montagu, and a decade later her brief affair with Charles of Orléans, the truest meeting of minds she had known. Now she could only live vicariously: smoothing the path of her godchildren, giving Tamsin a chance of winning a place in the world suited to her talents, and, she had thought, finding suitable husbands for the Stonor girls. And now Marlene had eloped with Caerleon. She shuddered at the prospect of telling Thomas and Jeanne.

They clattered over the palace drawbridge into its comfortingly familiar courtyard. Leo raced to greet them, wagging his tail ecstatically. She petted him as grooms bustled out of the stables to take their horses. Then she glanced up to Milo's habitual lookout bench in the guest lodgings gallery. It was empty.

'Has Harcourt's nasty little spy given up his scrutiny of our affairs?' she asked Martha Purbeck, who had come out of the buttery to greet them.

'I don't know, my lady. He went to Wallingford yesterday for some reason of his own. Just as well really. Leo has taken against him so much that he has to be tied up when Milo is around.'

Alyce gave a thin smile. 'They say that dogs know a rascal when they see one. Well, he needn't be tied up any more. I'll keep him by me.' She fondled Leo's sleek head.

'But there is good news,' Martha continued. 'Sybilla had a brief relapse, but she is now much better. I know she would dearly love to talk to you.'

Alyce breathed a sigh of relief. Two nagging worries removed for a while at least. 'I'll go over to the God's House as soon as I can. But, first, Jem will have told you about Marlene's elopement with Caerleon. Where is Bilton? I'm going to send him to Stonor Park to tell Thomas and Jeanne what has happened and to ask them to ride to Ewelme as soon as they can. We need to make a plan to avoid scandal.'

'Ben and Joseph Pek went to Swyncombe with a cart this morning soon after Jem arrived,' said Martha. 'They were planning to cut and collect wood. They aren't back yet.'

'Then Hugh will have to go. Better, really, as he knows all about what happened.'

She looked over at Eloise, who had collapsed weeping on a bench against the courtyard wall. Tamsin was trying to comfort her with whispered reassurances.

'Tamsin, take Eloise up to her room, then find Ella, and tell her to ride with Eloise and two grooms to Stonor. She needs to be with her parents. Then go and fetch the things that I'd put aside as comforts for Sybilla. We're going over to the God's House to see her.'

Watching as Tamsin persuaded Eloise to rise to her feet and go into the palace, she reflected on how well the girl was coping with her new position. 'She's a thoughtful little thing with a real love of books,' young William Stonor had said after he'd brought her back from Doll's. And Denzil had laughingly related her refusal to allow him to buy a little wooden mouse. Denzil. Her stomach churned.

Comfortably settled in a cushioned chair by the window of her cell, Sybilla gave a wave of welcome to Alyce and Tamsin as she saw them enter the cloister. She made an attempt to rise as they came in, but Alyce waved her back down, and knelt at her side.

'Sybilla. It is so good to see you recovered. I've brought you some things to make your cell better suited to you.' She turned to Tamsin.

'Undo the bundle, child.'

Sybilla shook her head at the sight of the linen sheets and the goose-feather quilt.

'They are too fine for a bedeswoman, Lady Alyce.'

'But not for my most faithful servant and oldest friend,' said the duchess. 'Take them upstairs, Tamsin.'

Then she unwrapped the folding shrine to St Botolph and handed it to her.

'Remember this? It was my mother's. I know she would love to know that it was now yours.'

Sybilla's face, still pale from her collapse, flushed with emotion. She held it, murmuring a prayer. Then she turned to her mistress.

'I shall treasure it. As I do all my long years with the Chaucer family. Your mother was rightly proud of you. Though she never dreamt of the adversities you have had to overcome.'

Alyce felt tears rising to her eyes. 'I couldn't have done so without your wise advice, Sybilla. I owe you more than words can say. As you well know.' She moved the fireside chair over, and sat down beside her.

'Are you strong enough to answer some questions?'

Sybilla gave a cautious nod.

'Have you any memory of how you came to be bitten by the vipers?'

'None at all, my lady. Farhang has told me that someone must have deliberately put them in my chamber, but I didn't notice anything when I returned after Lady Fulbert was safely delivered of her baby. I lay down without undressing and fell fast asleep. Snakes ever seek warmth, and they must have snuggled close to me. Perhaps I rolled over them accidentally – for they do not bite unless attacked or afraid. I was sorry to hear that they had been poisoned. And what of my cat? Is there any word of her?'

'She was terrified by the forcing of your door and rushed away. But Sir Brian sent word that she returned in the morning. We can have her brought down, if you like.'

'I would love to have Tibbs with me. Apart from being company, she's a notable mouser, and the God's House is sorely in need of one. How about my bundles? Not all mine in fact; many have been left with me for safekeeping until their owners can claim them.'

'We brought them all down on Wednesday. All, that is, except the relics of St Botolph. Sir Brian asked if his reliquary could be kept in the church, as they are much in demand with passing pilgrims. He is after all their patron saint.'

A spasm of anxiety crossed Sybilla's face. 'I suppose it is as safe there as anywhere. I trust it will be well guarded. But I would like to have everything else close by me. Where are the bundles now?'

'In Martha's charge in the courthouse. Along with some still unpacked cases of my own.'

There was a tap on the open window, and Vespilan looked in. Alyce smiled a welcome.

'Having you two near neighbours and close by me is a great relief. While I was away I worried constantly about your health. Rightly in your case, Sybilla. I'd no idea you were so frail.'

'We can give her all the care she needs in the God's House,' said Gerard. 'And she and I can talk over old times to our hearts' content.' He smiled at them both, and retreated to his own cell.

A moment later the great oak door to the cloister creaked open, and Alyce looked out to see Farhang with a small bottle in his hand. She hailed him. He veered towards the door of Sybilla's cell.

'Lady Alyce, welcome home! Good news of Dick Lawrence. He is on the road to recovery. And no one else has contracted his fever. So the God's House's complement of bedesmen – and woman – is complete.'

'Excellent news. I will go and congratulate him.'

Farhang shook his head firmly. 'Now is not a good time. I need to administer leeches to cleanse his blood thoroughly.'

Alyce grimaced. 'Then our meeting can wait. Will he be able to attend vespers tonight?'

'I think not. But Sunday should see him recovered. How is Sybilla?'

'Herself again, thank the Lord,' said Alyce. 'Though still weak, and she's pining for her cat.'

'I'd be happy to fetch it, my lady,' said Farhang. 'I'm about to go up to Swyncombe to make sure that Lady Fulbert and the new baby thrive.'

'Thank you, Farhang,' said Sybilla. 'Take a covered basket, though. Tibbs has decided ideas about where she wants to go.'

Once Farhang had left, she turned to Tamsin, who was sitting on a stool by the hearth. She looked at her through narrowed eyes.

'You've a familiar air about you. Aren't you Roger and Ellen's girl? And Nan's granddaughter?'

Tamsin nodded shyly. Sybilla turned to Alyce.

'I'm glad to see that you've had the sense to get rid of your last maid. She was a chuckle-headed wench, and not to be trusted. Ormesbys have always served the Chaucers loyally. Keep her by you.'

Alyce looked at Tamsin, whose cheeks had blushed fiery red, and smiled.

'I suspect I shall,' she said. 'Until she chooses to be wed.'

'Which I don't and I won't,' blurted out Tamsin, then turned and poked the fire to hide her embarrassment. Sybilla and Alyce exchanged amused glances.

Milo rode contentedly up the hill from Wallingford towards Ewelme, mentally replaying his meeting with Sir Robert

Harcourt's squire Hamel Turvey. He'd begun by boasting of his conquest of Marlene Stonor.

'A few days into my stay at the palace I saw her disappearing into the duchess's private garden and followed her. I guessed she had an assignation with someone.'

Turvey's eyes lit up. 'Who was it? Did you see them at it?'

'No. She was having a blazing row with a man called Denzil Caerleon. He's one of the duchess's most trusted servants. It seems that he'd got his leg over this wench while they were in Suffolk, and she's carrying his child. She wanted him to marry her.'

Turvey chuckled coarsely. 'I daresay she did. What did he say?'

'"What makes you so sure it was me?" Then he turned on his heel and left.'

'So what did you do?'

Milo grinned. 'I took it upon myself to comfort her. She'd given me the glad eye once or twice when we met in the palace. So I came out from where I'd been hiding. Gave her quite a jump, but I put my arm round her and said that she only had to stick to her story and he'd have to do right by her. I even said I'd testify that he'd admitted it. Then...' He glanced up at Turvey with a suggestive twinkle in his eye.

Turvey gave a vulgar guffaw that rang across the tavern. 'You had at her yourself.'

Milo put his finger to his lips, then nodded with mock modesty. 'I suspect the poor man was right to be suspicious. She knew what she was about. And it gave me a good deal of satisfaction to swive a de la Pole bastard.'

'What do you mean by that?' asked Turvey.

'Her grandfather was the late duke, she told me. Proud of

it, too. As if any connection with the Suffolks was something to boast of.'

Turvey was curious. 'You're not just doing this for the money, are you? It's personal, isn't it? What's your grudge against them?'

'That's my business,' said Milo curtly.

Hamel shrugged. 'So what happened next?'

'I explained to the young harlot that my support in hitching her to Caerleon and indeed my silence about our little tilt in love's lists both came at a price. I told her of Sir Robert's belief that there were traitors at Ewelme. She said that she had overheard two other palace servants, Simon Brailles and Ben Bilton, discussing a wounded man, a Lancastrian fugitive called John Trevelyan, who was concealed in a cell in the God's House. And two days ago I followed Caerleon, and heard him asking Farhang, the Ewelme infirmarer, how "his patient" did. On Thursday I followed Bilton again and discovered him with the recreant in one of the bedesmen's cells. I demanded money for my silence, then I locked them in and rode to Wallingford as fast as I could. Then I sent a courier to Oxford for you.'

'This will thoroughly damn the duchess!' Turvey crowed. He was a brawny giant of a man, with hands like hams and the shoulders of a bull. 'And when we've searched the anchorite's cell at Swyncombe and found the possessions of Lancastrian fugitives that you told us the old witch was hoarding there until you scotched her with the snakes, we can arrest all her henchmen as well. Well done, Milo. Here's your reward.'

He handed him a purse. 'You'll be able to ask Sir Robert for any position you fancy once he has taken possession of Ewelme. How does Master of God's House sound?'

'But what about my letters, Turvey? Sir Robert promised to return them.'

'Ah, yes.' Turvey took a scruffy bundle of papers out from an inner pocket of his jerkin and handed them to Milo. 'Destroy them – and his orders to you.'

'I hope they're all here,' said Milo, tucking the papers into the purse. 'And can I go back to Henley now? I'd rather not encounter Ben Bilton again. He has a violent temper.'

'Not yet. From what you say, they have no idea you are Sir Robert's man. Trevelyan will still be lying low in the God's House when we ride in with Lord Tiptoft and his men, and we'll need you there to bear witness to the treasons.'

Milo shivered. 'I really don't want to go back.'

'We'll ride for Ewelme as soon as we possibly can,' said Turvey. 'Probably tomorrow. Just lie low – and lock your door.'

Fantasising happily on the revenges he would wreak on the arrogant Ewelme servants once he was Master of God's House, Milo rode into the palace courtyard. Lady Alyce had returned. With Leo at her heels, she was walking across to the courthouse talking to a bent, white-haired woman who was leaning on her arm. His eyes narrowed. He had not bargained for this encounter. But, to his relief, Sybilla's rheumy eyes gazed through him rather than at him. Of course, she was probably purblind at her age. And he had looked very different on his visits to Swyncombe.

Leo gave a sharp bark, and Lady Alyce turned.

'So you have returned, Milo. Was your errand successful?'

Milo nodded his head and headed for the stables. He hoped that Sir Robert would be quick to act. He was not sure how much longer he could maintain his composure. But it was high time he did something about that brute of a hound. He went up the gallery staircase to his room. As far as he could tell, nothing been disturbed. So Bilton had not said anything. With a sigh of relief, he raised a loose plank in the floor, and tucked Turvey's purse, fattened further with Trevelyan's silver, under it. He also took out of his pocket a small packet that he had acquired two months earlier from the Wallingford apothecary.

Alyce and Sybilla were joined by Martha Purbeck and Tamsin as they entered the courthouse.

'Sybilla's bundles are over by the hearth,' the chamberlain said. 'Too many for her to keep with her in the God's House, I fear.'

'But I must have them near me,' said Sybilla, her voice unexpectedly forceful. 'I promised to keep the valuables that passing pilgrims entrusted to me safe.'

Alyce considered. 'How about the church strongroom above the vestry? Only Simon and William have keys to it. You can borrow a key when you feel strong enough to sort through them.'

'That would answer well,' said Sybilla, sitting down on a bench. 'By the by, who was the horseman Leo barked at as we were walking here?'

'Leo was right to bark,' said Alyce bluntly. 'He's Milo of Windsor, a spy of Queen Elizabeth. He was planted on us by the Harcourts on their visit last week. They'd heard there was a vacancy for a bedesman, but I told them it was filled. Thank the Lord that the snakes didn't make an end of you – if you had died, we'd have been forced to make Milo a bedesman.'

Sybilla frowned. 'Who knew that I was to come to the God's House? When was the decision made?'

Alyce thought for a minute. 'Well, Ben Bilton conferred with Peter Greene and Simon Brailles last Monday. Greene went up to Swyncombe early on Tuesday morning to ask you to replace Nicolas Webb, and when you said you were willing he came back, and Simon proposed it to me. I would trust all three of them with my life.'

'Did Peter meet anyone on his journey to Swyncombe and back on Tuesday morning?'

'Only a pedlar,' said Alyce. 'Tamsin asked one of the kitchen maids, and she said he had called at the manor just before Peter came to ask you to join the God's House.'

'Did you say a pedlar?' Sybilla asked. 'I remember him. That was the day that Lady Fulbert was in labour. He's been a regular visitor over the summer. He said he was on his way to Henley. I bought a length of fine white wool to make a robe for the baby.'

'What did you make of him?'

Sybilla shook her head. 'Just a pedlar, like any other. Long matted hair and beard, and a coarse-woven green cloak. I was only thinking of the baby.'

'He's been quite a regular at Ewelme,' said Tamsin.

'I did see a pedlar in the forecourt on the day I came home,' said Alyce.

'That was him,' Martha put in. 'Bearded and none too clean – and always avoided looking at me. Came from Bampton, he said. Goes as far as Henley. I thought him a sly devil.'

'When did he begin calling by?'

'Early summer, wasn't it, Tamsin? Every month or so. He

rarely called at the palace itself, just to the kitchen court, and the God's House.'

An unsettling idea struck Alyce. 'Has he visited since Milo moved in?' she asked. Tamsin and Martha shook their heads. Alyce turned to Sybilla.

'You said there was something familiar about Milo, Sybilla. Could he have been the pedlar shaven and barbered?'

Sybilla considered. 'My eyes are not what they were. Perhaps if I had a closer look at him…' Suddenly her face went white, and she began to fall forward. Martha rushed to catch her. Alyce turned to Tamsin.

'Help Martha take Sybilla back to the God's House, Tamsin, and tell Nan to tend her. Then get Hugh and Adam to take all her bundles into the church, and tell Marton and Greene to lock them safely in the strong-room.'

After vespers that evening, Alyce joined the priests in the master's chamber. They told her that the stuff brought down from Sybilla's cell was now safe in the strongroom. She asked Marton if anything had come to light concerning the letter that the Bishop's courier had handed to one of the bedesmen.

'No one I've spoken to remembers anything. The only person I haven't spoken to is poor Dick Lawrence. Farhang says that speaking to him will have to wait until he is fully recovered.'

Alyce thanked him and turned to Peter Greene. 'Peter, did you come across any strangers on your way up to Swyncombe to ask Sybilla if she would consider moving into the God's House.'

Greene pursed his plump lips thoughtfully. 'No one I'd call a stranger. A pedlar walked some of the way with me, but

I've seen him before. He has a regular route between Henley and Bampton. Calls at the God's House about once a month.'

'Did you mention Sybilla to him?'

'I said I was visiting her. He said he knew her well, and what a saint she was. Seemed to think the world of her. Then we chatted about the St Giles Fair. There'd been ructions there, he said. A flock of sheep broke out of their pen and were enjoying grazing in the courtyard of St John's College until the porters managed to chase them out.'

Alyce sensed Greene's attempt to change the subject. She did not.

'About Sybilla. Did you tell the pedlar that she might be moving down to the God's House?'

Greene reddened. Though over-inclined to talk, especially after some ale, he was by no means stupid. He realised that there was purpose behind the question, purpose linked to Sybilla's poisoning. Alyce waited.

'Er... I may have.' Gathering courage when his mistress's face remained pleasantly receptive, he added. 'In fact, yes, I think I did. I didn't see any harm in mentioning it. The whole of the village would find out soon enough, after all.'

'Of course they would,' said Alyce. 'Worry not, Peter. Sybilla is on the road to recovery.'

Ewelme

'I wonder if we are wise in going to Ewelme, John,' said Joan Moulton pensively as they rode past Dorchester Abbey early in the morning. They were followed at a short distance by Wenlock's secretary Francis Thynne and Monique de Chinon.

'Why not? When we talked at Neville's dinner, I promised to call on the duchess.'

'She'll welcome you, but I don't think she likes me at all. There was that unfortunate business about the stolen book. And on Thursday night at the feast I could read the disapproval in her eyes. Annoyed me rather, and I fear I acted up.'

Wenlock chuckled. 'That you did. But Alyce is a fair judge of people's true worth. I'm sure you can redeem yourself, especially since you are going to offer her some rare treasures. I wonder if anything has come of the investigations that Anthony Wydeville told you about. She left the feast so suddenly that I didn't have a chance to ask her. I wonder if...' He turned and called to his secretary. 'Francis, do you happen to know why the Duchess of Suffolk disappeared so suddenly last night?'

Thynne left Monique's side, and trotted up to him. 'Rumour has it that her man of business Denzil Caerleon has eloped with one of her ladies, Marlene Stonor.'

'Caerleon? But Alyce thought the world of him. Even though John Doll warned her that he was a bad lot when she took him into her service. Landless and penniless, apparently. The Stonors are a most respectable family. They will be appalled.'

Joan bridled. 'What do you mean, a bad lot? Denzil is a Caerleon, brother to my rascally late husband Walter. There's nothing wrong with his blood.'

'Why was he landless and penniless then?'

'I remember Walter telling me that he'd gone to the devil after his wife died in childbirth. She was the love of his life. He spent the next few years drunk, and gambled away everything he had. Walter took advantage of that, I'm afraid. But from what I heard, working for the duchess was the saving of him. Perhaps he genuinely loves this girl.'

'Eloping with her is a fine way to show it,' said Wenlock. 'It's more likely that he thinks she'll be handsomely dowered by her parents. Or by Lady Alyce. Who must be furious. No wonder she left the city.'

Turning east off the Henley road in Bensington half an hour later, they trotted along the deep-trodden lane beside Ewelme Brook. Soon the towers and turrets of Ewelme Palace came into view. Red and gold banners, some with the wheel of St Catherine sported by Alyce's father Thomas Chaucer, some with her mother Maud Burgersh's fork-tailed gold lion, announced the presence of its sovereign lady. Wenlock noticed that the de la Pole blue-and-gold was nowhere to be seen. Evidently Alyce now chose to leave the Suffolk blazon to her son and his wife.

Joan was awed. 'I had no idea it was so grand. It reminds me of Herstmonceux, Lord Dacre's seat in Sussex.'

'Other way about. Dacre's castle was inspired by Ewelme,' said Wenlock. 'His father Sir Roger Fiennes was a friend of the duke and duchess. He liked their palace so much that he persuaded its architect to design a similar one, as fitted his new position of King Henry's Treasurer.'

'I can see why he admired it,' said Joan, entranced at the harmonious grouping of the warm red brick and honey-coloured stone buildings nestling on the valley floor, skirted by a wide moat on which a single swan was swimming leisurely.

'What a handsome swan,' said Joan. 'It is said they mate only once. Perhaps this one is widowed like Lady Alyce. And are those cranes over by that pool?'

'Yes. Lady Alyce loves birds. Especially owls. She had a fine aviary at Wingfield, and the Ewelme mews have some splendid hawks.'

'I'd heard that she flew falcons. One of the books I'm hoping to tempt her with is Frederick II's *On the Art of Hunting with Birds*. I got it on my last trip to Bruges. In Latin, of course, and two hundred years old. The illustrations are exquisite.'

Just as the brook met a large pond, they drew level with a silver-haired man in a black robe with a red cross on its back. He was stooping over the bank of the pond gathering watercress. He looked up, and gave them a wave of greeting. They nodded in return as they rode onto the gatehouse.

'One of the bedesmen of the God's House?' asked Joan.

Wenlock nodded. 'Gathering salad stuffs, no doubt. They're a famously independent bunch. Most of them former Lancastrians, which adds to royal suspicions of the duchess.'

Simon Brailles was sorting through the theological texts which Lady Alyce had brought with her from Wingfield, reading out their titles for Tamsin to record in the various lists they were drawing up. One was of books to be kept in the palace chapel, one of those destined for his own study and a third of those to be kept by William Marton in the God's House. He was impressed to see what a neat hand she had, and how well controlled was the quill pen that she dipped in the rich black ink she had brought back for him from Oxford. He was grateful for her help, as there was no sign of Milo, who should have been assisting him. His eye travelled to her face, sullen with misery. It echoed the look on Lady Alyce's as she'd told them to start recording the titles of books she had brought from Wingfield and walked away despondently towards her private quarters. Caerleon's betrayal had hit them both hard, he knew, but he was unable to stifle a mean-spirited sense of elation that his mistress's posturing favourite had disgraced himself.

He stepped outside the courthouse at the sound of hooves in the base court. Could the Stonors already be here? Surely not. Then he realised that the foremost of the quartet of riders was Sir John Wenlock. He didn't know the flamboyant woman at his side, but she waved cheerfully at him as they stopped and dismounted. Wenlock hailed him.

'Well met, Brailles. Is your mistress receiving guests?'

'Good day, Lord Wenlock,' Simon replied as he bowed. 'Truth to tell, I am not sure whether she is or no. But I know how highly she values your friendship. I will send to find out.' He turned to Tamsin, who had followed him out of the courthouse. She was staring at Wenlock's companion.

'Tamsin, go and find Lady Alyce. Tell her that Lord Wenlock and… and…?'

'Mistress Joan Moulton,' supplied Joan. She winked at Tamsin. 'Didn't I see you in Doll's bookshop yesterday?' Tamsin nodded shyly, delighted that she had been remembered. Joan turned back to Simon.

'I met Lady Alyce in the evening, but there was no time to get acquainted. She left early, before I could tell her that I had some books that I think will interest her. So Sir John offered to bring me to Ewelme to meet her properly.'

Simon's heart sank. He had heard from Bilton about the acerbic encounter between Mistress Moulton and his mistress on her previous visit to Oxford.

'She is preoccupied with other things at present, I fear, Lord Wenlock. But Tamsin will let her know that you are here.'

Tamsin gave Joan a shy smile and scurried away.

Wenlock handed the reins of his horse to a stable lad. Thynne had taken Monique's arm, and guided her towards a bench below the magnificent gilded and enamelled sundial fixed against the south wall of the courtyard. Then he approached Simon.

'Master Brailles, Madame de Chinon is feeling a little weary,' he said. 'Could she have a little sustenance?'

'Of course,' said Simon. He called to the groom who was leading away the horses.

'Hugh, once you've seen to the horses, please find Martha, and tell her to bring refreshment for our visitors.' Then he turned back to Wenlock.

'Sir John, the truth is that we are in a state of uncertainty at present. Last night the duchess's lady-in-waiting Marlene Stonor disappeared from the Balliol guest house with her man of business Denzil Caerleon. The girl's parents have been sent for from Stonor Park. They will be distraught.'

'So we heard in Doll's bookshop this morning,' said Wenlock. 'But Mistress Moulton may be able to put Lady Alyce's mind at rest. She has some knowledge of the Caerleon family. They are of good standing, she says.'

Simon managed a hesitant smile. 'Pray God things are not as bad as we feared, then.' He turned to Joan. 'How do you know Denzil, Mistress Moulton?'

Before Joan could reply, Alyce emerged from the porch of the great hall, with Tamsin and Farhang behind her. Her face lit up when she saw Wenlock, then fell when she saw Joan Moulton at his side. Wenlock noticed her frown, but stepped forward to take the hand she held out for him to kiss. As he bowed over it, he spoke in a low whisper.

'Be of good heart, your grace. Mistress Moulton may be able to aid you in this sorry business. She has knowledge of Caerleon's family.'

Alyce sniffed. 'As do I. The Warden of New College told me on Monday that they cast him out and vowed never to have anything to do with him. For good reason, I now realise. When Chaundler said "What's bred in the bone will not out" I should have listened to him.'

Joan bustled forward. 'I must protest, Princess Alyce. Denzil was ever made a scapegoat by his brother Walter. He was blamed for razing a tenant's farm to the ground. But I know it was Walter's doing. He boasted of it to me when he was in his cups.'

Alyce blinked in surprise. 'And what do you know of Walter Caerleon?'

'Far too much, my lady. He was my fourth husband. He was the favourite son, and his parents always turned a blind eye to his sins. After his death, they realised that they were unfair, and sought to make reparation to Denzil. But he was too proud to accept anything from them.'

'How did Walter die?'

'Of the pox.' She pointed towards Monique. 'And this lady

is his one-time mistress, Monique de Chinon, once a great ornament of Queen Margaret's court. She too contracted the pox.'

Alyce gave Monique a nod, then turned back to Joan with less acrimony. 'I remember her well. And we met in Oxford on Thursday morning. She told me of the care you took of her after your husband's death. That was a Christian action.'

Joan shrugged carelessly. 'And a self-interested one. Monique is an intelligent companion and a notable needlewoman, with a talent for dressing hair and a knowledge of all manner of beautifying remedies.'

Alyce registered both Joan's modesty in disclaiming praise and the generosity of spirit she showed in her description of her companion's virtues. Her astute grey eyes met the bookseller's merry brown ones directly for the first time.

'You have eased my mind somewhat, Mistress Moulton. But you may not know that Caerleon has taken service with Sir Robert Harcourt, who is determined to find me guilty of treason. Apparently he has long had ears and eyes in Ewelme. And I fear it is Denzil who has been faithless.'

Wenlock broke in. 'How can that be, your grace? For the last two years Caerleon has been in Suffolk with you, not in Ewelme. Don't damn him out of hand. Maybe he has a story to tell.'

Alyce remained stony-faced.

Despite his jealousy of Caerleon, Simon could bear it no longer. 'Lady Alyce, Denzil is no traitor to you. He knew nothing of what we have been doing at Ewelme.'

Alyce turned to him in amazement. 'What have you been doing? And who is "we"?'

Simon swallowed, knowing that he had to tell his mistress

the truth. But could these visitors be trusted with it? He looked nervously at Lord Wenlock and Joan Moulton.

'Speak up, Simon,' said Wenlock. 'I assure you that I would never betray your mistress. I've valued her friendship since before you were born.'

'Nor need you fear that I would do so,' said Joan. 'Especially if what you have to say clears Denzil's name.'

Fixing his eyes on Alyce, Simon took a deep breath. 'It's a long story. Ewelme has always had a reputation for offering sanctuary for Lancastrians who had fallen on hard times. You yourself were proud of it. "Chaucers have served Lancaster since time out of mind," you always said. After you left for Suffolk, we continued that tradition, sure that we would have your blessing, though we knew you had to feign allegiance to York. While you were away, the battle of Hedgeley Moor ended the civil war and the country was full of fugitive Lancastrians. Instead of just providing for old and infirm loyalists, we began to help able men to escape. The God's House became a link in a chain running from London upriver to Thameside safe houses, then to Stonor Park, Swyncombe and Ewelme. From here, fugitives go to Donnington, then to High Clere Castle and so into the Solent and across to France.'

Alyce was dumbfounded. All her careful manoeuvrings brought to naught. If rumours of her misguided retainers' network had reached Harcourt, then her quitting Wingfield must have acted like a match to a powder keg.

Farhang moved to stand at Simon's side.

'We sought only to save lives, not to stir up rebellion,' he said. 'We followed the words of Rumi: *Your heart knows the way. Run in that direction.*'

'I doubt whether Lord Tiptoft will be swayed by Rumi when

he discovers what you have been doing,' said Alyce bitterly. 'So did Caerleon play no part in your rash activities?'

Simon summoned up his courage and spoke again. 'Only because he had to. When you announced you were returning for good, Ben Bilton said we should wind things down until we could be sure of your approval. But then John Trevelyan's fleet was attacked off Queenborough, and his men brought him, half-dead, to Deptford. He was nearly captured by Lord Tiptoft's men, but our London agent, the surgeon John Crophill, treated his wounds and persuaded Caerleon to take him on board one of your barges. We were going to conceal him in the God's House cell left vacant after Nicolas Webb's death, but then Bilton heard that the Harcourts were planning to force you to accept a placeman of the queen's and that he would be acting as a spy. So Peter Greene proposed Sybilla. You know the rest – though not that Trevelyan was concealed in Dick Lawrence's cell.'

Alyce's jaw dropped. 'You mean he was in the God's House when the Harcourts came to hunt?'

Simon nodded unhappily.

Alyce closed her eyes and sighed. 'Where, then, was Dick?'

'He agreed to be concealed in the attic of the Bridge Tavern in Wallingford.'

'Delighted by the prospect of unlimited ale, no doubt. He was ever a toper. Is Trevelyan still in the God's House?'

To Simon's relief, Farhang took up the story. 'While you were in Oxford, Milo followed Bilton into his cell. He promised not to tell of what he'd discovered if they rewarded him. Which they did – but he snatched Trevelyan's doublet and the money, locked them in and rode off. Sybilla raised the alarm, and I released them.'

'And John?' asked Alyce.

'He was still too weak to ride to Donnington, so Bilton and Pek hid him in the wood cart and took him up to Swyncombe.'

'Caerleon, Marton, Bilton, Greene, Pek, Sybilla, the Fulberts, the Stonors – was anyone not part of this madcap enterprise? Surely Martha Purbeck and Nan Ormesby had too much good sense to agree to it?'

But she could see from their downcast expressions that the women of the household had also been involved. How could they not have been, with wounded men to be tended and food and sleeping quarters to be provided?

'What of Milo? Sybilla and I saw him returning to Ewelme this morning. Where is he now?'

The silence that greeted her question was interrupted by the sound of horses' hooves. Alyce turned to see Thomas and Jeanne Stonor riding through the gatehouse, with Hugh and Ella behind them. Alyce braced herself for anger and blaming. But none came. Once she had dismounted, Jeanne walked up to her and held out her arms. Alyce felt tears welling in her eyes as she allowed herself to be folded into them.

'It is none of your doing, my lady,' said Jeanne. 'Marlene had her head turned by Lady Anne Vere when she was at Wingfield. She made a dead set at Caerleon, Eloise tells me, and one night when he was in his cups she seduced him. When he brought the barges to Ewelme, she told him he had made her pregnant. He was dumbstruck, Eloise told me, but he agreed to marry her.'

Perhaps there was hope, after all. Alyce's quick brain clutched at straws. Caerleon would have known that she would be angry with him for having made Marlene pregnant. He must have decided that he needed to leave her service and enter

Sir Robert's so that he could provide for Marlene. Marlene. She couldn't imagine a woman worse suited to Denzil. But then she thought again. Why on earth had he chosen Harcourt? He knew that the bullying knight was her mortal enemy. She sighed. No, Denzil had no excuse – he must be involved in plotting her downfall, and perhaps that of other links in the chain of Lancastrian refuges. She remembered his odd comings and goings in the days since he had arrived. Everything pointed to his having a hidden agenda. The handkerchief, bound in the Stonor colours, that she had found at the heart of her garden must have been left after he met Marlene there.

She stood up abruptly. 'We need a council of war.'

Stonor looked puzzled.

'Don't look surprised, Thomas. Simon and Farhang have confessed to me what has been going on – and that Stonor Park was part of the escape route for Lancastrian fugitives.'

'But I thought that was all ended when word came of your return for good,' said Jeanne. 'I was relieved, in truth. Too many people knew of what was going on.'

'Unfortunately, things didn't quite end. Denzil Caerleon brought a Cornish Lancastrian called John Trevelyan from London on one of the barges carrying my chattels from Suffolk. He'd been wounded and was in desperate need, and they knew him for a friend of mine. But the Harcourts planted a spy in my household when they came for the hunt – do you remember that ailing scrivener they brought with them? He discovered Trevelyan while I was in Oxford and has no doubt already passed word to the Harcourts. Bilton and Pek hustled Trevelyan away to Swyncombe as quickly as they could, but he will not be safe there for long. At any minute I fear Ewelme will be invaded by Yorkists bent on proving me a traitor. Led, no doubt by the Harcourts – and perhaps Denzil. Which is why we need a council of war. So who is with me, and who against me?'

There was total silence. Then Wenlock stepped forward. 'I will stand your friend through thick or thin, Lady Alyce. And my secretary is the most discreet man in the country.'

He turned to Joan, and raised his eyebrows.

'I disagree, Sir John,' said the bookseller.

Alyce's heart sank, but rose again at Joan's next words.

'Monique can match him without effort. As for me, I haven't known you for long, Lady Alyce, but I would like to better our acquaintance without being put to the inconvenience of visiting the Tower of London. And here's my hand on it.'

She held it out, muscled and weathered, the hand of a doer, not a watcher. Startled and moved, Alyce clasped it in her own slim, strong fingers. Then she turned to the Stonors, a question in her eyes.

'We have as much to lose as you do if the king's men find evidence of the escape route,' said Thomas. Jeanne nodded emphatically.

'Then we must plan our strategy,' said Alyce. 'The infirmary is the safest place to talk. Tamsin, go and fetch Martha Purbeck, and bring her over. Farhang, please could you fetch Vespilan. Nan Ormesby will already be there with Sybilla. But where is Ben Bilton?'

Planning was hungry work, but afterwards Martha rose to the occasion with aplomb, suggesting that they eat outside in the warm September sunshine. A long trestle table was erected in the base court close by the kitchen, and high-backed benches placed on each side. Alyce's chair of state stood at its head. Napery and horn beakers were brought, and the little company seated themselves – Lord Wenlock, Alyce, Thomas Stonor and Jeanne sat on one side of the table; Joan, Thynne and Monique on the other; Farhang and Simon at each end. Two heaped platters, one a salmagundi made from pheasant and partridge meat chopped with anchovies, onions and eggs; the other a leafy green salad with fresh fruits, grated carrots and Corinth currants. A jug of ale stood at each end of the table.

Once the cups were filled, Wenlock raised his in a toast: 'To friendship.'

They all raised their glasses, and were about to eat when Alyce rose: 'And to Lancaster.'

Everyone eyed each other nervously. Then they rose and raised their glasses again. Simon's and Farhang's eyes met. Alyce's shilly-shallying and havering were over. She had returned to the loyalty of her parents and grandparents.

They settled down to the meal in silence, uncertain what to talk about, minds crowded with thoughts of what the next few days would hold. Then Joan thought of a distraction.

'Lady Alyce, I have some books in my saddlebags that I brought from London because I thought they would appeal to you.' She smiled wickedly, then added, 'All of highly respectable provenance, I can assure you. Would you care to cast your famously discerning eyes over them?'

Alyce chuckled, liking the bold brash bookseller more and more.

'What better way could there be while we wait on our enemies? What have you brought with you?'

'The Emperor Frederick's *De Arte Venandi cum Avibus*. Although it's two hundred or more years old, it is still the best work on managing hawks. And my copy is sumptuously illustrated.'

As they ate, they talked about other books. Alyce became increasingly impressed by the breadth of Joan's knowledge. She asked if she had a copy of Christine de Pisan's love ballads. Joan looked wistful.

'That's the rarest of her works. I wish I did. I do have her *Tale of the Rose* Englished, though, and a French copy of her book about feats of arms and chivalry, *Le Livre des fais d'armes et de chevalerie*. But not with me. I hope that you'll visit the Sign of the Mole when you're next in London.'

Once the impromptu meal had been cleared away, Farhang and Brailles bowed and excused themselves. Then Thomas Stonor rose to his feet.

'Thank you, Alyce,' he said. 'It's time we went home. When we get back, we'll try to find out more about what Marlene has been up to.'

Once the Stonors were out of sight, Alyce turned to Joan. 'Shall we go to my closet? I'm eager to see the books you've brought. Tamsin, come with us, in case I think of anything Mistress Moulton might like to see from my own library.'

But before they reached the entrance to her wing of the palace, there was a shout from the gatehouse. They turned around. It was Pek's gruff bellow.

'Who goes there? Stop! Stop!' He was striding out of the porter's lodge to confront the invader. The lad on the rough-coated pony only just managed to rein it in before he knocked the old veteran over. Then he dismounted in one lithe leap. Tamsin recognised him with a lift of her heart. It was William Stonor.

'I bring warning of danger, Lady Alyce,' he gasped. 'The constable and his men, and the Harcourts, are on the road to Ewelme.'

'How do you know?' said Alyce.

'I was in Cornmarket when they rode past, and I heard Sir Robert boasting to Lord Tiptoft that he had proof that you had a Lancastrian outlaw hidden in a cell in the almshouse. I borrowed a nag and followed them. They stopped in Dorchester for lunch, so I did too, and I heard him say to Lord Tiptoft that someone called Milo would give evidence that he had seen a Cornish pirate called John Trevelyan in a bedesman's bed. And that the almshouse is steeped in immorality. One of the bedesmen is a woman.'

'Thank you, William. You've done well. How long do you think we have before they arrive?'

'They weren't hurrying over their meal. And their company rides more slowly than I do. But they won't be long.'

Alyce turned to Pek. 'Where is Milo?'

'I saw him return from Wallingford this morning, my lady, as did you. But I haven't seen hide or hair of him since then.'

'Go up to his room in the guest lodging, Joseph, and bring him to me. We must see if we can bribe him not to testify.' Pek limped away, and went up the outside stairs of the gallery across the front of the guest lodgings.

Minutes later a great company of horses and men led by Lord Tiptoft and Sir Robert Harcourt jostled through the still open gate of the palace. Nobody barred their way, not even Leo, who usually raced out at the advent of visitors.

'Dismount,' called Harcourt. 'And take the horses to the stables.'

He strode triumphantly towards Alyce with only a nominal

bow, nodded at Joan and Wenlock and ignored William and Tamsin completely.

'Where is Milo of Windsor, my lady? I believe he has some important news to impart to the constable. It seems that your much-lauded almshouse is in fact a nest of traitors and whores.'

Alyce drew herself up like a hawk preparing to strike.

'You presume, Sir Robert. And the spy that you planted here on behalf of your royal mistress can have discovered nothing because there is nothing to discover. I have just sent someone to search for him so that I can catechise him for telling lies.'

As she spoke, she searched the faces of the Harcourt men milling around in the base court. To her profound relief, there was no sign of Caerleon. That was a mercy. Suddenly she remembered Sybilla and her mysterious bundles. She looked round for Tamsin, nodded towards the God's House, and hoped she would read her mind aright. Then she turned to Lord Tiptoft.

'Sir John, I must protest most strongly at this invasion of my privacy. I have ever been a loyal friend of the Crown. Indeed, I made my nephew-in-law King Edward a considerable loan in the summer.'

Seeing that everyone's attention was focused on Alyce and Tiptoft, Tamsin took William's sleeve.

'Come away,' she whispered. 'We need to prepare Farhang and Sybilla for an invasion. I'm sure they will insist on searching the God's House and the infirmary. And I'll tell you what's been happening.' He followed her through the gatehouse obediently. None of the invaders noticed them go, except Lord Tiptoft, whose pale eyes followed their exit with interest.

With clumping footsteps, Joseph Pek descended from the

274

guest lodgings gallery, and nervously approached Alyce and Tiptoft.

'There's no sign of Milo, my lady. But I noticed that a plank in his floor was loose, and I found all manner of things hidden under it. It seems he has been pilfering ever since he arrived.' He laid a bundle of sacking on the ground and spread it out. There were various small trinkets that Alyce recognised. They had gone missing during the unpacking and sorting. There was also a plump purse of coins.

'And there was this letter.' Pek handed a folded piece of paper to Alyce. She opened it up and saw George Neville's untidy writing, his flamboyant signature. How had Milo got hold of this, when it had been sent four days before he arrived in Ewelme?

'That purse is yours, Sir Robert.' Hamel Turvey strode forward. 'It's the one I gave Milo as a reward. He asked if he could return to Henley because he was afeared for his life at Ewelme, but I told him he had to stay until we came, so that he could bear witness. Looks as if he was right to be scared.'

'Scared of being found out as a thief.' Lord Wenlock's commanding voice cut across the silence that followed Turvey's accusation. 'I suspect he is well on the way to some safe hole of his own knowing. Having made a fool of you, Harcourt.'

'I doubt that very much,' snarled Sir Robert. 'He had too much to gain. Why leave his valuables? Milo must be found before we can make sense of this.' He turned to Tiptoft.

'My Lord, I think our men should be sent to search the whole palace. Starting with the God's House and the church.'

Tiptoft gave a nod of assent. 'As the duchess has nothing to hide, I'm sure she won't protest.'

'Nor do I,' snapped Alyce. 'However, my people will follow

them round to make sure that no damage is done and no more valuables purloined.'

'As you wish,' said Harcourt coldly. 'Let's get started, Turvey. The God's House is this way.' He marched out of the gatehouse and down the village street.

'Sir John and I will go with them, Lady Alyce,' said Joan. 'And Thynne and Monique. The more eyes the better to oversee such street-sweepings as these rogues.'

Alyce was thankful for Joan's support. Behind the haughty mask she was presenting to the king's intelligencers she was desperately worried. Where on earth was Milo? And what was Caerleon up to? She had trusted him utterly. He'd been privy to all her secrets and, it seemed, to things that she hadn't known about. Had he told Harcourt all he knew? She desperately wanted to ask Sir Robert where he and Marlene were, and whether he had entered his service. But she was too proud to do any such thing. Moreover, the most important thing she had to do was to convince Lord Tiptoft of her innocence. She turned to him, her face all serenity.

'My lord, while this pointless search is taking place, I suggest that you and I adjourn to my bookroom. You mentioned your interest in my grandfather's writings at the feast on Thursday. I have all of his works, of course, some little known. Simon, please come with us. You know where everything is better than I do.'

'That would please me greatly,' said Tiptoft courteously, admiring her composure, but reflecting that an added inducement for proving the duchess a traitor to York was the prospect of confiscating her library. He offered Alyce his arm and they walked towards the palace, followed by Simon, blinking with anxiety.

Joan, on the other hand, had every intention of finding out what had happened to her former brother-in-law. She swept after Sir Robert, Wenlock in her wake.

'Sir Robert, what do you know of Marlene Stonor and Denzil Caerleon? The word in the city was that they had taken refuge with you at Stanton Harcourt. Is that true?'

Harcourt looked down at Joan, remembering her in all her finery at Neville's feast. An ample armful, indeed. And rumour had it that she was not averse to dalliance. He smiled wolfishly.

'Well to find out the truth of it, you'll have to visit my lady and myself at Stanton. All I can say at the minute is that the word in the city is not without some foundation in truth. My chaplain married them on Friday morning. The girl's condition meant that it needed to be speedily done. I don't envy Caerleon his wife. Who was it who said *The love of a shrew is briefer than the shadow of a cloud?*'

'Why did they take refuge at Stanton?'

A smirk spread over Harcourt's face. 'Marlene and my man Milo struck up a mutually beneficial acquaintanceship soon after he arrived in Ewelme. He realised how much she resented Lady Alyce and told her that I'd welcome with open arms anybody who had less than enthusiastic feelings for the duchess. I could see Caerleon was not keen, but he'd no option once Marlene ensnared him into promising to marry her. Young slut. She's the image of the French grandmother she was named for. Marlène de Cay. Whose affair with William de la Pole – he was the English commander by then – was the talk of Rouen. He didn't let his contract to marry Alyce stop him enjoying a much more congenial bedfellow than Lady High and Mighty can ever have been.'

Poor Alyce, Joan reflected. Rumours had long existed of

the coolness of her marriage to William, of how odd it was that they had had only one child, and he born eleven years after they were wed. Yet his last will and testament had given her total control over his estates, and the letter of advice he'd written for his son had been famously generous in her praise. Why, she wondered?

As Lord Tiptoft and Alyce walked across the great hall, Martha Purbeck appeared from the screens passage. She bowed at the constable, then turned to Alyce.

'My Lady, I would like a quick word with you in the kitchen as to the arrangements for feeding our guests. It shouldn't take many minutes.'

Alyce instantly realised that something was up.

'Of course. Excuse me, my lord. Simon, take the earl up to my turret closet to wait for me there. I'm sure he'll enjoy looking at my books.'

She walked towards the kitchen with Martha, heart pounding. John Cook was standing in front of the great hearth, directing a grease-covered boy who was thrusting a dozen chicken carcasses onto a long spit. He nodded as Alyce entered, and gestured towards the still room, a private place off the main kitchen where preserves and cordials were made. Once they were inside, Martha closed the door, and a sheepish Ben Bilton rose from a chair.

'So there you are,' said Alyce. 'Brailles tells me you have been merrily risking my heartland for the last two years.'

Bilton nodded, looking abashed. He opened his mouth to explain, but she waved his words away,

'Enough of excuses. What's done is done. And I gather it was no fault of yours that Trevelyan was brought here. But will Milo be able to prove the doublet and coins he took were Trevelyan's?'

'Trevelyan didn't think so. The coins were English, and the doublet an old one he was given in Southwark. But he had a Spanish silver St Christopher in its pocket.'

'What of the other new bedesmen? Are they wanted men as well?'

'No,' said Bilton. 'Just old and near senile. Deserving of care.'

'That's a mercy. But where is Milo? It's vital that we deal with him before he testifies to the constable. He may have discovered other incriminating matters.'

'I don't know,' said Bilton. 'Pek says he came back from Wallingford, but no one has seen him since. I'll seek him out.'

'Do so. For the nonce, we will just have to bluff it out. I must join the Earl of Worcester now. He'll be wondering what's become of me.'

Alyce's brain was whirling as she walked up to her chamber. Two weeks ago she had felt friendless, but safe. After hearing of Caerleon's desertion she had felt utterly forlorn. Now she seemed to have acquired dependable allies, but was in real peril of losing her heartland. And what had she been thinking of by toasting Lancaster? Rumi, she thought, wryly. *Your heart knows the way. Run in that direction.*

The God's House was in turmoil by the time Joan and Wenlock reached it. Sir Robert grinned as he saw several bewildered old men had gathered in a group in the centre of the courtyard while his henchmen were dragging chests out of their cells and creating general mayhem. Lord Wenlock frowned.

'Sir Robert, this is absurd. These poor dazed old men fought in France for England and St George, not for the warring factions of York and Lancaster.'

'Maybe, said Harcourt. 'But my spy was quite sure that the man he saw in one of these cells last Thursday was neither old nor loyal. As I said, he was the notorious pirate John Trevelyan of Whalesborough. Sorely wounded, too, apparently.'

'You only have Milo's word for this,' said Wenlock. 'How did he know who he was?'

'He heard the man with him – Ben Bilton, the duchess's own steward – say his name to the doctor who was treating him earlier in the week. Milo excels at skulking in shadows. He's been of great service to me for many years. And the queen herself endorsed his placing here. If anything has happened to him, she will be outraged.'

Voices were suddenly raised in consternation. One of the bedesmen must have asked one of Harcourt's men to haul up a bucket of water from the well. Now both were staring down into its depths. It was a large well, its smooth sides slimy with moss. The soldier had been turning the winding handle, and several turns of wet rope could be seen around the circular beam across the wellhead. But something had snagged on the bucket while it was still underwater. Something horribly recognisable, even though the shallow water over it was agitated by the tugging of the rope. A human hand. And, trailing from it into the depths, a human arm. The soldier crossed himself.

'Come and help, Piers,' he called to another of Harcourt's men. 'Happen there's been murder done.'

The two men bent over the flat top of the wellhead and hauled on the rope together. Slowly the bucket rose, and with it the corpse of a man. Harcourt's jaw sagged.

'God's wounds – it's Milo.' He stepped forward and helped the men haul out the body. A tangled loop of the rope attached to the bucket was pulled tight around its right wrist, biting into the white mottled flesh. Joan saw a thin, stooped bedesman step forward.

'This is not murder, Sir Robert,' he said. 'It's the sort of accident we have always dreaded. The paving around the wellhead is often slippery with spilt water. We usually leave raising water to the servants, which is why Brother Richard there asked your man for help. Milo must have been hauling the bucket out with the rope around his wrist to get a purchase, as one does with something heavy. Look – there's a bruise on his forehead. As if he slipped forward, then fell, hitting his head against the stone top of the well. The weight of the bucket would have pulled him after it.' He pointed to the flat stones that circled the top of the well.

'Look there. Traces of dried blood.'

'A likely story,' barked Harcourt. 'Which comes a great deal too pat. What's your name?'

'Gerard Vespilan, Sir Robert. I am the most senior member of the God's House, and hold the office of Minister of the Bedesmen.'

'And whose side did you fight on during the wars?' Harcourt asked accusingly.

Vespilan eyed him with a wry smile.

'Sir Robert, I am more than four score years of age. I worked for Lady Alyce's grandfather as a scrivener, and I've never raised anything more dangerous than a pen.'

Joan Moulton stepped forward. 'Your men should take this poor soul to the infirmary. Lady Alyce's matron can do what is necessary for his dignity.'

'And her surgeon Farhang can examine him,' said Wenlock. 'He'll likely confirm Gerard Vespilan's theory.'

'No doubt he will. You're all in this together,' snarled Sir Robert, staring round at them. 'The coroner will have to be summoned. I am quite sure that this was no accident, for all your facile explanation.'

He glared at Vespilan. '"Minister" is it? Well, you and your mistress are not going to get away with ministering to murder. She has overstepped the bounds with a vengeance this time. The queen will hear of this.'

While he waited for the duchess to finish her business with her chamberlain, Lord John Tiptoft looked around the sloping shelves of Alyce's bookroom with admiration. Never had he seen so many desirable volumes. Which, he reflected, could all come his way, if Harcourt proved her disloyalty. He leafed through the one in pride of place on her desk. Old Geoffrey Chaucer's wonderful Tales of the Pilgrims to Canterbury. How often he had relished hearing them acted out after feasts. Though its cover was battered, this copy was beautiful, the script elegant and even, the margins full of fanciful grotesques.

He wandered over to the table in the centre of the room. Careful scale drawings of an elaborate tomb were laid out on it. He picked up a drawing of the effigy that would lie on it. It was an astonishingly lifelike image of Alyce: long-jawed, a smooth brow, narrow nose and a lilt to the lips that suggested a sense of humour. She was in a simple blue mantle, very different from the elaborate robes of his own mother's brass effigy. He picked up a drawing concealed under the first. It had none of its serene calm but it too was of the duchess. Her head was arched back, the tendons of her neck prominent, her raddled breasts bare, one hand clutching a shroud over her groin. *Memento mori*, he murmured to himself. A reminder of the reality of death to be placed underneath the tomb itself. Here was a woman who knew herself and accepted her fate with rare courage.

The subject of the sketches appeared before him carrying an elaborately bound folio volume. She gave an odd half-smile when she saw him looking at the drawings.

'What do you think, my Lord? I insisted that Massingham represent me as I really am and as I really will be. He did them under protest, but I'm the piper and I call the tune. By the way, he told me a curious tale. He was attacked on his way from Henley by a squad of ruffians who claimed to be retained by King Edward. Was this your doing?'

The directness of the question startled Tiptoft. He walked to the window and looked out while he composed his thoughts. The attackers must have been Harcourt's men. He was beginning to regret that he had allowed his vendetta against Alyce free rein. But how could he have countered Elizabeth's will? The answer came to him suddenly. He must speak to the king as soon as possible.

He turned to face Alyce's level gaze, and said, truthfully, 'I knew nothing of it, my lady. And I will make enquiries as to who was responsible when I return to Windsor. But what new treasure is that?'

'This is the book I mentioned when we talked in Oxford. I've just collected it from my bedchamber, which delayed me somewhat as it had been moved from where I left it. It's the account of a pilgrimage to Jerusalem fifty years ago. It was dictated to a scribe by one Margery Kempe of Bishop's Lynn.'

Tiptoft pulled a face. 'I've read it. It is heartfelt, but reveals her as a trying companion. Always bursting into tears.'

Alyce nodded ruefully. 'Most tedious. Still, she showed that women were as able to reach Jerusalem as men. I'd love to hear about your own pilgrimage there. Did you take ship from La Serenissima? I yearn to visit Venice. I have long hoped to make a pilgrimage to the Holy Land myself, but at present the Turks and the Moors combine to make it too dangerous.'

'Now is certainly not the right time – unless you are a crusader,' said Tiptoft. 'But it seems doubtful that a new crusade will ever be mounted.'

He noticed that Alyce's fingers were nervously toying with the elaborate rosary looped around her girdle. Though her face was calm, something was worrying her.

'Your pardon, my lady, but I cannot help admiring your rosary. Is it oriental work?'

Alyce clutched at it, reminded of its near loss, of Tamsin finding it and so bravely fighting off those outlaws. Was it only two weeks since the child had been in her service?

'It was given to my grandfather by the Duke of Milan, and came to me at my birth, which was barely a year after he died. My father thought it Indian, but it could have come from farther east. The imagery is Christian, of course, used because such treasures sell well in Europe.'

'I have never seen its like,' said Tiptoft. 'You are fortunate to have a son to whom you can will it.' He looked searchingly at her, a hint of mockery in his eyes. Were his words intended to provoke her? He must know of the rift between her and Jack. Was he friend or foe? She was saved from saying anything more through the sudden entry of Sir Robert Harcourt, incandescent with anger.

'My Lord, murder has been done. Milo of Windsor, a valued servant of the queen, has been brutally killed. We have just discovered his body in the well in the God's House courtyard. I have sent for the coroner. He won't arrive until Monday, of course. Meanwhile, we must finish searching for evidence in the God's House today and start on the palace and the village tomorrow. God knows what other misprisions we will discover.'

He turned to Alyce. 'We will have to trespass on your hospitality overnight, Duchess. I hold a royal search warrant. I have no intention of allowing anything to be hidden or removed. Do I have your support in this, Constable?'

Tiptoft's already considerable dislike of Harcourt was hardening. What an unchivalrous and presumptuous bully he was. He shook his head.

'I doubt if Lady Alyce can accommodate so many at such short notice, Sir Robert. Of course, the search must go ahead, but when dusk falls we will find accommodation in hostelries in Bensington or Wallingford.'

'I have nothing to hide,' said Alyce with hauteur. 'And I would be happy to offer hospitality to yourself and Sir Robert. But it is very short notice. It would certainly ease the strain on my already disturbed household if your men could stay elsewhere. We already have four guests, Lord Wenlock, Joan Moulton and their attendants.'

'I will stay with my men in Bensington,' snapped Harcourt. 'But first I want you to see Milo's corpse for yourselves. It has been taken to the infirmary. Lord Wenlock and Mistress Moulton, who were with me when the body was found, thought that your surgeon Farhang could establish the cause of death. Your senior bedesman suggested that it was an accident, but I very much doubt that. Meanwhile the men and I will continue the search in the God's House.' He strode out of the room.

Alyce gave Tiptoft a nervous smile. He didn't respond. He knew she was hoping for his support, but he never put friendship, or gallantry to a woman, before what he regarded as his duty. He was a man with a strict code of honour. Which was why he had left England's shores on pilgrimage during the war between York and Lancaster. He had stayed in Milan for several years and only returned when its outcome seemed certain. And now he was unquestionably loyal to King Edward – and, for all his reservations about her, to Queen Elizabeth.

He made Alyce a courteous bow. 'Shall we, my lady...?'

She took his arm, unsure of almost everything, and wondering especially where Leo was. She hadn't seen him since he'd left her chamber that morning for his usual rough and tumble with the stable dogs.

Milo was laid out on a bed in the infirmary. Farhang was examining his swollen corpse carefully.

'There was water in his lungs, and that blow on his forehead looks severe enough to have caused loss of consciousness,' he told Wenlock and Joan. 'Did you notice any blood on the stone parapet of the well? If there was, Vespilan could be right about what happened.'

'Vespilan pointed out a stain that could well have been blood. Not that it made Sir Robert change his mind about it being murder. He's intent on proving the duchess a traitor. But why would Milo be drawing water from the well? He should have got a servant to do it for him, as the bedesmen do.'

From another bed in the infirmary, a quavering voice called. 'Farhang, I can speak to what happened.' It was Sybilla. She hauled herself up into a sitting position.

'Milo opened the door of my cell yesterday, around midday. He asked what I was doing there, and I explained that I was now a bedeswoman. He nodded in a nasty, knowing way. I said I was very thirsty, and asked him if he could fill my jug from the bucket of the well. He took my jug, but he never came back. I assumed that he had just gone away – but perhaps he tried to fill the bucket, then slipped, cracked his head and tumbled down after it.'

They stared at each other.

'Sybilla's story suggests his death was an accident,' said Joan.

'But Harcourt will say that there is no proof that an ill-wisher didn't take advantage of Milo after he left Sybilla's cell,' objected Wenlock. 'He could have seen him bending over the well, knocked him over and pushed him into it.'

Voices sounded outside, and several people crowded into the infirmary. The first was Harcourt. Next came Dick Lawrence, his arms pinioned to his sides. He was evidently drunk, and one of the men escorting him carried a leather bottle of ale.

'If this is the sort of worthy poor man the duchess harbours in her almshouse, the sooner she ceases to have management of it the better,' sneered Sir Robert. 'And the sot tells me that there was a woman in the cell next door to him. Just as Milo told my squire Hamel Turvey when he met him in Wallingford last Friday. Doubtless a whore, though she isn't there now.'

'Rubbish,' said Joan bluntly. 'All Ewelme knows that the duchess appointed the Swyncombe anchorite as a bedeswoman last week. She's in her eighties, and was a valued servant of the Chaucers all her life.'

Harcourt gave a guffaw. 'Valued servants of the Chaucers are Lancastrian loyalists. Milo can no longer give his testimony; nor have we found the wounded pirate he saw. But there is plenty of evidence to prove he spoke the truth. He was clad in a leather doublet which he told Turvey that he had from Trevelyan. And there was a Spanish silver St Christopher in its breast pocket. A trophy from piracy, no doubt.'

'Nonsense!' Alyce's clear voice rang across the infirmary. She and Lord Tiptoft had followed hard on Harcourt's heels. 'He was lying. It was I who gave the doublet to Milo, and I slipped a St Christopher into its pocket for good luck. Mistress Purbeck saw me doing so. As for poor Dick, that someone – probably Milo – smuggled beer in to tempt a man with a known weakness is their sin, not that of our God's House. And no one in their right mind could begrudge a cell in the God's House to Sybilla of Swyncombe. She is an exceptionally saintly woman, now very frail. My almshouses in Hull, Leighton Buzzard and Donnington all accept worthy women who have come upon hard times, and I am in the process of altering the Ewelme statutes to accord with theirs.'

She gestured to the pitifully thin Sybilla, who lay a few cots away from them. 'Look at her. Who could suppose her a whore, unless they had a personal grudge against me? Any of my tenants will testify that she has lived the holy life of an anchorite at Swyncombe for the last twelve years, healing the sick and praying for the souls of the departed. It was at the request of Sir Brian Fulbert that I brought her down here. She had been severely bitten by adders, and was sorely in need of expert medical attention.'

Tiptoft smiled inwardly. What a woman she was. Had had to be, indeed, to survive Dame Fortune's cruel arrows for the last sixteen years. But Harcourt thundered on, spittle flying from his mouth.

'Drunkards and illicit women are not all. We broke into the strongroom of the church and found goods belonging to notorious Lancastrians. Explain that away, Lady Alyce. I have arrested William Marton and Peter Greene on suspicion of aiding traitors. They claim that they knew nothing of them. A likely story, given that they have keys to the strongroom. My guess is that they did away with Milo to prevent him revealing what has been going on here.'

Alyce was lost for words, bewildered by this new accusation. But Sybilla intervened again.

'Hear me, Constable, this is none of the duchess's doing, nor of those she has trusted with her affairs. The fault lies with me, and me alone. Those bundles came from my cell in Swyncombe. They were left with me for safe-keeping by Lancastrian refugees travelling on the ridgeway high on the hills taken by those who are not minded to be seen. I listened to their confessions and they trusted their valuables with me. If you examine the directions left with them, you will see that they are intended to be collected by the dependants they had to leave behind. Beloved wives and children who they thought did not deserve to be deprived of the means to support themselves. And I agreed with them. I have never been one to judge; nor these days does right necessarily remain right. Sir John Fortescue was for years the most highly respected judge in England, but when I saw him he was a hapless fugitive. So was George Ashby, and so was Sir Gervais Clifton. And yet there was a time when all three were deemed loyal by England's king. The wheel of Fortune spins, and we are at its mercy. Do with me as you will. I am ready to meet my maker.'

She lay back, exhausted. Farhang drew her coverlet up and stood protectively beside her. For a few moments there was utter silence. Then a confusion of voices sounded. Harcourt's accusing, Wenlock's conciliatory, Joan's an indignant squawking. Finally, quelling them all with a sharp rap of his constable's staff on the floor, Tiptoft spoke.

'Let us adjourn to the palace and leave Doctor Farhang and his patient in peace. There is no question of Sybilla of Swyncombe fleeing from justice. We can only hope that she will survive the night. If she does, she will need to answer to the coroner, as she was the last person to see Milo alive. So will the man who found him in the well. What was his name, Sir Robert? He will be called as first finder, not that there is any question of his guilt.'

'Jake of Northmoor,' said Harcourt. 'He called his brother Piers to help him hoist up the bucket. So perhaps it was both of them.' He had calmed down. Which, Alyce reflected, probably made him more dangerous. He would be plotting new ways to justify arresting her for treason.

Sure enough, he soon spoke again. 'Turvey, I want you to extend the search to Swyncombe, if that is where those traitors' goods came from. Fulbert may have more hidden in his house. When you've finished around the God's House, take some men up there.'

He stalked away, followed by Lord Tiptoft and Alyce. Wenlock stayed at Joan's side, waiting to allow them to go ahead before taking her arm as they too returned to the palace. He bent his head towards her.

'Joan, Lady Alyce is still in danger,' he whispered. 'Harcourt will stop at nothing to prove her guilt. I must leave tomorrow to sort out certain matters in and around Oxford. Could you and Monique linger until I return? Her little wench Tamsin is fiercely loyal, but as a servant she has to do what she is bid. And there is no sign of Ben Bilton.'

'Of course,' said Joan. 'I'll stand by her. Such spirit. I begin to like her immensely. But where is Tamsin? She usually sticks as closely as a limpet to her mistress. I haven't seen her since she and young William Stonor sneaked off just after Harcourt and his ruffians arrived.'

Swyncombe

Having brought Sybilla to the infirmary, Tamsin and William had stayed concealed in Farhang's treatment room while the gaggle of the great milled about. Once they were alone, Farhang turned to them urgently.

'You two need to ride to Swyncombe as fast as you can. There are two ponies in the paddock behind the church. Get from Nan their bridles and a couple of apples to tempt them. Now that Harcourt intends to extend his search there, John Trevelyan must be taken to Stonor Park. And there is another threat. Sybilla has told me that the most compromising of all the things she had care of is hidden in St Botolph's reliquary in Swyncombe church. If it is found, she says it will utterly ruin Lady Alyce. You must ask Sir Brian Fulbert to have the reliquary taken to Stonor Park as well. William, you should go with Trevelyan and the reliquary. Give it to your father to conceal at Stonor. Tamsin, can you ride back and let us know all is well?'

They nodded, and slipped away to the God's House kitchen for the apples and bridles, then to the paddock, where the inquisitive ponies trotted over to them. When they reached Swyncombe, Sir Brian welcomed them with his usual warmth, but when they told him that Sir Robert Harcourt was planning to search his house he looked apprehensive.

'The sooner you take Trevelyan to Stonor Park the better. He is much recovered, thanks to the medicine that Farhang gave him. I think he will be able to ride. I'll send Roger with you, William. He's the only servant who knows who Trevelyan is, so he is best out of the way.' He summoned a page and sent him to tell Roger to prepare Trevelyan for the journey.

'Farhang also thinks that the St Botolph reliquary should be taken to Stonor,' said Tamsin. 'Apparently it contains something that threatens Lady Alyce.'

Sir Brian frowned. 'I'd rather not part with it. It is in itself immensely valuable, and the holy finger bones of the saint are what draw pilgrims to Swyncombe.'

'Then could we at least open it and take out whatever is so dangerous to the duchess?' asked William. 'It sounds as if it shouldn't be there anyway.' Fulbert thought for a moment, then nodded.

They walked over to the little flint-covered church. Behind the altar was an intricate screen with saints flanking a small central arch. Chained securely under the arch was a jewelled casket with a tiny set of double doors. Sir Brian pulled out his ring of keys, selected the smallest, put it in the keyhole on the right-hand door, and turned it. There was a click, and the door swung open. Putting in his hand, he pulled out an embroidered velvet pouch with a drawstring. He loosened the string, and gently emptied the contents of the pouch onto the altar slab. It contained about fifteen small bones – and a small, tightly rolled scroll sealed with a large black lump of wax into which a signet ring had been pressed. Three tiny lions' heads grouped around a chevron. He handed it to Tamsin.

'That's the Suffolk seal,' she said. 'I wonder what's on the scroll.'

'Whatever it is, it's none of our business,' said William. 'What matters is that Sybilla said that it must be safely hidden. But I don't like the idea of taking it with us to Stonor. We shouldn't have all our eggs in one basket in case Harcourt's men catch up with us. Tamsin, could you take it to Sybilla?'

Tamsin frowned. 'That might be dangerous if they are searching her things. But I'll find somewhere safe for it.'

Fulbert replaced the bones in the pouch and locked it up again inside the reliquary.

'I think you should get going, William. The sooner Trevelyan is away from here the safer for me and my family.'

He watched them trot away with relief.

'They should be at Stonor Park within an hour,' he said. 'Now, you must be off, Tamsin. I don't want that scroll to be found here.'

The jingling of harness made them turn. Led by a burly black-clad squire, seven men rode their horses into the yard in front of the manor house. The leader dismounted and made Sir Brian a cursory bow.

'I am Hamel Turvey, squire to Sir Robert Harcourt. We come from the Constable of England in search of traitors and evidence of treason. We are authorised to make a search of the church and the manor.'

Fulbert thought quickly, glancing at Tamsin, and hoping that Turvey had not recognised the girl from Ewelme.

'As you will, sir. Though you will find none such here. My wife has recently been delivered of a fine daughter, however, and I would appreciate courtesy in approaching her chamber. By your leave I will send her maid to prepare her.' He waved Tamsin towards the entrance of the house.

Tamsin nodded obediently and scuttled into the house. What should she do? She saw a kitchen maid crossing the hall and called to her.

'Sir Brian asks that you tell Lady Fulbert that men are about to search the house. But that there is no cause for alarm.'

Once the girl had disappeared, she looked around the hall. Which door had she gone through when she went into the kitchen on her last visit? Guessing, she went through the first one on her left. It was the buttery. She opened a door opposite and found that she was in the stable yard, busy now as lads led Turvey's men's mounts into stalls. One of them whistled at her, but she ignored him. Then she thought again, turning to him with a smile.

'Can you help me? I'm looking for my pony. Sir Brian has told me to return to Ewelme.'

The lad leered. 'Gonna make it worth my while?' His hand grabbed her shoulder. Tamsin froze.

Suddenly a tall groom advanced on the lad, cuffed him hard, and bowed to Tamsin.

'Apologies, little maid. Sir Brian told me to look out for you. I'll get your pony. He's been fed and watered. Will you be alright riding on your own? The coverts are wild places between here and Ewelme. This lad could go with you now I've taught him his manners.'

Deciding that such an escort might be as much of a menace as anyone she met on the road, Tamsin shook her head.

'Thank you, but no. It's still light, and I know the way.'

He shrugged and told the lad to fetch her pony. Making

a cup of his hands to help her mount, he smacked the little horse on its rump.

'God speed you. You're better away from these ruffians.'

Ewelme

Tamsin arrived in the village without incident, still unsure what to do about the scroll of paper she had hidden inside her bodice. From what Farhang had said, it represented a threat to the duchess. So perhaps she should just destroy it. But Sybilla had wanted it safely hidden. Tomorrow the palace itself was to be searched, so she couldn't conceal it in her room. As she cudgelled her wits to think of somewhere safe, Wat came to mind. Devoted to her, and now with a room of his own above Nan Ormesby's laundry. Had it been searched today? she wondered. If it had, it would be an ideal hiding place until she could ask Sybilla what to do with it.

Half an hour later, she reached the palace gatehouse. 'Where is Lady Alyce?' she asked Jem, who was on guard duty.

'In her garden with her visitors,' he answered. 'She was looking for you earlier. No one knew where you were.'

Tamsin felt a qualm of guilt as she slipped up the back stairs to her garret. She opened its window and craned her head. Sure enough, she could see several figures in Alyce's private garden, strangely foreshortened from this height. She decided to set the duchess's rooms to rights, hoping to forestall her anger, if angry she was. But when Lady Alyce eventually came in with Joan Moulton and Monique de Chinon, she was all smiles as she settled them on high-backed chairs around the long table in the centre of the solar. With them were Farhang and Lord

Wenlock, who gave her a broad wink and an approving nod. Farhang must have told him about her and William's errand.

'Ah, there you are, Tamsin,' said Alyce. 'We are a little more at ease now. Sir Robert has decided to stay in Bensington with his men, and Lord Tiptoft has left. He said he had urgent business in Windsor. Are young William and John Trevelyan on the road to Stonor Park?'

Tamsin nodded, relieved that Lady Alyce had approved their mission.

'Come and sit down, child,' said Joan Moulton. 'You've done well.'

She turned to Alyce. 'But now we must concentrate on saving you, Duchess. Somehow we have to convince the coroner that Milo's death was an accident. Perhaps one or more of the bedesmen saw something – or would obligingly say that they did so. But we must also persuade Lord Tiptoft that you are no threat to York. I think the best way of doing that would be to invite your son and your royal daughter-in-law for a visit. It would be a salutary reminder of your high position.'

Alyce looked unconvinced. 'Jack will be only too delighted to believe that I am a traitor.'

'But the young duchess will I think stand your friend,' said Monique de Chinon. 'She'll understand better than he does the risk to his inheritance.'

Alyce pursed her lips. She hated the thought of eating humble pie by appealing for support from Jack and Bess.

'There are more urgent things to attend to. I think that we may be able to lay two serious crimes at Milo's door.'

'I don't understand,' said Joan.

'I've been thinking hard. We have two mysteries to consider: the death of Nicolas Webb and the putting of adders into

Sybilla's anchorhold. I asked Vespilan after vespers yesterday if he had remembered anything else about the man he saw entering and leaving the cloister on the night before Webb died. He told me that he reminded him of the pedlar who started visiting Ewelme regularly this summer. Nan says that he came the day before Nicolas died. He commented on the size and freshness of the mushrooms Webb brought into the kitchen to cook for his supper. Suppose he added a poisonous one to them, so that there would be a vacancy among the bedesmen?'

'That seems a bit far-fetched,' said Joan. 'It's unlikely that he had a death cap or whatever with him.'

'But he might well have had some poison,' said Farhang.

'Let us imagine he did,' said Alyce. 'The pedlar also visited Swyncombe on the Monday that Simon and Bilton sent Peter Greene there to ask Sybilla to be a bedeswoman. He chatted to Peter on his way up the hill, and Peter told him that he was going to invite Sybilla to the God's House. Later the same day he visited Swyncombe and sold her a length of cloth. That was the night that Lady Fulbert's baby was born. Next morning, Sybilla was bitten after she returned to her cell for a well-earned rest. Suppose it was the pedlar who contributed a clutch of adders to the anchorhold?'

'All possible,' said Farhang. 'But not provable.'

'There's more,' said Alyce. 'I went to the infirmary to see Sybilla, and she told me that she thinks the pedlar was Milo. She and I saw him when he came back to Ewelme from Wallingford on Friday, and, despite his being clean-shaven and respectably dressed, she said then that he looked familiar.'

'If you are right, his accidental death was well deserved,' mused Joan. Silence fell. She looked around the room. 'Or did someone take it on themselves to exact justice? By the way, where is Ben Bilton?'

Tamsin felt a sinking feeling at the pit of her stomach. Ben had a hot temper. He could easily have murdered Milo.

Alyce said slowly, 'I asked him to find Milo this morning.'

'He might have gone to Wallingford,' said Tamsin. 'If he thought Milo was planning to escape by river.'

'Or have pushed Milo down the well and made himself scarce,' said Wenlock.

'But whatever happened, it seems to me that there is a case to be made against Sir Robert Harcourt if he foisted Milo on Ewelme not just as a spy but as an active agent who killed Webb. Though we can't prove anything, if he thought that we could it might be enough to make him hesitate to take further action. And I think Joan and Monique are right, Lady Alyce. You should send to your son at Windsor, inviting him and his wife to visit. It will remind the world that you are close kin to King Edward.'

Alyce looked stubborn. Then she imagined what calumnies Lord Tiptoft could be pouring into the receptive ear of the queen and sighed.

'I fear I must. Though it goes against the grain to do so.' She was recalling the terrible scene that decided her to leave Wingfield for good. Jack's accusing face. 'You hated my father. You caused his death!' he had shrieked, red in the face from too much wine.

'Tamsin, bring writing materials. I will pen a letter to Jack.'

As she climbed the stairs to Alyce's chamber, Tamsin remembered the first time she had entered the room, aching from the blows of the outlaws, and nervous of meeting the august lady of Ewelme. Now it was as familiar as her own snug attic.

When she returned with a small portable desk containing paper, pen and ink, and a silver sand shaker, she saw that Lord Wenlock had produced a long roll of parchment, and was spreading it out in front of Alyce.

'This is the formal document of trusteeship of the properties left to me for my lifetime by my late wife. I'd be grateful if you could sign here, Lady Alyce. And Mistress Joan, perhaps you would be kind enough to witness her signature.'

He watched as they did so, then shook fine sand over to absorb the excess.

'Tomorrow I will ride for Chalgrove and get Richard Harcourt to sign as second trustee. Some words in his ear on the subject of Milo will I think have an effect on his brother's belligerence. After that I have some other matters of business to settle in Oxford. I should be back by Thursday. Then I could escort you and Monique back to London, Joan, if you wish. Either by road or by river.'

Joan looked at Alyce. 'Does it suit you for us to stay on, Lady Alyce?'

Alyce considered. Solitude in her turret or continuing the literary conversation with this at times infuriating but never boring woman and her highly intelligent French companion. A little citadel of ladies. Christine de Pisan would approve, she was sure. She smiled.

'I'd welcome your company. But Tamsin, can you find out what's become of Leo? I haven't seen him since this morning.'

Tamsin nodded. 'I'll try the stables.' She hoped the dog would be there as she urgently needed to consult Sybilla about the scroll. But when she asked about Leo, Jem shook his head.

'Haven't seen him since the midday meal. I thought he'd be with the duchess.'

Tamsin tried the kitchen, another of Leo's favourite haunts. Cook also shook his head.

'Maybe he followed Wat back to the God's House. He brought some vegetables over from the bedesmen's gardens, and Leo's that fond of the boy.'

Thanking him, Tamsin hurried down the street towards the God's House. A horseman was riding towards her. It was Ben Bilton.

'Ben, where have you been?' she called. 'We are all at sixes and sevens. Milo's body has been found in the God's House well.'

Ben gave a snort of laughter as he dismounted. 'Good riddance to bad rubbish. But I fear the Harcourts will raise hell over it. But how? What happened?'

'We don't know.' Her eyes met his anxiously with an unasked question.

He shook his head impatiently. 'Not my doing. I've been looking for him, riding along the river in pursuit of a barge that the bridge warden said he'd seen a man like Milo climbing aboard. It was a wild-goose chase. Then Bayard cast a shoe, and I had to wait at old Job's forge.'

She looked at him doubtfully. Was he telling the truth? Mightn't he have killed Milo before riding away from the place?

He stared at her, then said accusingly, 'You don't believe me, do you?'

She blushed. 'I want to. But will the king's men?'

'The king's men can think what they like,' he said bullishly, and rode away.

Still wondering if he had been telling the truth, Tamsin continued along the lane in search of Leo. Just past the village pond, she slowed. A sodden shape, partly hidden by a clump of reeds, lay half in, half out, of the Ewelme Brook. She went closer. Leo. She tried to haul him out, and managed to get him onto the bank. As she tugged at his pelt his eyes opened and he whimpered. Not dead then. But close to death. His silky golden coat was saturated with vomit, and his hind legs were smeared with faeces. She got up and raced to the infirmary. Farhang was still in the palace, but her grandmother was there, talking to Sybilla.

'Nan!' she cried. 'Where's Wat? Leo is lying half-dead in the brook. I want him to help me carry him here, then fetch Farhang.'

Without wasting time on questions, Nan went to the back door of the infirmary and shouted to Wat, who was digging up potatoes. A few minutes later, he and Tamsin reached Leo's sodden body, and placed him on a wide board that Nan had given them. One at each end, they carried him to the infirmary. On their way, they were overtaken by Farhang returning from the palace.

'What's this?' he said, shocked by the sight of Leo sprawled on the board. 'Was he knocked over by a careless rider? He is forever jumping up at horsemen.'

'I think he may have been poisoned,' said Tamsin. 'There's vomit all over him. Smells foul.'

Farhang bent and smelt the noxious crud that caked the fur around Leo's mouth. 'You're right, It's henbane; the smell is unmistakeable. He's been poisoned. It must have been deliberate. No animal would go near the stuff. Perhaps seeds of it were mixed into food.'

He opened the dog's limp jaws, and pushed his finger as deeply down his throat as he could reach. Leo retched again, and another stream of vomit shot out. Farhang disappeared into his medicine closet and reappeared with a bowl of salt. He dropped a handful into a jug of water, opened Leo's jaws again, and poured it down his throat. The dog vomited again copiously, then retched dryly several times. Then he lay limp.

'Go and fetch Lady Alyce,' Nan said to Tamsin. She'll want to be with him.' Tamsin set off at a run. She found her mistress in her chamber, showing Joan her Tales of Canterbury.

'My lady, I've found Leo. Farhang thinks he has been poisoned.'

'Where is he?'

'Wat and I carried him to the infirmary.'

'Fetch my cloak. Then follow.'

Not wasting time apologising to Joan and Monique, Alyce hurried down to the gatehouse. Her rosary was clutched in her hand.

'To me, Pek,' she said curtly, and set off down the street. Tamsin was only a few yards behind her.

'What's up?' Pek asked. Tamsin turned back, but didn't slow up.

'It's Leo. He's close to death.'

Pek cursed, and shouted to a passing groom.

'Keep gate until I return.' Then he hurried after them.

Alyce had managed five heartfelt Hail Marys and a Paternoster by the time she reached the infirmary. She tucked the rosary safely into her pocket and ran to where Leo lay. Farhang had washed the vomit from his fur, and wrapped a thick blanket around him.

'Will he live?' she asked bluntly.

'I think so,' said Farhang. 'It was fortunate that Tamsin found him when she did. He must have been dizzy from vomiting, and fallen into the brook. He could easily have drowned.'

Careless of her gown, Alyce wrapped her arms around her beloved dog, and murmured endearments into his ear. The blanket stirred, and she smiled through her tears as she realised that he was trying to wag his tail.

'What makes you think he was poisoned?' she asked Farhang.

'He stank of henbane. He wouldn't have eaten it by accident. And violent vomiting and shitting is typical.'

His words triggered memories of Martha's description of Nicolas Webb's death: 'Guts like water, sick as a dog, sweating and dribbling.'

'Farhang, that sounds exactly like Nicolas Webb's symptoms. Did you attend him?'

'No, I was at Caversham, tending to the Countess of Warwick. He had been buried by the time I returned.'

'If we are right in thinking that Nicolas's murderer was Milo disguised as a pedlar, then he could have put henbane seeds both in his mushroom stew and in Leo's food.'

'Why poison a dog?' said Farhang.

'He feared him,' said Alyce. 'Leo rarely growls, but he snarled at Milo both on the day I arrived home, when he was seemingly a pedlar, and when he moved into the palace as Milo the scrivener. Perhaps he thought that someone would put two and two together. If only I'd done so.' She bent her head over the dog again, whispering comfort into his ear.

'I think it was just spite,' said Tamsin hotly. 'Begging your pardon, my lady. He knew how much Leo meant to you, and he wanted to make you feel alone and vulnerable.'

'She may be right,' said Farhang. 'If ever a man was an ill-wisher it was Milo. I felt it when I saw him looking at you in church. Such malevolence.'

Windsor

Lord Tiptoft, in full court dress, kneeled in front of the king and queen.

'How does my respected aunt of Ewelme?' inquired Edward. 'My sister Bess tells me that she left Wingfield in high dudgeon. Taking everything moveable that she could with her.'

'Disgraceful,' said the queen, waving Tiptoft to his feet. 'Such avarice deserves condign punishment.'

The king chuckled. 'The contents of Wingfield were Alyce's to do with as she chose. It was after all her personal fortune from her parents and her previous marriages that paid for them. Duke William had to pay over what little money he inherited as a ransom after he was captured at Jargeau. Nor is Bess much concerned at the loss of musty old-fashioned furniture, moth-eaten tapestries and boring books. When I send Duke John the next instalment of her dowry, they can be replaced.'

Lord Rivers, father to the queen and Treasurer of England, gave a little cough. 'I am not sure that we have enough in the coffers just now to do that.'

'I'm sure the dowager duchess would be happy to oblige with another loan,' offered Tiptoft. 'Naturally she will not want to offend you at present.'

Edward raised his eyebrows. 'How so?'

Tiptoft glanced at the queen, who sat expressionless. It was as he thought. Edward knew nothing of his wife's machinations with Harcourt. 'As I told you. I met her in Oxford on Thursday and called at Ewelme yesterday. There was some commotion over the accidental death of a scrivener. Sir Robert Harcourt is dealing with it.'

Elizabeth stirred. 'A scrivener? Not, I trust, the one that I proposed as a bedesman at the Ewelme God's House?'

'The very man,' replied Tiptoft. 'The Harcourts had left him with the duchess ten days ago.'

'And his death was an accident, you say. How did it come about?'

'It appears that he was obliging an elderly woman by hoisting up a bucket of water from the Ewelme God's House well and slipped on the wet paving surrounding it. Cracked his head on the stone wellhead and fell down the well. Harcourt has had the two priests in charge of the God's House arrested. The coroner is holding the inquest tomorrow.'

Bess of York, the young Duke of Suffolk's plump and amiable wife, put down her end of the bargello embroidery curtain she and her mother Cecily were working on, and looked up with concern.

'Poor Belle-mère. She was hoping for some peace in Oxfordshire. I'm afraid her grandsons tried her patience sorely at Wingfield. When she left, she was talking of becoming a vowess.'

'A wise precaution which will ensure that she isn't required to marry, as my sister was,' said her mother Cecily, fiercely jabbing a needle threaded with a new shade of blue into the heavy cloth draped over her knees. She glared at the queen.

'I hope planting a spy was none of your doing, Elizabeth. I saw you hugger-mugger with Harcourt last week.'

'It seems that the scrivener's death was just an unfortunate accident,' said Tiptoft. 'What was a little unusual was the discovery of a woman in the almshouse. But apparently she had just been appointed as a member of the community by Alyce herself.'

Elizabeth's eyes narrowed. 'Surely that runs counter to decency. It should be investigated.'

'With respect, your majesty, mixed communities are quite customary these days,' Tiptoft said. 'Moreover, the woman in question is in her ninth decade. A former anchorite and all but a saint, I was assured.'

'But what of the statutes? Do they allow for a woman?'

'Lady Alyce told me that she was in the process of having them altered to bring them into line with the rules in her other three almshouses.'

The doors of the presence chamber were flung open, and a flamboyantly dressed young nobleman in his mid-twenties marched into the room, bowed to the king and queen, kissed Bess's hand and sat down beside her. Tiptoft secretly found it extraordinary that the son of two such clever people as Alyce and William could be such a young popinjay. Jack was as plump as Bess was, and not much taller. But her delight at seeing him, and his pride in her even after eight years of marriage, were evident to all. Cecily Neville smirked, and King Edward looked benignly on them, though he drew the line at giving any responsibility to Roly-Poly, as he was universally known.

'Jack, dear, it appears that your mama is in trouble,' said Bess.

The young duke frowned. 'So what if she is? She probably deserves it. Sir Richard Harcourt told me that the reason she had stripped Wingfield Castle of its finest furnishings was to raise funds for the Lancastrian cause.'

King Edward raised his eyebrows in surprise. 'That hardly seems likely. Did Sir Richard offer any evidence?'

Jack changed tack. 'How has trouble come to her? Isn't she safely cloistered at Ewelme?'

'Trouble has come to her there,' said Tiptoft. 'An unfortunate accident, which is requiring the attendance of the coroner. Sir Robert Harcourt believes it to have been murder, and he has arrested the two men in charge of her almshouse.'

'God's wounds, I hope I'm not expected to go over, Bess. There's a hunt in the Great Wood tomorrow, and I want to ride that splendid horse you gave me for my birthday.'

'I think your mother will be able to manage without you,' said Tiptoft. 'She has several friends with her. The well-known London bookseller Joan Moulton and Lord Wenlock. To say nothing of her faithful secretary Brailles and, when he deigns to reappear, her steward Ben Bilton.'

Bess was looking thoughtful. She was every bit as clever as her brother and a good deal brighter than her husband. She had also observed the queen's tense interest in Tiptoft's account of his visit to Ewelme. She patted her husband's hand affectionately.

'If you're hunting, then I think I'll amuse myself by riding over to Ewelme. Belle-mère might appreciate a little support from the family. I'll go on to Woodstock and see Aunt Anne. She's always saying she doesn't see enough of me.'

Jack flushed. 'Oh. Do you really think of going? In that case I suppose I must come too, I might have known she'd find a way to spoil my fun.'

'You go hunting, dear heart,' said Bess. 'I'd prefer to go on my own. I can tell your mother about the new baby, and we can be womanish together. It'll take her mind off her troubles. I'll spend two nights with Aunt Anne and then come home.'

Tiptoft smiled. With Bess at Ewelme, it was unlikely that Harcourt would succeed in entrapping Alyce. Unless he did find conclusive evidence of the treason he was so sure existed. In which case, the duchess deserved her fate. And since neither Jack nor Bess was interested in literary pursuits, quite a few fine volumes might come his way. He bowed and backed out of the presence chamber.

Ewelme

Early on Monday morning Ralph Boteler, the Watlington coroner, clattered into the base court of Ewelme Palace with his clerks and marshalls. Milo's body had been moved to the courthouse, where a jury assembled from Ewelme village had inspected his rotting corpse. Despite Alyce's protestations, William Marton and Peter Greene had been kept chained in the cellar for the last two nights. They now stood in a makeshift dock at one side of the hall, Greene deflated and anxious, Marton pompous and indignant. Alyce sat in her chair of state at the side of the dais in the dauntingly splendid regalia of a duchess who was also aunt of the king. It sent, as she intended, a clear message. Beside her sat Joan Moulton and Monique, Simon Brailles and Ben Bilton. The jurors, local men all, filled two benches on the left-hand side of the hall, and the bedesmen sat behind them. At the end of their bench, Sybilla sat on a chair, with Tamsin beside her on a stool. Harcourt and his men, weary from their exhaustive but fruitless search of the great palace, filled the benches on the right-hand side of the courthouse. They all rose as Boteler entered and mounted the dais, followed by his clerk. He looked around the courthouse, relishing his power.

'Be seated. We are gathered here in the name of the king to investigate the death of Milo of Windsor. Witnesses will be on oath to speak the truth, the whole truth and nothing but the truth.' He rapped the table with his gavel, and sat down.

His clerk stood up. 'Call the first finder,' he intoned.

Jake of Northmoor and his brother Piers both stepped forward and presented themselves at the bar in front of the dais.

Boteler frowned. 'First, I said.'

The brothers looked at each other. Then Piers spoke.

'We were both bent over the well, hauling on the rope. Couldn't say which of us saw the fingers first.'

'The fingers?'

Harcourt rose and interrupted impatiently. 'They saw Milo's hand. Caught, or more likely fastened, around the handle of the bucket. Then they hauled the rest of him out.'

'So there was no question of these men being involved in his death? In that case, who was last to see the deceased?'

'It was, contrary to all custom of the God's House, a woman,' said Harcourt. 'The duchess flouted the statutes to instal her.'

Alyce stood up. 'The woman concerned is Sybilla of Swyncombe, your honour. I have had it in mind for some time to alter the God's House statutes to allow it to provide for worthy female candidates. When our revered anchorite Sybilla fell ill, the senior members of the community agreed with me that we should pre-empt that change slightly.'

She turned to the coroner. 'You know Sybilla's worth yourself, Ralph. She has provided succour for the physically and mentally sick of Pyrton parish for many years. I am sure you must endorse our action.'

Boteler saw Harcourt's angry glare, and hesitated. Then he reflected on the excellent dinner he had enjoyed at Ewelme Palace after a fine day's hunting only ten days earlier, and the attractive prospect of setting ferrets freely in the Ewelme warrens. His neighbour was best kept as a friend, for all Harcourt's vilification of her. He inclined his head.

'The action was not strictly legal, but in the circumstances understandable,' he announced. 'Call Sybilla of Swyncombe.'

Sybilla rose from the stool she had been sitting on, and, leaning on Tamsin, came forward.

'As far as I know, I was the last to see the poor man. I needed some water to wash in and came out of my room to get some. Milo was in the courtyard, so I asked him to fill the well bucket for me. Then I went back into my room. I busied myself building up the fire to heat the water, but Milo never brought it. And when I looked out to see what had become of him, there was nobody to be seen.'

Boteler looked at the shrivelled old woman. It was hard to imagine anyone less likely to have murdered somebody.

'Could anyone else have come out of their cells and killed Milo?' he asked her.

'I'm not sure if anyone else was in. It was midday, and most of the bedesmen were in the chapel for sext.'

'Most?' queried the coroner.

'My neighbour Gerard Vespilan was excused all but two of the hours. So perhaps he was in. And Dick Lawrence was ailing with a fever.'

'Downing ale from a firkin rather,' burst in Harcourt. 'When we searched the rooms after finding Milo's body, he was dead drunk.'

'And might he have pushed Milo down the well?'

Harcourt hesitated. He looked across the courtroom at the scraggy old bedesman's vacant expression and feeble frame and knew Lawrence would also cut a poor figure as murderer.

'I cannot say, your honour. But I feel that the responsibility for the death should lie with those responsible for the almshouse.

Which is why I arrested its master William Marton and the school's teacher Peter Greene.'

'Who were both taking the service of sext while Sybilla was asking Milo to fetch her some water,' interposed Simon Brailles, rising from his seat. 'I was in the church too, and I can vouch for them.'

'What of the other palace servants?' asked the coroner.

'None was seen in the God's House at that time. They were eating in the palace, and can vouch for each other.'

Boteler's next words caused Alyce to tense again.

'Call Gerard Vespilan.'

Gerard rose from the bedesmen's bench, walked with dignity to the bar, and bowed to Boteler. The coroner gave a courteous nod in response.

'I can see that your advanced years make it unlikely that you could have done any damage to a relatively strong man like Milo. But your cell is next to Sybilla's, and I must ask you if you had anything to do with his death.'

Vespilan shook his head. 'I saw nothing, your honour. I was weary after a wakeful night, and had nodded off in my chair. Mistress Ormesby had to knock hard to wake me for the midday meal.'

Boteler turned back to Simon Brailles.

'Master Brailles, what is the window of time between Sybilla seeing Milo on Saturday morning and his body being found by Sir Robert's men?'

'About four hours.'

'And were you with William Marton and Peter Greene all that time?'

'I was. We ate together in the servants' hall of the palace, and then sorted the holy books I had catalogued into their proper places in the palace chapel and the God's House.'

'Did you see anyone else in the God's House?'

'Nobody. It is always quiet in the early afternoon. Old folk like to take a nap.'

'In that case, the master and the Teacher of Grammar should be freed forthwith,' said Boteler. 'See that it is done. I know both you and them for honourable men.'

Alyce breathed a sigh of relief. Her courting of Boteler had paid off. His allegiance had shifted back to her from Harcourt. Another bang of the gavel. But as Boteler rose to send the jury out, a shout came from Sir Robert Harcourt.

'What about Ben Bilton? He was seen riding away that morning by the man I put on guard at the gatehouse.'

The coroner turned to Bilton.

'Can you explain yourself, Bilton?'

Bilton rose. 'I was searching for Milo. I thought he might have gone to Wallingford. The bridge warden saw me. And Job at the forge. Bayard cast a shoe.'

Boteler nodded. 'And I know you too for an honourable man. Jurors, you may leave the court to confer.' The twelve men trooped out, and there was a low buzz of voices. The minutes ticked by.

At last the jurors returned, and sat down again on their bench. Their foreman, a Bensington farmer, rose.

'How do you find?' asked Boteler.

'We find for an accidental death.'

'And is that the judgment of you all?'

'It is.'

'Then the court is adjourned. The dead man should be buried as soon as possible.'

Harcourt rose to his feet. 'This is an outrageous miscarriage of justice. I will appeal it.' Then he stalked out of the court-house, followed by his henchmen.

Boteler walked over to Alyce and bowed courteously.

'Thank you, Ralph,' she said with a smile. 'It is a relief to have such a fair-minded man as you as coroner. Sir Robert has made a mountain out of a molehill from this sad business because he placed Milo here himself with a mind to blackening the name of the God's House. We are, as you have heard, not above reproach in the matter of appointing a female to a cell in the God's House, but I can assure you that all will be set to rights as soon as possible.'

Boteler smirked, delighted at having put the Lady of Ewelme under an obligation.

After he had left and she had thanked the jurors, Alyce turned to Sybilla. 'You look exhausted, dear heart. Tamsin, help Sybilla to her room and make sure she is comfortably settled. I'll visit in the morning when she is rested.'

After they left, she looked at Joan.

'Mistress Moulton, I think I can at last look at the books you have brought. Shall we adjourn to my library? And Gerard, would you like to come too?'

Sybilla collapsed gratefully in her now sheepskin-lined chair by the hearth, watching Tamsin liven up the fire.

'You're a quick little thing. Tell me, what became of the reliquary? I hope it is safely at Stonor Park by now.'

'I'm afraid it isn't,' said Tamsin. 'Sir Brian didn't want St Botolph's relics to leave Swyncombe. But as you'd said there was something important to Lady Alyce in it, I thought we should see what it was. We opened the reliquary and found a little scroll in the pouch with the holy bones of the saint. Was that what you wanted hidden?'

'Yes!' Sybilla breathed a sigh of relief. 'William took it with him, I hope.'

Tamsin swallowed nervously. 'I'm afraid not. He and Sir Brian thought it was too risky for him to take both it and Trevelyan.'

Sybilla's face fell. 'But Harcourt's men left to search Swyncombe not long after you left.'

'I know. Sir Brian thought the best thing was for me to ride back to Ewelme with it. I was going to hide it in Wat's room above the laundry, but Nan told me that it hadn't been searched yet. So I took it up the hill to his old hideout in the hollow tree in the box copse. He never goes there now. I'm sure it will be safe. I tucked it deep into a cavity high inside the trunk.'

Sybilla paled. 'Tamsin, that is terribly dangerous. That scroll has the power to ruin the Duchess Alyce. She stubbornly refuses to destroy it. Her plan is to have it placed in her tomb, so that come the Day of Judgement truth will out. But if it falls into the hands of her enemies, she will lose everything she holds dear.'

'Then I'll go now and fetch it,' said Tamsin. 'Harcourt and his men have all gone. I'll bring it back to you and you can hide it somewhere else.'

'I don't know,' said Sybilla. 'It's getting dark. I think you had better leave it until the morning.'

'It isn't dark yet,' said Tamsin. 'I'll be there and back again before you know it.' She wrapped her russet cloak around her and left the room. A minute or two later, Sybilla watched her pick her way through the almshouse gardens and disappear up the steep slope of the graveyard. So too did another pair of eyes.

Stanton Harcourt

John Wenlock knew perfectly well that Robert Harcourt was far away in Bensington with the greater part of his retinue of ruffians, but he was a cautious man, and approached the gatehouse of Stanton Harcourt Manor hesitantly. Francis Thynne and his two grooms hung back even further. But there was no belligerent hail from the watchtower, and the gates were wide open. As they dismounted, Lady Margaret Harcourt came out with a welcoming smile.

'Lord Wenlock! This is an unexpected pleasure. I fear Robert is away at present. Are you just passing by, or do you have some business with him?'

'Not with Sir Robert, my lady. I'm looking for Denzil Caerleon and Marlene Stonor – now, I believe, his wife.'

'Not quite, for the banns have not been read in full, but you've come to the right place. Follow me.' She led the way into the main hall of the house, and through to a sunny chamber on its far side. Marlene was lying on a day bed, nibbling at sweetmeats; Caerleon was standing at a reading stand, seemingly absorbed in a massive volume. Neither turned to greet the visitors.

'The lovebirds,' said Margaret, with a grimace. 'Not that there seems much love between them.'

'I bring news from Ewelme, Denzil,' said Wenlock.

Caerleon's head whipped around. 'Of Lady Alyce?' he asked urgently.

'Who else?'

'Is she angry with me?'

'What did you expect?'

'I had hoped that Bilton would have made things right.'

Wenlock was puzzled. 'Bilton?'

'Didn't he get the letter I sent early on Saturday? I addressed it to him because I thought the duchess would refuse to read anything from me.'

'I don't think so.'

'Then I am utterly undone.' He stalked over to the great window giving on to the orchard outside the solar and gazed into the distance.

Wenlock cleared his throat. 'If you will excuse us ladies, I would like to talk to Caerleon alone.'

'Of course,' said Lady Margaret. 'Come along, Marlene. There is work to do in the still room.' She left the room, and the girl rose to follow her, heaving a noisy sigh of protest.

Wenlock quickly told Caerleon of the invasion of Ewelme, the discovery of Milo's corpse in the God's House well, and Brailles' confession to Lady Alyce.

'So her grace now knows about Trevelyan. Do you think she will forgive me for eloping with Marlene now she knows I saved a friend of hers from certain death?'

'What hurts her most is that you turned to Sir Robert rather than trusting yourself to her mercy.'

'I had little choice about seeking refuge here. It was Marlene's doing. She told me that she would never crawl to Lady Alyce. She even held a stiletto to her stomach and threatened to kill our child and herself.'

'Marlene is a conniving witch,' said Wenlock. 'I suspect that she has long been in league with Milo. How sure are you that the child she is expecting is yours?'

Denzil looked gloomy. 'Not at all. But it's true that I lay with her once at Wingfield after she got me drunk. And she told me she had a friend who would swear that I'd admitted it to him.'

'She doesn't seem much pleased with you as a husband. Why not see if you can get the truth out of her?'

Denzil considered for a moment, then strode out of the room, through the buttery and into the still room, where Marlene was sitting on a tall stool watching Lady Margaret boiling plums for jam. He took her by the shoulders and shook her.

'Tell me the truth, damn you. Am I the father of the whelp in your belly or not?'

A cat-like smile appeared on Marlene's disarmingly pretty face.

'Wouldn't you like to know?' she jeered. 'It might as well be you as the other one. Your prospects seemed the best to me, as he is promised to someone else. But now I'm not so sure. Anyway, it's too late. You agreed that we're to be wed.'

Denzil paled with anger, clenching his fists in frustration.

Wenlock was wondering if he was going to have to stop him hitting Marlene when help came from an unexpected quarter. Lady Margaret turned from the simmering pot.

'I'm not so sure about that, Marlene,' she said. 'I was talking to your parents at the hunt supper at Ewelme, and your father said that you were contracted to marry the son of his old friend Thomas Rokes of Wing.'

Marlene scowled. 'He's a spineless weakling. I told my father I wanted none of the match. And I've got a witness who heard you promise to marry me. Milo of Windsor. He's a favourite of the queen herself.'

Caerleon stared at her. 'Milo of Windsor? You were in league with him. Like Sir Robert.' He gave a jeering laugh. 'Much good may it do you. He's dead.'

Lady Harcourt spoke again. 'Marlene, if you are contracted, then you cannot enter in on another marriage until the contract has been declared void. Alyce is one of my oldest friends, and I've been worried by my husband's intriguing against her for a long time. Tricking her most valued retainer away from her is typical of him.'

Denzil's face lit up as what she had said sank in. 'Contracted to another? So I don't have to marry Marlene and become a Harcourt retainer. I can take her back to her family, and pay what compensation they demand.'

'Indeed,' said Wenlock. 'Which may not be ruinous. Thomas and Jeanne have no illusions as to their daughter's virtue, or rather lack of it. But I think we should leave as soon as we can. I'd rather not encounter Sir Robert.'

'A wise move,' said Lady Margaret. 'Go and get your things together, Marlene. Just *your* things, mind.'

Marlene stood still as stone. Then she turned and left the room. Lady Margaret turned to Wenlock.

'How does Princess Alyce, Sir John? My husband wouldn't tell me what he was up to, but I am sure that he intended new mischief.'

'Thankfully, I think it has been averted,' said Wenlock. 'And she will be all the better for knowing that Denzil is not an ally of your husband. We'll stay in Oxford tonight, and I'll return to Ewelme tomorrow. Caerleon can take Marlene to Stonor on his own.'

Ewelme

Dusk was falling around the great palace of Ewelme, and torches were being lit in its courtyards. As Tamsin climbed the steep footpath, she turned to admire its glories, and wondered once again at the change in her fortunes that had led to her becoming maid to Lady Alyce. But all that could alter if she failed in her mission.

She could still see her way clearly enough, and it was a path that she had used times without number as a child. Round the box copses, past the steep wall of the quarry from which much of the stonework of the church and almshouse had come, then up into the ancient forest where oaks of unimaginable age stood proudly despite being distorted by lightning strikes and branches snapped by storms. At last she came to Wat's hideout. She slipped into its hollow trunk, found handholds and footholds, and climbed up until she was level with the cavity in which she had stowed the scroll, wrapped in her kerchief. There it was. She gripped it tightly, and pulled. Just as she did so, she heard the crack of a broken twig below her, and the rustle of leaves. Looking down, she saw that someone had pushed inside the tree. Muscular fingers seized her leg and tugged mercilessly. With a cry, she tumbled down, crashing onto her assailant. But he recovered himself in a trice.

'So what have we here, my little maid?' She knew the voice instantly. Harcourt's squire Hamel Turvey grinned down at her in triumph.

'I thought I recognised you. Fulbert pretended you were one of his servants. But I'd seen you with Lady Alyce. Then I saw you slip out of the almshouse and head off up the hill. Got something to hide, have you? What is it, I wonder?'

He dragged her out of the tree, and saw the bundle in her hand. 'Something small, but something precious, I suspect. Evidence of the treason of the oh-so-arrogant Princess Alyce.'

He grabbed it from her and stuffed it in the front of his jerkin. Then he picked her up, tossed her over his shoulder, and strode through the trees to where his horse was tied up. Putting her down for a moment, he whipped out two lengths of cord from his saddlebag, and quickly lashed together first her wrists and then her ankles. He wrapped her cloak around her and flung her across his saddle. Then he untied the horse and mounted, his sweaty thigh horribly close to her face. Urging it forward, he held the reins with one hand, and made free of her body with the other, kneading her breasts and buttocks so brutally that she cried out in pain.

Just as the lane they had been riding along reached the main track, Turvey drew up his horse by a mounting block.

'I'm thinking that I've time for a bit of fun with you before we get to our camp – where quite a few other people will enjoy your charms. Little girls shouldn't wander in the woods when there are wolves about.'

He dismounted, and hauled her upright, pushing his head between her bound wrists and forcing her arms around his neck so that his foul breath sickened her. Tossing her cloak into the bushes, he seated her on the mounting block, drew her skirts up above her thighs, and tugged impatiently at the cord around her ankles. She stiffened, trying to protect herself, but he smacked her hard in the face, and soon had her legs hauled up on each side of his waist. He fumbled at the fastenings of his breeches. Desperate, she lunged forward and bit his nose as hard as she could. He swore angrily, and cuffed her again.

Out of nowhere came a feral growl, and a dark shape

hurtled towards them. It was Wat, determined on rescue. But this time he was up against a far more dangerous opponent than the beggarly outlaws he had worsted in Tamsin's defence a fortnight ago. Turvey threw the girl away from him into a patch of brambles, and turned on Wat with a snarl of rage. He pulled a dagger from his belt, and raised it high.

'No!' shouted Tamsin. 'Look out, Wat!'

Wat barrelled forward, knocking the blade away into the undergrowth. He gripped Turvey's throat with sinewy, muscled hands. Turvey wrenched them away, grabbed the lad round the waist in a bear hug, and lifted him high in the air, intending to throw him against a tree trunk. Tamsin watched in horror, but Wat twisted out of Turvey's grip like an eel, and leapt on his back, gouging at his eyes with his fingernails. Turvey screamed in agony and fury, then threw himself backwards on top of Wat, knocking every breath out of his body.

After checking the boy was unconscious, he turned back to Tamsin. 'Now, where was I?' He laid her face up across the stone mounting block, tore her dress clean away from her breasts and stomach, and began to force himself down on her with a broad grin. Which suddenly vanished as Wat dealt his head a crushing blow with an enormous tree branch. His eyes rolled, and he collapsed.

Tamsin wriggled out from underneath his senseless body and was about to run when she remembered the package. She hauled Turvey over onto his back and felt feverishly in his jerkin. There it was. She pulled it out, only to find a huge hand seizing her wrist. He had recovered. He hit her so hard that she fell backwards, her head meeting the stone of the mounting block with a crack. The world spun around her. Everything went dark.

Ewelme

Blithe Bessy, as she was familiarly known to her numerous brothers and sisters, had enjoyed her journey from Windsor. She had stopped overnight in Henley, and was now nearing Ewelme. Four harbingers rode ahead of her, to make sure that no unpleasant surprises awaited her grace the Duchess of Suffolk, own sister to King Edward. She also had two ladies-in-waiting and four grooms. Although she preferred the huge skies of Suffolk and the crags of her native Yorkshire to the undramatic Oxfordshire countryside, she loved the graceful sweep of the great valley of the Thames. As they trotted along the well-kept highway, its wide borders guaranteeing safety from ambushes, one of the harbingers returned.

'Your grace, it seems that there has been trouble. There is a man with a knife in his back beside the mounting block at the junction with the road to Ewelme, and a girl's body beside him. Perhaps they were set upon by outlaws last night.'

'Have you made sure that the miscreants are no longer close by?'

'Dafyd is doing just that, your grace. I suggest we halt until he returns. But I doubt they will be about in daylight.' He spat. 'Such carrion of the night will have disappeared with whatever they've stolen.'

They waited. Before long, Dafyd trotted into sight.

'All clear,' he called. 'But make haste. The wench is not yet dead.'

When the company reached the two bodies, Bess dismounted and bent over the girl. Tangled red hair and a freckled face. Brutally torn garments. A massive bruise on her cheekbone.

'She can't be much older than sixteen,' she said, pulling off her own cloak to cover the girl's nakedness. 'Dafyd, you know something of injuries. What wounds has she suffered?'

Dafyd dismounted and examined Tamsin's inert form, pulling up the lids of her eyes to reveal only whiteness. He raised her limp body, and saw clotted blood at the back of her head.

'Some nasty bruising to her face, and scratches on her arms and legs. It's the wound at the back of her head that's the trouble. Perhaps it struck that mounting block. We must get her to a physician.'

'Ewelme has a renowned infirmarian,' said Bess. 'Pray heaven he can save her. What about the man?'

'He's dead.'

What story lay behind the scene? Bess wondered. At least one other person must have been involved. Surely the girl could not have wielded the dagger that had ended the burly man's life. And was he protecting her or attacking her?

'What livery is the man wearing?' she asked one of the grooms. 'Turn him on his side, and see if he has a badge.'

The groom heaved the corpse half over. 'Red and gold stripes. That's the Harcourt badge. And there's an empty dagger sheath on his belt.'

A Harcourt man murdered a few miles from Ewelme. Belle-mère will be made to pay dearly for this if Sir Robert can blame the death on one of her servants, Bess reflected. And the unconscious girl must come from the village, if not the palace. Her torn clothes were of good quality, not those of a vagrant.

'Dafyd, can you cradle the little maid in front of you as you ride? Go carefully. We must leave Harcourt's man where he fell and summon the coroner when we reach Ewelme. I suspect he deserved to die. Those scratches on his cheeks look to be made by the girl's fingernails. It looks as if someone thought he had killed the girl and somehow managed to stab him with his own dagger. Then he fled.' She looked round at her retinue. Heads nodded in agreement.

'Good. Then that's the tale we'll tell the coroner.' She turned to her grooms. 'Hugo, you stay here until he comes. We'll take word to Ewelme. The sooner we get this poor maid to its infirmary the better.'

Dafyd picked Tamsin up gently, then noticed that she had a small packet in her hand. He prised it from her clenched fingers and held it up to Bess.

'Perhaps this will explain what happened, your grace.' Bess took it from him and unwrapped the kerchief around it. A scroll. With a seal she recognised. Suffolk's chevron between three lions' heads. She rewrapped it and tucked it into the pocket hanging from her girdle.

'This must belong to the dowager duchess. Which suggests that the girl is indeed from the palace. We must make all speed.'

Alyce walked into the great hall and looked around. No Tamsin. Only Martha Purbeck.

'Do you know where Tamsin has got to, Martha?' Alyce asked her chamberlain anxiously. 'She never returned from settling Sybilla yesterday afternoon. I missed her thoughtful little ministrations at bedtime and when I rose.'

'I do not,' said Martha. 'And it isn't like her to let you down. But perhaps Sybilla was took bad, and she thought she should stay with her.'

'That's probably it,' said Alyce with relief.

She turned to Joan Moulton, who was already making the most of the tempting array of dishes spread out on the dais table.

'Mistress Joan, when you've sufficiently broken your fast, shall we walk over to the God's House and see how Sybilla is this morning?'

Joan took a last swig of the light golden ale brewed from Ewelme's own hops, burped, and nodded her head. 'I'd enjoy that. And I'd like to have a look at your famous school. My late husband had it in mind to found one near St Paul's, and it would be a worthy memorial to him if I did so.'

'Nothing could please me more,' said Alyce. 'Learning is the best legacy. I'm glad you feel the same.'

Attended by Martha and Dominique, they donned pattens to protect their shoes from mud, and strolled down the village street towards the God's House. It was a splendid autumn day, and the leaves of the great oaks on the slope above the church shone with a coppery gleam in the autumn sunshine.

'You have a paradise of peace here, Lady Alyce,' said Dominique. 'It is a great achievement.'

Alyce opened her mouth to reply, but was distracted by the sight of a company of men and women trotting down Rabbit Hill. There were three women in sumptuous riding habits, and six men, one of whom had a limp figure cradled in his arms as he rode. Alyce gasped, instantly recognising Tamsin. She hurried forward. Then she saw the woman at the centre of the group.

'Bess! What in the name of heaven brings you here? And what has happened to Tamsin? Is she dead?'

'Not at present, Belle-mère,' said Bess, dismounting. 'But the man who attacked her is. We left him for the coroner to see. Where does he live? My harbinger will ride to fetch him.'

'Ralph Boteler in Berwick Salome,' stammered Alyce, horrified at the sight of her maid's scratched, chalk-white face. 'We must take Tamsin to Farhang Amiri straight away. What happened?'

'I've no idea,' said Bess. 'It looked as if she was ravished or was about to be. She has a nasty wound on her head that almost killed her. Who is she, by the way?' she asked as they approached the infirmary. 'I don't remember her in your retinue at Wingfield.'

'She's a village girl, who did me a great service by finding my grandfather's rosary. I took her into my service a few weeks ago. Where did you find her?'

'On the roadside where the track from Swyncombe joins the highway. With a dead man close by. One of Harcourt's retainers. His own dagger was stuck in his back.'

Alyce's heart sank. More trouble. Perhaps much more.

They reached the door of the infirmary and knocked. Nan Ormesby opened it, and gave a shocked cry at the sight of Tamsin. She crossed herself and called out for Farhang, who hurried out of his medicine closet.

'Bring her over here,' he said to Dafyd, and led him towards an empty bed, watching critically as he laid her gently down.

'Now I need peace,' he said firmly to the anxious faces peering in at the door of the infirmary. I will send when I have news.'

Alyce led the way back to the palace and directed servants

to stable the visitors' horses and take her daughter-in-law's retainers into the hall for refreshments. Then she ushered Bess and Joan towards her solar, calling back to ask Martha to have wine and sweetmeats brought to them there.

Once they were comfortably settled, she looked at Bess apprehensively. 'So has the king decided we are a nest of traitors? I suspect Lord Tiptoft will have apprised him of recent events here. Is that why you have come?'

'Lord Tiptoft has indeed told my brother of the death of Milo the scrivener, who it seems was wished on you by the queen herself. He said it seemed to have been an accident, and that your bedesmen – and indeed a bedeswoman – were likely to be exonerated by the coroner. But there was that in his manner and the queen's that made me think you should have family around you. Jack had an... er... earlier commitment, but I thought I would show our support by calling on you. And given what we found up the road, I'm glad I did come. Is Sir Robert Harcourt still at Ewelme?'

'Close by. He is quartered with his men down the road in Bensington, threatening to appeal the jury's verdict of accidental death. The murder of one of his men will incense him further, I fear.'

'From what we saw, the man deserved his fate, and we'll testify to it at the inquest. By the way, she was clutching this packet as if her life depended on it.'

She handed it over to Alyce, who hesitated for a moment, and then opened it. Her heart skipped a beat, and she gasped. She remembered the stiff little sealed scroll all too well from Newton Montagu. She stared at it silently, then sighed. Perhaps the time has come to confess. And who better to confess to than Jack's wife? Impulsively, she handed it to her.

Puzzled, Bess took it, looking questioningly at her. Alyce nodded, her stomach a jangle of nerves. 'Bess, it concerns you most nearly. Read it.'

The young duchess broke the seal and unrolled the stiff parchment. On it were a handful of words:

Date: 27 September 1442
Name: John de la Pole
Father: William de la Pole
Mother: Elsbeth de Burgh
Witnesses to the birth:
Alyce de la Pole, Sybilla of Berwick

Startled out of measure, she looked up at her mother-in-law.

'September 1442. Then you are not Jack's mother?'

Alyce shook her head, feeling a great lightening of spirit now that she had decided to reveal the truth. But the price of easing her conscience would be high. King Edward's wrath would be all-consuming when it was revealed that his sister was married to a bastard with no right to the title of Duke of Suffolk. She would lose her de la Pole inheritance, including much of her heartland, to Catherine Stapleton of all people. She also felt profound regret. Bess was a good woman, who had married Jack in good faith, believing him to be the rightful Duke of Suffolk. Her enemies would be quick to condemn her, and with good cause. She heaved a sigh.

'No. Jack's mother was Elsbeth de Burgh. She was William's favourite mistress. He liked royal connections, and Elsbeth was a bastard granddaughter of Edmund Mortimer, Earl of March.' She paused, then gave a short, hard laugh.

'So you need have no worries as to Jack's blood; it is rather more royal than mine. But it means that he too is a bastard.'

'How did this come about?' said Bess, struggling to take in the import of Alyce's words.

'Elsbeth lived at Clare Castle in Suffolk and William met her whenever he went to Cambridge to oversee King Henry's most prized project, the King's College. He installed her at Wingfield as one of my ladies.'

'Did you know she was his mistress?' asked Bess.

'I suspected she was – but I didn't know for certain until he brought her with him to Ewelme just before he left for France to look for potential brides for King Henry. She was limp as a doll, and he asked me to look after her.'

'Morning sickness?' asked Bess.

'So it turned out,' said Alyce. 'William was away all winter, and soon Elsbeth couldn't hide her condition from me. She begged me to help her conceal it, and I agreed. I took her to Newton Montagu, one of my Dorset estates. Sybilla came with us. Elsbeth gave birth early. Poor girl. We did our best – Sybilla is highly skilled – but she bled to death. However, we managed to save the child, a boy born with his father's deep blue eyes and the red Suffolk hair.'

'And it occurred to you that though you hadn't been able to give William an heir, here was one ready-made,' said Bess, frowning with concentration.

Alyce nodded. 'When William came back from France, I told him what had happened. And I put it to him that he now had what he longed for. He thought for a while, and then he agreed. Truth to tell, we were a happier couple after that. William made no further demands on me. Jack became the centre of his existence, his be-all and end-all.'

'What became of Elsbeth's body?' Bess asked.

'I informed her family of her death, though not of its cause.

We brought her embalmed body back to Ewelme, and then sent it to Clare Castle. She's buried there.'

Bess was still struggling with the implications of the ragged scrap of parchment. 'So Jack's mother is Elsbeth de Burgh. He is a bastard, not Duke of Suffolk. William had no legitimate issue. We have no right to Wingfield, or any of his father's estates.'

Alyce nodded sadly. 'The title and the estates will revert to the line of William's older brother Michael – to Catherine Stapleton, soon to be Catherine Harcourt. Sir Richard will be Duke of Suffolk by right of marriage.'

They had both forgotten Joan, who had witnessed the extraordinary scene without saying a word. But now she stepped forward intrepidly.

'Nonsense.' She grabbed the scroll and threw it into the fire that was burning merrily in the great hearth of the solar. Bess and Alyce stared open-mouthed.

'How does that old proverb run? *What's found is history. What's lost is mystery.* Jack isn't the first and he won't be the last convenient arrival for a dynasty. Far greater families than yours have found an unofficial way of continuing their line. Lancaster among them, in all probability.'

'But the scroll...' said Alyce faintly. 'The truth...'

'Who but us three know of this parchment?' demanded Joan. 'And what would be the good of noising its contents abroad? King Edward's sister swindled out of her duchy and William's true son deprived of what ought in any fair man's estimate to be his inheritance. The boy has been punished enough by having his father vilified and murdered. Now he has found happiness with you, Bess, let him keep it. But I advise you to tell him nothing of this.'

She turned to Alyce. 'Give away what you will of your own possessions, Lady Alyce, but don't destroy the happiness of others to appease an over-nice conscience,' she said fiercely. 'And don't give the Harcourts the satisfaction of ousting you.'

They gazed at the dwindling curls of the parchment, as it turned black, then crumbled into grey ash.

'But someone else does know,' said Alyce quietly. 'Sybilla was with me in Newton Montagu. That scroll has been in her keeping ever since. Even though William was happy enough to agree to it, the deception has always been on my conscience. Sybilla knowing too somehow helped to share its weight.'

'I'm sure that Sybilla would be the last person to disclose your secret,' said Joan. 'She has kept it for the last twenty-four years, after all.'

'Perhaps you and Mistress Moulton should go and ask her, Belle-mère,' said Bess. 'I think I'll stay here. I have much to reflect on.' She stood up, and walked to the window, her fingers linked over her stomach.

Neither Sybilla nor Gerard Vespilan was in their cell in the God's House. Alyce knocked at the door of William Marton's room, and asked him if he had seen them.

'Try the church,' said Marton. 'They often go there together to pray at terce.'

They walked up the steps to the great west door of the church and entered. Sure enough, two figures were seated close together in the Chaucer chapel, one white-haired, one mantled in black. Respectfully, Joan hung back, while Alyce walked up the north aisle towards them. She sat down behind them, expecting their heads to turn at the sound of the scrape of her stool. But neither moved. Alyce rose, walked to the front of the chapel and turned to look at them. They were as still as the wooden angels that edged the eaves of the chapel roof.

Alyce sank to her knees in front of them. She saw that their hands were linked, that they were propping each other up in death. In Vespilan's hand was a folded piece of paper. She opened it, and instantly recognised Caerleon's characterful italic script.

Friend Bilton, greetings. The last thing I want to do is to wed Marlene, but I see no way of escaping her coils. Tell Princess Alyce so, also that Milo caused both Webb's death and the near-death of Sybilla. He was disguised as a pedlar, and in the pay of Sir Robert Harcourt. I have no proof, but Sir Robert boasted of it in his cups last night.

Soberly, Alyce and Joan left the chapel and walked over to the infirmary. Farhang was at Tamsin's bedside. She was still unconscious, but now that her face and arms had been washed and she was decently clad, she looked more herself.

'Will she recover?' Alyce asked.

'It's too soon to know if there has been any damage to her brain. It was very fortunate that Duchess Elizabeth found her when she did. Longer out in the cold could have been the death of her.'

'Farhang, there is more bad news. We have just discovered Gerard and Sybilla in the church.'

Farhang looked at her sharply. 'Are they dead?'

'Yes. What made you say that?'

He hesitated a moment, then spoke. 'Because Peter Greene told me last night that they had asked him to hear their confessions. And yesterday Gerard asked for some aconite cordial for his headache.'

'They were seated side by side gazing at the statue of Mary Magdalene in the north chapel,' Alyce said quietly. 'Hand in hand.'

Joan and Alyce looked at each other, the same unspoken thoughts in their minds. Nicolas Webb's death. The attempt on Sybilla's life. Their semi-recognition of Milo. Caerleon's letter to Bilton, handed to Vespilan because Bilton was far away on the Thames towpath. Sybilla's story of Milo drawing up a bucket from the well, perhaps accidentally tumbling down it. Vespilan supposedly fast asleep in his cell. Mary Magdalene, famously both a sinner and Jesus' most trusted companion.

'But surely they wouldn't have had the strength!' Joan couldn't keep her astonishment stifled any longer.

'*The Lord gives power to the weak and strength to the powerless.* Isaiah 40, verse 29.'

Peter Greene's voice sounded across the infirmary with a forcefulness Alyce had never heard before. 'Best, I think to enquire no further. Suicide, even as atonement, is a mortal sin. And such notable members of our community should be given the funeral rites and burial that their long lives in the service of the Lord has earnt them.'

'What are you saying, Peter?' Alyce began. 'Did they...'

The Teacher of Grammar held up a hand. 'What was spoken in the shriving place is between those confessing and God.'

Ewelme

For three long days Tamsin lay unconscious, tended alternately by Farhang and her grandmother. Wat crouched on a window sill opposite her bed and refused to say a word. He had clearly been in a fight, but he wouldn't talk about that either. At long last, her eyelids fluttered open.

'Where am I?' she said. Wat gave a whoop of glee and rushed over to her. Nan, sitting at the bedside darning worn sheets, grabbed him before he could touch her.

'Gently, gently, Wat. Go and get Farhang. He's doing his rounds in the God's House.'

Once he had gone, she took Tamsin's hand and stroked her cheek tenderly.

'Are you back with us, my lamb? I feared we had lost you. What a troublesome little wench you are. There's no telling you. You're your father's own daughter.'

Tamsin gave her a wan smile, then frowned and tried to say something. Her words were hard to understand, and Nan hoped she had not lost her wits.

'Don't strain, child. Let time do its work. All is well. You have nothing to be feared of.'

A few minutes later Wat and Farhang returned. The physician took Tamsin's pulse and nodded approvingly.

'Much better. She's on the mend. Nan, could you go over to the palace and tell Lady Alyce.'

Nan nodded, and hurried away, pausing only to take off

her apron and put on the clean cap that she kept behind the infirmary door. The village was peaceful; the men and women of working age harvesting, the children in school or cared for by their grandparents. It was a relief not to have Harcourt's men trampling everywhere. She smiled as she remembered his angry departure two days ago, taking the corpse of his squire with him and swearing about the composition of the jury. Ralph Boteler, having listened respectfully to Bess of York's testimony, had accepted its verdict that Hamel Turvey was murdered by person or persons unknown. Now there were only two guests of note, the young duchess and Mistress Moulton. Martha had told her that they all seemed to be getting on splendidly, to judge by the merry conversations at mealtimes, and the late hours they kept in Alyce's chamber and her turret closet. 'They're just what our mistress needs,' the chamberlain had said. 'Friends who take her out of herself. She used to spend too much time on her lonesome.'

As she knocked on the door of Alyce's chamber, Nan could hear laughter. She smiled, glad that she was bringing good news.

'Come in!' called Alyce. She had a huge book open on her reading stand, and was slowly turning its colourfully illuminated pages for the benefit of Joan and Bess, who bent over it on each side of her. Monique de Chinon sat at a desk beside a window, studying a book of hours, and Leo lay on a thick cushion on the floor. When Alyce saw Nan, she stood up eagerly.

'Do you come from Tamsin?'

'Yes. She has opened her eyes. And Farhang says her pulse is steady now. Nor is she... nor is she deflowered. Just much scratched and bruised. But she's finding it hard to speak.'

337

'Let's go and see her,' said Joan eagerly. But Bess drew her back.

'Maybe it would be better for Belle-mère to go alone, Joan. We don't want to overwhelm the child. We can go on looking at this wonderful book.'

Following Nan over to the infirmary, Alyce was grateful for Bess's understanding forbearance. Joan in full spate was like a pump gushing. She fingered her rosary, as she walked. Her rosary. With which all this began. If I hadn't lost it, I'd never have picked the imp out from the gaggle of maids about the village. There would have been none of this troublesome… this most inconvenient affection for a rash and foolish chit.

But when she walked through the infirmary door and saw Tamsin sitting up against plump pillows looking anxiously towards her, her heart melted. She smiled. Time enough for recriminations.

'What happened, child?', she asked gently. 'How did you come by the scroll?'

'It was in St Botolph's reliquary. I was bringing it down from Swyncombe for Sybilla,' said Tamsin. 'But then I saw that Sir Robert's men were still searching the village and the palace, and so I hid it up the hill in Wat's den. Sybilla told me to fetch it, and Hamel Turvey followed me. He'd seen me up at Swyncombe and recognised me.'

'Do you know who killed him?'

'Killed him? Is he dead, then?'

'You were found unconscious and – er – very dishevelled beside him. And he had his own dagger stuck in his back.'

Tamsin's jaw dropped. Then she shut her mouth firmly. Alyce was vividly reminded of their first interview, when the girl had refused a dowry and begged to be taken into service.

And asked that Wat should not be punished. She raised her hand, palm outward, to show that she didn't want her to speak.

'I'm assuming that *you* didn't stab him. And I'm not going to ask you if you know who did, though I have my suspicions. The inquest is over, and the general opinion is that he deserved his fate. Harcourt has gone, and all his men with him. So there is nothing to fear.'

Relief flooded Tamsin, and tears welled in her eyes.

'None of that,' snapped Alyce. 'I want no blubbering ninnies in my service. If, that is, you still want to be my maid. I am in dire need of one, I have to say.'

With an abrupt nod, she left the infirmary. As she walked back to the palace, tears streamed down her cheeks. She had been disillusioned so often, had lost so many whom she had loved deeply, that she had long ago decided not to risk new attachments. Until by some strange chemistry this spirited, courageous child had become very dear to her. Still shaken from the shock of Caerleon's desertion and the deaths of Gerard and Sybilla, she realised that if Tamsin had died she would have felt utterly bereft.

Sir John Wenlock whistled a catchy tune that he had heard a student strumming on a lute as he and his secretary rode through Oxford's East Gate. He was looking forward to returning to Ewelme. Caerleon had left for Stonor Park soon after sunrise, with a yawning Marlene trailing after him, as sulky and contrary-minded as the Loathly Damsel in the comical Arthurian tale of the wedding of Sir Gawain and Dame Ragnild that Joan had given him last week. He wondered how Alyce and Joan had been getting on. They'd find that they had more in common than they had differences, could they only converse long enough to get to know each other properly. Which way would inclination tilt? He called back to Francis Thynne.

'What do you reckon, Francis? Will Lady Alyce and Mistress Moulton have hit it off?'

The cadaverous valet was silent for a moment of two.

'I think so. They seem like ice and fire, but opposites may attract as well as repel.'

When they rode into the base court of the palace, Wenlock discovered that Alyce had other visitors. Two grooms in flamboyant blue and gold Suffolk tabards were slouching on a bench. He smiled. It looked as if Alyce had taken his advice, although he was surprised that her son had arrived so quickly.

Jem and Adam hastened out of the stable as he dismounted.

'Welcome back, my lord,' said Jem.

'I see you have company,' said Wenlock. 'The young duke?'

'Nay, just the young duchess and her train. They arrived on Tuesday. Found little Tamsin on their way, more than half-dead. And Harcourt's squire Hamel Turvey dead beside her with a dagger in his back.'

'God in Heaven. How did that happen?'

'No one knows, my lord. Tamsin is still in the infirmary and the coroner's jury deemed Turvey's death murder by persons unknown and suggested he richly deserved it, given his assault on Tamsin. Sir Robert Harcourt was mightily displeased. He left straightaway.'

Wenlock gaped at the groom, lost for words for a good minute.

'Where is Princess Alyce?'

'She returned from the infirmary a half-hour ago. I expect she's with her daughter-in-law and Mistress Moulton in her chamber.'

Wenlock ascended the stairs to Alyce's chamber two at a time, followed at a more dignified pace by Thynne. He opened its door without ceremony, to be greeted by six sets of female eyes. Joan and Bess of York were playing at backgammon, watched by two ladies, presumably the young duchess's attendants. At the far end of the chamber, in the elegant curve of an oriel window, Lady Alyce and Monique were seated at a chessboard.

Alyce rose at the sight of him, and beckoned him towards her. 'Wenlock! We have much to tell you.'

'If it is the story of Hamel Turvey's attack on Tamsin and his unlamented death, Jem has already told it. But how does the child? What a knack she has for getting into scrapes.'

He saw a glitter appear in Alyce's grey eyes. Surely not tears?

'Pray God the child is not dying?' he said.

She shook her head, replying almost inaudibly.

'She has just come round. And Farhang thinks there will be no lasting physical damage.'

A raucous call came from the backgammon table.

'Welcome, Sir John. Come and pay your respects to Princess Elizabeth.' Joan, of course, determined to be the centre of attention. Or was she perhaps creating a distraction so that Alyce could gain command of herself?

He walked over to the backgammon table, and bowed deeply to the smiling young duchess.

'Lord Wenlock, it is very good to see you,' said Bess. 'And I hear that you have been a stalwart friend to my mother-in-law. Thank you.'

'But what have you been up to, John?' interrupted Joan. 'Do you have any news of the Harcourts?' She lowered her voice to a whisper. 'And of Caerleon? Lady Alyce frets deeply at his desertion.'

'I have been to Stanton Harcourt,' Wenlock answered, raising his voice so that Alyce could not but hear. 'It is as we thought. Marlene entrapped Denzil into promising to marry her. However, according to Lady Margaret, the banns had not been read, and moreover Marlene was not free to marry – she was contracted to the son of a friend of her parents. Denzil is even now on his way to Stonor Park with Marlene. His plan is to offer support for her unborn child – though it seems doubtful that he fathered it. She has brazenly confessed to another lover at Wingfield. My money is on Sir Richard Harcourt, but we'll never know.'

The room was silent except for the clack of the ivory gaming pieces on the backgammon board as Bess's ladies made their moves. Alyce had risen from the chess table, and stood gazing at the heraldic glass of the window, still as a statue. The slanting autumn sunlight dappled her grey and white gown with rainbow colours.

'What of the Harcourts themselves?' asked Joan.

'I rode to Chalgrove and talked at some length with Sir Richard. I told him of our suspicions, intimating that we actually had proof of Milo's perfidy. He feigned shock, but I suspect he was well aware of what his brother was up to but had decided to play no part in it in case it came to naught. Anyway, he will pass on the stuff of our conversation. I don't think that Sir Robert will be appealing either of the coroner's verdicts.'

Joan clapped her hands to applaud. 'An excellent outcome,

John. Nor does it seem that Caerleon has betrayed the duchess as she feared. Now, I think we have trespassed long enough on Lady Alyce's hospitality. If we set off presently we will reach Henley by nightfall. Then we can decide whether to travel on to London by road or by river.'

Half an hour later, the two duchesses, one pale and slender, the other rosy and rounded as a ripe peach, stood at the open window of the solar, hands raised in farewell as Wenlock and Joan, Monique and Francis Thynne rode out of the palace, followed by their grooms.

Bess was experiencing a curious sensation in her stomach. It was, she realised, the infant quickening inside her. She looked at Alyce.

'Belle-mère, I haven't told you.' She placed her hands over her gently rounded belly. 'I am expecting another baby. And it would please me immensely if she or he were born here at Ewelme when my time comes.'

Alyce trembled. How ironic it was that this lovely creature, whom she had, she now realised, envied rather than despised, should be suggesting something so generous. Tears pricking her eyes, she stepped forward and wrapped Bess in a warm embrace.

Ewelme

The young duchess and her company left Ewelme on Friday. On Saturday Alyce summoned Simon Brailles, Ben Bilton, Peter Greene and Martha Purbeck to her great chamber. They shuffled in sheepishly and stood with heads bowed in front of her chair of state.

She surveyed them silently for a few minutes, then spoke slowly, choosing her words with care.

'First, I know you all to be my faithful servants. What you were doing while I was at Wingfield was understandable, given the great love that we all have for King Harry and the great need of fleeing Lancastrians after the defeat at Hedgeley Moor. But it was misguided; a perilous course which led to two violent deaths and two narrow escapes from death, and came close to the forfeiting of my heartland. The saving of Ewelme, and of the God's House, has been at the cost of two more lives, those of my oldest and most valued members, Gerard Vespilan and Sybilla of Berwick. We will never know exactly how Milo came by his death, but I know that you, like me, will be assiduous in praying for their souls' release from purgatory.'

She crossed herself. Exchanging guilty glances, Ben, Simon and Martha did the same.

'As to loyalty to Lancaster, I know it will continue in all our hearts, but it must stay well hidden within them. Jack's marriage to a daughter of York means I am not a free agent.

Ironically, it was the Duchess Elizabeth who saved the life of Tamsin Ormesby. Moreover, she has promised to reassure her brother King Edward that there are no treasonous goings on at Ewelme Palace or the God's House.'

'B... bu... but surely...' Simon Brailles began to stutter. Ben Bilton glared at him, and he subsided.

Alyce smiled. 'You can't blame Brailles for finding that surprising, Bilton. Fortunately, Lady Bess is not enamoured of the new queen, or of the Harcourt brothers, though of course her loyalty to her brother is total. She is giving us a chance, and we must not betray her trust. From now on, Ewelme is to return to what it was originally intended to be: a haven of peace, a place where God's commandments are observed and learning promoted. We have escaped censure this time, but avaricious men will continue to covet my domain. From now on we must be without reproach.'

She gave the men a nod of dismissal, and turned to Martha Purbeck.

'How is Tamsin, Martha? I know she has been recovering in her sister Loveday's cottage.'

'We brought her back to her room in the palace this morning, my lady.'

'Then I'll go and see how she does myself.'

Martha made to follow her, but Alyce waved her away. She was puffing slightly by the time she'd reached the top of the attic stairs. When she opened the door, she saw that Tamsin was out of bed, craning out of the window. The girl, thin and pale, turned and gasped.

'My lady! You shouldn't have bothered.'

'What I bother about is up to me, child. How are you feeling?'

'Better, thank you. I'll be able to resume my duties soon I'm sure. If... if you still want me to.' Her mismatched green and hazel eyes met Alyce's calm grey ones.

The duchess hesitated. 'Tell me, did you know of the fugitives being lodged at Ewelme by my foolish servants while I was in Suffolk?'

Tamsin shook her head vigorously. 'No, my lady. I only began to fear something was amiss when Lady Stapleton asked me to spy for her. She gave me a silver penny. But I put it in the poor box and never told her anything of moment.'

'Why didn't you tell me about that?'

'I was frightened. That you would send me away.'

'Well, I might yet, unless you confess such things in future.'

In future. Used by now to interpreting her mistress's tart rejoinders, Tamsin's spirits soared. It sounded as if her probation was over. She summoned up her courage.

'And so may I stay in your service? My month's trial is up next week.'

Alyce smiled wryly. 'You can. And I have to thank you for all that you did, even at the near cost of your life. But never run such risks again.'

She paused, then felt inside her hanging pocket.

'By the way, it seems you have an admirer. Sir John Wenlock said that Denzil Caerleon asked him to give you this.' She handed Tamsin a small hard shape wrapped in a scrap of russet cloth.

Puzzled, Tamsin unwrapped it. Inside was the tiny carved mouse she had fondled on the High Street stall when she was in Oxford. Her face lit up.

'Oh! How kind of him. I wanted to buy it for Wat and didn't have any money.'

Alyce watched her with a sense of relief. It was obvious that Caerleon's present had been a disinterested one. One which she could chalk up on the credit side of his unpredictable actions. At vespers tonight she would say a prayer for him and light a tall candle.

She rose, patted Tamsin's cheek, and descended the stairs slowly. One more task awaited her. When she reached the solar, the black-gowned figure of William Marton rose to greet her.

'Your grace. Simon Brailles told me that you wanted me to wait for you here.' She saw his eyes shift nervously, and a twitch grip his cheek.

'Yes, William. I think that I am owed an explanation. I have shown you nothing but kindness and respect. But I believe that you have been profoundly dishonest. Why did you steal my grandfather's treatise on the astrolabe?'

He flushed scarlet. 'How did you know it was I, your grace? I suppose Mistress Moulton recognised me and told you. I thought I'd managed to keep out of her way...'

'You did. Very successfully. No, you damned yourself by knowing that the bookseller who offended me in Doll's shop was a woman. You referred to her as "she" before I did.'

He hung his head, looking so like a guilty child that Alyce had to stifle a smile.

'But why? You have a respected role here at the God's House, and are equally well thought of in the University.'

He muttered something inaudibly. 'Speak up, Marton,' said Alyce. 'Does someone have a hold over you?'

Marton nodded miserably.

Alyce remembered Thomas Chaundler's mention of having lunched with Marton during her visit to New College.

'Is it Thomas Chaundler?' she asked.

Marton gasped. 'How did you know?'

'I didn't but I do now. Tell me everything.'

All Marton's pomposity had gone. He was like a deflated football. He reached for a chair and sat down, something he would never normally do in her presence without being directed to.

'He knows... he knows about my... my shameful proclivities. There is a stable lad in Queen's College who I've been foolishly close to. And who feels the same about me. We've always been very discreet, but Chaundler got word of it, and said that he would force him to bear witness against me unless... unless I told him about doings at Ewelme. I didn't tell him about any specific fugitive, but I did say that there were a great many Lancastrians passing through. I fear that he told Harcourt what I told him.'

Alyce sighed. So it was Marton who had set the wolves running. 'But why did you steal my book?'

'I was trying to raise money so that Ralph – my young friend – could get away from Oxford. I thought that without his testimony I would be safe. He is the only person I have sinned with. And he's got a head on his shoulders. With money he will be able to better himself, buy an apprenticeship to a scrivener perhaps.'

Alyce thought for a while. As to what Marton called shameful proclivities, she had long been resigned to such things. Sinful though homosexuality was in the eyes of the Church, the court had been rife with such liaisons.

'And has Ralph now left the city?'

'Yes,' said Marton. 'He's gone to a scriptorium in Litchfield. And I am going to give up my post at Queen's. There is too

348

much temptation in Oxford. Nor do I suppose your grace will want me as master any longer.'

'On the contrary,' said Alyce. 'You are far too valuable a servant to lose. As you know, I have plans for future bedesmen to be poor scholars rather than veterans of the wars, and you will be an excellent judge of their worth. And keeping you will be one in the eye for Thomas Chaundler. I'll enjoy that. Oh – and if he ever threatens you again, tell him that I would like to speak to him personally about his visits to... er... a certain house in Cowley.'

Marton's eyes widened. 'You don't mean to say...?'

'Yes,' said Alyce, with a sly smirk. 'I have it from my own sources that he has a more common proclivity than yours – but not one that is seemly in the Warden of New College.'

She saw relief flood Marton's face. He bowed, and walked away, head once more proudly upright, almost visibly swelling as the defeated limpness left his portly frame.

Smiling, she returned to her desk, and began to compose a letter inviting her god-daughter Meg to Ewelme. It would be a pleasure to make over to Meg now the jewellery which had been given to her on her marriage to Thomas Montagu, rather than risk it going astray after her death.

There was a tap at the door.

'Come in,' she called, expecting it to be Martha. But it was Joseph Pek, holding a small box and looking embarrassed.

'What is it, Pek?' she said.

The old soldier hesitated, then cleared his throat and spoke. 'It's this, my lady.' He held the box out to her.

I found it under the floorboards in Milo's room. I kept it back because... because it was writings. And I didn't know if you'd want others to see them.'

'Did you read them?'

Pek shook his head. 'I don't read, my lady. But I know that writings can betray secrets. So I kept the box back.'

She smiled at his worried face. 'Thank you Pek. You did the right thing. Writings can indeed be perilous.'

He bowed, and left the room.

Alyce opened the box, and took out a sheaf of letters inside it. None was sealed, but she was only too familiar with Sir Robert Harcourt's sprawling handwriting. She read them with growing anger. They began in May, setting Milo on his covert mission disguised as a pedlar. In August Harcourt described his visit to Ewelme and finding that there was no vacancy for a bedesman. 'Make sure there is one as soon as you can,' the letter ended. Then a summons to Windsor, to meet the queen. Then came one praising Milo for his quick independent action when he discovered that Sybilla was to be invited to replace the man he'd poisoned.

She sat down. Here was abundant evidence of Sir Robert's plot against her. Though the chances of successfully arraigning someone with the backing of Queen Elizabeth were vanishingly small, this would stand her in good stead if he ever resumed his persecution of her.

She began to replace the letters in the box, but saw that there was another folded paper tucked under the crossed ribbons in its lid. She pulled it out.

To Sir Robert Harcourt of Stanton Harcourt

Know that Milo of Windsor, the carrier of this letter, was heinously cheated out of his patrimony by William Duke of Suffolk, who twenty years ago seized his father's holding at Kelmscott on his death. I, the vicar of St Beornwald, Bampton, hold proofs of this. The Duke had Milo outlawed and his mother whipped out of Bampton. He has now returned from Paris, where he learnt the craft of a scrivener and acted as a courier for the Duke of Burgundy. I believe you will find him a useful tool in furthering your cause against the Dowager Duchess of Suffolk and her false progeny.

Yours in God,

Dom. Robert Hiat.

She sighed. Here, then, was the explanation for Milo's hatred. Wronged by Duke William, he doubtless had noxious fuel added to the flames of his anger by Harcourt. If only Robert Hiat had advised him to appeal to her after William's death. But at that time she had, for her own protection, cultivated a reputation for being unapproachable and intractable.

She reread the letter's last sentence. *Her false progeny.* Who, she wondered, was this Bampton vicar to be impugning Jack's legitimacy? Was it just a casual insult, or could the house of Suffolk still be in danger?

Ewelme

Eight weeks later, Alyce sat in her high-backed throne in Ewelme's church, her fingers stroking the worn heads of the lions on the ends of its arms. How her mother would have welcomed this outcome: the imminent arrival of a new baby, to be lodged in the ancient oak cradle that had held both Jack and his father. She had sent to Wingfield for it and other necessaries.

The church was packed with worshippers. Advent was the most popular feast of the year, but the presence of young Duke John and his wife made it even more of an occasion. They sat close to her, on the left-hand side of the nave, with their two sons beside them, each attended by a white-clad nursemaid. The oldest boy John was four, and loved coming up to her turret cabinet to learn his letters. Little Geoffrey had a great sense of humour and his father's red hair and deep blue eyes. She smiled ruefully at the realisation that she would miss them when they returned to Wingfield. She wondered if Bess had told Jack of the scroll, and hoped not. He was not a good keeper of secrets, even one so much to his benefit as this was. The truth was that, until she had ascertained who murdered his father, Jack would remain as resentful of her as ever.

The Stonors sat to the right of the nave. Thomas and Jeanne had their heads bowed in prayer. Their son William looked across at her and smiled, then shifted his gaze to Tamsin, who was standing behind Alyce, and smiled again. Next to him was Eloise, less nervous now her domineering sister had moved to her new husband's farm. The Rokes had voided their contract, but John Yeme had been sweet on Marlene since she turned thirteen, and hadn't minded her condition. Especially as she came well dowered. Thomas had told Alyce that they had had an unexpected visit from Sir Richard Harcourt, who said he felt for her plight, asked to be her godfather and presented her with a bridal gift of £100, unthinkable wealth for a tenant farmer. Marlene had protested at the marriage, but been given no choice. Besides, Yeme was remarkably handsome.

Sir John Wenlock and Joan Moulton were also on chairs of state. Alyce's friendship with them both had deepened when she went to London in November to shop for Christmas, and she had been so impressed by the bindings of the books she had bought from Joan that she decided that she would entrust the binding of her beloved Tales of Canterbury to the Sign of the Mole.

Near the front of the nave stood her senior servants, Ben Bilton and Simon Brailles. Ben was still too bullish, Simon still too nervy, but both were as loyal as ever. The absence of Caerleon remained as painful as a newly pulled tooth, but it was a huge relief to know that, though he had left her service, he had not, after all, betrayed her. John Wenlock had found him a position as a royal courier, and he was on his way to Milan with despatches for the new duke, Don Galeazza Sforza. She said a silent prayer for his survival, hoping against hope that somehow the friendship between them, a friendship that she prized above any other, might be renewed.

She looked across at the bedesmen in the front four ranks of the Chaucer Chapel. Joseph Pek had been left in her London home, Montagu Inn, so that he was safe from any further inquiries into the recent events, and Dick Lawrence had joined Vespilan and Sybilla in the graveyard. Before he died, he confessed that he had traded Neville's letter to Marlene Bishop in return for a tankard of ale. There were four new faces: aged scholars recommended by William Waynflete as worthy of support, and fitting in well with her resolution that the occupants of the God's House would be elderly and needy men – or women – of learning or holiness rather than veterans of the French wars. Trevelyan, now safe in St Veep, his remotest Cornish manor, was the last Lancastrian fugitive to be sheltered at Ewelme.

But what of her own loyalty to Lancaster? Was there any hope at all of ousting Edward and reinstating Henry, now incarcerated in the Tower of London? Would he emerge as the 'Once and Future King' secretly toasted by those loyal to him? In her heart she wanted to support him as his father and grandfather had supported her father and grandfather. But at forty-four he cut a sorry figure beside the splendid twenty-four-year-old Edward.

She gazed at Jack and his family. They were the future, bridging the two warring houses. She had become closely allied to Bess over the threat to her heartland, and she was looking forward to giving her the copy of her book of recipes which Joan had had bound for her – with plenty of blank pages for new ones. What remained was to resolve the hatred that remained a canker in Jack's heart, a hatred that might become as destructive as that lodged in Milo.

She sighed, and Tamsin stepped forward, a question in her eyes. Alyce waved her back with a smile. What a treasure she had found on the day she had lost her rosary.

The congregation rose as William Marton and Peter Greene swept up the aisle, followed by the choir, each holding a candle and singing the advent carol.

All the world in woe was wound
Until he crept into our kin,
A lovely girl he lit within,
The worthiest that ever was.

Afterword

Although this is a fiction, not a biography, I've enjoyed knitting what is known about Alyce into my story. Details of Alyce's books appear in Karen K. Jambeck's 'The Library of Alice Chaucer, Duchess of Suffolk' (Misericordia International, 1998). Her copy of *The Canterbury Tales* is based on the Ellesmere manuscript now in the Huntingdon Library, San Marino, California; it is described in detail by the British Library (www. bl.uk/collection-items/ellesmere-manuscript). John Goodall's *God's House at Ewelme* (Routledge, 2001) gives both the history of the almshouse and that of Ewelme Palace, now vanished except for a corner of the guest lodgings known as Ewelme Manor. It includes inventories of what Alyce brought to Ewelme from Suffolk, and the inventory of what survived of the Palace in the seventeenth century. I have borrowed the names of several characters from Henry Napier's *Historical Notices of the Parishes of Swyncombe and Ewelme* (1858), which also contains fascinating details of the de la Poles' occupation of Ewelme. I have added imaginary crimes to the unflattering biographies of Sir Robert and Sir Richard Harcourt which appear in *The House of Commons 1422–1461*, edited by Linda Clark (7 vols, History of Parliament Trust, 2020). I have invented doings of Sir John Wenlock and Sir John Tiptoft, who both appear in the *Dictionary of National Biography*. My version of Alyce's marriage to William de la Pole and his 'false progeny' is also invented, though plausible.

This book's title, *The Serpent of Division*, is taken from the title of a life of Julius Caesar commissioned by Duke Humfrey of Gloucester, youngest brother of the Lancastrian King Henry V and Henry VI's uncle. I've adopted it as it seems to me to suit not only the divided loyalties of the period but also the villainess of my piece: Elizabeth Wydeville, the Lancastrian widow who married the Yorkist King Edward IV in 1464. She proudly claimed descent from the snake fairy Melusine.

It would be tedious to detail here the ups and downs of the Wars of the Roses, which began in the 1450s. But crucial to this book and those that follow is the fact that, though the Yorkist Edward IV seized the throne in 1460 and from 1465 held Henry VI a prisoner in the Tower of London, the cause of Lancaster was not lost. Supporters of the 'Once and Future King' continued to plot against Edward and, after gaining the support of the immensely powerful Earl of Warwick, managed to oust him in 1470 and reinstate Henry VI.

Six months later Edward returned from exile and raised an army. The Earl of Warwick and Henry VI's son were killed at the Battle of Tewkesbury; Henry was captured, then quietly murdered. Edward IV ruled for the next thirteen years. After Edward's marriage to Elizabeth Wydeville had been declared illegitimate he was succeeded by his brother, who became Richard III. Two years later, Richard was defeated by Henry Tudor, grandson of Henry V's widow, who became Henry VII. Whether Richard or Henry engineered the murder of Edward's sons, the 'Princes in the Tower', is still debated.

Acknowledgements

With thanks to Claire Bodanis, Nicolas Soames, Fiona Maddocks, Richard Mayon-White, Alex Hammond, Daisy Griffith, Susie Billings, Tilly Connor and Ellie Danby for their encouragement and helpful criticism; to Joe and Lenny Billings for website work; to Dr Linda Clark, editor of the fifteenth-century volumes of the *History of Parliament*, for letting me read early drafts of the biographies of members and casting an erudite eye over the finished book. Professor Nicolas Orme gave advice on the medieval church, and Katherine Swift of Morville on medieval gardens. Ros and Phil Danby lent me Aunty Lucy's bungalow in Arnside, and Lucy and Andrew Penny allowed me to roost unsociably to write in the sunroom of Clwyd-Waen-Hir and enjoy their cooking and company of an evening.

Most of all, thank you Lucy Morton and Robin Gable of illuminati book design & editing, for making it look so lovely, correcting innumerable errors and much invaluable advice.